E R

W9-BSA-445

Wizard at Large

By Terry Brooks
Published by Ballantine Books:

THE SWORD OF SHANNARA

THE ELFSTONES OF SHANNARA

THE WISHSONG OF SHANNARA

MAGIC KINGDOM FOR SALE—SOLD!

THE BLACK UNICORN

WIZARD AT LARGE

Wizard at Large

Terry Brooks

DEL REY

A Del Rey Book

BALLANTINE BOOKS • *NEW YORK*

A Del Rey Book
Published by Ballantine Books

Copyright © 1988 by Terry Brooks
Map by Shelly Shapiro

Library of Congress Cataloging-in-Publication Data

Brooks, Terry.
  Wizard at large.
  "A Del Rey book."
  I. Title.
PS3552.R6596W55 1988   813'.54   88-47805
ISBN 0-345-34773-0

Designed by Ann Gold

Manufactured in the United States of America

First Edition: October 1988

10 9 8 7 6 5 4 3 2 1

For Alex

Who is something of a wizard at large himself . . .

At that word the young man let his glass slip through his fingers, and looked upon Keawe like a ghost.

'The price,' says he; 'the price! You do not know the price?'

'It is for that I am asking you,' returned Keawe. 'But why are you so much concerned? Is there something wrong about the price?'

'It has dropped a great deal in value since your time, Mr. Keawe,' said the young man, stammering.

'Well, well, I shall have the less to pay for it,' says Keawe. 'How much did it cost you?'

The young man was white as a sheet. 'Two cents,' said he.

'What?' cried Keawe, 'two cents? Why, then, you can only sell it for one. And he who buys it—' The words died upon Keawe's tongue; he who bought it could never sell it again, the bottle and the bottle imp must abide with him until he died, and when he died must carry him to the red end of hell.

Robert Louis Stevenson, The Bottle Imp

Contents

Wizard
at
Large

Sneeze

*B*en Holiday sighed wearily and wished he were somewhere else besides where he was. He wished he were anywhere else.

He was in the garden room at Sterling Silver. The garden room was probably Ben Holiday's favorite of all the many rooms at the castle. It was bright and airy. Flower boxes criss-crossed the tiled floor in dazzling swatches of color. Sunshine streamed through floor-length windows that ran the length of its southern wall, tiny motes of pollen dancing on the broad bands of light. The windows stood open and fragrant smells wafted in. The room looked out on the gardens proper, a maze of flower beds and bushes that spread their way downward to the lake on which the island castle rested, mixing and mingling their colors like paints run together on a rain-soaked canvas. The flowers bloomed year-round, reseeding themselves with commendable regularity. A horticulturist from Ben's old world would have killed to study such treasures—species that grew only in the Kingdom of Landover and nowhere else.

Just at the moment, Ben would have killed to escape them.

". . . Great High Lord . . ."

". . . Mighty High Lord . . ."

The familiar calls of supplication grated on him like rough stones and reminded him anew of the cause of his disgruntle-

ment. His eyes rolled skyward momentarily. *Please!* His gaze
shifted furiously from flower box to flower bed and back again,
as if somewhere among all those tiny petals the escape he so
desperately sought might be found. It wasn't, of course, and
he sagged back further in his cushioned chair and contemplated
the unfairness of it all. It wasn't that he was trying to shirk his
duty. It wasn't as if he didn't care about these things. But this
was his *refuge*, for Pete's sake! This was supposed to be his place
for time away!

". . . and took all of our hard-earned berry stores."

"And all of our ale kegs as well."

"When all we did was to borrow a few laying hens, High
Lord."

"We would have replaced those that were lost, High
Lord."

"We intended to be fair."

"We did."

"You must see that our possessions are returned . . ."

"Yes, you must . . ."

They went on, barely pausing for breath.

Ben studied Fillip and Sot the way his gardener studied
weeds in the flower beds. The G'home Gnomes rambled on
unself-consciously and endlessly, and he thought about the va-
garies of life that permitted misfortunes such as this to be visited
on him. The G'home Gnomes were a pitiful bunch—small,
ferretlike burrow people who begged, borrowed, and mostly
stole everything with which they came in contact. They mi-
grated periodically and, once settled, could not be dislodged.
They were regarded in general as a blight upon the earth. On
the other hand, they had proven unswervingly loyal to Ben.
When he had purchased the Kingdom of Landover from Rosen's
Department Store Christmas Wishbook and come into the valley—almost two years ago now—Fillip and Sot, on behalf of
all of the G'home Gnomes, had been the first to pledge their
loyalty. They had aided him in his efforts to establish his king-

ship. They had helped him again when Meeks, the former Court Wizard, had slipped back into Landover and stolen his identity and his throne. They had been his friends when there were precious few friends to be had.

He sighed deeply. Well, he owed them something, certainly—but not this much. They were taking advantage of his friendship in a way that was totally unconscionable. They had traded on it to bring this latest complaint before him, deliberately circumventing the regular channels of a court administration he had worked hard to implement. They had brandished it like a fiery torch until he was hounded to this, his last sanctuary. It wouldn't be so bad if they didn't do this every single time there was a complaint of any sort—which was every five minutes, it sometimes seemed—but, of course, they did. They didn't trust anyone else to be fair and impartial. They wanted their "Great High Lord" and their "Mighty High Lord" to hear them out.

And hear them out, and hear them out . . .

". . . a fair disposition would be a return of all things stolen and a replacement of all things damaged," said Fillip.

"A fair disposition would be for you to order to our service several dozen trolls for a reasonable period of time," said Sot.

"Perhaps a week or two," said Fillip.

"Perhaps a month," said Sot.

It would also help matters if they didn't bring most of their problems on themselves, Ben thought darkly. It was difficult to be either objective or sympathetic when he knew before the first word was out of their mouths that they were *at least* as guilty of causing the dilemma as whomever their latest complaint was to be lodged against.

Fillip and Sot rambled on. Their grimy faces twitched as they talked, their eyes squinting against the light, their fur wrinkled and worn. Their fingers curled and straightened as they gestured, and bits of dirt crumbled and broke away from beneath the nails where it was caked from digging. Their shabby clothes hung on them, leather and sackcloth, colorless save for a single incongruous red feather stuck in the headband of their caps. They were bits of wreckage that had somehow washed up on the shores of his life.

"Perhaps a tribute would help serve as recompense," Fillip was saying.

"Perhaps a token gift of silver or gold," Sot echoed.

Ben shook his head hopelessly. This was quite enough. He was about to cut them off when he was saved from the need to do so by the sudden, unexpected appearance of Questor Thews. His Court Wizard burst through the garden room doors as if catapulted by some giant sling, arms waving, white beard and long hair whipping about, gray robes with their colorful patches trailing after in what appeared to be a desperate effort to keep up with their wearer.

"I have done it, I have done it!" he proclaimed without any preliminaries. He was flushed with excitement, his owlish face made positively glowing by whatever it was that he had done. He seemed oblivious to the presence of the G'home Gnomes, who mercifully stopped their presentation in mid-sentence and simply stared at him openmouthed.

"What is it that you have done?" Ben inquired mildly. He had learned to temper his enthusiasm where Questor was concerned, because it was often sadly misplaced. Questor accomplished on the average about one half of what he thought he had accomplished.

"The magic, High Lord! I have found the magic! Finally, I have found the means to . . ." He stopped, hands gesturing emphatically. "No, wait a moment! The others must hear this, too. All of our friends must be present. I have taken the liberty of sending for them. It should only be a few, brief . . . This is such a glorious . . . Ah, ah, here they are now!"

Willow appeared in the open door, stunning as always, more beautiful than all the flowers about her, her slender form a whisper of white silk and trailing lace as she slipped into the sunlit room. Her pale green face glanced toward Ben, and she smiled that special, secret smile that she reserved only for him. A fairy creature, she seemed as ephemeral as the warmth of the midday air. The kobolds, Bunion and Parsnip, trailed after, gnarled bodies skittering along, wizened monkey faces grinning doubtfully, all teeth and sharp angles. Fairy creatures, too, they had the look of something conjured from a nightmare. Abernathy came last, resplendent in his scarlet and gold Court Scribe uniform, no fairy creature, but a soft-coated Wheaten Terrier who seemed to think he was human. He held his dog's body erect and dignified, his soulful eyes darting at once to the hateful, carnivorous G'home Gnomes.

"I see no reason to be present in the same room as these loathsome creatures . . ." he began indignantly and was cut short by the sight of Questor Thews advancing on him with arms stretched wide.

"Old friend!" the wizard gushed. "Abernathy, the best of news for you! Come, come!"

He seized hold of Abernathy and propelled him into the center of the room. Abernathy stared at the wizard in disbelief, finally shaking himself free of the other entirely.

"Have you lost your mind?" he demanded, brushing at his garments to straighten them. His muzzle twitched. "And what is this old friend business? What are you up to now, Questor Thews?"

"Something you cannot begin to imagine!" The wizard was beaming with excitement as he rubbed his hands together and beckoned them all closer. They crowded in, and Questor's voice lowered conspiratorially. "Abernathy, if you were to wish for that which you most desire in all the world, what would it be?"

The dog stared at him. Then he glanced momentarily at the G'home Gnomes, then back again. "How many wishes do I get?"

The wizard lifted his bony hands and brought them to rest

gently on the other's shoulders. "Abernathy." He breathed the scribe's name. "I have found the magic that will change you from a dog back into a man!"

There was stunned silence. Everyone knew the story of how Questor had used the magic to change Abernathy from a man into a dog to protect him from the old King's spiteful son some years earlier, when that reprobate was in one of his more hateful moods, and then had been unable to change him back again. Abernathy had lived since then as an imperfect dog who retained human hands and speech, always with the hope that one day a way would be found to restore his human self. A chagrined Questor had searched in vain for that way, frequently claiming he would find it when he found certain books of magic hidden by Meeks on his departure from Landover. But the books had been destroyed while being recovered, and not much had been heard on the subject since.

Abernathy cleared his throat. "Is this simply an overgenerous dose of your usual nonsense, wizard?" he asked cautiously. "Or can you really change me back?"

"I can!" Questor declared, nodding vehemently. He paused. "I think."

Abernathy drew back. "You think?"

"Wait a minute!" Ben was out of his chair and between them with as much speed as he could manage, nearly tripping headfirst over a box of gardenias in his effort to prevent bloodshed. He took a deep breath. "Questor." He waited until the other's eyes found his. "I thought that kind of magic was beyond you. I thought that when you lost the books of magic, you lost any way of even studying the arts mastered by your predecessors, let alone trying to . . ."

"Trial and error, High Lord!" the other interrupted quickly. "Trial and error! I simply expanded on what I already knew, taking matters a step further each time, learning a bit more as I went until I had learned it all. It has taken me until now to master the magic, but master it I have!"

"You think," Ben amended.

"Well . . ."

"This is a waste of time—as usual!" Abernathy snapped, turned, and would have stalked away except that he was hemmed in by the G'home Gnomes, who had crowded close to hear better. Abernathy wheeled back. "The fact of the matter is, you never get *anything* right!"

"Rubbish!" Questor cried out suddenly, quieting them all. He straightened. "For ten long months I have worked on this magic—ever since the old books of magic were destroyed with Meeks, ever since then!" His sharp eyes locked on Abernathy. "I know how much this means to you. I have dedicated myself to mastering the magic that would make it possible. I have used the magic on small creatures with complete success. I have proven so far as it is possible to do so that it can be done. It only remains to try it with you."

No one said anything for a moment. The only sound in the room was the buzz of a solitary bumblebee as it meandered from flower box to flower box. Abernathy frowned at Questor Thews in determined silence. There was disbelief reflected in his eyes, but it couldn't quite mask the hope.

"I think we should give Questor the opportunity to finish his explanation," Willow spoke up finally. She stood a pace or two back from the others, watching.

"I agree," Ben added his approval. "Tell us the rest, Questor."

Questor looked offended. "Rest? What rest? That is the whole of it, thank you—unless you expect technical details on how the magic works, which I am not going to give you, since you would not understand them anyway. I have developed a means to complete the transformation from dog to man and that is that! If you wish me to use the magic, I will! If not, I will dismiss the matter from my mind!"

"Questor . . ." Ben began soothingly.

"Well, really, High Lord! I work hard to discover a difficult and elusive magical process and I am greeted with insults, jeers, and accusations! Am I Court Wizard or not, I ask myself? There certainly seems to be some doubt!"

"I simply asked . . ." Abernathy tried.

"No, no, you need not apologize for the truth of your feelings!" Questor Thews seemed to relish thoroughly the role of martyr. "Throughout history, all great men have been misunderstood. Some have even died for their beliefs."

"Now, look here!" Ben was growing angry.

"That is not to say that I feel my own life is threatened in any way, you understand," Questor added hastily. "I was simply making a point. Ahem! It only remains for me to repeat that the process is complete, the magic is found, and we can use it if you wish. Simply say so. You have all the facts." He stopped suddenly. "Oh. Except one, that is."

There was a collective groan. "Except one?" Ben repeated.

Questor tugged uncomfortably on one ear and cleared his throat. "There is one small matter, High Lord. The magic requires a catalyst for a transformation of this magnitude. I lack such a catalyst."

"I knew it . . ." Abernathy muttered under his breath.

"But there is an alternative," Questor continued hastily, ignoring the other. He paused and took a deep breath. "We could use the medallion."

Ben stared at him blankly. "The medallion? What medallion?"

"Your medallion, High Lord."

"My medallion?"

"But you would have to take it off and give it to Abernathy to wear during the transformation process."

"My medallion?"

Questor looked as if he were waiting for the ceiling to fall in on him. "It would only be for a few moments, you understand—that would be all. Then you could have your medallion back."

"I could have it back. Right."

Ben didn't know whether to laugh or to cry. "Questor, we just spent weeks trying to get the damn thing back when it wasn't really gone in the first place, and now you want me to take it off for real? I thought I was *never* supposed to take it off. Isn't that what you yourself have told me on more than one occasion? Isn't it?"

"Well, yes . . ."

"What if something goes wrong and the medallion is damaged or lost? What then?" A dark flush was beginning to creep up Ben's neck. "What if . . . what if, for whatever reason, Abernathy *can't* give it back? Great balls of fire! This is the most half-baked idea I ever heard, Questor! What are you thinking about, anyway?"

Everyone had sort of shrunk away from him during this explosion, and now Ben found himself alone amid the flower boxes with the wizard. Questor was standing fast, but looking none too comfortable.

"If there were another choice in the matter, High Lord . . ."

"Well, find one, confound it!" Ben cut him short. He started to elaborate, then stopped, glancing instead at the others. "How much sense does this make to anyone else? Abernathy? Willow?"

Abernathy did not answer.

"I think you have to consider carefully what is at risk, Ben," Willow said finally.

Ben put his hands on his hips, looked at them each in turn, then gazed out wordlessly into the gardens beyond. So he had to consider what was at risk, did he? Well, what was at risk was the thing that had made him King of Landover and kept him there. It was the medallion that summoned the Paladin, the knight-errant who served as the King's champion and protector—*his* champion and protector on more than one occasion already. And it was the medallion that let him pass back and

forth between Landover and other worlds, including the one
he had come from. That's what was at risk! Without the medallion, he was in constant danger of winding up as just so much
dog meat!

He regretted that last comparison almost immediately.
After all, what was also at risk was Abernathy's permanent
future as a canine.

He frowned blackly. What had begun as a fairly uneventful
day was turning into a quagmire of unpleasant possibilities. His
memory tugged at him. Ten months ago, he had been tricked
into conveying the old wizard Meeks back into Landover when
he had thought his worst enemy safely exiled. Meeks had then
used his considerable magic to steal Ben's identity and the
throne and—most important of all—to convince Ben that he
had lost the medallion. It had almost cost Ben his life—not to
mention Willow's—to discover what had been done to him and
to defeat the old troublemaker once and for all. Now he was
King again, safely ensconced at Sterling Silver, comfortably
settled, the reins of kingship firmly in hand, his programs for
a better life nicely underway, and here was Questor Thews
playing around again with the magic!

Damn!

He stared at the flowers. Gardenias, roses, lilies, hyacinth,
daisies, and dozens of variations of other familiar species along
with a truckload of ground cover and flowering vines—all
spread out before him like a vast patchwork quilt, scented and
soft as down. It was so peaceful here. He didn't get to enjoy
the garden room that often. This was his first morning in weeks.
Why was he being hounded like this?

Because he was the King, of course, he answered himself.
Let's not be stupid here. This wasn't a nine-to-five job. This
wasn't why he had left his profession as a successful trial lawyer
in Chicago, Illinois, to apply for the position of High Lord of
Landover, a kingdom of magic and fairy folk that wasn't anywhere near Chicago or anywhere else anyone there had ever

heard about. This wasn't why he had chosen to alter his life so completely that he was no longer even recognizable as the person he had been in his old world. He had wanted to change all that; that was why he had come here. He had wanted to escape the purposelessness of being who and what he had become—a bitter and reclusive widower, a disillusioned practitioner of a profession that had lost its character. He had wanted a challenge that would again give meaning to his existence. He had found that here. But the challenge was constant and not circumscribed by time or place, by need or want. It was simply there, always new, always changing; and he understood and relished the fact that he must always be there to meet it.

He sighed. It was just a little difficult sometimes.

He was conscious of the others watching him, waiting to see what he would do. He took a deep breath, inhaled the mix of fragrances that filled the noonday air, and turned to face them. Whatever doubts he'd had were gone. The decision wasn't really all that hard after all. Sometimes he just had to do what felt right.

He smiled. "Sorry to be so touchy," he said. "Questor, if you need the medallion to make the magic work, then you've got it. As Willow said, I have to consider the risks involved, and any risk is worth helping Abernathy get back to himself." He looked directly at his scribe. "How about it, Abernathy? Want to take the chance?"

Abernathy seemed undecided. "Well, I don't know, High Lord." He paused, thought, looked down briefly at his body, shook his head, and looked up again. Then he nodded. "Yes, High Lord, I do."

"Splendid!" Questor Thews exclaimed, promptly coming forward. The others murmured, hissed, and chittered their approval. "Now, this won't take a moment. Abernathy, you stand here, right in the center of the room, and the rest of you stand back a bit behind me." He adjusted them accordingly, beaming all the while. "Now then High Lord, please give the medallion to Abernathy."

Ben reached for the medallion where it rested about his neck and hesitated. "You're certain about this, Questor?"

"Quite certain, High Lord. All will be well."

"I mean, I can't even speak or write Landoverian without the medallion!"

Questor brought his hands up quickly in a gesture of re-assurance. "Here, now. A simple spell will solve that problem." He motioned briefly, muttered something, and nodded in sat-isfaction. "There we are. Go ahead. You can take it off."

Ben sighed, took off the medallion, and handed it to Ab-ernathy. Abernathy slipped it carefully about his shaggy neck. The medallion lay against his tunic front, sunlight dancing off its polished silver surface, detailing the etching of a knight riding out of an island castle at sunrise—the Paladin riding out of Ster-ling Silver. Ben sighed again and stepped back. He felt Willow come up beside him and take his hand in hers.

"It will be all right," she whispered.

Questor breezed back about Abernathy again, adjusting him first this way and then that, telling him all the while that things would take only a moment. Satisfied at last, he moved directly in front of the scribe and took two careful steps right. He tested the air with a wet finger. "Ah!" he declared mysteriously.

He brought his arms high out of the gray robes, flexed his fingers, and opened his mouth. Then he paused, his nose twitch-ing. One hand dropped quickly to rub at it in irritation. "Drat-ted sunshine tickles," he muttered. "Pollen does nothing to help, either."

The G'home Gnomes crowded close again, pressing up against the wizard's robes, their ferret faces peering out at Ab-ernathy in anxious anticipation.

"Could you move those creatures back?" the dog snapped and even growled a bit.

Questor glanced down. "Oh. Well, yes, of course. Back now, back with you!" He shooed the gnomes away and resumed his stance. His nose twitched again, and he sniffed. "Quiet, please!"

He began a long incantation. Bizarre gestures accompanied words that brought frowns of puzzlement to the faces of his listeners. They edged forward a pace or two to listen: Ben, a lean, fit man of forty standing firm against the advancement of middle age; Willow, a child in a woman's body, a sylph, half-human, half-fairy; the kobolds Parsnip and Bunion, the first thick and stolid, the second spindle-legged and quick, both with sharp, glittering eyes and teeth that suggested something feral; and the G'home Gnomes Fillip and Sot, furry, unkempt ground creatures that appeared to have just poked their heads up from their earthen dens. They watched and waited and said nothing. Abernathy, the focus of their attention, closed his eyes and prepared for the worst.

Still Questor Thews went on, looking for all the world like some scarecrow escaped from the fields, his recitation seemingly as endless as the complaints of the G'home Gnomes.

Ben was struck suddenly with the incongruity of things. Here he was, until recently a member of a profession that stressed reliance on facts and reason, a modern man, a man from a world where technology governed most aspects of life, a world of space travel, nuclear power, sophisticated telecommunications and a hundred-and-one other marvels—here he was, in a world that was all but devoid of technology, fully expecting a wizard's magic to transform completely the physiological makeup of a living creature in a way that the sciences of his old world had barely dreamed was possible. He almost smiled at the thought. It was just too bizarre.

Questor Thews' hands swooped down suddenly and then up again, and the air was filled with a fine silver dust that sparkled and shimmered as if alive. It floated in breezy swirls all about Questor's hands for a moment, then settled over Abernathy. Abernathy saw none of it, his eyes still tightly closed. Questor continued to murmur, his tone changing, growing sharper, becoming more a chant. The silver dust swirled, the light of the room seemed to brighten, and there was a sudden coldness in the air. Ben felt the G'home Gnomes shrink back behind his legs, muttering guardedly. Willow's hand closed tighter about his own.

"Ezaratz!" Questor cried out suddenly—or something like it—and there was a brilliant flash of light that ricocheted off Ben's medallion and caused them all to flinch away.

When they looked back again, there stood Abernathy— unchanged.

No, wait, thought Ben, his hands are gone! He has paws!

"Oh, oh," Questor said.

Abernathy's eyes blinked open. "Arf!" he barked. Then, in horror, "Arf, arf, arf!"

"Questor, you've turned him completely into a dog!" Ben exclaimed in disbelief. "Do something!"

"Drat!" the wizard muttered. "A moment, a moment!" His hands gestured, and the silver dust flew. He resumed the incantation. Abernathy had discovered paws where his hands had been. His eyes had snapped wide open and his muzzle had begun to quiver.

"Erazaratz!" Questor cried. The light flashed, the medallion flared, and the paws disappeared. Abernathy had his hands back. "Abernathy!" the wizard exulted.

"Wizard, when I get my hands on you . . . !" the scribe howled. Clearly, he had his voice back as well.

"Stand still!" Questor ordered sharply, but Abernathy was already advancing on him, moving out of the ring of silver dust. Questor moved quickly to stop him, brushing at the dust where it formed a screen between them. The dust darted away from him as if alive and flew suddenly into his face.

"Erazzatza!" Questor Thews sneezed suddenly.

A well of light opened up beneath Abernathy, a cloudy

brightness that seemed to fasten about the dog's legs with tiny feelers. Slowly, the light began to draw Abernathy down.

"Help!" Abernathy cried.

"Questor!" Ben screamed.

He started forward and tripped over the G'home Gnomes, who had somehow edged in front of him.

"I . . . I have him . . . High Lord!" Questor Thews gasped between sniffles. His hands tried desperately to regain control of the swirling dust.

Abernathy's eyes had opened even wider, if that were possible, and he was struggling to climb free of the pooled light, calling out to them frantically. Ben tried to untangle himself from the G'home Gnomes.

"Be . . . calm!" Questor urged. "Be . . . ca . . . ah, ah, ah . . . ACHOOO!"

He sneezed so hard, he lurched backward into Ben and the others and knocked them all sprawling. The silver dust flew out the windows into the sunlit gardens. Abernathy gave one final cry and was sucked down into the light. The light flared once and disappeared.

Ben pushed himself up on his hands and knees and glared at Questor Thews. "Gesundheit!" he snapped.

Questor Thews turned crimson.

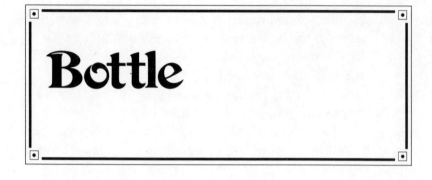

Bottle

"*W*ell?" Ben demanded. "Where is he? What's happened to him?"

Questor Thews didn't seem to have a ready answer, so Ben diverted his attention from the flustered wizard long enough to help Willow up, then turned quickly back again. He wasn't angry yet—he was still too shocked—but he was going to be very angry any second. Abernathy had disappeared just as surely as if he had never been—vanished, just like that. And, of course, Ben's medallion, the medallion that protected the kingship and his life, the medallion Questor had assured him would be perfectly safe, had vanished as well.

He changed his mind. He wasn't going to be angry after all. He was going to be sick.

"Questor, where is Abernathy?" he repeated.

"Well, I . . . the fact of the matter is, High Lord, I . . . I am not entirely certain," the wizard managed finally.

Ben seized the front of the wizard's robes. He was going to be angry after all. "Don't tell me that! You've got to get him back, damnit!"

"High Lord." Questor was pale, but composed. He didn't try to draw away. He simply straightened himself and took a deep breath. "I am not sure yet exactly what happened. It will take a little time to understand . . ."

"Well, can't you guess?" Ben shouted, cutting him short.

The owlish face twisted. "I can guess that the magic misfired, of course. I can guess that the sneeze—that wasn't my fault, you know, High Lord, it simply happened—that the sneeze confused the magic in some fashion and changed the result of the incantation. Instead of transforming Abernathy from a dog back into a man, it seems to have *transported* him instead. The two words are quite similar, you see, and the magics likewise are similar. It happens that the results of most incantations are similar where the words are similar . . ."

"Skip all that!" Ben snapped. He started to say something further, then caught himself. He was losing control of the situation. He was behaving like some B-picture gangster. He released the front of the wizard's robes, feeling a bit foolish. "Look, you think that the magic sent him somewhere, right? Where do you think it sent him? Just tell me that."

Questor cleared his throat and thought a moment. "I don't know," he decided.

Ben stared at him, then turned away. "I don't believe this is happening," he muttered. "I just don't believe it."

He glanced momentarily at the others. Willow stood close, her green eyes solemn. The kobolds were picking up a planter that had been knocked over in the struggle. There was dirt and broken flowers scattered in a six foot circle about them. The G'home Gnomes were whispering together anxiously.

"Perhaps we should . . ." Willow started to say.

And then there was a bright flash of light from the spot where Abernathy had disappeared, a popping sound as if someone had pulled a cork free, and something materialized from out of nowhere, spun wildly about, and came to rest on the floor.

It was a bottle.

Everyone jumped, then stared. The bottle lay there quietly, an oval-shaped container about the size of a magnum of champagne. It was corked and wired tightly shut and it was painted white with red harlequins dancing on its glass surface, all in varying poses of devilish gaiety, all grinning madly.

"What in the world is that?" Ben muttered and reached down to pick it up. He studied it wordlessly for a moment, hefting it, peering into it. "Doesn't appear to be anything inside," he said. "It feels empty."

"High Lord, I have a thought!" Questor said suddenly. "This bottle and Abernathy may have been exchanged—transposed, one for the other! Transpose sounds like transform and transfer, and I think the magics are close enough that it is possible!"

Ben frowned. "Abernathy was exchanged for this bottle? Why?"

Questor started to reply and stopped. "I don't know. But I am quite positive that is what happened."

"Does this help determine where Abernathy is now?" Willow asked.

Questor shook his head. "But it gives me a starting point. If I can trace the source of the bottle, then perhaps . . ." He trailed off thoughtfully. "Odd. This bottle seems familiar."

"You've seen it somewhere before?" Ben wanted to know immediately.

The wizard frowned. "I am not sure. It seems as if I might have and at the same time it seems I must be mistaken. I do not quite understand it."

Along with just about everything else, Ben thought rather unkindly. "Well, I don't give a hoot about this bottle," he declared, "but I do care about Abernathy and the medallion. So let's find a way to get them back. Whatever it takes, Questor, you do it and do it quickly. This mess is your responsibility."

"I realize that, High Lord. You need not remind me. It was not my fault, however, that Abernathy tried to move out of the incantation's sphere of influence, that the dust flew into my face when I tried to stop him, and that I thereupon sneezed. The magic would have worked as it was intended to work if I had not . . ."

Ben impatiently brushed the explanation away with a wave of his hand. "Just find him, Questor. Just find him."

Questor Thews bowed curtly. "Yes, High Lord. I will begin at once!" He turned and started from the room, muttering, "He *might* still be in Landover; I will begin my search here. The Landsview should help. He should be safe for the moment in any event, I imagine—safe even if we do not reach him immediately. Oh! Not that there is any reason he shouldn't be safe, High Lord," he added, turning hastily back. "No, no, we have time." He started away again. "The sneeze was not my fault, drat it! I had the magic perfectly under my control, and . . . oh, what is the point of belaboring the matter, I will simply start looking . . ."

He was almost through the door, when Ben called after him, "Don't you want this bottle?"

"What?" Questor glanced back, then hastily shook his head. "Later, perhaps. I have no immediate need for it. Odd, how familiar . . . I wish my memory were a little bit better on these things. Ah, well, it cannot mean much if I cannot summon even a faint recollection . . ."

He disappeared from view, still muttering—the Don Quixote of Landover, searching for dragons and finding only windmills. Ben watched him go in frustrated silence.

It was difficult to think about anything beyond the lost medallion and the missing Abernathy, but there was nothing to be done about either until Questor reported back. So while Willow went into the gardens to pick fresh flowers for dinner and the kobolds went back to their work about the castle, Ben forced himself to resume consideration of the latest complaint of the G'home Gnomes.

Intriguingly enough, the gnomes were no longer so anxious to pursue the matter.

"Tell me whatever you have left to tell me about the trolls," Ben ordered, resigned to the worst. He settled himself wearily in his chair and waited.

"Such a beautiful bottle, High Lord," said Fillip instead.

"Such a pretty thing," echoed Sot.

"Forget the bottle," Ben advised, remembering for the first time since Questor had departed that it was still there, sitting where he had put it down on the floor next to him. He glanced at it in irritation. "I'd like to."

"But we have never seen one like it," persisted Fillip.

"Never," agreed Sot.

"Can we touch it, High Lord?" asked Fillip.

"Yes, can we?" pleaded Sot.

Ben glared. "I thought we were here to discuss trolls. You seemed anxious enough to do so earlier. You practically cried to do so. Now you don't care anymore?"

Fillip glanced hastily at Sot. "Oh, we care a great deal, High Lord. The trolls have mistreated us grievously."

"Then let's get on . . ."

"But the trolls are gone for now and cannot be found again immediately in any case, and the bottle is right here, right in front of us, so can we touch it for a moment, Great Lord—just for a moment?"

"Can we, Mighty High Lord?" echoed Sot.

Ben wanted to take the bottle and beat them over the head with it. But instead he simply picked it up and handed it over. It was easier than arguing. "Just be careful," he cautioned.

There really wasn't much to worry about on that count, he realized. The bottle was heavy glass and looked as if it could endure a good deal of mistreatment. Actually, it seemed almost something more than glass—almost a metal of some sort. Must be the paint, he thought.

The G'home Gnomes were fondling and caressing the bot-

tle as if it were their most precious treasure. They stroked it
and loved it. They cradled it like a child. Their grimy little paws
moved across its surface almost sensuously. Ben was disgusted.
He glanced out into the gardens at Willow and thought about
joining her. Anything would be better than this.

"How about it, fellas," he said finally. "Let's finish up with
the trolls, okay?"

Fillip and Sot stared at him. He beckoned for them to
return the bottle, and they reluctantly handed it back. Ben set
it down next to him again. The gnomes hesitated, then resumed
their complaint against the trolls. But the effort was halfhearted
at best. Their eyes kept straying back to the bottle, and finally
they gave up on the trolls altogether.

"High Lord, could we have the bottle?" asked Fillip
suddenly.

"Oh, yes, could we?" asked Sot.

Ben stared. "Whatever for?"

"It is a precious thing," said Fillip.

"It is a treasure," said Sot.

"So beautiful," said Fillip.

"Yes, beautiful," echoed Sot.

Ben closed his eyes and rubbed them wearily, then looked
at the gnomes. "I would love to be able to give it to you, believe
me," he said. "I would love to say, 'Here, take this bottle and
don't let me see it ever again.' That's what I would love to do.
But I can't. The bottle has some connection with what happened
to Abernathy, and I have to know what."

The G'home Gnomes shook their heads solemnly.

"The dog never liked us," muttered Fillip.

"The dog never did," muttered Sot.

"He growled at us."

"And even snapped."

"Nevertheless . . ." Ben insisted.

"We could keep the bottle for you, High Lord," interrupted Fillip.

"We would take good care of it, High Lord," assured Sot.

"Please, please," they implored.

They were so pathetic that Ben could only shake his head in wonder. They were just like little children in a toy store. "What if there were an evil genie in the bottle?" he asked suddenly, leaning forward with a dark frown. "What if the genie ate gnomes for breakfast?" The gnomes looked at him blankly. Obviously they had never heard of such a thing. "Never mind," he said. He sighed and sat back again. "You can't have it, and that's that."

"But you said you would love to give it to us," Fillip pointed out.

"That is what you said," agreed Sot.

"And we would love to have it."

"We would."

"So why not give it to us, High Lord?"

"Yes, why not?"

"Just for a little while, even?"

"Just for a few days?"

Ben lost his temper once again. He snatched up the bottle and brandished it before him. "I wish I have never seen this bottle!" he yelled. "I hate the damn thing! I wish it would disappear! I wish Abernathy and the medallion would reappear! I wish wishes were candy and I could eat them all day long! But they aren't, and I can't, and neither can you! So let's drop the whole subject of the bottle and get back to the trolls before I decide I don't want to listen to you anymore on *anything* and send you on your way!"

He put the bottle down again with a thud and sat back. The gnomes glanced at each other meaningfully.

"He hates the bottle," whispered Fillip.

"He wishes it would disappear," whispered Sot.

"What did you say?" Ben asked. He couldn't quite hear them.

"Nothing, Great High Lord," answered Fillip.

"Nothing, Mighty High Lord," answered Sot.

They went quickly back to their tale of woe about the trolls, a tale which they wrapped up rather quickly. While they were telling it, they never took their eyes off the bottle.

The remainder of the day slipped by rather quicker than Ben had expected. The gnomes finished their tale and departed for their quarters. Guests were always invited to spend the night, and Fillip and Sot invariably accepted the invitation because they loved Parsnip's cooking. That was all right with Ben so long as they stayed out of trouble. Before they were even through the garden room door, Ben was moving to join Willow. Belatedly, he remembered the bottle, still sitting next to his chair amid the flower boxes. He retraced his steps, picked it up, glanced around for a safe place to put it, and decided on a cabinet that displayed a series of ornate flower pots and vases. He slipped the bottle inside, where it blended quite nicely, and hurried out.

He walked the gardens with Willow for a time, reviewed his agenda for the following day—how in the world was he going to get along without Abernathy to remind him of his appointments and to keep his calendar?—stuck his head in the kitchen to see what Parsnip was preparing, and went for a run.

Running was the one exercise he still practiced faithfully. He kept what he could of his boxer's routine—a holdover from his days as a silver gloves champion and after—but he lacked the sophisticated punching equipment that would let him train as he would in a Chicago gym, so he relied heavily on the running, together with rope work and isometrics. It was enough to keep him fit.

He dressed in his sweats and Nikes, crossed from the island to the mainland in the lake skimmer—his private skiff, a vessel that ran without any power but that of his own thought—climbed the hills beyond, and began to run along the rim of the valley. Fall was in the air, a brief hint of color already beginning to show in the green of the trees. Days were growing short, the nights cold. He ran for almost two hours, trying to work through the day's frustrations and disappointments; when he was sufficiently tired, he crossed back again.

By now the sun was slipping quickly into the west, already partially masked by a screen of forest trees and distant peaks. He watched the dramatic outline of the castle loom up before him as he sat in the skimmer, thinking how much he loved it here. Sterling Silver was the home he had always searched for—even when he didn't know he was searching for it. He remembered how forbidding she had seemed that first time, all worn and discolored from the Tarnish, the loss of magic in the land having sickened her. He remembered how huge and empty she had seemed. That was before he had discovered that she was alive and that she was as capable of feeling as he. He remembered the warmth he had felt in her that first night—a warmth that was real and not imagined. Sterling Silver was a singular bit of magic, a creation of stone and mortar and metal that was nevertheless as human as any creature of flesh and blood. She could extend warmth, she could provide food, she could shelter, she could comfort. She was a wondrous magic, and he never ceased to marvel that she could actually be.

He received word from Willow on his return that Questor had surfaced long enough to report that he had determined that Abernathy definitely wasn't still in Landover. Ben accepted the news stoically. He hadn't really expected things to be that easy.

Willow came to him and washed him in his bath. Her tiny hands were gentle and loving, and she kissed him often. Her long, green hair swept down about her face as she worked, and it made her seem veiled and mysterious.

"You must not be too angry with Questor," she said finally as he was toweling himself dry. "He tried to do what he thought best for Abernathy. He wanted desperately to help."

"I know that," Ben said.

"He holds himself responsible for Abernathy's condition,

and such responsibility is a terrible burden." She looked out the window of his bedchamber into the darkening night. "You should understand better than anyone what it can be like to feel responsible for another person."

He did. He had carried the weight of that responsibility more times than he cared to remember. A few times he had carried it when it was not really his to carry. He thought of Annie, his wife, gone now almost four years. He thought of his old law partner and good friend, Miles Bennett. He thought of the people of Landover, of the black unicorn, of his new friends Willow, Abernathy, Bunion, Parsnip, and, of course, Questor.

"I just wish he could manage to control the magic a little better," he said softly. Then he stopped in the middle of what he was doing and looked over at the sylph. "I'm scared to death of losing that medallion, Willow. I remember all too well what it was like when I thought I'd lost it last time. I feel so helpless without it."

Willow came to him and held him. "You will never be helpless, Ben. Not you. And you will never be alone."

He hugged her close and nodded into her hair. "I know. Not while you're around. Anyway, I shouldn't worry. Something will come up."

Something did come up, but it wasn't until dinner was nearly over that it did, and it wasn't what either of them expected. Dinner was a sparsely attended affair. The G'home Gnomes did not show up—an astonishing occurrence—nor did Questor. Bunion dropped by briefly and was off again, and Parsnip stayed in the kitchen. So Ben and Willow sat alone at the great dining hall table, eating dutifully and listening to the silence.

They were just finishing when Questor Thews burst into the room, his owlish face so distraught that Ben was on his feet instantly.

"High Lord!" the wizard gasped. "Where is the bottle?"

"The bottle?" Ben had to think a moment. "In the garden room, in a display case. What's wrong?"

Questor was trying so hard to catch his breath that Ben and Willow felt obliged to help him to a chair. Willow gave him a glass of wine, which he quickly drained. "I remember now where I saw the bottle, High Lord!" he said finally.

"Then you *did* see it before! Where?" Ben pressed.

"Here, High Lord! Right here!"

"But you didn't remember that earlier when you saw it?"

"No, of course not! That was over twenty years ago!"

Ben shook his head. "You're not making any sense, Questor."

The wizard lurched to his feet. "I will explain it all to you as soon as we have that bottle safely in hand! I will not feel comfortable until we do! High Lord, that bottle is extremely dangerous!"

Bunion and Parsnip had appeared as well by now, and the bunch of them hastened down the castle halls toward the garden room. Ben tried to find out more as they went, but Questor refused to elaborate. They reached the garden room in moments and pushed through the closed doors in a knot. The room was dark, but a touch of Ben's hands on the castle walls brought light.

He crossed the room to the display cabinet and peered through its glass doors.

The bottle was gone.

"What, what in . . . ?" He stared in disbelief at the empty space on which the bottle had rested. Then he knew. "Fillip and Sot!" He spit their names out like loose stones. "Those damn gnomes, they couldn't leave well enough alone! They must have stayed behind at the door to see where I put it!"

The others pushed forward, facing past him to the cabinet.

"The G'home Gnomes took the bottle?" Questor asked incredulously.

"Bunion, go search for them," Ben ordered, already fearing the worst. "If they're still here, bring them—quick!"

The kobold was gone instantly and back again just as quickly. His monkey face grimaced and his teeth showed.

"Gone," Ben cried in fury.

Questor looked faint. "High Lord, I am afraid that I have some very bad news for you."

Ben sighed stoically. Somehow, he wasn't surprised.

Graum Wythe

*A*bernathy came awake with a start. He didn't come awake in the ordinary sense because he had never really been asleep, just wishing he was, his eyes squinched closed, his breath held like a swimmer underwater. It seemed as if he came awake, however, because first the light was there, all around him, so intense he could feel its brightness even with his eyes closed, and then all of a sudden it was gone.

He blinked and looked around. A screen of shadows and half-light masked everything. He took a moment to let his vision clear fully. There were bars in front of his face. He blinked again. There were bars all around! Good heavens, he was in a cage!

He tried to scramble up from the sitting position in which he found himself and discovered that his cage would not permit it. His head was right up against the ceiling. He maneuvered one arm—he could barely move that either—to touch the ceiling experimentally, then the bars . . . Wait, what was this? He touched the bars again. They were set in glass of some sort—and weren't really bars, but some sort of latticework, very ornate, very intricate. And the cage wasn't square, it was hexagonal!

Who ever heard of a hexagonal cage?

He glanced down. A pair of delicate-looking vases were squashed between his legs and the glass, looking for all the world as if they would shatter with his next breath.

Nevertheless, he did breathe, mostly from astonishment. He wasn't in a cage; he was in some sort of display case!

For a moment he was so bewildered that he was at a complete loss as to what to do next. He stared out beyond the case into the shadows and half-light. He was in a massive stone and timber hall filled with cabinets and shelving, cases and pedestals, all displaying various artifacts and art objects. The light was so poor that he could barely make any of it out. A scattering of windows that were small and set high on the walls allowed in what little light there was. Tapestries decorated the walls at various intervals, and a floor of stone flagging was covered with scattered squares of what appeared to be handwoven carpet.

Abernathy scowled. Where in the name of all that was good and decent in the world was he? That confounded Questor Thews! He might still be in Sterling Silver for all he knew, locked away in some half-forgotten room of old art, except . . . He let the thought trail away unfinished. Except that he wasn't, he sensed. His scowl deepened. That muddleheaded wizard! What had he done?

A door opened at one end of the room and closed softly. Abernathy squinted through the gloom. Someone was there, but he couldn't see who. He held his breath and listened. Whoever was there apparently didn't know about him yet. Whoever was there was strolling idly about the room, moving very slowly, stopping from time to time, looking things over. A visitor, Abernathy decided, come to look at the art. The footsteps grew closer, off to his left now. His display case sat rather far out from the wall, and he could not see clearly behind him without turning his head and shoulders. If he did that he was afraid he might break something in the case. He sighed. Well, maybe he should. After all, he couldn't just sit there indefinitely, could he?

The footsteps passed behind him, slowed, came around, and stopped. He looked down. A small girl was looking up. She was very young, he decided, no more than maybe twelve, with a tiny body, a round face and curly honey-blond hair cut short. Her eyes were blue and there was a scattering of freckles on her nose. She was apparently trying to decide what he was. He held his breath momentarily, hoping that she might lose interest and go away. She didn't. He tried to stay perfectly still. Then he blinked in spite of his resolve, and she drew back in surprise.

"Oh, you're alive!" she exclaimed. "You're a real puppy!"

Abernathy sighed. This was turning out about the way he had expected it would—about the same as the rest of his day.

The little girl had come forward again, eyes wide. "You poor thing! Locked in that case like that, no food or water or anything! Poor puppy! Who did this to you?"

"An idiot who fancies himself a wizard," Abernathy replied.

Now her eyes *really* opened wide. "You can talk!" she whispered in a voice of conspiratorial elation. "Puppy, you can talk!"

Abernathy frowned. "Would you mind not calling me 'puppy'?"

"No! I mean, no, I wouldn't mind." She edged closer. "What's your name, puppy? Uh, I'm sorry. What's your name?"

"Abernathy."

"Mine's Elizabeth. Not Beth or Lizzy or Liz or Libby or Liza or Betty or anything else, just Elizabeth. I hate those cute abbreviations. Mothers and fathers just stick you with them without asking you what you think about it, and there they are, yours forever. They're not real names, just half-names. Elizabeth is a real name. Elizabeth was my great-aunt's name." She paused. "How did you learn to talk?"

Abernathy frowned some more. "I learned as you did, I imagine. I went to school."

"You did? They teach dogs how to talk where you're from?"

Abernathy was finding it hard to stay patient. "Of course not. I wasn't a dog, then. I was a man."

Elizabeth was fascinated. "You were?" She hesitated, thinking. "Oh, I see—a wizard did this to you, didn't he? Just like *Beauty and the Beast*. Do you know the story? There was this handsome prince and he was changed into an ugly beast by a wicked spell and couldn't be changed back again until he was truly loved." She stopped. "Is that what happened to you, Abernathy?"

"Well . . ."

"Was the wizard a wicked wizard?"

"Well . . ."

"Why did he change you into a dog? What kind of dog are you, Abernathy?"

Abernathy licked his nose. He was thirsty. "Do you suppose you could open the door to this display case and let me out?" he asked.

Elizabeth hurried forward, curls bouncing. "Oh, sure." She stopped. "It's locked, Abernathy. These cases are always locked. Michel keeps them that way to protect his things. He's very mistrustful." She paused. "Oh, oh. What's happened to the bottle that was in there? There was a white bottle painted with dancing clowns and now it's gone! What's happened to it? Are you sitting on it, Abernathy? Michel will be furious! Is it under you somewhere, maybe?"

Abernathy rolled his eyes. "I have no idea, Elizabeth. I cannot see anything under me because I cannot move out of the way to look. I will probably never see anything under me again if I do not get out of here!"

"I told you, the door's locked," Elizabeth repeated solemnly. "But maybe I can get a key. My father is steward of

Graum Wythe. He has keys to everything. He's gone right now, but let me check his room. I'll be right back!" She started away. "Don't worry, Abernathy. Just wait here!"

Then she was gone, out the door like a cat. Abernathy sat quietly in the silence and thought. What bottle was she talking about, who is Michel, where is Graum Wythe? He had known a Michel once. And a Graum Wythe. But that was years ago, and that Michel and that Graum Wythe were best forgotten. . . .

He felt a sudden chill steal up his spine as the almost forgotten memories took shape once more. No, it couldn't be, he told himself. It was just a coincidence. Probably he heard wrong. Probably Elizabeth said something else and he misunderstood.

The minutes slipped away, and finally she was back. She appeared noiselessly through the door, crossed to the display case, inserted a long iron key into the lock, and twisted. The glass and iron-mesh door opened, and Abernathy was free. Gingerly, he extricated himself.

"Thank you, Elizabeth," he said.

"You're welcome, Abernathy," she replied. She straightened the upended vases, searched about in vain for the missing bottle, and finally gave up. She closed the display case door and locked it once more. "The bottle isn't there," she announced solemnly.

Abernathy straightened himself and brushed off his clothing. "I give you my word, I know nothing of its whereabouts," he advised her.

"Oh, I believe you," she assured him. "But Michel might not. He isn't very understanding about such things. He doesn't even allow people in this room normally unless he invites them in—and then he stays right there with them. I can get in alone only because my father is steward. I like to come here to look at all the neat things. Do you know that there's a picture on the far wall with people in it that really move? And a music box that will play whatever you ask it to? I don't know what was in the bottle, but it was something special. Michel never let anyone near it."

A picture with people that moved and a music box that played requests? *Magic,* Abernathy thought instantly. "Elizabeth," he interrupted, "where am I?"

Elizabeth looked at him curiously. "In Graum Wythe, of course. Didn't I tell you that before?"

"Yes, but . . . where is Graum Wythe?"

The blue eyes blinked. "In Woodinville."

"And where is Woodinville?"

"North of Seattle. In Washington State. In the United States of America." Elizabeth watched the confusion on Abernathy's face grow. "Doesn't any of this mean anything to you, Abernathy? Don't you know any of these places?"

Abernathy shook his head. "These are not places in my world, I am afraid. I do not know where . . ." Then suddenly he stopped. There was alarm in his voice. "Elizabeth," he said slowly, "have you ever heard of a place called Chicago?"

Elizabeth smiled. "Sure. Chicago is in Illinois. But that's a long way from here. Are you from Chicago, Abernathy?"

Abernathy was beside himself. "No, but the High Lord is—or was! This is a nightmare! I'm not in Landover anymore! I have been sent to the High Lord's world! That fool wizard!" He stopped in horror. "Oh, good heavens—and I have the medallion! The High Lord's medallion!"

He fumbled desperately at the chain and medal that hung about his neck while Elizabeth cried, "Abernathy, it's all right, it's okay, don't be frightened, please! I'll take care of you, really I will, I'll look out for you." And all the while she petted him soothingly.

"Elizabeth, you do not understand! The medallion is the High Lord's talisman! It cannot protect him while I have it in this world! He needs it to be with him in Landover! This is no longer his worl . . . !" Again, he stopped. There was new horror in his eyes. "Oh, for . . . His world! This is his world, his *old* world! Elizabeth! You say this place is called Graum Wythe—and that its master is called Michel. What is his full name, Elizabeth? Quickly, tell me!"

"Abernathy, calm down!" Elizabeth kept trying to pet him. "His name is Michel Ard Rhi."

Abernathy looked as if he were about to have a heart attack. "Michel Ard Rhi!" He breathed the name as if to speak it too loudly would bring on the pending heart attack for sure. He took a deep, calming breath. "Elizabeth, you must hide me!"

"But what's wrong, Abernathy?"

"It is quite simple, Elizabeth. Michel Ard Rhi is my worst enemy."

"But why? What happened to make you enemies?" Elizabeth was full of questions, her blue eyes dancing. "Is he a friend of the wizard who changed you into a dog, Abernathy? Is he a bad . . ."

"Elizabeth!" Abernathy tried to keep the desperation from his voice. "I will tell you everything, I promise—after you hide me! I cannot be found here—not with the medallion, not with . . ."

"Okay, okay," the little girl assured him quickly. "I said I would take care of you, and I will. I always keep my promises." She thought. "You can hide in my room. You won't be found there for a while. No one comes there much except for my dad, and he won't be back for a few days." She paused. "But we have to find a way to get you there first. That might not be easy, you know, because there's always someone wandering about the halls. Let me see . . ."

She studied him critically for a moment, Abernathy wishing he could make himself invisible or something, and then she clapped her hands excitedly.

"I know!" She grinned. "We'll play dress-up!"

It was the low point of Abernathy's life, but he did it because Elizabeth assured him it was necessary. He trusted Elizabeth instinctively, the way you will a child, and did not question that she truly intended to help him. He was frantic to get out of the open and into hiding. The worst thing in any world that could happen to him was to be found again by Michel Ard Rhi.

So he let Elizabeth tie a makeshift collar and leash about his neck, he dropped down on all fours still wearing his silks with their silver clasps, and he walked out of that room like a real dog. It was uncomfortable, disgraceful, and humiliating. He felt like a complete fool, but he did it anyway. He even agreed to sniff at things as he walked and wag his stubby tail.

"Whatever you do, don't talk," Elizabeth cautioned as they stepped through the door into a hallway beyond. The hallway was as shadowed and closed away as the room filled with art, and Abernathy could feel the cold of the stone on his feet and hands. "If anyone sees us, I'll just tell them you're my dog and we're playing dress-up. I don't think they will question it much when they see those clothes you're wearing."

Charming, thought Abernathy, irritated. And exactly what is wrong with my clothes? But he didn't say anything.

They passed down a long series of corridors, all rather poorly lit by a combination of tiny windows and lamps, all constructed of stone and timber. Abernathy had seen enough of Graum Wythe by now to know that it was a castle much like Sterling Silver. That suggested that perhaps Michel Ard Rhi was living out his boyhood fantasies, and that in turn made the scribe curious to know more. But he didn't want to think about Michel just now; he was almost afraid that thinking of him might somehow make the man appear, so he forced the matter from his mind.

Elizabeth had brought him quite some distance through Graum Wythe's halls without encountering anyone when they rounded a corner and found themselves face to face with a pair of men in black uniforms. Elizabeth stopped. Abernathy immediately edged back behind her legs, finding them entirely too skinny to hide behind. He sniffed the floor dutifully and tried to look like a real dog.

"Afternoon, Elizabeth," the men greeted.

"Good afternoon," Elizabeth replied.

"That your dog?" one asked. She nodded. "All dressed up, eh? Bet he doesn't like it much."

"Bet he hates it," the other agreed.

"What's he got on his nose, glasses? Where'd you find those, Elizabeth?"

"Pretty fancy stuff for a dog," the other observed. He started to reach down, and Abernathy growled, almost before he realized what he was doing. The man pulled his hand back quickly. "Not very friendly, is he?"

"He's just frightened," Elizabeth offered. "He doesn't know you yet."

"Yeah, guess I can understand that." The man started on his way again. "Let's go, Bert."

The other hesitated. "Does your father know about this dog, Elizabeth?" he asked. "I thought he told you no pets."

"Oh. Well, he changed his mind," Elizabeth said. Abernathy slipped out from behind her, pulling on the leash. "I have to go now. 'Bye."

"'Bye, Elizabeth," the man said. He started away, then turned back. "Hey, what kind of dog is that anyway?"

"I don't know," Elizabeth called. "Just a mutt."

It was all Abernathy could do to keep from biting her.

"I am not a mutt," he told her when it was safe to talk again. "I happen to be a soft-coated Wheaten Terrier. My bloodlines are probably better than your own."

Elizabeth blushed. "Sorry, Abernathy," she said softly, eyes downcast.

"Oh, well, that's all right," he soothed, trying to make up for his gruffness. "I simply wanted you to know that I possess pedigree despite my condition."

They sat in her room on the edge of her bed, safe for the moment. Her room was bright and sunny in contrast to what they had seen of the rest of the castle, the walls paneled and papered, the floor carpeted, and the furniture soft and feminine with stuffed animals and dolls scattered about. Books lined a case on one wall beside a small writing desk, and pictures of teddy bears and puffins were hung casually about. A poster of something or someone called Bon Jovi was taped to the back of the closed door.

"Tell me about you and Michel," Elizabeth asked, eyes lifting once more.

Abernathy sat back stiffly. "Michel Ard Rhi is part of the reason that I am a dog," he said. He thought for a moment. "Elizabeth, I honestly don't know if I should tell you this or not."

"Why, Abernathy?"

"Well . . . because much of it is going to be very hard for you to believe."

Elizabeth nodded. "Like what you told me about the wizard changing you from a man into a dog? Like you being from another world?" She shook her head and looked very solemn. "I can believe things like that, Abernathy. I can believe there are things most people don't know anything about. Like magic. Like make-believe places that really aren't make-believe. My dad tells me all the time that there are all kinds of things people don't believe just because they don't understand them." She paused. "I don't tell anyone this—except for my best friend Nita—but I think that there are other people living out there somewhere on other worlds. I do."

Abernathy regarded her with new respect. "You happen to be right," he said finally. "This is not my world, Elizabeth. It is not Michel Ard Rhi's world either. We are both from a world called Landover, a kingdom really, not very big, but very far away. It is a crossroads for many worlds besides yours, all leading into the mists where the fairy people live. The mists

are the source of all magic. The fairies live entirely in the magic;
other worlds and peoples do not—at least, not for the most
part."

He stopped, trying to think how to proceed. Elizabeth was
staring at him with amazement, though not disbelief. He
reached up and shoved his glasses further back on his nose.

"What happened to me happened more than twenty years
ago. Michel's father was King of Landover then. He was in the
final year of his life. I was his Court Scribe. Michel was about
your age—but other than that, he was nothing like you, of
course."

"Was he bad?" Elizabeth wanted to know.

"He was."

"He's not very nice now, either."

"Well, then, he has not changed much from when he was
your age." Abernathy sighed. The memories came flooding
back, painful images that lingered and refused to go. "I played
with Michel while he was growing up. His father asked me to
and so I did. He was not a very pleasant child, especially after
Meeks took him under his wing. Meeks was the old Court
Wizard, a very bad man. He made friends with Michel and
taught him bits of magic. Michel liked that. He was always
pretending he could do anything he wanted to do. When I
played with him, he always pretended he had a castle called
Graum Wythe, a fortress stronghold that could stand against a
hundred hostile armies and a dozen wizards. He liked the idea
of having so much power at his command."

Abernathy shook his head. "He played at this and he
played at that, and I went along with it. It was not my place
to question what was happening to the boy—or what I thought
was happening. The old King did not seem to see it as clearly
as I did . . ." He shrugged. "Michel was quite a little monster,
I'm afraid."

"Was he mean to you?" Elizabeth asked.

"He was, but he was much meaner to others. I had some

protection because I was Court Scribe. Others were not so fortunate. And Michel was really cruel toward animals. He seemed to take great delight in tormenting them. Particularly cats. He really hated cats for some reason. He was always finding strays and throwing them off the castle walls . . ."

"That's horrible!" Elizabeth exclaimed.

Abernathy nodded. "I told him so. Then one day I caught him doing something so unspeakable that even now I cannot bear to talk about it. In any case, that was the end of my patience. I picked up that boy, turned him over my knee, and beat him with a switch until he howled! I did not think about what I was doing, I just did it. When I was finished, he ran screaming from the room, furious at me for what I had done to him."

"Well, he deserved it," Elizabeth announced, certain of it even without knowing what it was he had done.

"Nevertheless, it was a terrible mistake on my part," Abernathy continued. "I should have left well enough alone and simply advised the King on his return. The King was gone, you see, and Michel had been left to the care of Meeks. He went immediately to Meeks, therefore, and demanded that I be punished. He wanted my hand cut off. Meeks, I learned later, laughed and agreed. Meeks never cared much for me, you see. He felt I influenced the old King against him. So Michel summoned his guards and they came looking for me. There was no one to protect me. Meeks was acting regent in the King's absence. I would most certainly have had my hand removed had they found me."

"But they didn't." Elizabeth was anxious to help the story along.

"No. Questor Thews found me first. Questor was Meeks's half brother, a wizard as well, albeit a lesser talent. He was visiting for the week, hoping the old King would find him a position somewhere or other. We were friends, Questor and I. He did not care much for his half-brother or Michel either, and

when he heard what was happening he came to warn me. There
was no time for me to escape from the castle and no place to
hide within it. Michel knew them all. So I allowed Questor
Thews to change me into a dog so I would not be harmed. I
wasn't, fortunately, but afterward Questor was unable to
change me back again."

"So it wasn't a bad wizard who changed you after all,"
Elizabeth said.

Abernathy shook his head. "No, Elizabeth—just a poor
excuse for one."

Elizabeth nodded solemnly, her freckled face lined with
thought. "And you've been a dog all these years? Sorry. A . . .
a soft-coated Wheat Terrier?"

"Soft-coated *Wheaten* Terrier. Yes. Except for my fingers
and my voice and my thinking, which are still the same as they
were when I was a man."

Elizabeth smiled a sort of sad child's smile. "I wish I could
help you, Abernathy. Help change you back, I mean."

Abernathy sighed. "Someone tried that already. That's
how I ended up here, scrunched up in that display case. Questor
Thews again, I'm afraid. He is not any more adept at his art
now than he was thirty years ago. He thought he had finally
found a way to change me back. Unfortunately, the magic failed
him once again, and here I am, trapped in the castle home of
my worst enemy."

They were silent for a moment, staring at each other. Afternoon sunshine spilled through the curtained windows and
warmed the room. The speckled blue and violet wildflowers in
the vase on the dresser smelled of meadows and hills. From
somewhere distant, there came the faint sound of laughter and
a scraping of boxes or crates. Abernathy was reminded of home.

Elizabeth was speaking. "My father once told me that
Michel could be very mean to animals," she was saying. "He
said that was why I couldn't have a pet—because something

might happen to it. No one at Graum Wythe has a pet. You never see any animals here."

"I don't wonder," Abernathy replied wearily.

She looked at him. "Michel mustn't be allowed to find you."

"No, he certainly mustn't."

"But the watch will say something about my having a dog, I'll bet." She frowned at the thought. "The watch tells him everything. They keep this place guarded just like a prison. Even my father can't go everywhere—and he is chief steward of Graum Wythe. Michel relies on him completely. He runs everything—well, almost everything. He doesn't run the watch. They report directly to Michel."

Abernathy nodded, saying nothing, thinking suddenly of the medallion concealed beneath his tunic, imagining what would happen if he were caught wearing it.

Elizabeth sighed. "I don't like Michel very much—even though he's really never done anything to me. He just isn't very friendly. He always looks so . . . creepy."

Abernathy didn't know what "creepy" meant, but he was sure it was something Michel Ard Rhi could be. "I have to get away from here, Elizabeth. You have to help me."

"But, Abernathy, where will you go?" she asked immediately.

"It really doesn't matter so long as it is far away from here," he advised. He paused, frowning. "I still cannot understand why I am here rather than somewhere else. Here, of all places. How could that happen?" He shook his head.

"I think I should go with you," Elizabeth said suddenly.

"No! No, you cannot do that!" Abernathy replied at once. "No, no, Elizabeth, I have to go alone."

"But you don't even know where you're going!"

"I can find my way, believe me. There is a way back into Landover if you wear the medallion. The High Lord told me something of it once—a place called Virginia. I can find it."

"Virginia is at the other end of the country!" Elizabeth exclaimed, horrified. "How will you get there?"

Abernathy stared at her. He had no idea, of course. "There are ways," he said finally. "But I have to get out of here first. Will you help me?"

Elizabeth sighed. "Of course, I'll help you." She stood up, walked over to the window, and looked out. "I have to think of a way to sneak you through one of the gates. They check everyone going out." She thought. "It's too late today to do anything. Maybe tomorrow. I have to go to school, but I get home by four. Or maybe I'll pretend to be sick and stay home. I can't hide you here for very long." She looked over. "I still think I should go with you."

Abernathy nodded. "I know. But you can't, Elizabeth. You are too young. It would be too dangerous."

Elizabeth frowned, then turned back to the window. "My dad says that sometimes when I ask to do things."

"I suppose he does."

Elizabeth turned back again and looked over with a smile. He saw himself fleetingly in the mirror behind her, saw himself as she saw him, a dog in red and gold silk clothing sitting on her bed, glasses on his furry nose, soulful brown eyes looking back at her. He suddenly thought how ridiculous he must seem to her. He looked away, embarrassed.

But she surprised him. "Are we going to stay good friends, Abernathy," she asked, "even after you're gone?"

He would have smiled if it were possible for dogs to do so. "Yes, Elizabeth, we are."

"Good. I'm really glad that I'm the one who found you, you know."

"I am, too."

"I still wish you would let me come with you."

"I know."

"Why don't you think about it."

"I will."

"Do you promise?"

Abernathy sighed. "Elizabeth?"

"Yes?"

"I could think much better if I had something to eat. And maybe something to drink?"

She bounced out of the room. Abernathy watched her go. He liked Elizabeth. He had to admit that he didn't mind so much being a dog around her after all.

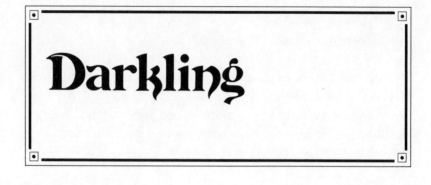

Darkling

"*T*here is something that lives in the bottle," Questor Thews said.

He sat with Ben, Willow, and the kobolds in the garden room. Night's shadows cloaked everything in shawls of gray and black, save only where a single dimmed light from a smokeless lamp lent muted shades of color to a small circle of space where four listeners sat hunched over in silence, waiting for the wizard to continue. Questor's owlish face was gaunt and craggy with worry, his brow furrowed more deeply than usual, his eyes bits of silver glitter. His hands were folded in his lap, gnarled sticks of deadwood that had become inextricably locked together.

"The thing is called a Darkling. It is a kind of demon."

Like the bottle imp, Ben thought suddenly, remembering the old Robert Louis Stevenson story. Then he remembered what the creature of that story had done to its owners and he experienced a sudden twinge of uneasiness.

"The Darkling is very like the genie of the lamp in the old tales," Questor continued. Ben felt the uneasiness begin to subside. "It serves the holder of its bottle, appearing when summoned, doing its master's bidding. It uses various forms of magic to accomplish this." He sighed. "Unfortunately, the magic it uses is all bad."

"How bad?" Ben asked quietly. The uneasiness was back.

"That depends, High Lord." Questor cleared his throat and rocked back in thought. "You have to understand the nature of the magic the Darkling employs. It isn't a magic that is self-contained; it is a magic that is derivatory."

"Which means what?"

"Which means that the Darkling draws its strength from the holder of the bottle. Its magic is fed by the strength of character of the one who calls upon it—not by what is good and kind in that character, but by what is bad and hurtful. Anger, selfishness, greed, envy, other emotions that you can name as well as I, destructive emotions that lurk within all of us to some degree—the Darkling draws the power for its magic from these."

"It feeds on human failing," Willow observed softly. "I have heard of such creatures, long ago banished from the mists."

"Well, that is not yet the worst of it," Questor went on wearily. His mouth had twisted into a scowl that threatened to pull his nose down into his beard. "I mentioned before that the bottle seemed somehow familiar to me. It is—or was, a very long time ago. It has been more than twenty years since I last saw it. It was only just this evening that I was able to remember where." He cleared his throat nervously. "I last saw it in the hands of my half-brother. The bottle belonged to him."

"Oh, oh," Ben groaned.

"But how did it get here?" Willow asked.

The wizard sighed his deepest sigh yet. "To explain that, I have to go back in time."

"Not too far back, I hope?" Ben pleaded.

"High Lord, I will go no further back than is necessary for the purpose of completing my explanation." Questor was slightly indignant. "You must appreciate the fact that the amount of time either of us might believe necessary is somewhat subjective when one . . ."

"Just do it, Questor—please!" Ben urged helplessly.

Questor hesitated, shrugged, nodded, then rocked back once more. He was seated on a bench that offered no back support at all and appeared at every rock to be in danger of going over altogether. He tugged up his legs beneath his robe as a child would, drawing them close to his chest, and his owlish face assumed a faraway look. His brows knitted, and his lips tightened. He appeared to Ben to be a man who had eaten something disagreeable.

Finally, he was ready. "You will remember that my half-brother was Court Wizard to the old King," he began. They all nodded, the kobolds included. "I was without position at the Court, but I would visit from time to time anyway. The old King often gave me small tasks that took me to other parts of the kingdom—tasks that were of no particular interest to my half-brother. My half-brother had been named tutor to the old King's young son shortly after the boy's eighth year, and the whole of my half-brother's time thereafter was occupied with teaching that boy. Unfortunately, he was teaching the boy all the wrong things. He saw that the old King was weakening, aging more quickly, sick from ailments which could not be cured. He knew that the boy would be King after his father was gone, and he wanted control of the boy. Michel was his name. Michel Ard Rhi."

He cocked his head. "Michel had never demonstrated much character, even before he began spending all his study time with Meeks. But after my half-brother got his hands on him, he became a thoroughly despicable lad in no time at all. He was cruel and mean-spirited. He took great delight in tormenting everyone and everything. He was obsessed with the magic Meeks employed and he begged after it as would a hungry man for food. Meeks used the magic to win the boy over and then finally to subvert him altogether."

"Delightful," Ben observed. "So what has this got to do with the bottle, Questor?"

"Well." Questor had assumed his best professorial look. "One of the toys that Meeks gave to Michel to use was the bottle. Michel was allowed to summon the Darkling and order him about. The demon was extremely dangerous, you understand, but not if one appreciated his uses. My half-brother understood enough to keep the creature under control, and Michel's play presented no real threat to him. Michel used the Darkling in quite frightful ways—often in terrible games with animals. It was during one of these uses that Abernathy lost patience with the boy and thrashed him, and I was then forced to change my good friend from a man to a dog in order that he not be harmed.

"It was shortly after that the old King saw what was happening to the boy and ordered all tutoring to stop. Meeks was forbidden to engage in magic thereafter when the boy was about. All the boy's magic things were ordered destroyed—the bottle, in particular."

"But that didn't happen, obviously," Ben interjected.

Questor shook his head. "The old King was weak, but he was still protected by the Paladin. Meeks was not about to challenge him. My half-brother was content to wait for the old man to die. He was already planning his future with the boy, already planning to abandon Landover for other worlds. Time would eventually give him everything, he believed. On the other hand, he was not about to give up the bottle—certainly not about to let it be destroyed. But he couldn't simply hide it; the old King might learn of his deception. And even if he did, he couldn't convey the magic out of Landover when he left, in any case; the natural law of things would not permit it. What was he to do, then?"

Questor paused as if expecting an answer. When he failed to get one, he bent forward conspiratorially and whispered, "What he did was to order the Darkling to convey himself *and* his bottle out of Landover to a place where both would remain hidden until my half-brother came for them once more. Very ingenious.''

Ben frowned impatiently. "Questor, what does all this have to do with the price of apples and oranges?" Questor looked befuddled. "What about the bottle?" Ben snapped.

Questor grimaced and held up his hands imploringly. "My half-brother promised it to the boy. That bottle was the boy's favorite possession. My half-brother assured Michel that his bottle would not be destroyed. He said they would recover it later, after the death of the old King, after they had taken up residence in another land and begun selling kingships to Landover. It was to be their secret." He shrugged. "I would have informed the old King, of course, had I known. But I did not learn of all this until later when the old King was gone. That was when Meeks first chose to tell me about it."

"He *told* you about it?" Ben was appalled.

Questor looked mortified. "Yes, High Lord. There was no reason not to. There was nothing I could do about the matter. My half-brother was quite proud of himself, and his pride insisted that he share his satisfaction in his accomplishments with someone. I was always his first choice when it came time to bestow such honors."

Ben was thinking. Questor glanced at him nervously. "I regret that it took me until now to remember all this, High Lord. I realize I should have remembered sooner. But it has been over twenty years, and the bottle simply didn't recall itself to my memory until . . ."

"Wait a minute!" Ben cut him short. "What *about* the bottle? What happened to it?"

"What happened to it?" Questor repeated.

"Yes. That was the question. What happened to it?"

Questor looked as if he wanted to disappear into himself. "My half-brother retrieved it and gave it back to Michel."

"Gave it back . . ." Ben stopped, horrified.

"Well, there was no reason not to give it back, you see," Questor tried to explain. "My half-brother had made the boy a promise, you remember. There was little danger in keeping it. They were in a new world, and the magic of the bottle was considerably diminished by the fact that not much of anyone in that world believed in or practiced magic. It was relatively harmless there, and . . ."

"Wait a minute!" Ben interrupted. "We're talking about *my* world!"

"Your old world, yes . . ."

"My world! The bottle was in my world! You said . . . ! That means . . . !" Ben was beside himself. He took a quick breath. "Your errant magic worked an exchange, didn't it? That was what you said, wasn't it? And if the magic brought the bottle *here*, it must have sent Abernathy *there*! What in the hell have you done, Questor? You've sent Abernathy to my world! Worse, you've sent him to this nut Michel, haven't you?"

Questor nodded dismally.

"Along with my medallion, damnit, so that now I can't even get back into my world to help him!"

Questor cringed. "Yes, High Lord."

Ben sat back without a word, glanced at Willow, then glanced at the kobolds. No one said anything. The room was still, the sounds of the night distant whispers. Ben wondered why these things always seemed to happen to him.

"We have to get the bottle back," he said finally. He looked at Questor. "And when we do, you had better find a way to exchange it back again for Abernathy!"

The wizard's face screwed into a knot. "I will do my best, High Lord."

Ben shook his head hopelessly. "Whatever." He stood up. "Well, we can't do much until sunrise. It's too dark out there to try to track down those confounded gnomes now. Even Bunion would have trouble. Hardly any light at all—clouded over, no moon. Damn the luck!" He strode to the windows

and back again. "At least Fillip and Sot don't know what they've
taken. They think of the bottle as a pretty possession. Maybe
they won't open it before we find them. Maybe they'll just sit
there and look at it."

"Perhaps." Questor looked doubtful.

"But perhaps not?" Ben finished.

"There is a problem."

"Another problem, Questor?"

"Yes, High Lord, I am afraid so." The wizard swallowed.
"The Darkling is a very unpredictable creature."

"Meaning?"

"Sometimes it comes out of the bottle on its own."

Not a dozen miles from where Ben Holiday was staring in horror at Questor Thews, Fillip and Sot lay huddled together in
the concealing blackness of the night. They had scooped out an
abandoned badger den and backed their way in, two chubby,
furry bodies disappearing inch by inch into the earth until nothing remained but pointed snouts and glittering eyes. They
crouched within their makeshift warren, listening to the sounds
that rose about them, as still as the leaves hanging limp from
the surrounding trees in the windless, peaceful air.

"Shall we take it out one more time?" asked Sot finally.

"I think we should keep it hidden," replied Fillip.

"But we need only take it out for a moment," argued Sot.

"That might be one moment too long," insisted Fillip.

"But there is no light," persisted Sot.

"Some need no light," declared Fillip.

Then they were quiet again, eyes blinking, noses sniffing.
Somewhere distant, a bird cried out sharply.

"Do you think the High Lord will miss it?" asked Sot.

"He said he wished he had never seen it," answered Fillip.
"He said he wished it would disappear."

"But he still might miss it," said Sot.

"He has many other bottles and vases and pretty things," said Fillip.

"I think we should take it out one more time."

"I think we should leave it where it is."

"Just to look at the dancing clowns."

"Just to give someone else a chance to steal it."

Sot hunched down irritably, squirming in a way that would leave no doubt in his brother's mind as to how he felt about the matter. Fillip ignored him. Sot squirmed some more, then sighed and stared out again into the night. He was thinking of the tasty meal and the warm bed he had left behind at the castle.

"We should have stayed with the High Lord until morning," he said.

"It was necessary that we leave at once with the bottle," replied Fillip, a tad weary now of the other's talk. His nose wrinkled. "The High Lord was disturbed by the presence of the bottle. It gave him great pain even to look upon it. It reminded him of the dog. The dog was his friend—although I admit I will never understand how anyone can be friends with a dog. Dogs are good to eat, but have no other purpose."

"We should have told him we were taking the bottle," argued Sot.

"That would only have caused him more pain," rebutted Fillip.

"He will be angry with us."

"He will be pleased."

"I think we should look at the bottle again."

"Will you stop . . . ?"

"Just to be certain that it is still all right."

". . . asking that same . . . ?"

"Just to be sure."

Fillip sighed a deep, wheezy sigh that sent dust flying from their burrow entrance. Sot sneezed. Fillip glanced at him and blinked. Sot blinked back.

"Perhaps just for a very, very brief moment," said Fillip finally.

"Yes, just for a moment," agreed Sot.

Their wrinkled, grimy fingers pawed at the cluster of sticks and leaves that concealed a narrow hole they had dug in the earth directly before them. When the clutter was pushed aside, they reached in together and gingerly extracted a cloth-bound bundle. Holding it close, they loosened the wrappings and pulled out the bottle.

Carefully, they set it on the ground in front of their noses, its painted white surface gleaming faintly, its red harlequins at their dance. Two pairs of gnome eyes glittered with excitement.

"Such a pretty thing," whispered Fillip.

"Such a beautiful treasure," echoed Sot.

They stared at it some more. The allotted moment stretched into several and then into many. Still they stared, transfixed.

"I wonder if there is anything inside," mused Fillip.

"I wonder," mused Sot.

Fillip reached out and shook the bottle gently. The harlequins seemed to dance faster. "It seems empty," he said.

Sot shook it as well. "It does," he agreed.

"But it is difficult to tell without looking," said Fillip.

"Yes, difficult," said Sot.

"We might be mistaken," said Fillip.

"We might," said Sot.

They sniffed it and pawed it and studied it in silence for long moments, turning it this way and that, moving it about, trying to learn something more of its contents. Finally Sot began poking at the stopper. Fillip moved the bottle quickly away.

"We agreed to open it later," he pointed out.

"Later is too long," countered Sot.

"We agreed to open it when we were safely home."

"Home is too far away. Besides, we are quite safe right here."

"We agreed."

"We could re-agree."

Fillip felt his resolve begin to slip. He was as anxious as Sot to discover what, if anything, was concealed within their precious bottle. They could open it—just for a moment—then close it again. They could look down its neck, take just a quick peek . . .

But what if whatever was within the bottle spilled out in the dark and was lost?

"No," said Fillip firmly. "We agreed. We will open the bottle when we are home again and not before."

Sot glowered at him, then sighed his defeat. "When we are home and not before," he echoed with measurable dejection.

They lay without talking for a time, staring at the bottle. They blinked their eyes weakly, trying to keep it in focus, their sight so poor that they could barely do so. G'home Gnomes relied almost entirely on their other senses to tell them what was happening about them. Their eyes were practically useless.

The bottle sat there, a vaguely luminescent oval against the dark. When the stopper wiggled experimentally in its seating, they missed it completely.

"I suppose we should put it away," said Fillip finally.

"I suppose," sighed Sot.

They reached for the bottle.

"Hsssstt!"

Fillip looked at Sot. Sot looked at Fillip. Neither had spoken.

"Hssssstt!"

It was the bottle. The hissing sound was coming from the bottle.

"Hsssstt! Set me free, masters!"

Fillip and Sot froze, ferretlike faces twisted into masks of terror. The bottle was talking!

"Masters, open the bottle! Let me come out!"

Fillip and Sot jerked their extended hands back as one and

scrunched down into their burrow until nothing showed but the tips of their noses. Had they been able to get further down into the earth, they would have done so gladly.

The voice from the bottle began to whine. "Please, please, masters, let me out? I won't hurt you. I am your friend. I can show you things, masters. Set me free. I can show you wonderful things."

"What sort of wonderful things?" ventured Fillip from his refuge, a disembodied voice in the black. Sot didn't say a word.

"Things of bright magic!" the bottle said. There was a long moment of silence. "I won't hurt you," the bottle repeated.

"What are you?" asked Fillip.

"Why can you talk?" asked Sot.

"Bottles don't talk."

"Bottles *never* talk."

The bottle said, "It isn't the bottle speaking to you, masters. It is I!"

"Who's I?" asked Fillip.

"Yes, who?" echoed Sot.

There was a moment's hesitation from the bottle. "I don't have a name," was the answer.

Fillip inched out of the burrow. "Everyone has a name," he said.

Sot inched out with him. "Yes, everyone," he agreed.

"Not I," the bottle said mournfully. Then it became brighter. "But perhaps you can give me a name. Yes, a name you find fitting for me. Why don't you let me out so you can name me?"

Fillip and Sot hesitated, but their fear was already giving way to curiosity. Their marvelous treasure was not just a pretty thing; it was a talking thing as well!

"If we let you out, will you be good?" asked Fillip.

"Will you promise not to hurt us?" asked Sot.

"Hurt you? Oh, no!" The bottle was shocked. "You are

the masters! I must never hurt the masters of the bottle. I must do as they bid me. I must do as I am told."

Fillip and Sot hesitated further. Then Fillip reached out his hand tentatively and touched the bottle. It felt warm. Sot did the same. They looked at each other and blinked.

"I can show you wonderful things," the bottle promised. "I can show you things of bright magic!"

Fillip looked at Sot. "Should we open the bottle?" he asked in a whisper.

Sot looked back at him. "I don't know," he replied.

"I can give you pretty things," the bottle promised. "I can give you treasures!"

That was good enough for the G'home Gnomes. Fillip and Sot reached for the bottle as one, fastened their hands about its neck, and pulled the stopper free. There was a puff of reddish smoke that glittered with bits of green light, then a popping sound, and something small, black, and hairy crawled out of the bottle. Fillip and Sot jerked their hands back at once. The thing crawling from the bottle looked like an oversized spider.

"Ahhhh!" The thing on the lip of the bottle sighed contentedly. It perched there and looked down at them. It was barely a foot tall. Red eyes blinked like those of a cat. It looked less like a spider now. It had four limbs, all seemingly the same, a rat's tail that switched and jerked, an arched back with a spine of bristling black hair, whitish hands and fingers like those of a sickly child, and a face that was thick with hair and blunted— as if it had been pushed in once and never came back again to its original shape. Pointed ears pricked up and listened to the night sounds. A mouth crooked with teeth and wrinkled skin smiled in something close to a grimace.

"Masters!" the creature soothed. The fingers of one limb picked at its body as if there were something irritating hidden in all that black hair.

"What are you?" asked Fillip in a whisper. Sot just stared.

"I am what I am!" the creature said. The grimace broadened. "A wondrous child of magic and wizardry! A being far better than those who gave me life!"

"A demon!" whispered Sot suddenly in terror.

The creature winced. "A Darkling, masters—a poor unfortunate made prisoner to this repulsive body by . . . chance. But keeper of the bottle, too, masters—keeper of all its wonders and delights!"

Fillip and Sot were barely allowing themselves to breathe. "What . . . what wonders do you keep in the bottle?" Fillip ventured finally, unable nevertheless to keep his voice from shaking.

"Ahhhh!" the Darkling breathed.

"Why . . . are they kept there?" asked Sot. "Why not in your pocket?"

"Ahhhh!" the Darkling said again.

"Why do you live in the bottle?" asked Fillip.

"Yes, why?" echoed Sot.

The spiderlike body arched and turned on the lip of the bottle like some feeding insect. "Because . . . I am bound!" The Darkling's voice was an excited hiss. "Because it is my need! Would you like it to be yours, too, perhaps? Would you like to feel its touch? Little masters, would you dare? Would you dare to see how it shapes and molds and reworks life?"

Fillip and Sot were inching further back down into their burrow with every word, trying to make themselves disappear altogether. They were wishing they had kept the bottle closed as they had agreed they would. They were wishing they had never opened it up.

"Ohhhh! Are you frightened?" the Darkling asked suddenly, whining the words, teasing with them. "Are you frightened of me? Oh, no, you mustn't be frightened. You are the masters; I am but your servant. Command me, masters! Ask for something and let me show you what I can do!"

Fillip and Sot just stared at him wordlessly.

"A word, masters!" the Darkling pleaded. "Command me!"

Fillip swallowed the dryness in his throat. "Show us something pretty," he ventured tentatively.

"Something bright," added Sot.

"But that is such a simple task!" the Darkling pouted. "Ah, well. Something pretty, masters, something bright. Here, then!"

It rose from a half-crouch and seemed to swell slightly in size. Fingers flicked this way and that, and tiny bits of green light sparked. All about it flying insects caught fire, turning into brilliant bits of rainbow color. The insects darted madly as the flames consumed them, tiny trailers of brightness as they swept past the astonished gnomes to form intricate patterns against the night.

"Ohhhh!" breathed Fillip and Sot as one, transfixed by the kaleidoscope of color, only vaguely disturbed after the first insect or two by a sense of repulsion.

The Darkling smiled a crooked smile and laughed gleefully. "Here, masters! More colors for you!"

Skeletal white fingers flicked the night air once more, and the bits of green light flew higher this time, exploding with showers of brightness that flared and rainbowed out. A night bird had been set aflame, its cry quick and final as it perished. Others joined it, flaming rainbows of wondrous, terrible color in the dark, stars falling from the heavens. The gnomes watched, their delight growing strangely more demanding as the birds died, their sense of what was being lost gradually becoming submerged in some distant, darkened place within them.

When the birds had been consumed as well, the Darkling turned back to Fillip and Sot. Its eyes glittered a smoky red. That same light was reflected now—just a touch—in the eyes of the gnomes.

"You can see many such things, masters," the Darkling

whispered, its voice a low hiss of promise. "The magic of the bottle can give you all you wish—all the delights and wonders of your imagination and beyond! Do you wish these, masters? Do you wish to enjoy them?"

"Yes!" breathed Fillip rapturously.

"Yes!" sighed Sot.

The Darkling hunched over, black hair bristling out, a thing of perverse shape and fawning gestures. "Such good masters," it whispered. "Why don't you touch me?"

Fillip and Sot nodded obediently. Already they were reaching out their hands.

The Darkling's eyes closed in satisfaction.

Spellbound

*B*en Holiday slept poorly that night, troubled by dreams of the bottle and the demon that lived within it. He dreamed that the demon came out of the bottle on its own—just as Questor had warned it might—a huge, gargoyle monster that could swallow men whole. It did that with Fillip and Sot, did it with half a dozen others, and was in close pursuit of Ben when he mercifully came awake.

The day was gray and rainy, not an auspicious omen. They had delayed their search for the missing G'home Gnomes until morning to assure favorable tracking conditions and had merely ended up swapping darkness for rain. Ben glanced out the windows as he dressed, watching the rain fall in sheets. The ground was puddled and glistening; it must have been raining for some time. Ben sighed heavily. It would be difficult finding any trail at all in this weather.

Nevertheless, Bunion, whose job it was to track the gnomes, seemed unperturbed by the situation. Ben came downstairs to the dining hall to have breakfast with the others before leaving and found the kobold engaged in earnest conversation with Questor Thews on just that subject. Ben was able to follow most of the conversation, having spent enough time with the kobold to pick up a good deal of his difficult, guttural language, and Bunion was indicating that despite the rain he felt he would have no difficulty. Ben nodded in satisfaction and ate more of the breakfast than he thought he would.

When the meal was finished, he adjourned with Questor and Bunion to the front court. Willow was already there, supervising the selection of the horses they would ride and overseeing the loading of the pack animals. Ben was always surprised at how organized the sylph was, taking on duties that weren't necessarily hers, wanting to make certain of the thoroughness of the work. She smiled and kissed him, the rain trailing off her hooded cloak onto her nose and mouth. Ben hadn't particularly wanted her to accompany him, always worried for her safety, but she had insisted. Now he was glad she was doing so. He kissed her back and gave her a reassuring hug.

They ferried the animals across to the mainland, and by midmorning they were underway. Ben rode Jurisdiction, his favorite mount, a bay gelding, Questor sat atop an elderly gray with one white sock, and Willow had chosen a blue roan. The kobolds, as usual, walked, having little use for horses and vice versa. Ben liked to joke that wherever he went on horseback, he always had Jurisdiction. He said it again this morning, but it sounded flat. Everyone was bundled up in their rain gear, heads lowered against the wet and the wind, bodies hunched up against the morning chill, and they were not particularly interested in jokes. They were mostly interested in trying to ignore their discomfort.

Bunion went quickly on ahead, leaving the others to follow at a slower pace. There wasn't much question in Ben's mind where the G'home Gnomes would go; they were fairly predictable creatures. With a treasure of the sort that they believed the bottle to be, they would head directly for the safety of their burrow home. That meant they would travel north out of the forestlands of Sterling Silver through the western borders of the Greensward and finally to the hill country beyond to their gnome community. They would not travel fast; they were slow

creatures under the best of circumstances and they were preoc-
cupied with the bottle. Ben was half-convinced that the little
guys really didn't view what they were doing as theft in any
event and would not be concerned with anyone following. That
meant they would not be running, and Bunion might find
them—rain or no rain—before the day was out.

So they meandered north, picking their way through the
raindrops and puddles, waiting patiently for Bunion to return
with the news that he had found them. Bunion would find
them, of course. Nothing could escape a kobold once he made
up his mind to track it. The kobolds were fairy creatures who
could move from place to place almost swifter than the eye
could follow. Bunion would catch up to the gnomes in nothing
flat once he came across their trail, and Bunion had seemed
certain he would do so quickly. Ben hoped so. He was worried
about this demon.

A Darkling, Questor had called it. Ben tried to envision
it as he rode and failed to find a satisfactory image. Questor
had not seen the creature for better than twenty years, and his
memory as usual was a bit hazy. Sometimes it was little and
sometimes it was big, Questor had said. Ben shook his head,
remembering the wizard's confusion. Big help. What mattered
most, in any case, was the magic the Darkling wielded—magic
that was always bad news for whoever came up against it. But
maybe Fillip and Sot had not yet opened the bottle and let the
Darkling free. Maybe they could manage to stifle their curiosity
long enough for him to catch them before they gave in to it.

He sighed, shifting uncomfortably atop Jurisdiction as the
rain blew into his face on a sudden gust of wind. Maybe the
sun would come out if he clapped his hands, too.

"I think it might be clearing a bit, High Lord," Questor
called out suddenly from just behind him.

Ben nodded wordlessly, never believing it for a moment.
It was probably going to rain like this for forty days and forty
nights, and they ought to be out building an ark instead of

chasing around the countryside after those pinheaded gnomes.
It had been almost a full day now since Abernathy had disappeared into the light with his medallion, and he was beginning
to despair. How was Abernathy going to take care of himself
in Ben's world? Even if he did somehow manage to elude
Michel Ard Rhi, where could he go? He didn't know anyone. He didn't know the first thing about the geography of
Ben's world. And the minute he opened his mouth to ask
someone . . .

Ben quickly blocked the rest of that scenario from his
mind. There was no point in dwelling on Abernathy or the
medallion. He had to concentrate his energy on getting the bottle back from Fillip and Sot. Even without the services of the
Paladin, he felt confident he could do that. Bunion and Parsnip
were more than a match for the gnomes, Darkling or no, and
Questor Thews ought to be able to use his own magic to coun-
teract that of the demon if it should become necessary to do
so. If they were quick enough, they would get the bottle back
again before Fillip and Sot even knew what had happened.

Still, it would have been nice to be able to rely on the
Paladin, he thought—as frightening as his alter ego was to him.
Ben could still remember the times he had been transformed
into the knight-errant—armor closing him about, straps and
buckles clinking into place, the smell of fighting and the memories of battle filling his senses. It was both terrifying and ex-
hilarating, and he was repelled and drawn to it at the same time.
He breathed the wet, cold air and pictured it again in his mind.
Sometimes, when he let himself consider the possibility, he was
afraid that, with enough exposure, the experience of becoming
the Paladin could become an addiction . . .

He shrugged the thought away. Such thoughts didn't matter just now. Without the medallion, there could be no transformation. Without the medallion, the Paladin was just a dream.

Morning stretched into midday, and they paused long
enough to consume a cold lunch within the shelter of a stand

of crimson maple. There was still no sign of Bunion. No one spoke of the matter, but all were concerned. Time was quickly slipping away. They rode out again after a short rest, edging now into the Greensward. Long, grassy stretches of flatland spread away before them east and north. The rain had begun to diminish, fulfilling Questor's expectations, and the air warmed slightly. Daylight was gray and hazy through a vast blanket of gauzy, rumpled clouds.

A short time later, Bunion appeared. He appeared not from the north as expected, but from directly west. He came up to them so swiftly that he was almost on top of them before they saw him, his wiry body skittering and dancing through the damp. His eyes were bright, and he was grinning like a delighted child, all his sharp teeth in evidence. He had found Fillip and Sot. The G'home Gnomes were not on their way north after all. As a matter of fact, they did not appear to be on their way to much of anywhere. They were scarcely two miles distant, engrossed in watching raindrops fall from trees and turn into brightly colored gemstones.

"What?" Ben exclaimed in disbelief, certain he had heard wrong.

Questor hastily said something to Bunion, listened to the kobold's reply, and turned back to Ben. "They have opened the bottle, High Lord. They have set the Darkling free."

"And the Darkling is turning raindrops into gems?"

"Yes, High Lord." Questor looked decidedly uneasy. "Apparently it amuses the gnomes."

"I'll bet it does, those little ferret-faced bozos!" Ben scowled. Why wasn't anything ever easy? "Well, so much for getting the bottle back unopened. Now what, Questor? Will the Darkling try to stop us from putting it back in the bottle?"

Questor shook his head doubtfully. "That depends on Fillip and Sot, High Lord. Whoever holds the bottle controls the demon."

"So the real question is, will Fillip and Sot refuse to give the bottle back to us?"

"The magic is a powerful lure, High Lord."

Ben nodded. "Then we need a plan."

The plan he came up with was fairly simple. They would ride over to a place just out of sight of the gnomes. Parsnip would remain with the horses while the others went forward afoot. Ben, Questor, and Willow would approach from the front, openly. Bunion would sneak around behind. If Ben was unable to persuade the gnomes to return the bottle willingly, Bunion would snatch it away before they could do anything to stop him.

"Remember, Bunion, if you see me rub my chin with my hand, that's your signal," Ben finished. "You get in there as fast as you can and you get that bottle!"

The kobold grinned wolfishly.

They turned west, Bunion showing the way, Parsnip trailing with the pack animals, and rode the short distance to where the G'home Gnomes were at play with their treasure. They pulled into a stand of fir behind a low ridge while still hidden from view, dismounted, gave the horses over to Parsnip, sent Bunion on ahead to get into place, and began walking up the ridge. When they reached its crest, they stopped short.

Fillip and Sot sat beneath a massive old willow, legs tucked up underneath, hands outstretched, laughing gleefully. The old willow's boughs were heavy with rain, and as the droplets slipped free they became sparkling gemstones. The gnomes tried to catch those that fell close, but most tumbled earthward out of reach and collected in shimmering piles. There were gemstones everywhere, heaps of them, flashing rainbow colors through the afternoon gray and damp, a seeming mirage come to life.

The bottle sat upon the ground between the G'home Gnomes, forgotten. An ugly, spiderlike creature danced upon the bottle's rim where the stopper had been pulled and flicked bits of green fire at the raindrops. Each bit of fire changed another droplet into a gemstone.

It was the weirdest scene Ben Holiday had ever witnessed. Fillip and Sot looked as if they had gone nuts.

"All right! That's enough!" he yelled sharply.

The G'home Gnomes froze, shrinking down against the earth like wilted flowers. The Darkling crouched catlike on the lip of the bottle, eyes glittering. Ben waited a moment to be certain that he had their attention, then started down the slope of the ridge, Questor and Willow in tow. When he reached the outer curtain of the willow's broad canopy—not more than a dozen yards from the gnomes—he stopped.

"What do you think you're doing, guys?" he asked quietly.

Fillip and Sot looked terrified. "Leave us alone!" they cried. "Let us be!" The words all jumbled together as they spoke them, and Ben couldn't tell who was saying what.

"There is a small problem that needs solving first," he said evenly. "You have something that belongs to me."

"No, no," whined Fillip.

"Nothing," whined Sot.

"How about the bottle?" he asked.

The moment he said the word "bottle" the gnomes had their hands on it, snatching it back away from him. The Darkling stayed perched on the open lip, clinging to the glass as if it had suction cups on its fingers. Ben had a clear view of the creature now; it was an ugly little thing. The red eyes glittered hatefully, and Ben looked quickly away.

"Fillip. Sot." He tried to keep his voice calm. "You have to give the bottle back. It doesn't belong to you. You took it without permission."

"You said you wished you had never seen it!" insisted Fillip.

"You said you wished it would disappear!" added Sot.

"You put it away!"

"You didn't want it!"

"Great High Lord!"

"Mighty High Lord!"

Ben held up his hands quickly to silence them. "You have to give it back, fellas. That's all there is to it. Close it up and hand it over—right now."

The gnomes pulled the bottle closer still. Their eyes narrowed, and something of the look he had seen in the Darkling's eyes reflected suddenly in their own. Fillip's muzzle was drawing back to show teeth. Sot was stroking the demon's arched spine.

"The bottle belongs to us!" snapped Fillip.

"The bottle is ours!" grated Sot.

The terror was still evident in their eyes, but Ben had mistaken completely its source. He had thought them frightened of him; in truth, they were frightened, not of him, but of losing the bottle.

"Nuts!" he muttered and looked at Questor.

The wizard stepped forward. His scarecrow form straightened. "Fillip and Sot, you are hereby charged with theft of royal property and flight to avoid return of same!" He cleared his throat officiously. "Return the property now—the bottle, that is—and all charges will be dropped. Otherwise, you will be arrested and placed in the castle dungeons." He paused hopefully. "You don't want that, do you?"

The G'home Gnomes cringed. Then suddenly they leaned down to the bottle as the Darkling whispered something up to them. When they looked back again, the defiance was evident.

"You lie to us!" declared Fillip.

"You wish to hurt us!" declared Sot.

"You want the bottle for yourselves!"

"You want its treasures for your own use!"

"You try to trick us!"

"You play hateful games!"

They were on their feet now, holding the bottle between them, backing slowly toward the base of the tree. Ben was appalled. He had never seen the gnomes like this; they were actually ready to fight!

"What's happening here?" he whispered urgently.

"It is the demon, High Lord!" Questor whispered back. "It poisons everyone it touches!"

Ben was already regretting that he had even bothered trying to talk the gnomes out of the bottle. It would have been smarter just to send Bunion in to steal the damn thing and be done with it.

Willow appeared suddenly at his other side. "Fillip!" she called out. "Sot! Please, do not do this to the High Lord! Remember how he came to you when no one else would? Remember how he helped you?" Her voice softened. "He has always helped you when you needed it; you owe him much. Return the bottle to him. He needs the bottle to help find Abernathy and bring him safely back. Do not obstruct him like this. Listen to what is inside of you. Give him back the bottle."

For just a moment, Ben thought they would. They seemed to respond better to Willow; they looked sheepish and guilty. They started forward a step or two, tenuous shufflings, muttering something unintelligible, appearing themselves once more. Then the Darkling darted from the bottle onto first Fillip's shoulder and then Sot's, hissing wickedly, then dropped back again, dancing as if maddened. Fillip and Sot stopped abruptly and began retreating once more. The look of fear and defiance returned.

That was enough for Ben. It was time to call on Bunion. He brought his hand up to his chin and rubbed it as if thinking matters over.

Bunion shot out of nowhere, a blur of darkness against the gray haze of the rain. Fillip and Sot never saw him. He was on them before they realized what was happening. But, by then, the attempt to regain possession of the bottle had already failed. One instant Bunion seemed to have his hands on the bottle; in the next he was flung back, thrown by an invisible force. In-

credibly, the Darkling had taken matters into its own hands.
The demon hissed, spit like a cat, and threw a massive bolt of
green fire at the kobold. Bunion was picked up again and hur-
tled backward through the air to disappear completely from
view.

Ben was already rushing forward, but he was not nearly
quick enough. The G'home Gnomes screamed in warning, and
the Darkling was quick to respond. It whirled on Ben, fingers
flicking at the air. Raindrops turned to knives and whistled toward the High Lord in a lethal barrage. Ben had no chance to
dodge them.

Fortunately, he didn't have to. For once, Questor Thews
got the magic to work right the first time, and the knives were
turned aside at the last possible moment. Ben blinked, shied
away out of reflex, came around again when he realized he
wasn't a pincushion after all, and yelled for Questor and Willow
to run. Already the Darkling was lashing out again, this time
with a bewildering array of rocks and loose stone, thrown from
the earth as if scooped by some giant's hand. Questor's shield
held firm, however, and the three friends backed quickly away,
crouching down against the strange assault as it hammered toward them.

Then the stones were obscured in a gust of hailstones and
winter sleet that suddenly took shape out of the falling rain and
came at them with frightening purpose. Questor cried out
sharply, threw out his hands, and a flash of blinding light obscured everything. But the protective shield was beginning to
give and the hailstones to break through. They struck with
stinging, painful blows, and Ben staggered back, trying to protect Willow as they edged toward the summit of the ridge.

"Get down, High Lord!" he heard Questor yell frantically.

Pulling Willow close, he stumbled over the summit and
down the far slope. Questor's shield gave way completely. Hail
and sleet were all about, a blinding flurry of white, striking at

them. Ben fell to the ground and rolled, Willow going down with him, tumbling wildly through scrub and bare earth.

Then, miraculously, the sleet and hail were gone. Rain fell softly once more, the day gray and empty and still. Ben let his eyes slip open, met Willow's as they lifted to find him, then caught a glimpse of Questor over her shoulder as he struggled up woodenly and brushed himself off.

There was no sign of the gnomes or the demon.

Ben was shaking. He was frightened and angry and grateful to be alive. The Darkling had very nearly killed them. He reached over impulsively and hugged Willow close.

They found Bunion snarled in some brush several hundred yards off, bruised and battered, but conscious. He should have been dead, considering the beating he had taken, but kobolds were very tough creatures. Willow worked over him carefully for a time, using the healing powers common to the once-upon-a-time fairy people of the lake country, touching him gently, taking away the worst of the hurt. After less than half an hour, Bunion was back on his feet, stiff and sore, but grinning wickedly. The kobold hissed a few words of unmistakable meaning at Questor. He wanted another crack at the demon.

But the Darkling had disappeared along with the bottle and Fillip and Sot, and there was no trace of where they might have gone. Ben and company searched for a time, scouring the surrounding countryside for a trail. They found nothing. Apparently the demon had used his magic to conceal their tracks.

"Or maybe they simply flew out of here, High Lord," Questor advised solemnly. "The Darkling has such power."

"Are there any limits to what this thing can do?" Ben asked.

"The only limits imposed on it are those imposed by the character of the holder of the bottle. The worse the character, the stronger the demon." Questor sighed. "Fillip and Sot are not really bad creatures. The strength the Darkling can draw from them should exhaust itself quickly."

"I feel sorry for them, Ben," Willow said quietly. "For Fillip and Sot."

He looked at her in surprise, then nodded wearily. "I suppose I do, too. I don't imagine they even know what's happened to them." He turned. "Parsnip, bring the horses!"

The kobold hurried away. Ben glanced skyward momentarily, thinking. The rain was ending, the day edging quickly toward dusk. There wasn't enough time left to accomplish much of anything before nightfall.

"What do we do now, High Lord?" Questor asked him. The others crowded close.

Ben's jaw tightened. "I'll tell you what we do, Questor. We wait until morning. Then we go after Fillip and Sot. We hunt for them until we find them, and when we find them we get the bottle back and shut the Darkling away once and for all!"

He glanced over at a grinning Bunion. "And next time we'll be ready for the little monster!"

Michel
Ard Rhi

*A*bernathy spent his first full day in Ben's world shut away in Elizabeth's room, discovering how much trouble he was really in. Elizabeth had considered the possibility of staying home sick from school in order to be with him, but had discarded the idea when she realized being sick would bring the housekeeper on a determined crusade of mercy and Abernathy would likely be discovered in the process. Besides, she hadn't come up with a plan to sneak him out of Graum Wythe yet, so she needed the day to think the matter over.

So off she went to school while Abernathy stayed hidden in her room, reading old magazines and newspapers. He asked her for the reading material, and she brought it to him from her father's study before she left. Abernathy was Court Historian as well as Court Scribe in Landover and he knew something of the histories of other worlds as well as his own. He had made it a point to study the history of Ben's world when Meeks moved over there and began recruiting men willing to pay for Landover's throne. It had been pretty frightening stuff. Most of what Abernathy remembered had to do with machines and sciences and any number of wars. Since he was wearing the medallion, he could read and speak the language of any world he was in, so learning what Ben's world was like wouldn't be difficult. But it would be necessary if he was to find a way back to his own.

So he picked through the stack of magazines and newspapers, propped up on Elizabeth's bed amid stuffed animals and dolls, a scattering of pillows at his back, and tried to figure out how things worked. Most of his reading was superfluous. There were an abnormally large number of stories about wars and killing, most the result of politics and economics, many having no rational purpose. There were a number of stories having to do with investigations of one sort or another as well. Abernathy read a few and gave up, concluding that he was trapped in a world full of crooks and thieves. Some of the magazines offered stories of romance and adventure, but Abernathy skipped those. He read more closely the advertisements—that's what they were called, he discovered—and learned most of what was useful from them.

The advertisements told him what was for sale in the way of goods and services, and that let him discover several things. It let him discover that no one traveled by horse or carriage; everyone rode or even flew in machines developed by the world's sciences. It let him discover that in order to use these machines, he had to pay for the privilege with money or something called credit, and he, of course, had neither. Finally, it let him discover—forgetting for the moment the fact that he was a talking dog—that no one dressed anything like the way he did, talked anything like the way he did, or shared much of anything else in the way of a common social, economic, or cultural background. Once beyond the walls of Graum Wythe, he would stand out from everyone else as clearly as day from night.

One of the magazines included a map of the United States, which he quickly realized was Ben's country. He found the state of Washington, where he was, and the state of Virginia, where he had to go. The topography of the country between was clearly delineated on the map. A legend advised him of the distance he would have to travel. Elizabeth had been right—it was a long, *long* way from here to there. He might walk it, but it looked as if the walk could take him forever.

After a time, he put down the newspapers and the magazines, got off the bed, walked over to the twin latticework windows that opened to the south, and looked out. The countryside immediately surrounding the castle was planted with vineyards. There were a few small patches of open space, a tiny stream that meandered about, and several distant houses that dotted the landscape, but not much of anything else. The houses intrigued Abernathy. He had seen pictures of such houses in the magazines, and neither those nor these were anything at all like the houses in Landover. Graum Wythe seemed sorely out of place amid such structures, as if it had been picked up and plunked down without thought to whether it belonged or not. Abernathy assumed it was here solely because it was the prideful re-creation of Michel Ard Rhi's imaginary fortress from his childhood—the place he had occupied in his mind most of his life. There was a moat about it, guardhouses at either end of the drawbridge leading over, a low stone wall farther out with wire and sharp barbs atop it, and a gate. Abernathy shook his head. Michel hadn't changed.

Elizabeth had prepared a sandwich and something called potato chips for Abernathy's lunch, and he ate them at midday before settling back down to read further from the magazines and newspapers. He hadn't been at it for more than a few minutes when he heard footsteps come up to the bedroom door, saw the door handle turn, and watched in horror as it swung open.

There wasn't time to hide. There wasn't time to do anything but drop down amid the newspapers and magazines and play dead. So that was what Abernathy did.

A woman came into the room carrying an armful of what appeared to be cleaning supplies. Abernathy could see this through slitted eyes. She was humming to herself, unaware yet that there was anyone else in the room. Abernathy had curled himself into a ball, trying hard to blend in with the stuffed animals. Was this the dreaded housekeeper Elizabeth had thought to avoid by going on to school instead of playing sick? Why hadn't Elizabeth warned him that she might come into the room to clean anyway? He tried hard not to breathe. Maybe she wouldn't notice him. Maybe she would leave if he just . . .

She turned around and looked right at him. She stiffened in surprise and put her hands on her hips. "Well, what's this? What are you doing here? There's not supposed to be any dogs in here! That Elizabeth!"

She smiled then and laughed—a private joke of some sort, Abernathy decided. There was nothing for him to do now but to play along. He lay there and thumped his stubby tail as best he could, trying to appear like a normal dog.

"Well, well, well! You are a cute thing! All dressed up like a little doll!" The cleaning lady came right up to him, reached down, and gave him a suffocating hug. She was rather stout to begin with, and Abernathy felt the breath leave his body in a rush. "Now what am I supposed to do with you?" she went on, stepping back, giving him an appraising look. "I'll bet no one else knows you're here, do they?"

Abernathy kept thumping his tail, trying to appear cute.

"You've sure made a mess of this room—look at these magazines and newspapers!" The woman bustled about, picking up, straightening up. "Did you eat this sandwich, too? Where'd you get that? I tell you, that Elizabeth!" She laughed some more.

Abernathy lay patiently waiting as she finished moving about, then looked up expectantly as she came back to give him a pat on the head. "None of my business," she muttered and patted him some more. "Tell you what," she said conspiratorially. "You stay right here, don't move. I'll clean the room like I'm supposed to and be on my way. It's not up to me to worry about you. I'll leave you to Elizabeth. Okay?"

Abernathy thumped his tail some more, wishing it were longer. The cleaning lady put a cord in the wall and ran a rather noisy machine about the floor and rugs for a time, ran a cloth over the furniture, picked and straightened up some more, and was done.

She came back over. "Now you be good," she admonished, ruffling his ears. "Don't let anyone know you're here. I'll keep your secret if you will, okay? Now give me a kiss. Right here." She bent down, offering her cheek. "C'mon, just a little kiss."

Abernathy licked her dutifully on the cheek.

"Good dog!" She patted him on the head and rubbed his muzzle. Then she picked up her cleaning gear and headed out the door. "'Bye, old boy," she called back.

The door closed softly and the footsteps moved away.

Abernathy wished he had something to wash out his mouth.

Elizabeth returned around mid-afternoon, unremittingly cheerful. "Hi, Abernathy!" she greeted, pushing through the door and closing it tightly behind her. "How was your day?"

"It would have been better," Abernathy replied archly, "if you had thought to warn me that the housekeeper might clean!"

"Oh, that's right, it's Monday!" Elizabeth groaned and dropped her books on the writing desk with a thud. "Sorry about that. Did she see you?"

"She did. But she thought I was a pet and said I was your responsibility and not hers. I don't think she plans to tell anyone."

Elizabeth nodded solemnly. "Mrs. Allen is my friend. When she gives her word, she keeps it. Not like some I know." She frowned menacingly. "Nita Coles used to be my friend, but she isn't anymore. Know why? Because she told everyone I like Tommy Samuelson. I don't know why she did that. He isn't even my boyfriend or anything, I just said I sort of liked him. He is cute. Anyway, she told Donna Helms, and Donna tells everyone everything, so the first thing you know, the whole school is talking about me and Tommy Samuelson, and I am embarrassed beyond tears! I bet even Mr. Mack, my teacher, knows! I told Eva Richards, my other friend, that if Nita doesn't take it all back and right now, I won't . . ."

"Elizabeth!" Abernathy cut her short with something very much like a bark. "Elizabeth," he said her name again, this time more gently. She stared at him. "Have you come up with a way to get me out of here?"

"Sure." She said it matter-of-factly, as if there had never been any question about it. She dropped herself down on the bed next to him. "A real good way, Abernathy."

"How, Elizabeth?"

She grinned. "We'll send you out with the laundry!" The look on Abernathy's face sent the grin scurrying for cover. "Look, it's simple, really. A truck from the cleaners picks up the laundry every Tuesday. That's tomorrow. Several big canvas hampers go out, full of sheets and stuff. You can hide in one. The guards never check the laundry. You ride out in the back of the truck and when it stops to unload, out you jump. By then, you'll be miles away." She grinned again. "What do you think?"

Abernathy thought. "I think it might work. But what about when they load me in the truck? Won't they think the laundry is a bit heavy?"

Elizabeth shook her head firmly. "No way. The towels and stuff go out wet all the time. They weigh a ton. I've heard Mr. Abbott say so. He's the driver. He won't think anything about it when he puts you in the truck. He'll just think you're a load of wet towels or something."

"I see." Abernathy was undecided.

"Believe me, it'll work," Elizabeth assured him. "All you have to do is sneak down to the laundry early in the morning.

I'll go with you. If we go early enough, we won't run into anyone. I can set my alarm. On the clock," she added, pointing.

Abernathy looked at the time-telling device doubtfully, then back at the little girl. He sighed. "Can you give me a good map of the country to take with me, Elizabeth—something that will help me find my way to Virginia?"

Elizabeth immediately shook her head no. "I have an idea about that, too, Abernathy. You can't go trekking across the country on foot all the way to Virginia. It's just too far. There are mountains between here and there, and it's almost winter. You might freeze!"

She reached over and put her hand on his head. "I've got some money saved. I want to give it to you. I'll have to make up something for Dad, but I can do it. I'll give you the money, and here's what you do. You wrap yourself all up in bandages so no one can see what you look like. They'll think you're all burned or something. Then you go to the airport and buy a standby ticket to Virginia. They're real cheap—I'll show you how to do it. You can fly back in a couple of hours. You'll still have to walk a bit when you get there, but not nearly so far as from here—maybe a hundred miles or so. And it will still be warm there; you won't freeze."

Abernathy didn't know what to say. He just stared at her for a moment. "Elizabeth, I cannot take your money . . ."

"Shhhh, shhhh!" She cut him short with a hiss. "Don't say that. Of course you can. You have to. I can't sleep thinking about you out there wandering across the country. I have to know that you're all right. Really, I should go with you. But since you won't let me, you at least have to take the money." She paused. "You can pay me back later, if you want— sometime."

Abernathy was overwhelmed. "Thank you, Elizabeth," he said quietly.

Elizabeth reached over and gave him a big hug. It was a much better hug than the one he had received from Mrs. Allen.

Abernathy stayed in Elizabeth's room when she went down to eat dinner, waiting patiently for her to bring something edible back for him. He passed the time reading idly through something called *TV Guide,* which he didn't understand. He expected Elizabeth to return in short order, just as she had the previous night, but the minutes slipped by and she failed to show. He began listening at the door for her and even risked a quick look down the empty hall. No Elizabeth.

When she finally appeared, she was ghost white and visibly distressed.

"Abernathy!" she exclaimed with a hiss, closing the door quickly behind her. "You've got to get out of here immediately! Michel knows about you!"

Abernathy went cold. "How did he find out?"

Elizabeth shook her head in anguish, tears starting down her cheeks. "It was all my fault, Abernathy," she sobbed. "I told him! I had to!"

"Now, now," he soothed, kneeling down in front of her, paws coming up to rest on her shoulders reassuringly. He wanted nothing so much as to run from that room as quickly as he could, but first he needed to know what he was up against. "Just tell me what happened," he said, trying to sound calm.

Elizabeth sniffed back her tears and sobs and faced him. "The watch told Michel about you, just as I was afraid they would. They came up to us just after dinner to make their report and happened to mention it to him. They remembered it because they saw me standing there, and one of them asked if I still had the dog. He mentioned the odd clothes you were wearing and the way your paws didn't quite look like paws. He described you. Michel got this funny look on his face and started asking me questions. He asked me where I found you, and I . . . Well, I couldn't lie to him, Abernathy, I couldn't! He has this way of looking at you, kind of mean, like he can see everything . . ."

She broke into sobs again, and Abernathy quickly hugged her against him, holding her until the tears began to subside. "Go on," he urged.

"Well, I told him I found you near the art room. I didn't tell him you were in it or anything, but it didn't matter. He went right to the art room, telling me to stay where I was, and when he came back he was furious! He wanted to know what had happened to his bottle. I said I didn't know. He wanted to know what had happened to *you*! I said I didn't know that, either. I started crying, telling him I just wanted someone to play dress-up with and that when I found you, you were wandering about in these old clothes, so I just put you on a leash and took you for a walk, and . . . Then he wanted to know if you *said* anything to me! He seemed to know you could talk, Abernathy!"

Abernathy felt as if the walls were closing in on him. "Hurry up, Elizabeth," he urged. "Tell me the rest as quick as you can!"

She took a deep, steadying breath. "Well, as I told you, I couldn't lie—not completely, not to him. So I said, 'Yeah, he did!'—as if I was real surprised he knew. I said that was why I sent you away, because I was afraid of you. I just turned you loose and you ran off. I said I hadn't seen you since. I said I hadn't said anything to anyone because I was afraid they wouldn't believe me. I said I was waiting to tell my father when he came back Wednesday." She took hold of him with her hands. "He believed me, I think. He just told me to go to my room and wait there for him. He ordered the watch to start a search. But he was yelling at them like he was crazy, Abernathy! You have to get out of here!"

Abernathy nodded wearily. "How do I do that, Elizabeth?"

The little girl's hands tightened on his arms. "Just the way I said you would—except that you have to go down to the laundry room right now!"

"Elizabeth, you just said they were searching for me!"

"No, no, Abernathy—listen!" Her roundish face bent close, brow furrowed with determination. Her nose freckles seemed to dance. "They've already searched the laundry room. That's where they started. I told them that was where I let you go. So no one's there anymore. They're looking around everywhere else. The laundry room is down the hall, around the corner to the right, on the ground floor—not far. If you go out the window . . . listen to me . . . if you go out the window and down the vines, you can slip around the corner and through the window!"

"Elizabeth, I can't climb down . . ."

"The catch is off, Abernathy! I took it off over the weekend when I was playing hide-and-seek with Mrs. Allen! You can slip right through the window into one of the hampers and wait! If not, just wait in the bushes; I'll come down and open it as soon as I can! Oh, I'm so sorry, Abernathy! This is all my fault! But you have to go! You have to hurry! If they find you here, they'll know I lied, that I helped you . . ."

There was the sound of voices and footsteps in the hall beyond, rapidly approaching.

"Abernathy!" Elizabeth whispered fearfully.

Abernathy was already moving for the windows. He released the catch, pushed open the twin latticework frames, and peered down. It was dark, but he could just make out a thick tangle of trailing vines. They appeared strong enough to hold him.

He turned back to Elizabeth. "Good-bye, Elizabeth," he whispered. "Thank you for your help."

"It's the fifth window around the corner!" she whispered back. Then she put her hands to her mouth in horror. "Abernathy, I haven't given you the money for the airplane ticket!"

"Never mind that," he said, already swinging carefully out the window, testing his weight on the vines. His fingered paws gripped poorly. He would be lucky if he didn't break his neck.

"No, you have to have the money!" she insisted, practically beside herself. "I know! Meet me tomorrow at noon at
the school—Franklin Elementary! I'll have it then!"

There was a knock at the door. "Elizabeth? Open the
door."

Abernathy recognized the voice immediately. "Good-bye,
Elizabeth!" he whispered again.

"Good-bye!" she whispered back.

The latticework windows swung silently shut above him,
and he was left hanging in the dark.

It seemed to Abernathy that it took him an impossible amount
of time to get down. He was terrified of being caught out there,
but he was equally terrified of falling. He compromised his fears
by making his way at something of a snail's pace, taking time
to find each handgrip and foothold as he inched downward
through the vines, pressed as close as he could get to the stone
block. Lights had come on in the courtyard below, electric
lamps—he had read about them—and the darkness was no
longer quite so concealing. He felt like a fly waiting for the swat
that would end its purposeless life.

But the swat didn't come, and he finally felt the reassuring
firmness of the ground touch his feet. He crouched down instantly, eyes sweeping the yard, searching for movement. There
was none. Quickly, he made his way along the wall, staying
close against its dark shadow, out of the illumination of the
lamps. A door opened from somewhere behind, and he heard
voices. He scurried along faster, reaching the bend in the wall
that would take him to the promised laundry window. It was
darker here, the wall turning back into a deep, shadowed alcove.
He slipped along silently, counting windows as he went. The
fifth window, Elizabeth had said. One, two . . .

Behind him, a beam of light shot across the dark, sweeping
the courtyard to the low outer wall and the moat and back again.
A flashlight, Abernathy thought. He had read about those, too.

A flashlight meant that someone was out there on foot, searching the grounds. He practically ran now, counting three, four . . . five!

He skidded to a stop, almost passing by number five without seeing it because it was partially concealed in a clump of bushes. He looked at it. It was smaller than the previous four— smaller, too, than the ones that followed. Was this the right window? Or was he not supposed to count this one? There was light inside, but there was light in the next one as well. He began to panic. He bent close and listened. Did he hear voices in there? He glanced back frantically. The flashlight was coming closer in the dark, the sound of voices back there as well.

He looked forlornly at the window. There was nothing to do but chance it, he decided. If he stayed where he was, he was certain to be found. He reached down to the window and pushed carefully inward. The window gave easily at his touch. He caught a glimpse of linens in a basket. Relief flooded through him. He knelt down quickly and started to crawl in.

Several pairs of hands reached up to help him.

"We found him sneaking in through the laundry room window," said a guard, one of three from the watch that had captured Abernathy. They held him firmly by the arms. "It was lucky we went back or we would have missed him. We'd searched there first and hadn't found a thing. But Jeff here says he thinks maybe one of the windows was left unlatched, that we ought to check it. We did, and that's when we found him, crawling in."

They stood in a study, a room filled with books and files, desks and cabinets—Abernathy and his captors and Michel Ard Rhi.

The guard speaking paused and glanced uncertainly at Abernathy. "Exactly what sort of creature is he, Mr. Ard Rhi?"

Michel Ard Rhi ignored him, the whole of his attention centered on Abernathy. He was a tall, rawboned man with a

shock of black hair and a narrow, pinched face that suggested
he had just eaten something sour. He looked older than he was,
his brow lined, his skin sallow. He had dark, unfriendly eyes
that registered immediate disapproval with everything in view.
He stood ramrod straight, affecting an air of complete
superiority.

"Abernathy," he whispered almost soundlessly, as if in
answer to the guard's question.

He took a moment longer to study his captive, then said
to the guards without bothering to look at them, "Wait
outside."

The guards left, closing the study door softly behind them.
Michel Ard Rhi left Abernathy standing where he was and
moved over to sit behind a huge, polished oak desk littered
with paperwork. "Abernathy," he said again, as if not yet convinced of it. "What are you doing here?"

Abernathy was no longer shaking. When the guards had
captured him he had been so terrified that he could barely stand.
Now he accepted his situation with the weary resignation of
the condemned, and his acceptance gave him a small dose of
renewed strength. He tried to keep his voice calm. "Questor
Thews sent me here by mistake. He was trying something with
the magic."

"Oh?" Michel seemed interested. "What was the old fool
trying this time?"

Abernathy showed nothing. "He was trying to change me
back into a man."

Michel Ard Rhi looked at him appraisingly and then
laughed. "Remember how he changed you into a dog in the
first place, Abernathy? Remember how he botched it? I'm surprised you let him come near you." He shook his head hopelessly. "Questor Thews never could manage to do anything
right, could he?"

He made it a statement of fact, not a question. Abernathy
said nothing. He was thinking of the High Lord's medallion,

still concealed beneath his tunic. He was thinking that whatever else happened, Michel Ard Rhi must not be allowed to discover he wore it.

Michel seemed to know what he was thinking. "Well," he mused, drawing the word out. "Here you are, you say, delivered to me by your inept protector. Such irony. But you know what, Abernathy? Something isn't right about all this. No one human—or dog—crosses through the fairy mists without the medallion. Do they, Abernathy?"

He waited. Abernathy shook his head carefully. "The magic . . ."

"The magic?" Michel interrupted at once. "The magic of Questor Thews? You want me to believe that the magic was the cause of your passage out of Landover into this world? How . . . incredible!" He thought a moment and smiled unpleasantly. "I don't believe it. Why don't you prove it to me? Why don't you satisfy my curiosity? Open your tunic."

Abernathy went cold. "I have told you . . ."

"Your tunic. Open your tunic."

Abernathy gave it up. Slowly he unclasped the tunic front. Michel leaned forward as the silver medallion came into view. "So," he said, his voice a slow hiss. "It *was* the medallion."

He got up and walked out from behind the desk, coming to a stop directly in front of Abernathy. He was still smiling, a smile without warmth. "Where is my bottle?" he asked softly.

Abernathy held his ground, fighting down the urge to step back. "What bottle are you talking about, Michel?"

"The bottle in the case, Abernathy—where is it? You know where it is and you're going to tell me. I don't believe for a moment that you just happened to appear in my castle. I don't believe that this is all just the result of errant magic. What sort of fool do you think I am? The medallion brought you here from Landover. You came to Graum Wythe to steal the bottle, and that's what you've done. It only remains for me to discover where you have hidden it." He paused thoughtfully. "Maybe it's in Elizabeth's room. Is that where it is, Abernathy? Is Elizabeth your accomplice in all this?"

Abernathy tried to keep any trace of fear for Elizabeth from his voice. "The little girl? She just happened to stumble on me, and I had to pretend with her for a bit. If you want, search her room, Michel." He tried to sound disinterested.

Michel watched him like a hawk. He leaned forward a bit. "Do you know what I am going to do with you?"

Abernathy stiffened slightly. "I am sure you will tell me," he replied.

"I am going to put you in a cage, Abernathy. I am going to put you in a cage just as I would with any stray animal. You'll be given dog food and water and a pad to sleep on. And that is where you will stay, Abernathy." The smile was gone completely now. "Until you tell me where the bottle is. And . . ." He paused. "Until you take off the medallion and give it to me."

He bent closer still, his breath strong in Abernathy's nostrils. "I know the law of the medallion. I cannot take it from you; you must give it to me. It must be given freely, or the magic is useless. You will do that, Abernathy. You will give me the medallion of your own choice. I grow tired of this world. I think perhaps I might return to Landover for a time. I think I might *like* being King now."

He stared into Abernathy's eyes for a moment, searching for the fear concealed there, found it, and stepped back again in satisfaction. "If you don't give me the bottle and the medallion, Abernathy, you will be left in that cage until you rot." He paused. "And that could take a very long time."

Abernathy didn't say a word. He simply stood there, paralyzed.

"Guard!" Michel Ard Rhi called. The men without reappeared. "Take him down to the cellar and put him in a cage.

Give him water and dog food twice a day and nothing else. Don't let anyone near him."

Abernathy was dragged roughly through the door. Behind him, he heard Michel call out in a singsong, taunting voice, "You should never have come here, Abernathy!"

Abernathy was inclined to agree.

Slight
Miscalculation

*F*illip and Sot fled north with the bottle, intent on putting as much distance between themselves and the High Lord as was possible. They had escaped in the first place because the Darkling had transported them from the site of battle to a point some miles north, enveloping them in a shroud of smoke and brightly colored lights and whisking them off with all the ease that true magic allows. They had no idea what had become of the High Lord and his companions and they frankly didn't want to know. They didn't even want to think about it.

They ended up thinking about it anyway, of course. All the while they fled north, they thought about it, even without speaking to each other about it, even without acknowledging by covert glances or gestures what they were doing. They couldn't help it. They had committed the most unpardonable, treasonable act imaginable—they had defied their beloved High Lord. Worse, they had actually attacked him! Not directly, of course, since it was the Darkling who had done the attacking, but it was all at their behest and that was the same thing as if they had struck the blows. They couldn't imagine why they had done such a thing. They couldn't conceive of how they had allowed it to happen. They had never even dreamed of challenging the wishes of the High Lord before. Such a thing was unthinkable!

Nevertheless, it had happened, and there was no turning back from it now. They were fleeing because they didn't know what else to do. They knew the High Lord would come after them. He would be furious at what they had done and he would hunt them down and punish them. Their only hope, they sensed, was in flight and, eventually, in hiding.

But where to run and where to hide?

They hadn't resolved the dilemma by the time nightfall and exhaustion made further flight impossible, and they were forced to stop. They wormed their way down into an abandoned badger nest and lay there in the dark listening to the pounding of their hearts and the whisper of their consciences. The bottle was open before them, the Darkling perched on its rim, playing with a pair of frantic moths it had captured and secured with long strands of gossamer webbing. Moon and stars were hidden behind a bank of low-hanging clouds, and night sounds were strangely muted and distant.

Fillip and Sot held hands and waited for the fear to go away. It refused to budge.

"I wish we were home!" Sot whined over and over to Fillip, and Fillip nodded each time without speaking.

They huddled close, too frightened even to think of eating, though they were hungry, or sleeping, though they were tired. They could do nothing but crouch there and think on the misfortune that had befallen them. They watched the Darkling cavort about the bottle, flying the moths like tiny kites, turning them this way and that as the mood struck. They watched, but it was different from what it had been the night before. They no longer found the demon or the bottle so wonderful a treasure.

"I think we did a terrible thing," ventured Fillip finally, his voice a cautious, frightened whisper.

Sot looked at him. "I think so, too."

"I think we made a very bad mistake," Fillip went on.

"I think so, too," said Sot again.

"I think we should never have taken the bottle," finished Fillip.

Sot just nodded this time.

They glanced over at the Darkling, who had stopped playing with the moths and was looking intently at them.

"It might not be too late to give the bottle back to the High Lord," suggested Fillip tentatively.

"No, it might not," agreed Sot.

The Darkling's eyes flared bright red in the dark, blinked once, and fixed on them.

"The High Lord might forgive us if we return the bottle," said Fillip.

"The High Lord might be grateful," said Sot.

"We could explain that we did not understand what we were doing," said Fillip.

"We could tell him how sorry we were," said Sot.

They were both sniffling a bit, wiping at their eyes and noses. The Darkling pointed once at the moths and turned them to bits of blue fire that flared and were gone.

"I do not want the High Lord to hate us," said Fillip softly.

"Nor I," said Sot.

"He is our friend," said Fillip.

"Our friend," echoed Sot.

The Darkling spun suddenly about the lip of the bottle, throwing bits of colored light all about the darkness, the light sparking and exploding in brilliant streamers. Strange images formed and faded and formed again. The G'home Gnomes watched, intrigued anew. The demon laughed and danced, and there were jewels raining down about them as flying moths crystalized and tumbled from flight.

"The bottle is so pretty," said Fillip in awe.

"The magic is so wondrous," sighed Sot.

"Perhaps we could keep the bottle just a bit longer," ventured Fillip.

"Perhaps for just a day or two," agreed Sot.

"What could it hurt?"

"What harm could there be?"

"Perhaps . . ."

"Maybe . . ."

They began and stopped talking at the same moment, turning suddenly to each other, seeing the red glare of the demon's bright eyes reflected in their own and recoiling from it. They tightened their clasped hands and blinked with dazed incomprehension.

"I'm frightened," said Sot, tears in his eyes.

Fillip's voice was a wary hiss. "I don't like the bottle anymore," he said. "I don't like how it makes me feel!"

Sot nodded voicelessly. The Darkling was watching them, the lights and colors and images gone back into the night. The demon hunched down on the lip of the bottle and its red eyes were slits.

"Let's put it back in the bottle," suggested Fillip quietly.

"Let's," agreed Sot.

The demon curled down into a ball and spit suddenly.

"Go away!" said Fillip bravely, making shooing motions with one hand.

"Yes, go away!" echoed Sot.

The demon hissed sharply. "Where would you have me go, masters?" it asked, a bit of a whine in its voice.

"Back into the bottle!" answered Fillip.

"Yes, into the bottle!" agreed Sot.

The demon studied them a moment longer, and then the strange spiderlike body skittered back into the bottle and was gone. Fillip and Sot reached up as one, grabbed the bottle almost frantically, and jammed the stopper back into place.

Their hands were shaking.

After a moment, they set the bottle back down again, just

in front of them, hidden in leaves and twigs at the forefront of their little den. They watched it silently for a time, and then their eyes began to droop, and sleep began to steal through them.

"Tomorrow we will return the bottle to the High Lord," murmured Fillip.

"Give it back to the High Lord," yawned Sot.

They were asleep in moments, reassured that all would be well. Soon, their snores grew steady and their breathing deep.

Immediately, a dull red glare began to emanate from the bottle.

Sot dreamed of brightly shining jewels. He dreamed that they were falling all about him like raindrops, shimmering as they tumbled down from clouds of rainbow-lined fleece and skies of depthless blue. He sat upon a hill of fragrant grasses and wildflowers and watched them gather all about him in mounds. Sunshine shone from somewhere, warming him, and there was a sense of endless peace.

Beside him sat the bottle—his precious, wondrous bottle. It was the bottle and the Darkling locked within that made the jewels fall.

"Set me free, little master!" the Darkling pleaded suddenly, a small, frightened voice. "Please, master!"

Sot stirred within his dream, and he knew somehow that if he did as the demon had asked that the jewels that fell about him would increase in number and beauty beyond anything he could imagine. He knew that if he obeyed, the demon would give him precious things beyond all comprehension.

It all seemed so easy and right.

He reached over, still asleep, still in his dream, it seemed, and he pulled the stopper free . . .

It was raining when Fillip and Sot came awake again, the skies leaden and clouded over. The rain fell in great, heavy drops that splattered noisily as they struck the earth. Puddles and streams were already forming, mirrors of silver and trickles of gray. It was barely dawn, and everything in the haze of damp and new light was a shimmer of vague images and phantoms.

Coarse, gnarled hands wrenched Fillip and Sot from their slumber and dragged them roughly to their feet. The G'home Gnomes stood shivering with the cold, their weak eyes blinking in bewilderment. Bulky, dark shapes encircled them, a ring of grotesque shadows that lacked clear definition. Fillip and Sot squirmed and wriggled, trying to break free, but the hands held them fast.

One of the shapes detached itself from the ring. It bent close, a body consisting of heavy limbs, bent spine, and matted, dark hair, with a face that was almost featureless under a covering of skin like rough hide.

"Good morning, little gnomes," the troll greeted in his rough, guttural language.

Fillip and Sot shrank back, and trolls all about them laughed with delight.

"Can't you talk?" the speaker asked, feigning sadness.

"Let us go!" pleaded the gnomes in unison.

"But we just found you!" the other said, aggrieved now. "Must you run off so quickly? Have you somewhere to go?" A meaningful pause. "Might you be running from someone, perhaps?"

Fillip and Sot both shook their heads vigorously.

"From someone looking for this?" the troll asked slyly.

He held forth one massive hand. In that hand was their precious bottle, unstoppered once more, the Darkling dancing along its rim, withered child's hands clapping merrily.

"The bottle is ours!" cried Fillip angrily.

"Give it back to us!" wailed Sot.

"Give it back?" the troll said in disbelief. "A thing as wonderful as this? Oh, I think not!"

Fillip and Sot kicked and fought like trapped animals, but

the trolls holding them just tightened their grip. The speaker
was bigger than the others and obviously in charge. He reached
out suddenly with his free hand and thumped them hard on
their heads to quiet them down. The force of the blows knocked
them to their knees.

"It appears to me that you've been thieving again," the
troll continued thoughtfully. "Stealing what doesn't belong to
you." The gnomes managed to shake their heads once more in
denial, but the troll ignored them. "I think this bottle cannot
belong to you. I think it must belong to someone else, and
whoever that someone is, he has clearly suffered a great misfortune because of you." He brightened. "Still, another's misfortune need not necessarily be passed on. One man's loss is
another man's gain, as the old saying goes. We cannot be certain
whom the bottle formerly belonged to. So it seems best that it
now belong to me!"

Fillip and Sot looked at each other. These trolls were scavengers, common thieves! They looked quickly to the Darkling
where it danced along the neck of their precious bottle.

"Don't let them do this!" pleaded Fillip desperately.

"Make them give you back to us!" begged Sot.

"Stop them, stop them!" they cried together.

The demon did handstands and backflips and watched
them through slitted eyes that glittered redly in the haze. A bit
of multicolored fire spurted to life at the end of the fingers of
one hand, and it blew the fire toward them in a shower of sparks
that flared, died, and turned to ashes that caused them to choke
and cough and go silent again.

The troll who held the bottle looked down at the Darkling.
"Do you belong to these gnomes, tiny fellow?" he asked
solicitously.

The Darkling went still. "No, master. I belong only to
the holder of the bottle. I belong only to you!"

"No, no!" wailed Fillip and Sot. "You belong to us!"

The other trolls laughed with glee, the sound as chill as the rain that fell all about them.

The speaker bent close. "Nothing belongs to a G'home Gnome, foolish ones! Nothing ever has and nothing ever will! You haven't learned how to keep your possessions safe! How do you think we found you? Who do you think brought us here? Why, gnomes, it was this very creature you now call upon for help! It showered the skies with its brightly colored fire! It *asked* that we take it from you! It *asked* that it not be left your prisoner!"

The G'home Gnomes stared wordlessly, their last shred of hope gone. The Darkling—their friend, their maker of wondrous magic—had deliberately betrayed them. It had given them over to their worst enemies.

"Ho, hum," the speaker said with a yawn. "Time to dispose of you, I think."

The other trolls growled their assent and stamped their feet impatiently. They were growing bored with this game. Fillip and Sot struggled anew.

"What shall we do with them?" the speaker mused. He glanced about at the others. "Cut their throats and spike their heads? Pull off their fingers and toes? Bury them alive?"

Roars of approval sounded from all about, and the G'home Gnomes cringed down into small puddles of despair.

The troll leader shook his head. "No, no, I think we can do better than that!" He looked down at the cavorting demon. "Little fellow, what do you say should be done with these gnomes?"

The Darkling danced and balanced on fingers and toes, a wicked spiderlike shape clinging to the bottle's slick surface. "They might make good feeding for the animals of the forest," it teased.

"Ah!" the troll leader exclaimed. The others joined in a chorus of raucous approval, and the early morning stillness was filled with the sound.

So it was that Fillip and Sot were thrown to the ground, bound hand and foot with cord, hoisted feet first from a line slung over a low branch of a nearby hickory, and left to dangle with their down-turned heads some four feet above the ground.

"Not so close as to drown you in a rain wash and not so far as to prevent the scavengers from reaching you," the speaker advised as the trolls turned away north. "Farewell, little gnomes. Keep your chins up!"

The pack laughed and shoved playfully at one another as they departed. The Darkling sat upon the speaker's broad shoulder and looked back, eyes a blood red glitter of satisfaction.

In moments, Fillip and Sot were left alone, hanging upside down from the hickory. They swayed gently in the wind and rain and cried.

One-Way Ticket

*I*t was raining and blowing on Ben Holiday as well as he began his day some twenty miles south of where the G'home Gnomes had been strung up by their heels. He unwrapped himself from the warmth of Willow and his sleeping gear and shivered with the early morning chill as he dressed. They were encamped within a sheltering stand of giant fir that sat back against a rocky bluff, but the damp seemed to penetrate even there. The kobolds were already up and moving about, Bunion making ready to begin scouting ahead for the fleeing gnomes. Questor staggered about sleepily, attempted to make breakfast with his magic, and succeeded in producing five live chickens that flapped about madly and a cow that scattered Parsnip's cooking gear. Within minutes, wizard and kobold were yelling at each other irritably, and Ben was wishing he were back at Sterling Silver in the comfort and seclusion of his own bedchamber.

But there wasn't much point in wishing for what he couldn't have, so he consumed a stalk of Bonnie Blue and a little water, mounted Jurisdiction and set off with the others in tow. Bunion quickly went on ahead, disappearing into the shadows and half-light like some aberrant wraith. The others rode after in a line, Ben leading, Willow and Questor following, Parsnip bringing up the rear on foot with the pack animals.

They traveled in silence. It was cold, rainy, and dark, and no one felt much like talking. It was the kind of day that you wished on your enemies or, at the very worst, on yourself when you knew you were going to be comfortably settled indoors before a warm fire. It was not the kind of day in which you traveled. Ben sat atop Jurisdiction and wondered why things had to be like this. He was thoroughly discomforted within minutes of setting out. The rain gear kept the water off his body, but the damp and the chill permeated everything. His toes were numb through his boots, his fingers through his gloves. What good thoughts he might have started out with trickled away with the speed of the puddles and streams that passed underfoot.

He began brooding about his life.

Oh, sure, he liked his life well enough. He liked being King of Landover, High Lord of a fantasy realm in which mythical creatures were real and magic was a fact of existence. He liked the challenge of what he did, the diversity of its demands, the constant ebb and flow of the feelings it generated. He liked his friends, even at their worst. They were good and loyal, and they genuinely cared for one another and for him. He liked the world in which he had placed himself and would not have traded it back again for the world he had left, even in the darkest of times.

What disturbed him was how little he felt like what he was supposed to be—a King.

Jurisdiction snorted and shook his head lazily, and a shower of water flew into Ben's face. Ben brushed it away and kicked the horse reproachfully with his boots. Jurisdiction ignored him, plodding ahead at his own pace, blinking against the rain.

Ben sighed. He just didn't feel as if he really was a King, he told himself gloomily, picking up his train of thought. He felt that he was just playing at it, that he was filling in for the *real* King, someone who had been called away unexpectedly, but who would return and prove infinitely more capable than he. It wasn't that he didn't try to do the job right; he did. It wasn't that he couldn't understand its demands; he could. It was more a question of not ever being quite in control. He seemed to spend all his time trying to extract himself from situations he should have avoided in the first place. After all, look at this latest mess—Abernathy dispatched to God-knew-where, his medallion gone the same way, and now the G'home Gnomes run off with the bottle. What sort of King allowed these things to happen? He could excuse matters by arguing that events beyond his control were responsible for everything that had happened, but wasn't it a bit ridiculous for him to try to blame everything on a sneeze?

He sighed again. Well, it most certainly was. He had to accept whatever responsibility needed accepting; that was what Kings were for, after all. But the minute he did that, he was confronted once again with that nagging sense of inadequacy—that sense that he really didn't have a handle on things and never would.

Willow saved him from further self-degradation by riding up next to him and offering a quick smile. "You seem so alone up here," she said.

"Alone with my thoughts." He smiled back. "This day is depressing me."

"You mustn't let it," she said. "You must keep its un-pleasantness from you and make it serve your own needs. Think of how good the sunshine will feel after the rain has gone away. Think of how much better its warmth will seem."

He rocked back slightly in his saddle, stretching. "I know. I just wish some of that sunshine and warmth would hurry up and appear."

She looked away for a moment, then back again. "Are you worried about the gnomes and the bottle?"

He nodded. "That, Abernathy, the medallion, and a dozen other things—mostly the fact that I don't feel like I'm doing much of a job as King. I can't seem to get it right, Willow. I just sort of muddle around, trying things out, trying to get out of trouble I shouldn't have gotten into in the first place."

"Did you think it would be different from this?" Her face was shadowed and distant beneath her riding hood.

He shrugged. "I don't know what I thought. No, that's not so. I knew what it would be like—at least, I knew once I was here. That's not the problem. The problem is that things keep happening that I don't seem to have any control over. If I were a real King, an honest-to-God true King, that wouldn't be the case, would it? Wouldn't I be able to anticipate and prevent a few of these things from happening? Wouldn't I be better at this?"

"Ben." She said his name quietly and for a moment didn't say anything more, simply riding there next to him, looking over. Then she said, "How long do you think Questor Thews has been trying to get the magic right?"

He stared at her. "What do you mean?"

"I mean that you have been a King for a much shorter time than Questor has been a wizard. Should you expect so much of yourself when you see how hard it still is for him? The truths of what we undertake in our lives are never quickly mastered. No one is born with those truths; they must always be learned." She reached over and touched him briefly on the cheek. "Besides, was there ever a time in your life when events you could neither anticipate nor control did not intrude on your plans and disrupt them? Why should it be different now?"

He felt suddenly foolish. "It shouldn't, I suppose. And I shouldn't be moping about like this, I know. But it just seems that I'm not really what everyone thinks I am. I'm just . . . me."

She smiled again. "That is what we all are, Ben. But it doesn't stop others from expecting us to be more."

He smiled back. "People should be more considerate."

They rode on in silence, and he consigned his brooding to the back burner, concentrating instead on formulating a plan for getting the bottle back from Fillip and Sot. Morning passed steadily away, and it was nearing midday when Bunion reappeared from out of the mist.

"He has found the gnomes, High Lord," Questor advised hurriedly after a brief conference with the tracker. "It appears that they are in some sort of trouble!"

They spurred their horses ahead and rode at a fast canter through the gloom, the rain and wind blowing into their faces as they sought to keep the elusive Bunion in sight. They passed along a ridge line and down a wash to a grassy hillock beyond. Bunion stopped them at its base and pointed.

There, halfway up, suspended head downward from an aging hickory, were Fillip and Sot. The G'home Gnomes dangled in the wind like a pair of rather bizarre pods.

"What the heck's going on here?" demanded Ben.

He urged Jurisdiction forward, slowly, cautiously, the others following. When he was several dozen yards away, he dismounted and looked guardedly about.

"Bunion says they are alone," Questor offered over one shoulder, his owlish face poking out of his rain cloak's hood. "The bottle and the Darkling appear to be gone."

"Great High Lord!" called out Fillip weakly.

"Mighty High Lord!" echoed Sot.

They sounded as if they were just about all done in, their voices a faint gurgle of rain water and exhaustion. They were sodden and muddied and presented the most pathetic spectacle Ben had ever witnessed.

"I should just leave them there," he muttered half to himself, thinking of the missing bottle.

It was as if they had heard him. "Don't leave us, High Lord, please don't leave us!" they implored as one, whining like beaten pups.

Ben was disgusted. He shook his head hopelessly, then looked at Bunion. "All right, Bunion. Cut them down."

The kobold skittered forward, climbed the hickory, and

cut the ropes suspending the gnomes. Fillip and Sot dropped headfirst into the muck. Serves them right, Ben thought darkly.

Willow hastened forward, rolled them out of the mud and water, and cut the bonds that secured their hands and feet. Gently, she helped them sit up, rubbing their wrists and ankles to help restore the circulation. The gnomes were crying like babies.

"We are so sorry, Great High Lord," whimpered Fillip.

"We meant no harm, Mighty High Lord," whimpered Sot.

"It was the bottle—it was so beautiful."

"It was the creature—it could do wondrous magic things!"

"But it heard us say we would return it."

"It made us free it in our sleep!"

"Then it brought the trolls, High Lord!"

"It used magic lights to guide them!"

"And they captured us!"

"And tied us like dogs!"

"And hung . . . !"

"And left . . . !"

Ben put his hands up quickly. "Whoa, stop! I can't follow any of this! Just tell me what happened, all right—but slowly, please. Just tell me where the bottle is now!"

The G'home Gnomes told him everything. They dissolved into tears of repentance numerous times, but they finally got through it. Ben listened patiently, glancing once or twice at Questor and Willow, wondering for what must have been the hundredth time in the past few days why these things always seemed to happen to him.

When the gnomes were finished and lapsing once more into tears, Questor said something to Bunion, who moved away for a few moments and then returned. He spoke with the wizard, who turned to Ben.

"The trolls left several hours ago, it seems. But it is unclear where they have gone. Their tracks appear to lead off in several different directions." Questor paused uneasily. "Apparently, the Darkling knows we are following and is using its magic to confuse us."

Ben nodded. Hardly a surprise, he thought. Murphy's Law was kicking into high gear. He asked Willow to do what she could to help the shaken gnomes recover, then stood up and walked away to look out into the gloom and think.

What to do?

He felt a sudden resurgence of the insecurities that had plagued him earlier. Damn! He was just not getting anywhere! The longer he spent traipsing around the countryside in search of the bottle, the farther away it seemed to get! Not to mention Abernathy and the medallion, he reminded himself bitterly. God only knew what had happened to them by this time, sent into a world where animals were simply pets and magic medallions were scorned as tools of the devil. How long could they last before something happened to them, something for which he would have to hold himself forever accountable?

He breathed the chill air to clear his thoughts and lifted his face to let the rain cool it. It was no use berating himself. It was pointless to stand there and wish that things were different, that he were more a King, or that he had a better sense of what to do about things. Just shove the insecurities and doubts back into their cubicles and keep them there, he admonished himself. Just decide what to do and do it!

"High Lord?" Questor inquired anxiously from somewhere behind him.

"In a minute," Ben answered.

He had already decided that he was going about matters in the wrong way, that he had reversed his priorities. It was more important that he retrieve Abernathy and his medallion than it was that he retrieve the stolen bottle. It was going to take time to track down that demon and force it back into the bottle, and Abernathy simply didn't have that kind of time. Besides, it was going to take either luck or magic to subdue the

Darkling, and Ben didn't feel he could rely on the former. He needed his medallion back.

So the problem then became, how did he get Abernathy and the medallion back without being able to switch the bottle for them?

"Questor," he called suddenly, turning to where the others huddled in a knot beneath the hickory. He saw that Willow had gotten Fillip and Sot back to their feet and had stopped their crying. She was talking to them in a low, quiet voice, her eyes straying momentarily to find him as she heard him call.

Questor Thews shambled over quickly, tall form stooped against the wind, rainwater dripping off his hooked nose. "High Lord?"

Ben looked at him critically. "Have you sufficient magic to send me back after Abernathy? Could you employ something of the same sort of magic you used on him to send me back to wherever he is now? Or do we have to have the medallion? Is the medallion the only way?"

"High Lord . . ."

"Is the medallion necessary, Questor? Yes or no."

Questor shook his head. "No. The medallion was needed only for the purpose of interacting with the magic to separate out the animal from the man in Abernathy. That was the difficult part of the incantation. Simply sending one somewhere is a relatively easy magic."

Ben grimaced. "Please don't say that. It always worries me when you say something involving the magic is easy. Just tell me that you can send me back after Abernathy, okay? Can you do that? No sneezing, no mistakes—just send me back in one piece, right to where he is?"

The wizard hesitated. "High Lord, I do not think this a good . . ."

"No editorials, Questor," Ben interrupted quickly. "No arguments. Just answer the question."

Questor rubbed his rain-drenched beard, tugged his ear, and sighed. "The answer is yes, High Lord."

"Good. That's what I wanted to hear."

"But . . ."

"But?"

"But I can only send you there; I cannot bring you back again." Questor shrugged helplessly. "That is all I have been able to learn of that particular magic. After all, if I knew more, I could simply bring Abernathy and the medallion back myself, couldn't I?"

True enough, Ben thought dismally. Well, you takes your chances in this world, just like you do in any other.

"High Lord, I really wish you would think this . . ."

Ben brought his finger up quickly and made a hushing sound. "Just give me a moment to consider this, Questor. Please?"

He glanced away into the gloom once more. If he did this thing, it meant that he couldn't come back again unless he regained the medallion. He would have to stay in his old world, whatever happened, until he could locate it. This all presumed, of course, that Questor could get the magic right this time and actually send him where he was supposed to go and not to some other place and point in time.

He looked back at the wizard, studying the owlish face. Questor Thews. Wizard at large. He would have to leave Questor in control of Landover's affairs. That was a pretty scary proposition all by itself. He had allowed Questor to act in his place once before when he had been forced to return to his old world, but he had only been gone three days. He was likely to be gone much longer this time out. Maybe forever.

On the other hand, who else could he trust to assume the duties of the throne? Not Kallendbor or any of the other Lords of the Greensward. Not the River Master and his lake country fairies. Certainly not Nightshade, the witch of the Deep Fell. Willow, perhaps? He thought about that a moment. Willow would defer to Questor, he decided. Besides, Questor's confidence in himself would be shattered if he were not named ruler in Ben's absence. The Court Wizard was supposed to be the second most powerful figure in the monarchical structure.

Supposed to be. Those were the operative words, of course, Ben thought wryly. The truth of the matter might be something else altogether.

Well, Questor Thews had been a friend to him when he had no others. Questor had stood by him when it seemed foolish for anyone to do so. Questor had done everything asked of him and more. Maybe it was time to repay his loyalty with a little trust.

He brought his hands up to the narrow shoulders and gripped them firmly. "I've decided," he said quietly. "I want you to do it, Questor. I want you to send me back."

He kept the other's gaze locked onto his own, waiting. Questor Thews hesitated once more, then nodded. "Yes, High Lord. If you wish."

Ben walked him back to where the others waited and gathered them about. Fillip and Sot started to sob again, but he quickly quieted them with assurances that all was forgiven. Bunion and Parsnip hunched down against the trunk of the old hickory, their gnarled bodies glistening wetly. Willow stood apart, an uneasy look to her. She had seen something she didn't like in Ben's eyes.

"I have asked Questor to use the magic to send me after Abernathy," Ben announced brusquely. "He has agreed to do so." He avoided Willow's startled eyes. "I have to do what I can to help Abernathy and to regain possession of the medallion. When I have done that, I'll come back to you."

"Oh, Great High Lord!" cried Fillip dismally.

"Mighty High Lord!" sobbed Sot.

"We are so sorry, High Lord!"

"Oh, yes, we are!"

Ben patted them on the head. "Questor will assume the duties of the throne in my absence. I want you all to do your best to help him." He paused and looked directly at his Court

Wizard. "Questor, I want you to continue to try to find a way
to get the Darkling back into the bottle. That little monster is
too dangerous to be allowed to remain loose. See if Kallendbor
or the River Master will agree to help you. But be careful."

Questor nodded wordlessly. The others continued to stare
at him, waiting.

"I guess that's all I have to say," he finished.

Willow came right up to him then, the determination in
her face unmistakable. "I am going with you, Ben."

"Oh, no." Ben shook his head quickly. "That would be
much too dangerous. I could be trapped over there, Willow. I
might never get back. If you were with me, you would be
trapped there as well."

"Which is why I must go with you, Ben. I cannot risk
that you might be separated from me forever. What happens
to you happens to me as well. We are one person, Ben. It was
foretold by the weaving of the flowers in the garden where I
was conceived. Even the Earth Mother knows of it." She took
his hand in her own. "Do you remember her admonishment
to you? Do you remember what she said?" She waited until he
nodded yes. He had forgotten about the Earth Mother—that
strange elemental who aided them in their search for the black
unicorn. Willow's hand tightened suddenly. "You are to be my
protector; that was what she said. But, Ben, I must be your
protector as well. I must be because if I am not, then my love
for you is meaningless. There is no argument that you can offer
that will dissuade me. I am going with you."

He stared at her, so in love with her in that instant that he
could scarcely believe it. She was so much a part of him. It had
happened almost without his realizing it, a gradual strength-
ening of ties, a binding of feelings and emotions, a joining of
their lives. He recognized the truth of it and marveled in his
recognition that such a thing could be.

"Willow, I . . ."

"No, Ben." She put a finger to his lips, and her beautiful, flawless face lifted to kiss his own. "It is decided."

Ben kissed her back and held her. He guessed it was.

He decided that they would depart at once.

He had Questor use the magic to outfit them both in jogging suits and Nikes, giving Willow a sweatband to hold back her long hair and sunglasses to help mask her startling eyes. There was nothing he could do about her green complexion; he wouldn't risk allowing Questor to try anything with magic. They would simply have to make something up if there were questions. He had the wizard conjure up some folding money so he could pay whatever expenses he might incur while trying to find Abernathy. He hoped there wouldn't be any, of course. He hoped he would find his missing scribe and the medallion right off the bat. But he doubted that he would be that lucky. He hadn't been very lucky so far in trying to straighten out this mess.

Questor did a superior job of suiting them up in the sweats and running shoes, right down to the appropriate logos. He did yeoman work on the money as well; it felt like the real thing. It was fortunate, Ben thought, that he had shown the wizard some samples on earlier occasions. He gave the money a hasty glance and shoved it down into his pocket.

"And, Questor, you'd better spell Willow to speak English when we get there," he added.

Willow came over to stand next to him, her slim arms wrapping about his waist to hold him. He wanted to ask her once more if she was still certain about going with him, but he didn't. Such a question was pointless now.

"Ready, Questor," he announced. He glanced doubtfully at the gloom and damp that surrounded them, a gray and misty haze. He looked down through the wash to the grasslands beyond, to the hills and forests. He wished he could see it all in

a better light, in sunshine, in bright color. He wanted to remember it all. He was afraid he would never see it again.

Questor Thews moved the others behind him, back against
the trunk of the hickory. The kobolds were grinning fiercely,
the gnomes whining as if they were about to be strung up again.
Questor shoved back the sleeves of his robes and lifted his
hands.

"Be careful," Ben said quietly, his arms tightening about
Willow.

The wizard nodded. "Good luck to you, High Lord."

He began the incantation, the magic words spilling out in
a steady stream of meaningless rhetoric. Then came the gestures, the appearance of the silver dust, and the coming of the
light. Rain and gloom faded, taking with them the kobolds and
the gnomes, then Questor Thews as well. Ben and Willow were
alone, holding each other close.

"I love you, Ben," he heard the sylph say.

Then everything disappeared in a flash of light, and they
closed their eyes tight against its brilliance.

They drifted for a time, a long, slow drifting that lacked direction or focus, the sort of drifting one sometimes experiences
when sleep grows into gradual wakening. Then the light grew
less intense, the drifting stopped, and the world about them
grew distinct again.

They were standing on a street corner in a city, the air
filled with the sounds of cars and people. Willow clung to Ben,
burying her face in his shoulder, clearly frightened. Ben looked
quickly about, shaken himself by the sudden rush of noise.

Good heavens, it was hot! It was as if it were the middle
of summer instead of fall! But that couldn't be . . .

"Holy mackerel!" he breathed.

He knew exactly where he was. He would have known
whatever the circumstances of his being there.

He was right in the middle of the Las Vegas strip.

Castles and Cages

Questor Thews stared thoughtfully at the empty space that had been occupied by Ben Holiday and Willow only seconds before, then rubbed his hands together in satisfaction and said, "Well, I believe they are safely on their way."

Bunion and Parsnip came forward, peered at the emptiness, and hissed their agreement. Their teeth showed and their yellow eyes blinked like signal lamps.

"Great High Lord," whimpered Fillip from somewhere in the shadows behind them.

"Mighty High Lord," whimpered Sot.

"Come, come! The High Lord is safe and sound," Questor assured them, wondering briefly if he had remembered correctly all the words and gestures to the part of the incantation having to do with the place to which he had sent them. Yes, he was certain that he had. Reasonably certain, at any rate.

"Got to concentrate on dealing with matters here," he announced, mostly to himself. "Hmmmmmm. Let me see."

He straightened himself beneath his robes, tugged on his beard, and peered out into the gloom. It was still raining heavily, the drops spattering into ever-widening puddles and streams that interlocked across the whole of the landscape as far as he could see. Clouds hung low against the horizon, and the day seemed to be growing darker. The haze of mist that had shrouded the valley since dawn was thickening.

Questor frowned. It would be a perfectly reasonable decision to return to Sterling Silver here and now and forget about chasing after that confounded demon.

On the other hand, there was nothing waiting at Sterling Silver that wouldn't keep a few days more—and he had promised the High Lord that he would do his best to retrieve the bottle. Although he didn't care to dwell on it, he knew he was at least partially responsible for the bottle being in Landover in the first place; therefore, he should do his best to set matters right again—especially since the High Lord had placed such great trust in him.

"I think, perhaps, that we should continue our hunt," he declared. "Bunion? Parsnip? Shall we keep after the Darkling a little while longer?"

The kobolds glanced at each other and hissed their approval.

"Excellent!" Questor turned to the G'home Gnomes. "I should be less charitable with you than was the High Lord, Fillip and Sot, if the choice were mine. Still, all was forgiven, so you are free to go."

Fillip and Sot stopped whimpering and shivering long enough to glance about at the gray, empty landscape and then at each other. Their eyes were wide and frightened.

"Good and kind Questor Thews!" said Fillip.

"Wondrous wizard!" declared Sot.

"We will stay with you!"

"We will give you our help!"

"Please let us stay?"

"Please?"

Questor Thews looked down at them with undisguised suspicion. The gnomes were asking to stay only because they were afraid of being left alone come nightfall with the Darkling still on the loose. He hesitated, then shrugged. Well, after all, what could you expect of G'home Gnomes?

"Just be sure you stay out of the way if we come across the trolls and that bottle," he admonished sternly.

The gnomes could not agree quickly enough, falling all over each other in their efforts to assure him that such would be the case. Questor had to smile in spite of himself. He was quite certain they were telling the truth on this occasion.

So they struck out north through the weather, Bunion sweeping the land ahead in an effort to pick up some true sign of the trolls' passing, Questor and the others trailing after at a slower pace. Questor rode his old gray, letting Parsnip and the gnomes follow afoot, with Parsnip leading Jurisdiction, Willow's mount, and the pack animals. The rain continued to fall steadily, its gray haze mingling with the mist to wrap the land in ribbons of shadow. Daylight faded as nightfall approached, and still there was no sign of the trolls.

Bunion returned at sunset, and the company made camp within a gathering of rain-drenched cyprus along a river whose swollen waters churned by in sluggish, monotonous cadence. It was relatively dry beneath the great, hanging limbs, and Questor was able to produce a small, cheerful fire by using his magic. Parsnip cooked a delightful dinner which was quickly consumed. Then, buoyed by his earlier success, Questor employed the magic once more to produce blankets and pillows. He would have done better to let well enough alone, but he decided to try one last incantation, a spell that would have produced an enclosed, heated, waterproof shelter complete with bath. The effort failed abysmally. One of the trees actually toppled over on the spot, allowing the rain to douse the fire and leaving the entire company exposed to the weather. They were forced to move their camp farther back within the remaining trees, salvaging what they could of the now-dampened blankets and pillows, and that was that.

Questor apologized profusely, but the damage was never-

theless done and couldn't be undone. It was most embarrassing.
While the others slept, Questor Thews lay awake within his
blankets and thought long and hard about the vicissitudes of a
wizard's life. Teaching oneself reliable use of the magic was not
an easy task, he lamented. Nevertheless, he must do so. After
all, he stood now in the shoes of the High Lord and he was
responsible for the well-being of all Landover.

Daybreak brought more rain. The dawn was iron gray and
thick with mist stirred by sluggish winds and a mix of cool air
and warm earth. The little company ate breakfast and struck
out once more across the grasslands of the Greensward. Bunion
roamed ahead, still searching for some sign of the trolls, while
the rest followed at a slower pace. Everyone was soaked
through and thoroughly discomforted. Questor thought briefly
to dry them off with the magic, then decided against it. He had
resolved during the night not to employ the magic again except
when he could be certain of its results or in time of desperate
need. He would conserve himself; he would focus his concentration on specific and limited conjuring. That way, he felt, he
would be at his best.

Midday came and went. They were well into the grasslands by now, far north and east of Sterling Silver, deep in the
country of the Lords of the Greensward. Plowed fields decorated the landscape in checkerboard fashion, most of the crops
taken from them now, the earth black and hard looking. Farm
buildings and cottages were scattered about, brightened by gardens and hedgerows blooming with flowers of all colors and
shapes, rainbow streaks across the rain-swept, gray land.

Questor's eyes surveyed the misted countryside. Less than
a dozen miles distant was Rhyndweir, the fortress castle of Kallendbor, the most powerful of the Lords of the Greensward.
The wizard permitted himself a small sigh of expectation. Tonight, he promised himself, they would sleep beneath a dry
roof, in dry beds, with steaming baths to remove all memory
of the damp and the chill.

It was nearing midafternoon when Bunion abruptly appeared from out of the haze, his hard, dark body glistening with the wet. He approached at something very close to a run—unusual for him—and spoke hurriedly to Questor, his breath hissing from between his sharp teeth, his eyes narrowed and furtive.

The wizard caught his breath. Bunion had found the trolls—but not as any of them had imagined.

The company pressed at a quicker pace, Questor saying nothing to the others yet, still stunned by what Bunion had told him. They passed across a series of fields and a small, quick-flowing stream into a stretch of timber.

The trolls lay in a clearing, amid a close gathering of pine, dead to a man. They were sprawled on the rain-drenched earth in grotesque positions, throats cut, bodies stabbed, tangled together in an orgy of death. The G'home Gnomes took one look and shrank back behind the pack animals, whining in fear. Even Parsnip shied away. Questor went forward with Bunion because it was expected. Bunion whispered again what he had whispered earlier. This tragedy had not been caused by some third party. The trolls had evidently set upon themselves. They had killed one another.

Questor listened patiently and said nothing, but he knew what had happened. He had seen the Darkling's work before. The chill of the day worked into him more deeply. He was suddenly very frightened.

Bunion pointed ahead into the gloom. One of the trolls had escaped the massacre. One had survived, wounded, and staggered ahead into the woods. That one had taken the bottle.

"Oh, dear," Questor Thews murmured.

The wounded troll was heading directly for Rhyndweir.

"Abernathy!"

The scribe lifted his head from the straw matting on which he lay to peer into the near-blackness beyond. "Elizabeth?"

She appeared out of the shadows of an alcove set into the far wall, slipping through a break in the stone that he could have sworn hadn't been there a moment before. She crossed the dungeon passageway on tiptoe and put her face up against the bars of his cage. Abernathy, unable to stand erect in the small enclosure, crawled over on all fours to greet her. He could just make out the roundish face with its scattering of nose freckles.

"Sorry I couldn't come sooner," she whispered, glancing left and right cautiously. "I couldn't chance trying. I couldn't let my dad or Michel know I cared about what happened to you or they might have been suspicious. I think Michel already is."

Abernathy nodded, grateful that she had come at all. "How did you get in here, Elizabeth?"

"Through a secret passage!" She grinned. "Right there!" She pointed behind her to the break in the wall, a seam of light still faintly visible against the black. "I found it months ago when I was exploring. I doubt anyone else even knows that it's there. It leads all up and down the south wall." She hesitated. "I didn't know how to get to you at first. I didn't even know where you'd be. I just found out this afternoon."

"This afternoon? Is it night, then?" Abernathy asked. He had lost all track of time.

"Yep. Almost bedtime, so I have to hurry. Here, I brought you something to eat."

He saw then that she was carrying a paper bag. She reached into it and produced several sandwiches, some raw vegetables, fresh fruit, a bag of potato chips, and a small container of cold milk.

"Elizabeth!" he breathed gratefully.

She passed the items through, and he tucked them into the straw to hide them—all but the first sandwich, which he began to devour hungrily. He hadn't been given anything to eat but stale dog food and a little water in almost three days now, the time that he had been imprisoned there. He had been shut away in the bowels of Graum Wythe, ignored except for periodic visits from his uncommunicative jailers, who either came to make certain he was still there or to give him his rations. He hadn't seen sunlight the entire time. He hadn't seen Michel Ard Rhi, either.

"How are you, Abernathy?" Elizabeth asked as he ate. "Are you all right? They didn't hurt you, did they?"

He shook his head and continued to chew. Ham and cheese—one of his favorites.

"I talked to my father about you a little bit," she ventured after a moment. Then she added hastily, "I didn't tell him about you and me, though. I just told him that I had found you wandering about and Michel didn't seem to like you and I was worried about you. I told him I thought it was wrong. He agreed, but he said he couldn't do anything. He said I knew better than to get involved with strays in the first place, that I knew how Michel was. I said sometimes you had to get involved."

She hunched down thoughtfully. "I know you aren't being given any food. I found out from one of the guards, a sort of friend." She bit her lip. "Why is Michel doing this to you, Abernathy? Why is he being so mean? Does he still hate you so much?"

Abernathy stopped chewing, swallowed, and lowered what remained of the sandwich. He couldn't have eaten it at all if he hadn't been so hungry. His cage smelled of sick animals and excrement, and the walls were dark with mold.

"It's simple, really—he wants something from me." He decided it couldn't hurt to tell her the truth now. "He wants this medallion I am wearing. But he cannot take it from me. I have to give it to him. So he has locked me away down here until I agree to give it up." He brushed some straw from his muzzle with one paw. "But the medallion isn't his; it isn't even mine. It was just loaned to me, and I have to return it to its owner.''

He thought, for the first time in quite a while now, about the High Lord and the problems he faced in Landover without the medallion to protect him. Then he sighed and began eating again.

Elizabeth looked at him a moment, then nodded slowly. "I talked to Nita Coles about you today. We're friends again, see. She explained all about Tommy Samuelson and said she was sorry. Anyway, I told her about you, 'cause we tell each other everything. But we keep it all secret. Most of the time, anyway. This was a sworn, double-locked finger secret, so neither of us can tell *anyone* or we'll have seven years bad luck and Tad Russell for a husband for life! She says you can't be real, of course, but I told her you were and that you needed us to help. So she said she would think about it, and I said I'd think about it, too.''

She paused. "We've got to get you out of here, Abernathy.''

Abernathy pushed the last of the sandwich into his mouth and shook his head vehemently. "No, no, Elizabeth, it's gotten much too dangerous for you to try to help me anymore. If Michel finds out . . .''

"I know, I know,'' she interrupted. "But I can't keep sneaking food down to you like this. Michel is going to figure out that you're not starving or anything, that someone's feeding you. And how will you get out of here if I don't help you?''

Abernathy sighed. "I'll find a way,'' he insisted stubbornly.

"No, you won't,'' Elizabeth declared, just as stubborn. "You'll just be down here in this cage forever!''

There was a sudden barking from somewhere down the hallway through a closed door. Abernathy and Elizabeth both turned to look, freezing into motionless statues. The barking lasted only a few seconds and died away.

"Real dogs," Abernathy whispered after a moment. "Michel keeps them locked away down here, poor things. I don't even want to speculate why. I hear them cry out sometimes, calling. I can understand something of what they are saying . . ."

He trailed off, distracted. Then he looked quickly back at the girl. "You have to stay out of this, Elizabeth," he insisted. "Michel Ard Rhi is very dangerous. He would hurt you if he knew what you were doing—even if he suspected! It wouldn't make any difference to him that you were a little girl. He would hurt you anyway—maybe your father, too, for that matter."

There was immediate concern reflected in her eyes when he mentioned the danger to her father. He felt bad about suggesting such a thing, but he had to make certain that she did not take any further chances on his account. He knew what Michel Ard Rhi could be like.

Elizabeth was studying him intently. "Why do you try to scare me like that, Abernathy?" she asked suddenly, almost as if she could read his mind. "You are trying to scare me, aren't you?"

She made it a statement of fact. "Yes, of course I am, Elizabeth," he answered immediately. "And you should be scared. This isn't a game for children!"

"Just for dogs and wizards, I suppose!" she snapped back angrily.

"Elizabeth . . ."

"Don't try to make up to me!" There was hurt now in her eyes. "I am not a child, Abernathy! You shouldn't call me one!"

"I was just trying to make a point. I think you would . . ."

"How are you going to get out of here without me?" she demanded again, cutting him short.

"There are certainly ways that . . ."

"There are? How? Name one. Just one. Tell me how you're going to get out. Go on, tell me!"

He took a deep breath, his strength deserting him. "I don't know," he admitted wearily.

She nodded in satisfaction. "Do you still like me, Abernathy?"

"Yes, of course I do, Elizabeth."

"And would you help me if I needed helping, no matter what?"

"Yes, of course."

She bent forward against the bars of the cage until her nose was only inches from his. "Well, that's how I feel about you, too! That's why I can't just leave you here!"

The dogs began barking again, more insistent this time, and someone yelled at them to shut up. Elizabeth began backing away toward the alcove.

"Finish your food so you'll stay strong, Abernathy!" she whispered hurriedly. "Shhh, shhhh!" she cautioned when he tried to speak. "Just be patient! I'll find a way to get you out!"

She paused halfway through the break in the wall, a slight shadow in the half-light. "Don't worry, Abernathy! It'll be all right!"

Then she was gone, the break disappearing once more into blackness.

The barking down the hall was punctuated by several sharp yelps and then faded slowly into silence. Abernathy listened for a time, then pulled out the medallion from beneath his tunic, and studied it silently.

He was scared to death for Elizabeth. He wished he knew what to do about her. He wished he could find some way to protect her.

After a time, he put the medallion back in place again. Then he uncovered the rest of his food and slowly began to eat.

Charades

*B*en Holiday squinted through the glare of the hot Nevada sun in total disbelief. Massive hotel and casino signs lined the street in both directions, jutting up against the cloudless desert horizon like some bizarre, twentieth-century Druidic Stonehenge, garish even without the dance of the bright, flashy lighting that would come with nightfall. The Sands. Caesar's Palace. The Flamingo.

"Las Vegas," he whispered. "For crying out loud, what are we doing in Las Vegas?"

His mind raced. He had assumed that when he was transported from Landover into his old world, he would emerge just as he always did when coming out of the fairy mists into the Blue Ridge Mountains of Virginia. He had assumed, quite reasonably he thought, that Abernathy must have been dispatched to that same point when the magic went awry. But now, it seemed, he had been wrong on both counts. The magic must have gone sufficiently bonkers to send them both to the other end of the country!

Unless . . .

Oh, no, Ben thought. Unless Questor had messed up yet again and sent Abernathy to one place and Willow and him to another!

He caught himself. He wasn't thinking this through clearly. The magic had exchanged Abernathy and the medallion for the bottle and the Darkling. Abernathy would have been sent to wherever the bottle was being kept by Michel Ard Rhi—assuming Michel still had the bottle. In any case, Abernathy would have been sent to *whomever* it was that had the bottle. And Ben had asked Questor to send him to wherever Abernathy was. So maybe Las Vegas was exactly the place he was supposed to be.

Willow still had her body turned into him protectively, but she brought her face up from his shoulder long enough to whisper, "Ben, I don't like all this noise!"

The strip was jammed with cars even at midday, the air filled with the sounds of engines, horns, brakes and tires, and shouts from everywhere. Cabs zipped past and a descending airliner passed overhead with a frightening roar.

Ben glanced around once more, still confused. Passersby and motorists were beginning to rubberneck in his direction. Must be the jogging suits, he thought at first, then realized it was nothing of the sort. It was Willow. It was a girl with emerald green hair that tumbled to her waist and flawless sea-green skin. Even in Las Vegas, Willow was an oddity.

"Let's go," he said abruptly and started walking her south up the street. Las Vegas Boulevard, the sign said. He tried to remember something useful about Las Vegas and couldn't remember a thing. He had only been there once or twice in his life, and that had been for only a day or two and on business at that. He had visited a few casinos and recalled nothing about any of them.

They reached the intersection of Las Vegas Boulevard and Flamingo Road. Caesar's Palace was on the left, the Flamingo on the right. He hurried Willow across, pushing through a knot of people going the other way.

"Far out, honey!" one called back and whistled.

"You been to the Emerald City?" another asked.

Great, thought Ben. This is all I need.

He swept Willow on, ignoring the voices, and they faded behind him. He had to come up with a plan, he thought, irritated at how matters had worked out. He couldn't just wander about the city indefinitely. He glanced at the two massive hotels bracketing the boulevard on the south side of the intersection. The Dunes and Bally's. Too big, he thought. Too many people, too much going on, too . . . everything.

"Where's the circus, doll?" he heard someone else shout.

"Ben," Willow whispered urgently, clutching at him tighter.

Questor, Questor! You better be right about this! Ben walked faster, sheltering Willow as best he could, moving her to the inside of the street traffic, hurrying her past the crush of people coming and going through the entrance to Bally's. The Shangri-La loomed ahead, then the Aladdin and the Tropicana. He had to pick one of them, he admonished angrily. They had to spend the night somewhere—had to get their bearings, decide where to begin their search for Abernathy. Maybe it would be better if he *did* choose one of the larger hotels. They might be less noticeable there, blend in a bit easier with all the other bizarre sorts . . .

He turned Willow about abruptly and walked her through the entrance of the Shangri-La.

The lobby was jammed. The casino beyond was jammed. There were people everywhere, the sounds of cards and dice and roulette wheels and one-armed bandits a steady, low-level din mixed with the excited voices of the game players. Ben took Willow through it all, ignoring the stares that followed them, and went directly to the registration desk.

"Reservation for . . ." He hesitated. "Bennett, please. Miles Bennett."

The clerk looked up perfunctorily, looked down, looked up again quickly on seeing Willow, then nodded and said, "Yes, sir, Mr. Bennett."

Willow, confused about the name, said, "Ben, I don't understand . . ."

"Shhhh," he cautioned softly.

The clerk checked his reservations sheet and looked up again. "I'm sorry, sir, I don't have a reservation for you."

Ben straightened. "No? Perhaps you'll find it under Fisher then. Miss Caroline Fisher? A suite?"

He took a deep breath while the registration clerk looked again. Naturally, the result was the same. "Sorry, Mr. Bennett, I don't find a reservation under Miss Fisher's name, either."

He smiled apologetically at Willow and for a very long moment was unable to look away from her.

Ben stiffened in feigned irritation. "We have had that reservation for months!" He lifted his voice just loud enough to draw attention. A small scattering of people slowed and began to gather to see what was happening. "How can you not have any record of it? It was confirmed only last week, for God's sake! We have a shooting schedule that begins at five o'clock in the morning, and I cannot afford to waste time on this!"

"Yes, sir, I understand," the clerk said, understanding only that something had gone wrong for which he was not to blame.

Ben pulled out the wad of bills Questor had given him and began to thumb through them absently. "Well, our luggage will be here from the airport shortly, so I see no point in arguing about the matter. Please arrange whatever you can for us, and I'll speak with the manager later."

The clerk nodded, looked back at the reservation sheet, looked next at the bookings on the computer, then said, "Excuse me just a moment, Mr. Bennett."

He went out while Ben, Willow, and the small crowd gathered behind them waited expectantly. He was back quickly, another man in tow. Someone with more authority, Ben hoped.

He was not disappointed. "Mr. Bennett, I'm Winston Allison, Assistant Manager. I understand that there has been some sort of mix-up in the reservations you booked? I'm sorry about that. We do have rooms available for you and Miss Fisher." He smiled broadly at Willow, clearly assessing her potential for star status. "Would you still like a suite?"

"Yes, Mr. Allison," Ben replied, "Miss Fisher and I would like that very much."

"Well, then." Allison spoke quietly to the clerk, who nodded. "For how long will you need the suite, Mr. Bennett?" he asked.

"A week at the outside." Ben smiled. "Our shooting schedule only calls for three, possibly four days."

The clerk began writing, then passed Ben the registration forms. Ben filled them out quickly, using a bogus studio reference for a business name, still playing his role to the hilt, and passed the forms back. The crowd behind them began to disperse again, moving on to find some new attraction.

"I hope you enjoy your stay with us, Mr. Bennett, Miss Fisher," Allison said, smiled once more, and went back to wherever he had come from.

"The rate for the suite is four hundred and fifty dollars a night, Mr. Bennett," the clerk advised, consulting the registration forms officiously. "How will you be paying for this?"

"Cash," Ben answered nonchalantly and began thumbing through the roll of bills. "Is one thousand dollars a sufficient deposit?"

The clerk nodded, stealing another quick glance at Willow, smiling warmly when she noticed him looking.

Ben proceeded to count out the sum of five hundred dollars in fifties, then noticed something odd about one of the bills. He paused, slowly worked a new bill free of the roll as if the bills were sticking, and looked closely at its face.

Ulysses S. Grant's picture wasn't on the bill. His was.

He surreptitiously checked another bill and another. His picture was on every one, bigger than life, and looking not a thing like Grant's. He felt his heart drop. Questor had messed up again!

The clerk was looking at him now, sensing that everything was not quite right. Ben hesitated; then, unable to think of anything else, lurched forward suddenly against the counter, hands clutching at the bills, his breath coming in gasps.

"Mr. Bennett!" the clerk exclaimed, reaching out to catch him.

Willow's hands clutched at him as well. "Ben!" she cried before he could do anything to stop her.

"No, no, I'm quite all right," he assured them both, praying the clerk hadn't noticed that she had used a different name. "I wonder . . . could I go directly to my room and lie down a bit? Finish this later, perhaps? The sun was a bit too much, I think."

"Certainly, Mr. Bennett," the clerk agreed hastily, summoning a bellhop instantly. "Are you certain you don't need medical help? We have someone on staff if . . ."

"No, I'll be fine . . . once I've rested a bit. I have my medicine. Thank you again for your help."

He smiled weakly, pocketed the bills once more, and gave a silent sigh of relief. With Willow and the bellhop both holding tightly onto him, he moved off through the crowded lobby. Another silver bullet dodged, he thought gratefully.

He prayed that Abernathy was having the same sort of good fortune.

"All right, students, quiet down now! Everyone find a seat! Let's have your attention, please!"

The energetic young principal of Franklin Elementary in Woodinville, Washington, walked to the center of the gymnasium floor, microphone in one hand, other hand held high and signaling for order, voice booming out over the loudspeaker system. The K through sixth graders slowly settled down on their bleacher seats, the din of their voices dying into a rustle of anticipation. Elizabeth sat six rows back with Eva Richards. She watched the principal glance at a man who stood to one side, his lanky frame slouched, a smile on his bearded face. The man reached down and scratched the ears of a small black poodle who sat obediently beside him.

"We have a special treat for you this afternoon, something many of you have enjoyed before," the principal announced, looking around with a broad grin. "How many of you like dogs?"

Hands shot up everywhere. The man with the dog smiled some more and waved hello to a section of students close at hand. They waved back eagerly.

"Well, we've got some special dogs for you this afternoon, some dogs who can do things that even some of you can't do!" A titter of laughter sounded. Elizabeth grimaced. "I want you to watch closely and listen to what our guest has to say. Students, please welcome Mr. Davis Whitsell and his *Canine Review*!"

Applause and whistles sounded as Davis Whitsell took the floor, accepting the microphone from the departing principal. He waved and pretended not to notice that the little black poodle was trailing after.

"Good afternoon, everyone!" he greeted. "Such an enthusiastic group! I am delighted to have you all here, happy you came—even if you had to come, this being one of those required assemblies." He made a face and there were hoots of laughter. "But maybe we can have some fun together. I'm here to tell you about dogs—that's right, dogs! And since your parents don't want you going to the dogs, I'm bringing the dogs to you!"

He raised his hands and everyone clapped in response.

"Now, I want you to listen up, because I have to tell you something important. I have to tell you . . ."

He paused, acting as if he had just noticed Sophie tugging dutifully at his pants leg. "Hey, hey, what's this? Let go now, Sophie, let go!"

The little black poodle released her grip and sat back,
watching.

"Now, as I was saying, I have something to tell you
that . . ."

Sophie began tugging at him again. Elizabeth laughed with
the others. Davis Whitsell looked down, distracted once more
from his speech.

"Sophie, what is it? You want to say something first?"
Sophie barked. "Well, why didn't you say so? Oh, you just
did, didn't you? Well, I don't think the kids heard. Maybe you
better say it again." Sophie barked once more. "What, you want
to show them how smart you are?" Sophie barked. "How smart
all dogs like you are?" He looked up at the bleachers. "What
do you say, kids? You want to see how smart Sophie is?"

They all yelled that they did, of course. He gave an ex-
aggerated shrug. "Okay. Let's see what you can do, Sophie.
Can you jump?" Sophie jumped. "Can you jump higher?" Sophie jumped almost to his shoulder. "Whoa! Bet you can't do
a back flip." Sophie did a back flip. "Hey, how about that, kids?
That's not bad, is it? Now, how about . . ."

He took Sophie through one trick after another, jumps
through hoops and over hurdles, more flips, retrieving and carrying off, and a dozen and one other marvelous stunts. When
she was finished, the students gave her a tumultuous round of
applause, and Davis Whitsell sent her off. Then he began to
talk about the need for proper pet care. He gave a few statistics,
talked about the good work of the ASPCA, stressed the ways
a little love and understanding could affect the lives of animals,
and pointed out the need for every student there to involve himself or herself in this ongoing project.

Elizabeth listened intently.

Then, back came Sophie. She appeared from the edge of
the floor leading a big tan boxer by the leash about his neck.
Davis Whitsell expressed surprise, then went through the whole
routine all over again, asking Sophie what she was doing there

with Bruno, pretending he understood what she was saying when she barked, carrying on a conversation with her just as if she were human.

Elizabeth began to think.

Then came a whole new repertoire of stunts involving Sophie and Bruno, the former riding the latter, the two of them jumping through hoops and over hurdles, racing about in leaps and bounds, playing tag, and conducting contests of skill and daring.

The program closed with a reminder of the need for responsibility where animals were concerned and a wish for a good school year for all of them. Whitsell went off with a wave to the cheers and applause, Sophie and Bruno in tow. The principal shook his hand, took back the mike, thanked him publicly, then dismissed the students to their classes.

Elizabeth made up her mind.

As the other students filed out, one after the other, Elizabeth hung back. Eva Richards tried to stay with her, but Elizabeth told her to go on ahead. Davis Whitsell was watching as the students passed by, returning their smiles. Elizabeth waited patiently. The principal came up and thanked Whitsell once more, saying he hoped he'd be back next year. Whitsell replied that he would.

Then the principal moved off as well, and Davis Whitsell was alone.

Elizabeth took a deep breath and walked up to him. When he looked down at her, she said, "Mr. Whitsell, do you think you could do something to help a friend of mine?"

The bearded man grinned. "Depends, I guess. Who's your friend?"

"His name is Abernathy. He's a dog."

"Oh, a dog. Well, sure. What's his problem?"

"He needs to go to Virginia."

The grin broadened. "He does? Hey, what's your name?"

"Elizabeth."

"Well, look, Elizabeth." Whitsell put his hands on his knees and bent forward confidentially. "Maybe he doesn't really need to go to Virginia. Maybe he just needs to get used to living in Washington, you know? Tell me something. Are you planning to go back to Virginia with him? Did you used to live there, too, maybe?"

Elizabeth shook her head firmly. "No, no, Mr. Whitsell, you don't understand. I didn't even know Abernathy until about a week ago. And he's not really a dog, in any case. He's a man who was turned into a dog. By magic."

Davis Whitsell was staring at her open-mouthed. She hurried on. "He can talk, Mr. Whitsell. He really can. He's a prisoner right now in this . . ."

"Whoa, back up!" the other interrupted quickly. He shifted into a crouch. "What are trying to tell me? That this dog can talk? Really talk?"

Elizabeth backed off a step, beginning to wonder if she had done the right thing coming to this man. "Yes. Just like you and me."

The bearded man cocked his head thoughtfully. "That's some imagination you've got there, Elizabeth."

Elizabeth felt stupid. "I'm not making this up, Mr. Whitsell. Abernathy really can talk. It's just that he needs to get to Virginia, and he doesn't know how. I thought maybe you could help him. I was listening to what you said, about how dogs need proper care and how all of us should involve ourselves in helping. Well, Abernathy is my friend, and I want to be sure that he's taken care of, even if he isn't a real dog, and I thought . . ."

Davis Whitsell raised one hand quickly, and she went still. He stood up and glanced around the gymnasium, and Elizabeth glanced with him. The last few students were filing out. "I have to go," she said quietly. "Can you help Abernathy?"

He seemed to consider. "Tell you what," he said suddenly. He took out a wrinkled card that bore an imprint of his name and address. "You bring me a talking dog—a genuine talking dog, now—and I'll help him for sure. I'll take him anywhere he wants to go. Okay?"

Elizabeth beamed. "Do you promise?"

Whitsell shrugged. "Sure."

Elizabeth beamed some more. "Thanks, Mr. Whitsell! Thanks a lot!" She clutched her books tightly to her chest and hurried off.

The minute her back was turned, Davis Whitsell dismissed the matter with a shake of his head.

Miles Bennett, lawyer-for-hire, sat in the study of his suburban Chicago home amid a clutter of *Northeast Reporters* and *ALRs* and seriously considered having a drink. He had been working on this damn corporate tax assessment case since Monday a week ago, and he wasn't any closer to a resolution of its multiple legal dilemmas now than he had been when he had first picked it up. He had been working on it day and night, at the office and at home, living it, sleeping it, eating it, and he was sick of it, both figuratively and literally. Yesterday, he had caught the flu, the unpleasant kind that attacks you from both ends, and he was just now beginning to shake its effects. He had spent the afternoon in no small amount of discomfort tramping around the subject properties, a vast office complex in Oak Brook, and he had brought his notes home with him in an effort to decipher them while everything was still fresh in his mind.

If it was possible that *anything* could be fresh in his mind at this point, he thought dismally.

He leaned back in his leather desk chair, his heavy frame sagging. He was a big man with thick dark hair and a mustache that seemed to have been tacked on as an afterthought to a face that in happier times was almost cherubic. Eyes perpetually lidded at half-mast peered out with a mix of weary resignation and sardonic humor on a world that viewed even hardworking, conscientious lawyers such as himself with unrelenting suspicion. Still, that was all right with him. It was just part of the price you paid to do something you really loved.

His sudden smile was ironic. Of course, sometimes you loved it more than others.

That made him think unexpectedly of Ben Holiday, formerly of Holiday & Bennett, Ltd., their old law partnership, of when it was Ben and him against the world. His smile tightened. Ben Holiday had loved the law—knew how to practice it, too. Doc Holiday, courtroom gunfighter. He shook his head. Now Doc was God-knew-where, off fighting dragons and rescuing damsels in some make-believe world that probably existed only in his own mind . . .

Or maybe for real. Miles wrinkled his brow thoughtfully. He had never been quite sure. Maybe never would be.

He brushed the extraneous thoughts from his mind and bent back over the law books and yellow pads. He blinked his eyes wearily. His notes were beginning to blur. He needed to get this done and get to bed.

The phone rang. He glanced over at it, sitting on the end table next to his reading chair. He let it ring a second time. Marge was at bridge and the kids were up the block at the Wilson house. No one home but him. The phone rang a third time.

"Damnit all, anyway!" he swore, lifting himself heavily out of the desk chair. Phone was never for him, always for the kids or Marge; even if it was for him, it was always some ditsy client who didn't have sense enough not to bother him at home with questions that could just as easily wait until morning.

The phone rang a final time as he lifted the receiver. "Hello, Bennett's," he rumbled.

"Miles, it's Ben Holiday."

Miles stiffened in surprise. "Doc? Is that you? I was just thinking about you, for God's sake! How are you? *Where* are you?"

"Las Vegas."

"Las Vegas?"

"I tried to reach you at the office, but they said you were out for the day."

"Yeah, tramping all over hell and gone."

"Listen, Miles, I need a big favor." Ben's voice crackled on the connection. "You'll probably have to drop everything you're doing for the rest of the week, but it's important or I wouldn't ask."

Miles found himself grinning. Same old Doc. "Yeah, yeah, butter me up so you can toss me into the frying pan. What do you need?"

"Money, to begin with. I'm staying at the Shangri-La with a friend, but I don't have any money to pay for it."

Miles was laughing openly now. "For Christ's sake, Doc, you're a millionaire! What do you mean you don't have any money?"

"I mean I don't have any here! So you have to wire me several thousand first thing in the morning. But listen, you have to send it to yourself, to Miles Bennett. That's how I'm registered."

"What? You're using *my* name?"

"I couldn't think of another on the spur of the moment, and I didn't want to use my own. Don't worry, you're not in any trouble."

"Not yet, anyway, you mean."

"Just send it to the hotel directly to my account—your account, that is. Can you do it?"

"Yeah, sure, no problem." Miles shook his head in amusement, settling down comfortably now into the reading chair. "Is that the big favor you needed, money?"

"Partly." Ben sounded subdued and distant. "Miles, you remember how you always wanted to know something about what happened to me when I left the practice? Well, you're going to get your chance. A friend of mine, another friend, not the one with me now, is in trouble here, somewhere in the

United States, I think—maybe not, though, we have to find out. I want you to call up one of our investigating agencies and have them find out anything they can about a man named Michel Ard Rhi." He spelled it out and Miles hastily wrote the name down. "I think he lives in the U.S., but, again, I can't be certain. He should be pretty wealthy, probably somewhat reclusive. Likes to use his money, though. Have you got all that?"

"Yeah, Doc, I got it." Miles was frowning.

"Okay. Now here's the rest—and don't argue. I want you to check to see if there is any news—anything at all, rumors, gossip, anything, anywhere—about a dog who talks."

"What?"

"A dog who talks, Miles. I know this sounds ridiculous, but that's the other friend I'm looking for. His name is Abernathy. He's a soft-coated Wheaten Terrier, and he talks. Did you write that down?"

Miles did so hastily, shaking his head. "Doc, I hope you're not putting me on about this."

"I'm dead serious. Abernathy was a man who was turned into a dog. I'll explain it all later. Get what you can on either subject and catch a plane out here as quickly as possible. Bring me whatever sort of file the investigators can put together. And tell them you need it right away, no delays. First of the week at the latest." He paused. "I know this won't be easy, but do what you can, Miles. It really is important."

Miles shifted himself, chuckling. "The part that's going to be hard about this is finding a way to tell the investigators that we're looking for a talking dog! Christ, Doc!"

"Just pick up whatever bits of information there are about any sort of dog that's supposed to talk. It's a long shot, but we might get lucky. Can you break away to fly out?"

"Sure. It'll be good for me, actually. I've been working on a tax assessment case, and it's about to bury me in a sea of mathematics. So you're at the Shangri-La? Who's with you?"

There was a pause. "You wouldn't believe me if I told you, Miles. Just show up and see, okay? And don't forget to wire the money! Room service is the only thing keeping us alive!"

"Don't worry, I won't forget. Hey!" Miles hesitated, listening to the static in the line. "Are you all right, Doc? I mean, other than this thing? You okay?"

There was a pause at the other end. "I'm fine, Miles. I really am. We'll talk soon, okay? You can reach me here if you need me. Just remember to ask for yourself—don't get confused."

Miles roared. "How could I possibly be any more confused than I am now, Doc?"

"I suppose. Take care, Miles. And thanks."

"See you soon, Doc."

The line went dead. Miles placed the receiver back on its cradle and stood up. How about that? he thought, grinning. How about *that*?

Humming cheerfully, he went over to the cupboard and took out a bottle of the Glenlivet scotch Ben Holiday liked so much. Damned if he wasn't going to have that drink after all!

Button,
Button

Abernathy lay in his darkened cage and dreamed fitfully of Landover's sunshine and green meadows. He hadn't been feeling very well the past day or so, a condition he attributed to a combination of his confinement and the food—mostly the lack thereof. He half suspected that something in the environment of this land in general was having a debilitating effect on his system, something apart from his present circumstances, but there was no way to test his theory. In any case, he spent most of his time dozing, finding what small refuge he could in his dreams of better times and places.

Elizabeth hadn't been to see him in more than two days now. He noticed that the guards had been checking on him more frequently, and he assumed that her failure to appear was due in part at least to fear of discovery. Michel Ard Rhi had come once. That, too, had been at least two days ago. He had looked at his prisoner quite dispassionately, asked him once if he had anything to give him, then left without another word when Abernathy advised him in no uncertain terms that he was wasting his time.

No one else had come at all.

Abernathy was beginning to grow frightened. He was beginning to believe that he actually was going to be left there to die.

The thought stirred him from his sleep, his dreams faded away, and the reality of his situation intruded once more. He grappled momentarily with the prospect of dying. It might not be so frightening if he were to confront it directly, he decided. He considered his choices in the matter of Michel Ard Rhi and the medallion. There were none. He certainly could not relinquish the medallion; his conscience and his duty would not allow it. Such a powerful magic must not be allowed to pass into the hands of so evil a man. Even death was preferable to that.

Of course, once he was dead, what was to prevent Michel from just taking the medallion off his lifeless body?

He was despondent all over again, thinking of that possibility, and he closed his eyes once more in an effort to escape back into his dreams.

"Hsssst! Abernathy! Wake up!"

Abernathy's eyes slowly opened and he found Elizabeth standing outside his cage. She was gesturing impatiently. "Come on, Abernathy, wake up!"

Abernathy rose stiffly, straightened his soiled clothing, fumbled in his waistcoat pocket for his spectacles, and slipped them over his nose. "I am awake, Elizabeth," he insisted sleepily, shoving the spectacles carefully into place.

"Good!" she whispered, fumbling now with the cage door. "Because we're getting you out of here right now!"

Abernathy watched in befuddlement as the little girl located the lock, inserted a key, twisted it, and pulled. The cage door swung open. "How about that?" she murmured in satisfaction.

"Elizabeth . . ."

"I took the key off the rack in the guard room where they keep the spares. They won't miss it right away! I'll have it back before they know it's gone. Don't worry. No one saw me."

"Elizabeth . . ."

"Come on, Abernathy! What are you waiting for?"

Abernathy couldn't seem to think, staring vacantly at the open cage door. "This seems awfully dangerous for you to . . ."

"Do you want out of here or not?" she demanded, a trace of irritation in her voice.

From down the hall, beyond the passageway door, the imprisoned dogs suddenly began barking, yelps and howls of dismay. "Yes, I do," Abernathy answered quickly and crawled through the open door.

He stood erect in the passageway beyond for the first time since his imprisonment, feeling immediately better. Elizabeth closed the cage door once more and locked it. "This way, Abernathy! Hurry!"

He followed her across the passageway and through the break in the wall to a stairway beyond. Elizabeth turned and pushed the hidden door in the wall section closed. The sounds of the barking dogs died away into silence.

They stood there in the blackness a moment until Elizabeth clicked on a flashlight. Abernathy was pleasantly surprised to discover that he still retained sufficient faculties to remember reading about flashlights in one of the little girl's magazines that first afternoon he had hidden out in her room. He guessed he wasn't as debilitated as he had imagined.

Elizabeth led the way up the stairs, Abernathy dutifully following. "We don't have much time," she was saying. "The Coles are already here to take me to the school chorus program. You remember my friend Nita? They're her parents. They're visiting with my dad while I finish dressing." Abernathy noticed she was wearing a ruffled pink and white dress. "That's what I'm supposed to be doing now. Nita's up there in my room, keeping watch, pretending she's helping me. When we get back, she'll go down and tell her parents and my dad that I'll be right there. While she's doing that, I'll sneak you downstairs the back way to a door that leads out to the yard. The Coles' car is parked there and we can hide you in the trunk.

The release is on the dash. It's perfect! The guards won't bother to check the Coles—not with my dad with them."

Abernathy started. "An automobile, one of those mechanical . . . ?"

"Shhhh! Yes, yes, an automobile! Just listen, will you?" Elizabeth had no time for interruptions. "Once at the school, we'll all go in to get ready, but I'll tell the Coles I have to go back out for my purse, which I'll leave in the car. When I come out, I'll open the trunk and let you out. Okay?"

Abernathy was shaking his head doubtfully. "What if you cannot get me out? Will I be able to breathe in there? What if I . . . ?"

"Abernathy!" Elizabeth turned, exasperated. "Don't worry, all right? I'll get you out. And you can breathe just fine in a car trunk. Now, listen! I found someone to help you get to Virginia."

They had reached a landing where the stairs stopped at a door. Elizabeth turned, eyes bright. "His name is Mr. Whitsell. He's a dog trainer. He goes around to the schools and talks about animal care and things. He said if I brought you to him, he would help you. Now wait here."

She pushed open the door on the landing, handed the flashlight to Abernathy, disappeared through the opening, and pushed the door shut again. Abernathy stood there pointing the flashlight at the wall and waiting. Things were happening much too rapidly to suit him, but there was nothing to be done about it. If there was even the slightest chance that he might escape Graum Wythe and Michel Ard Rhi, he had to take it.

Elizabeth was back almost at once, bundled in a coat, scarf, and gloves. "Put this on," she instructed, handing him an old topcoat and brimmed hat. "I took them from the storage closets where they keep the old stuff."

She took the flashlight from him while he struggled into the hat and coat. The coat felt like a tent on him, and the hat wouldn't stay in place. Elizabeth looked at him and giggled. "You look like a spy!"

She led him through the wall opening into a closet filled with brooms, mops, and buckets. She paused, peered through the door leading out, then beckoned him after her. They slipped quickly down a hallway to a back stairs that wound downward to the ground floor and a set of double doors that opened onto the back yard.

Abernathy peered through a glass panel in the door over Elizabeth's shoulder. An automobile was parked close against the castle wall. Lights bathed the yard in their muted yellow glow, but no one was about.

"Ready?" she asked, turning to look up at him.

"Ready," he answered.

She pulled open the double doors and rushed for the automobile. Abernathy followed. She had the driver's door open and the trunk release pulled by the time he reached her. "Hurry!" she whispered and helped him climb hastily inside. "Don't worry!" she said when he was safely settled, pausing momentarily with her hands on the lid. "I'll be back to get you out when we reach the school! Just be patient!"

Then the lid slammed down and she was gone.

Abernathy lay hidden in the automobile for only a few minutes before he heard voices approach, the passenger doors open and close again, and the engine start up. Then the automobile began to move, jouncing and bumping him all over the place as it twisted and wound down the roadway and steadily picked up speed. The trunk was carpeted, but there wasn't much padding underneath, and Abernathy was thoroughly knocked about. He tried to find something to hold onto, but there wasn't anything to grasp, and he had to settle for bracing himself against the top and sides.

The ride seemed to go on interminably. To make matters worse, the automobile gave off a rather noxious odor that quickly upset Abernathy's stomach and gave him a headache. He began to wonder if he was going to survive the experience.

Then, finally, the automobile slowed and stopped, the

doors opened and closed, the voices faded away, and all went still except for the muffled and somewhat distant sounds of other doors opening and closing and other voices calling out. Abernathy waited patiently, letting cramped muscles relax again, rubbing strained ligaments and bruised bones. He promised himself faithfully that if he could just get safely back to Landover, he would never, under any circumstances, even *think* of riding in another of these horrendous, mechanical monsters.

Time slipped away. Elizabeth did not come. Abernathy lay in the dark and listened for her, thinking that the worst had happened, that she had been prevented somehow from returning, and that now he was trapped there indefinitely. He began to doze. He was almost asleep when he heard the sound of footsteps.

The car door opened, the trunk latch was sprung, the lid popped up, and there was Elizabeth. She was gasping for breath. "Hurry, Abernathy, I have to get back right away!" She helped him from the trunk. "I'm sorry it took so long, but my dad wanted to come with me and I had to wait until he . . . Are you all right? You look all bent over! Oh, I'm sorry about this, really I am!"

Abernathy shook his head quickly. "No, no! No need to be sorry about anything. I am just fine, Elizabeth." A few latecomers were passing in the distance, and he pulled the topcoat close about him and adjusted the brimmed hat. He bent down to her. "Thank you, Elizabeth," he said softly. "Thank you for everything."

She put her arms about him and hugged him, then stepped quickly back. "Mr. Whitsell lives a couple of miles north. Follow this road out here." She pointed. "When you reach a road with a sign that says Forest Park, turn right and count the numbers until you find 2986. It'll be on the left. Oh, Abernathy!"

She hugged him again, and he hugged her back. "Don't worry. I will find it, Elizabeth," he assured her.

"I have to go," she said and started away. Then she turned

and hurried back. "I almost forgot. Take this." She thrust an envelope into his paw.

"What is it?"

"The money I promised, for an airplane ticket or whatever. It's okay to keep it," she added hastily as he tried to give it back. "You might need it. If you don't, you can give it back when we see each other again."

"Elizabeth . . ."

"No, you keep it!" she insisted, turning and starting quickly away. "Good-bye, Abernathy! I'll miss you!"

She ran toward the school building and was gone.

"I'll miss you, too," Abernathy whispered after her.

It was approaching midnight by the time Abernathy turned up the walk to 2986 Forest Park, still wearing the brimmed hat and the trench coat. He had made a wrong turn some distance back and had been forced to retrace his steps. As he approached the little house with the shuttered windows and flower boxes, he could see a man dozing in a chair through the partially drawn blinds of the front window. The light next to him was the only light burning in the house.

Abernathy went up to the door cautiously and knocked. When there was no response, he knocked again.

"Yeah, what is it?" a voice growled.

Abernathy didn't know what to say, so he waited. After a moment, the voice said, "Okay, just a minute, I'm coming."

Footsteps approached. The front door opened, and the man from the chair stood there, bearded and sleepy-eyed, wearing jeans and a work shirt open to the waist over a sleeveless undershirt. A tiny black poodle stood next to him, sniffing. "Are you Mr. Whitsell?" Abernathy asked.

Davis Whitsell stared, his mouth dropping open. "Uh . . . yeah," he said finally.

Abernathy glanced around uneasily. "My name is Abernathy. Do you suppose that . . ."

The other man started; then he seemed to understand and

managed a slight smile. "The little girl at Franklin!" he exclaimed. "You're the one she told me about! You're the one she said was locked up somewhere, right? Sure, you're the talking dog!"

"I'm a man who was turned into a dog," Abernathy said rather stiffly.

"Sure, sure, she told me about that!" Whitsell backed off a step or two. "Well, come in, come on in . . . Abernathy! Sophie, get back. Here, let me take that coat from you. Way too big, anyway. Hat doesn't do a thing for you either. Here, sit down."

"Who is it, Davis?" a woman's voice called from somewhere down the hall.

"Uh, no one, Alice—just a friend," Whitsell replied hurriedly. "Go back to sleep." He leaned close. "My wife, Alice," he whispered.

He took Abernathy's coat and hat and beckoned him across the living room to the couch. Sophie wagged her tail and whined softly, sniffing at Abernathy with dismaying enthusiasm. Abernathy nudged her away.

The TV was on. Whitsell turned the volume down carefully, then seated himself across from Abernathy. He leaned forward eagerly, his voice hushed. "Well, tell you the truth, I thought the little girl was kidding me. I thought she was making all this up. But . . ." He stopped, as if trying to gather his thoughts. "So, you were changed into a dog, were you? Terrier breed, right? Uh, English breed, I'd guess."

"Soft-coated Wheaten Terrier," Abernathy advised, looking around doubtfully.

"Sure, that's it." Whitsell got up again. "You look all done in, you know that? Would you like something to eat, drink maybe? Uh, real food, right—you being human and all? Come on into the kitchen, I'll fix you something."

They walked from the living room to a kitchen that looked out into the back yard. Whitsell poked through the refrigerator and came up with some cold ham, potato salad, and milk. He made Abernathy a sandwich, commenting over and over again on how amazing he was. God almighty, he said, a real live talking dog! He must have said it a dozen times. Abernathy was offended, but he kept it to himself. Finally Whitsell finished, carried the food to a small folding table with four chairs, made Abernathy sit down, grabbed a beer for himself, and sat down as well.

"Look, the little girl . . . uh, what's her name?"

"Elizabeth."

"Yeah, Elizabeth said you had to get to Virginia. That right?"

Abernathy nodded, his mouth full of sandwich. He was starved.

"What do you have to go to Virginia for?"

Abernathy considered his answer. "I have friends there," he said finally.

"Well, can't we just call them up?" the other asked. "I mean, if you need help, why not just give them a call?"

Abernathy was confused. "A call?"

"Sure, by phone."

"Oh, telephone." He remembered now what that was. "They don't have a telephone."

Davis Whitsell smiled. "That so?" He sipped at his beer and watched while Abernathy finished his food. The dog could feel him thinking.

"Well, it won't be easy getting you all the way to Virginia," he ventured after a moment.

Abernathy looked up, hesitated, then said, "I have some money to pay my way."

Whitsell shrugged. "Maybe so, but we can't just put you on an airplane or a train and ship you out. There would be all sorts of questions about who or what you were. Uh, pardon me for saying that, but you got to understand that people aren't used to seeing dogs who dress up and walk about and talk like you do."

He cleared his throat. "Other thing is, the little girl said something about you being held prisoner. That right?"

Abernathy nodded. "Elizabeth helped me escape."

"Then this might be dangerous business, me helping you. Someone's going to be pretty unhappy once they find you gone. Someone's liable to be coming after you. That means we have to be extra careful, don't it? 'Cause you're pretty special, you know. Don't find dogs like you every day. Sorry. Men like you, I mean. So best to get in quick, get out quick. Make what we can off this, eh?" He seemed to be thinking his way through the matter. "Won't be easy. You'll have to do exactly what I tell you."

Abernathy nodded. "I understand." He drank the last of his milk. "Can you help at all?"

"Sure! You bet I can!" Whitsell rubbed his hands briskly. "Best thing for now, though, is to get some sleep, then we'll talk about it in the morning, come up with something. Okay? Got the spare room down the hall you can use. Bed's all made up. Alice won't like it, doesn't like anything she can't under- stand, but I'll handle her, don't you worry. Come on with me."

He took Abernathy down the hall to the spare room, showed him the bed and the bath, provided him with a set of towels, and got him settled in. All the while he was thinking out loud, talking about missed opportunities and once-in-a- lifetime chances. If he could just figure out a way to make things work, he kept saying.

Abernathy pulled off his clothes, climbed into bed, and lay back. He was vaguely bothered by what he was hearing, but he was too exhausted to give the matter proper consider- ation. He closed his eyes wearily. Whitsell switched off the light, stepped outside, and pulled the door shut behind him.

The house was very still. Just outside, the branches of a tree brushed against the window like claws.

Abernathy listened for only a moment. Then he was asleep.

Jericho

*I*t was approaching nightfall when Questor Thews, the kobolds, and the G'home Gnomes arrived at Rhyndweir. The sky
was hazy blue-gray with tiny strips of pink where the sun still
lingered as it fled from the encroaching darkness. Mist clung
to the Greensward in gauzy strips, turning the land to shadows
and blurred images. Rain still fell, a thin veil of damp that
seemed to hang on the air. Sounds were muted and displaced
in the murkiness, and it was as if life had lost all substance and
drifted bodiless.

Bunion led the way cautiously as they crossed the bridge
spanning the juncture of the rivers that fronted the towering
plateau on which the fortress castle of Lord Kallendbor had been
built. The town beneath was closing down for the day, a jumbled mix of grunting men and animals, of clanging iron and
creaking wood, and of weariness and sweat. The little company
passed down the roadway through the shops and cottages; the
buildings were dim, squat mounds in the mist, from which
slivers of candlelight peeked out warily. The roadway was rutted and muddied from the rain, a morass that sucked at their
boots and the horses' hoofs. Heads turned to watch them pass,
evidenced momentary interest, then turned quickly away again.

"I'm hungry!" whined Fillip.

"My feet hurt!" added Sot.

But Parsnip hissed softly in warning, and the gnomes went still again.

Then Rhyndweir materialized before them out of the mist and rain. Walls and parapets, towers and battlements, the whole of the great castle slowly took shape, a monstrous ghost hunkered down against the night. It was a massive thing, lifting skyward over a hundred feet, its uppermost spires lost in the low-hanging clouds. Flags hung limply from standards, torches flickered dimly from within their lamps, and dozens of sodden guards kept watch upon the walls. The outer gates yawned open, huge wooden and ironbound jaws fronting a lowered portcullis. The inner gates stood closed. It was a forbidding sight, and the little company approached with mixed feelings of wariness and trepidation.

The gate watch stopped them, asked them to state their business, and then moved them into the shelter of an alcove in the shadow of the wall while a message was carried to the Lord Kallendbor. Time dragged slowly past as they stood shivering and weary in the gloom and the damp. Questor was not pleased; a King's emissary was not to be kept waiting. When their escort finally arrived, a pair of lesser nobles dispatched directly from Kallendbor with perfunctory apologies for the delay, the wizard was quick to voice his displeasure at their treatment. They were representatives of the King, he pointed out coldly—not supplicants. The escort merely apologized once again, no more concerned about the matter than before, and beckoned them inside.

Leaving the horses and pack animals, they circumvented the portcullis and inner gates by slipping through a series of hidden passages in the walls, crossed the main courtyard to the castle proper, entered an all but invisible side door which first had to be unlocked, and then passed down several corridors until they reached a great hall dominated by a huge fireplace at its far end. Logs burned brightly in the hearth, the heat almost suffocating. Questor winced away and squinted into the light.

The Lord Kallendbor turned from where he stood before the blaze—so close to the fire, it seemed to Questor, that he must be scorched. Kallendbor was a big man, tall and heavily muscled, his face and body scarred from countless battles. He wore chain mail tonight beneath his robes, armored boots, and a brace of daggers. His brilliant red hair and beard gave him a striking appearance—more so against the flames of the hearth. When he came forward, it was as if he brought the fire with him.

He dismissed the lesser nobles with a brief nod. "Well met, Questor Thews," he rumbled, extending one callused hand.

Questor accepted the hand and held it. "Better met, my Lord, if I had not been kept waiting so long in the cold and the wet!"

The kobolds hissed softly in agreement, while the G'home Gnomes shrank back behind Questor's legs, their eyes like dinner plates. Kallendbor took them all in at a glance and dismissed them just as quickly.

"My apologies," he offered Questor, withdrawing his hand. "Things have been a bit uncertain of late. I must be cautious these days."

Questor brushed the loose water from his cloak, owlish face twisting into a frown. "Cautious? More than that, I would guess, my Lord. I saw the deployment of your watch, the guards at all the entrances, the portcullis down, and the inner gates closed. I see the armor you wear, even in your own home. You behave as if you are at siege."

Kallendbor rubbed his hands briskly and looked back at the fire. "Perhaps I am." He seemed distracted. "What brings you to Rhyndweir, Questor Thews? Some further bidding of the High Lord? What does he require now? That I battle demons with him? That I chase after that black unicorn again? What does he wish now? Tell me."

Questor hesitated. There was something in the way Kallendbor asked his questions that suggested he already knew the answers. "Something has been stolen from the High Lord," he said finally.

"Ah?" Kallendbor kept his eyes on the blaze. "What might that be? A bottle, perhaps?"

The room went still. Questor held his breath.

"A bottle with dancing clowns painted on it?" Kallendbor added softly.

"You have the bottle in your possession, then." Questor made the question a statement of fact.

Kallendbor turned now, smiling as wickedly as the kobolds ever thought of doing. "Yes, Questor Thews, I have it. A troll gave it to me—a miserable, thieving troll. He thought to sell it to me, actually, this thief. He had stolen it from some other trolls after they had quarreled among themselves. He survived the quarrel, wounded, and came to me. He would not have done so—come to me, that is—if he had been thinking clearly, if he had not been so badly hurt . . ."

The big man trailed off, shaking his head. "He told me there was magic in the bottle, a little creature, a demon, a Darkling he said, who could give the holder of the bottle anything he wished. I laughed at him, Questor Thews. You can understand. I have never had much faith in magic; only in strength of arms. Why would you want to sell anything so dear, I asked this troll? Then I saw the fear in his eyes and I knew why. He was frightened of the bottle. Its power was too great. He wanted to be rid of the bottle—but there was enough greed left in him to wish something in return."

Kallendbor looked away. "I think he believed the bottle was responsible somehow for the destruction of his companions—that in some way this creature that lives within caused it."

Questor said nothing, waiting. He wasn't sure yet where this was leading and he wanted to find out.

Kallendbor sighed. "So I paid him the price he asked, and then I had his head cut off and spiked on the gateway. Did you see it when you entered? No? Well, I put it there to remind anyone who needs reminding that I have no use for thieves and swindlers."

Fillip and Sot were shivering against Questor's legs. Questor reached down surreptitiously and slapped them. He straightened again as Kallendbor looked around.

"You claim the bottle belongs to the High Lord, Questor Thews, but the bottle does not bear the mark of the throne." Kallendbor shrugged. "The bottle could belong to anyone."

Questor bristled. "Nevertheless . . ."

"Nevertheless," the big man cut in quickly, "I shall give the bottle back to you." He paused. "After I am finished with it."

The flames in the hearth crackled loudly in the silence as they consumed the wood. Questor was buffeted by a mix of emotions. "What are you saying?" he asked.

"That I have a use for this bottle, Questor Thews," the other said quietly. "That I intend to give the magic a chance."

There was something in the big man's eyes that Questor could not identify—something that wasn't anger or determination or anything else he had ever seen there before. "You must reconsider," he advised quickly.

"Reconsider? Why, Questor Thews? Because you say so?"

"Because the magic of the bottle is too dangerous!"

Kallendbor laughed. "Magic doesn't frighten me!"

"Would you challenge the High Lord on this?" Questor was angry now.

The big man's face went hard. "The High Lord isn't here, Questor Thews. Only you."

"As his representative!"

"In my home!" Kallendbor was livid. "Let the matter rest!"

Questor nodded slowly. He recognized now what was reflected in Kallendbor's eyes. It was an almost desperate need. For what, he wondered? What was it that he wanted the bottle to give him?

He cleared his throat. "There is no reason for us to argue, my Lord," he said soothingly. "Tell me—to what use will you put the magic?"

But the big man shook his head. "Not tonight, Questor Thews. Time enough to talk about it tomorrow." He clapped his hands and a scattering of servants appeared. "A hot bath, some dry clothes, and a good meal for our guests," he instructed. "Then to bed."

Questor bowed reluctantly, turned to go, then hesitated. "I still think . . ."

"And I think," Kallendbor interrupted pointedly, "that you should rest now, Questor Thews."

He stood there, armor glinting in the firelight, eyes flat and hard. Questor saw there was nothing more to be accomplished at this meeting. He must bide his time.

"Very well, my Lord," he said finally. "Good night to you."

He bowed and departed the room with the kobolds and gnomes in tow.

Later that night, when his companions were sleeping and the castle was at rest, Questor Thews went back. He slipped down the empty corridors, hiding himself with small touches of magic from the few guards he encountered, moving on cat's feet through the stillness. His purpose was rather vague, even in his own mind. He supposed he needed to satisfy himself about Kallendbor and the bottle—that matters were as Rhyndweir's Lord had declared them to be and not as Questor feared.

He reached the great hall without being seen, bypassed its entrance and the sentries standing watch in favor of a connecting anteroom, eased the anteroom door open, then closed it softly behind him. He stood there in the darkness for a moment, let-

ting his eyes adjust. He knew this castle as he knew all the castles
of Landover. This one, like most of the others, was a maze of
connecting halls and rooms, some known, some secret. He'd
learned much that he wasn't necessarily intended to learn while
carrying messages in the service of the old King.

When his sight grew sharp enough to permit it, he moved
across the room to a shadowed nook, touched a wooden peg
in the wall, and pushed gently on the panel it secured. The panel
swung back, giving him a clear view of what lay beyond.

Kallendbor sat in a great chair facing the hearth, the bottle
with its painted clowns resting loosely in his lap. His face was
flushed and his smile an odd grimace. The Darkling skittered
about the room, going first to this, then to that, eyes as bright
as the flames blazing in the hearth, but infinitely more wicked.
Questor found he could not stare into those eyes comfortably
for more than an instant.

Kallendbor called, and the Darkling scampered up his arm
and rubbed itself against him like a cat. "Master, great master,
such strength as I feel in you!" it purred.

Kallendbor laughed, then said to it, "Leave me, creature!
Go play!"

The Darkling dropped down again, skittered across the
stone floor to the open hearth, and leaped into the fire. Dancing
about, the creature played with the flames as if they were cool
water.

"Black thing!" Kallendbor hissed. Questor saw him raise
an ale mug rather unsteadily, the contents splashing down his
front. Kallendbor was drunk.

Questor Thews thought seriously then of stealing the bottle and its loathsome inhabitant from the Lord of Rhyndweir
and ending this nonsense once and for all. There would be little
risk to himself. He could simply wait until the man tired of his
game and returned the bottle to its hiding place, then nip the
treasure for himself, collect the Kobolds and the G'home
Gnomes, and disappear.

It was a most tempting thought.

But he decided against it. First, everyone who had stolen the bottle had come to a bad end. Second, Questor had never been a thief and did not relish the thought of starting now. Finally, Kallendbor had said he would return the bottle after he finished with it and he deserved the benefit of the doubt. He had always been—despite his other obvious failings—a man of his word.

Reluctantly, Questor set the thought aside.

He risked a final look into the room. Kallendbor sat slumped in his chair, staring at the hearth. Within its flames, the Darkling was laughing and dancing gleefully.

Questor let the wall panel swing shut again, shook his grizzled head doubtfully, and departed for his room.

Dawn brought an end to the rains, with skies swept clear of clouds and gloom and colored once more a vast, depthless blue. Sunshine flooded the valley, and even the dark, catacombed recesses of Rhyndweir seemed bright and new.

Questor and his companions were awakened at first light by a knock on their bedchamber door and a message from Kallendbor. They were to dress and join him for breakfast, the young page announced. After that, they would be going for a ride.

The G'home Gnomes had long since had enough of Kallendbor and begged Questor to be allowed to stay in their rooms where they could draw the window coverings closed again and snuggle safely in the darkness. Questor shrugged and agreed, inwardly relieved that he would not have to contend with their constant whining while dealing with the problem of how to get the bottle back from Kallendbor before he caused any mischief with it. He assigned Parsnip to keep watch over them and arranged for breakfast to be delivered to their rooms. Then, with Bunion in tow, he hurried out to join Rhyndweir's Lord.

Breakfast was almost completed, however, before Kal-

lendbor appeared, armored head to foot and bristling with
weapons. In one gloved hand he carried a sack containing an
object that was almost certainly the bottle. He greeted Questor
perfunctorily and beckoned him to follow.

They went down to the main courtyard. Several hundred
knights in full battle dress waited with their mounts. Kallendbor
called for his own horse, saw to it that Questor was provided
with his gray, mounted, and wheeled the knights into formation. Questor had to hurry to keep up. The gates opened, the
portcullis rose with a screech of metal, and out the column rode.

Questor Thews was brought to the forefront to ride directly beside Kallendbor. Bunion raced off on his own, on foot
as always, anxious to keep himself clear of the dust and noise
of the horsemen. Questor looked once or twice to find him,
but the kobold was as invisible as air. The wizard quickly gave
up searching and directed his efforts instead to the task of discovering what Kallendbor was up to.

The Lord of Rhyndweir appeared to have no intention of
disclosing that information, all but ignoring Questor as he led
his men down the rutted roadway through the town. People
appeared in the doors and windows of the shops and cottages,
and a few halfhearted calls and whistles trailed after. No one in
the town had any idea what Kallendbor was about, or cared
much, for that matter. They wanted to be kept safe—that was
all that really mattered to them. Kallendbor had never been a
popular ruler—just a strong one. Twenty Lords ruled the
Greensward, but Kallendbor was the most powerful and his
people knew it. He was the one Lord to whom the others all
deferred. He was the Lord no one dared challenge.

Until now, it seemed.

"I am betrayed, Questor Thews!" Kallendbor was suddenly telling him. I am beset at every turn in a way I would
never have believed possible! Betrayed, mind you, not by my
enemies, but by my fellow Lords! Stosyth, Harrandye, Wilse!
Lords I thought I could trust—Lords who, at least, were too

cowed to act if I did not approve!" Kallendbor's face was scarlet. "But Strehan is the one who surprised and disappointed me most, Questor Thews—Strehan, the closest of them all to me! Like an ungrateful child who bites its father's tending hand!"

He spit into the dirt as they rode, the column winding down across the bridge and out into the grasslands. Leather battle harness creaked, metal fastenings clanked, horses snorted and nickered, and men called out. Questor tried to picture the tall, shambling, dour Strehan as a child of any sort, ungrateful or otherwise, and found the task beyond him.

"They have built this . . . this tower, Questor Thews!" Kallendbor snapped in fury. "The four of them! Built it at the falls of the Syr, at the juncture of my lands! They tell me it is an outpost, nothing more. They apparently take me for a fool! It stands taller than the walls of Rhyndweir, and its battlements shadow the whole of my eastern borders! If they should choose, they could close off the river itself and dam up the waters that feed my fields! This tower offends me, wizard! It hurts me in ways I would not have thought I could be hurt!"

He bent close as they rode. "I would have destroyed it the moment I discovered it but for the fact that the combined armies of these four dogs guard it as one! I have not the strength to break them without so decimating my own armies as to leave me weakened and vulnerable to all! So I have been forced to endure this . . . this aberration!"

He jerked upright again, eyes bits of ice. "But no more!"

Questor saw it all instantly. "My Lord, the magic of the bottle is too dangerous . . ."

"Dangerous!" Kallendbor cut him short with a vicious chop of one hand. "Nothing is more dangerous than this tower! Nothing! It must be destroyed! If the magic can serve my needs, then I will chance whatever danger it poses and gladly!"

He wheeled ahead, and Questor was left with a mouthful of dust and a feeling of helplessness in the face of what was surely to come.

They rode northeast toward the Melchor through the remainder of the morning until at last, as the midday approached,
the falls of the Syr came into view. There was the tower, a
massive, stone-block fortress situated on the bluff at the edge
of the falls where they spilled down into valley. It was indeed
a monstrous thing, all black and bristling with battlements and
repelling devices. Armed men stalked its parapets, and riders
patrolled its causeways. Trumpets and shouts sounded at the
approach of Kallendbor's knights, and the tower stirred to life
as if a sluggish giant.

The Lord of Rhyndweir signaled for a halt, and the column
pulled up at the river's edge some several hundred yards beyond
the base of the bluff and the fortress tower. Kallendbor sat looking at the tower for a moment, then called forward one of his
knights.

"Tell those in the tower that they have until midday to
leave," he instructed. "Say to them, at midday the tower will
be destroyed. Now, go."

The knight rode off and Kallendbor had the column stand
down. They waited. Questor considered once again saying
something to Kallendbor about the danger of using the bottle's
magic, but decided against it. It was pointless to argue the matter further; Kallendbor's mind was made up. The wiser course
of action was to allow Rhyndweir's Lord to have his way for
the moment, but to get the bottle back from him immediately
after this business was finished. Questor Thews was not happy
with the prospect, but it seemed to him that he had no other
reasonable choice.

He stood next to his gray, his tall frame stooped beneath
his patchwork robes as he stared off into the distance and
thought suddenly of the High Lord and of Abernathy. Thinking of them distressed him further. He certainly had not done
much to help either of them in this matter so far, he thought
dismally.

The messenger returned. The men in the tower would not

be leaving, he reported. They had simply laughed at the ultimatum. They had suggested that Kallendbor leave instead. Kallendbor grinned like a wolf when he heard the messenger's report, fixed his gaze on the tower, and did not look away again as he awaited the arrival of midday.

When it came, Rhyndweir's Lord grunted in satisfaction, climbed back aboard his mount, and said, "Come with me, Questor Thews."

Together, they rode forward along the river's edge for about a hundred yards, then stopped and dismounted. Kallendbor stood so that the horses blocked what he was doing from his waiting men. Then he brought out the sack from a saddle pouch and produced the brightly painted bottle.

"Now, we shall see," he whispered softly, cradling his treasure.

He pulled free the stopper and out climbed the Darkling, squinting its reddened eyes against the sunlight. "Master!" it hissed softly, stroking its hands along Kallendbor's gloved fingers. "What is it you wish?"

Kallendbor pointed. "Destroy that tower!" He paused, glancing briefly at Questor. "If your magic is strong enough, that is!" he added in challenge.

"Master, my magic is as strong as your life!" The demon spit the words out with a curl of its lip.

It climbed down from the bottle and skittered off across the ground, over the river's waters as if they were nothing more than a walkway, and out into the plains directly below the bluff where the fortress stood. There it stopped. It did nothing for a moment, gazing upward. Then it seemed to jump and whirl, to dance about in a sudden profusion of colored light, and a monstrous horn appeared out of nowhere. The demon darted away to a point another hundred yards along the base of the bluff, and a second horn appeared. It darted away again, and a third appeared.

The demon stood back then and pointed, and the horns

began to sound—a long, deep, mournful howl like the wailing
of some great wind through an empty canyon.

"See!" Kallendbor whispered in delight.

The wailing was causing the whole of the land about them
to quake, but nowhere more so than atop the bluff where the
offending tower sat. The tower shuddered as if it were a stricken
beast. Cracks began to appear along its seams, and stone blocks
began to loosen. Kallendbor and Questor Thews braced. The
sound of the horns rose, and now the horses were stamping
and rearing, and Kallendbor had to seize the reins of both and
hold them fast to keep them from fleeing.

"Demon spawn!" the Lord of Rhyndweir cried with a
howl.

The horns reached a new pitch, and the land split apart all
about them in deep cracks and crevices. The bluff was shattered,
and the tower was turned into an avalanche of crumbling rock.
Men screamed from within. The walls exploded into rubble in
an instant's time, and the whole of the tower collapsed. Down
it tumbled to the plains and the river's waters and was gone.

Then the horns disappeared, and the sound of their wailing
faded into silence. The land was still again, empty save for the
awestruck men of Rhyndweir and the cloud of dust and silt
that rose above the rubble of the shattered tower.

The Darkling skittered back across the river and bounded
up once more onto the lip of the bottle, its grin wicked and
sharp. "Done, master!" it hissed. "Done at your command!"

Kallendbor's face was alive with excitement. "Yes, demon!
Such power!"

"Your power!" the Darkling soothed. "Yours only,
master!"

Questor Thews did not care one bit for the look that
crossed Kallendbor's face when he heard that. "Kallendbor . . ." he started to say.

But the big man waved him into silence. "Back into the
bottle, little one," he commanded.

The Darkling slipped obediently from view, and Kallendbor replaced the stopper.

"Remember your promise," Questor tried again, stepping
forward to claim the bottle.

But Kallendbor snatched it away. "Yes, yes, Questor
Thews!" he snapped. "But only when I am finished! Only then.
I may have . . . other uses yet."

Without waiting for the wizard's response, he mounted
his horse and rode quickly away. Questor Thews stood there,
staring after him. He turned back one final time to gaze up at
the empty space where only moments earlier the tower had
stood. All those men dead, he thought suddenly. And Kallendbor barely gave them a thought.

He shook his head worriedly and pulled himself back up
on his frightened gray.

He knew already that Kallendbor was never going to return the bottle to him. He was going to have to take it back.

He returned to Rhyndweir lost in thought, the day slipping into
evening almost before he knew it. He ate dinner in his room
with the gnomes and Parsnip. Kallendbor left him there willingly, making no effort to insist on his presence in the dining
hall. Kallendbor did not attend himself. There were clearly other
matters of more pressing concern for the Lord of Rhyndweir.

Questor was halfway through his meal when he realized
that Bunion had failed to return. He had no idea what had become of the little kobold. No one had seen anything of him
since early morning.

When dinner was finished, Questor took a walk to clear
his thoughts, found that they were too murky to do so, and
returned to his bedchamber to sleep. He went to bed still wondering what had become of Bunion.

It was after midnight when the bedchamber door burst
open and Kallendbor stalked through. "Where is it, Questor
Thews?" he shouted in fury.

Questor looked up from his pillow, sleepy-eyed, and tried to figure out what was happening. Parsnip was already between him and the Lord of Rhyndweir, hissing in warning, teeth gleaming brightly. The G'home Gnomes were cowering under the bed. Torchlight cast a harsh glare from the hallway beyond and there were armed men milling about uncertainly.

Kallendbor loomed over him, an angry giant. "You will return it to me at once, old man!"

Questor rose, indignant now. "I haven't the faintest idea what you . . ."

"The bottle, Questor Thews—what have you done with the bottle?"

"The bottle?"

"It is missing, wizard!" Kallendbor was livid. "Stolen from a room locked all around and guarded at every entrance! No ordinary man could have accomplished that! It would have required someone who could enter and leave without being seen—someone like yourself!"

Bunion! thought Questor instantly. A kobold could go where others could not and not be seen doing it! Bunion must have . . .

Kallendbor reached for Questor, and only the sight of Parsnip's bared teeth kept him from seizing the wizard's thin neck. "Give it to me, Questor Thews, or I'll have you . . . !"

"I do not have the bottle, my Lord!" Questor snapped in reply, pushing forward bravely to confront the other. Kallendbor was as big as a wall.

"If you do not have it, then you know where it is!" the other rasped in fury. "Tell me!"

Questor took a deep breath. "My word is known to be good everywhere, my Lord," he said evenly. "You know that to be so. I do not lie. The truth is exactly as I have told you. I do not have the bottle nor do I know where it is. I have seen nothing of it since this morning when you took it away." He cleared his throat. "I warned you that the magic was dangerous and that—"

"Enough!" Kallendbor wheeled away and stalked back to the open door. When he reached it, he wheeled back again. "You will stay as my guest a few days more, Questor Thews!" he said. "I think you would do well to pray that the bottle reappears in that time—one way or the other!"

He walked out, slamming the door behind him. Questor could hear the locks snapping into place and the sound of men taking up watch.

"We are being made prisoners!" he exclaimed in disbelief.

He started across the room, stopped, started forward again, stopped again, thought angrily of what the High Lord would do when he learned that his representatives were being held against their will by a land baron, and then remembered that the High Lord would do nothing because Ben Holiday wasn't even *in* Landover anymore and wouldn't know a thing about any of this.

In short, Questor realized dismally, he was on his own.

It was several hours later that Bunion reappeared. He did not come through the door, being no fool, but through the window of the tower wall. He tapped softly on the shutter until Questor opened it in curiosity and found him perched there on the window ledge. Below, it was a straight drop of at least sixty feet to the battlement wall.

The little kobold was grinning broadly, his teeth flashing. In one hand was a length of knotted rope. Questor peered out. Somehow Bunion must have scaled the castle wall to reach them.

"Come to rescue us, I see!" Questor whispered in excitement and smiled back. "You were right to do so!"

Bunion, it happened, had been as suspicious of Kallendbor's intentions as Questor and had decided to keep an eye on things from a distance after witnessing the destruction of the

tower. Kobolds, of course, could do that; you couldn't see them
if they didn't want you to. That was the way of things with
true fairy creatures. Bunion understood all too well the awe-
some power of the magic wielded by the Darkling and he did
not think Kallendbor strong enough to resist its lure. Better
that he remain hidden, he had decided, until he could be certain
that Questor and the others would not become victims of Kallendbor's misguided ambition. It was fortunate he had done so.

Questor helped the kobold crawl inside, and together they
began tying one end of the knotted rope about a wall hook.
The others were awake now as well, and Questor was quick
to hush the gnomes into silence. The last thing he needed was
for Fillip and Sot to start whining. They worked quickly and
quietly, and the rope was firmly fastened in minutes. Then out
the window they all went, one after the other, hand over hand
down the castle wall. It was easy going for the kobolds and the
gnomes, and only Questor was forced to work a bit at it.

Once safely down, they followed Bunion along the castle
wall to a stairway and down that to a passage leading to an iron
door that opened to the outside. Slipping through the dark,
keeping within the shadows, they crossed to the back of the
town and arrived at a shed where waited the horses and pack
animals Bunion had somehow managed to retrieve.

Questor mounted his gray, put Fillip and Sot together on
Jurisdiction, left the remaining animals to Parsnip's care, and
signaled for Bunion to lead them out. Slowly, cautiously, they
made their way through the sleeping town, crossed the bridge,
and disappeared into the night.

"Farewell and good riddance, Lord Kallendbor!" Questor
shouted back once they were safely into the grasslands.

He was feeling considerably better about things. He had
extracted himself and his friends from a difficult situation before
any harm had been done to them. He neatly sidestepped the
fact that it was Bunion who had actually rescued them by telling
himself that it was his leadership that had made it all possible.

He was free now to resume his duties and to carry out the responsibilities that had been given him. He would prove his worth to the High Lord yet!

There was only one problem. Bunion, it turned out, didn't have the missing bottle after all. Someone else had stolen it—someone who, like Bunion, could get in and out of a heavily guarded room without being seen.

Questor Thews knotted his owlish face in thought.

Now who could that someone be?

Show Time

*W*hen the phone finally rang, Ben Holiday almost broke his leg falling over a chair in his eagerness to catch the call.

"Damn! Hello?"

"Doc? I'm here, finally," Miles Bennett said through the receiver. "I'm downstairs in the lobby."

Ben breathed a long, audible sigh of relief. "Thank God!"

"You want me to come up?"

"Immediately."

He hung up the phone, collapsed onto the nearby sofa, and rubbed his sore leg ruefully. Salvation, at last! He had been waiting four days for Miles to arrive with the information on Michel Ard Rhi and Abernathy—four long, endless days of being couped up in the opulent confines of the Shangri-La. Miles had wired the promised money, so at least he had been able to avoid starvation and eviction. But it hadn't been possible to leave the room for more than an hour or two each day— always late at night or early in the morning. Willow simply drew too much attention.

Besides, the sylph had not been feeling well ever since their arrival from Landover.

He glanced over to where she sat naked in a pool of sunlight on the balcony just outside the sliding glass doors that opened off the living room of their suite. She sat there every day, sometimes for hours, staring out into the desert, face lifted toward the sun, perfectly still. It seemed to help her to be exposed like that, so he left her alone. He figured that it had something to do with her amorphous physiology, that the sunlight was good for both the animal and plant parts of her. Nevertheless, she seemed listless and wan, her coloring not quite right, her energy mysteriously depleted. At times, she appeared disoriented. He was very worried about her. He was beginning to believe that something either present or lacking in the environment of his world was causing the problem. He wanted to finish this business with Abernathy and the missing medallion and get Willow safely back to Landover.

He got up, walked into the bathroom, and splashed some cold water on his face. He hadn't slept well these past few days, too keyed up, too anxious to do something and end this waiting. He toweled his face dry and gazed at himself in the mirror. He looked healthy enough, he decided, except for his eyes. His eyes were tiny roadmaps. That came from lack of sleep and reading two or three paperback novels a day to keep from going stir crazy.

A knock sounded on the door. He tossed aside the towel, crossed the room, and squinted into the peephole. It was Miles. He released the latch and pulled open the door.

"Hiya, Doc," Miles greeted, extending his hand.

Ben took it and pumped it vigorously. Miles hadn't changed a bit—still the big, baby-faced teddy bear with the rumpled suit and the winning smile. He was carrying a leather briefcase under one arm. "You look good, Miles," he said and meant it.

"You look like a damn yuppie," Miles replied. "Running suit and Nikes, camped out in the Shangri-La, waiting for nightfall and the lights of the city. Except you're too old. Can I come in?"

"Yeah, sure you can." He stepped aside to let his old friend into the room, checked both ways down the outside hall, then closed the door behind them. "Find a comfortable seat, why don't you?"

Miles moved across the room, admiring the furnishings, whistling softly at the fully stocked bar, and then suddenly stopped dead in his tracks. "For Christ's sake, Doc!"

He was staring through the sliding glass doors at Willow.

"Nuts!" Ben exclaimed in dismay. He had forgotten all about Willow.

He went into the bedroom, took down a bathrobe, and went out onto the balcony. He placed the robe gently around Willow's slender shoulders. She looked up at him questioningly, her eyes distant and haunted.

"Miles is here," he told her quietly.

She nodded and rose to join him. They walked back into the living room to confront the still-paralyzed man who was clutching his briefcase like a shield. "Miles, this is Willow," he said.

Miles seemed to remember himself. "Oh, yeah, pleased to meet you . . . Willow," he stammered.

"Willow is from Landover, Miles," Ben explained. "From where I live now. She's a sylph."

Miles looked at him. "A what?"

"A sylph. A mix of wood nymph and water sprite."

"Sure." Miles smiled uneasily. "She's green, Doc."

"That's just her coloring." Ben was suddenly uncomfortable. "Look, why don't we sit down on the sofa and have a look at what you brought, Miles."

Miles nodded, his eyes still on Willow. The sylph smiled briefly, then turned and moved off into the bedroom. "You know, it's a good thing I'm standing here having this conversation with you, Doc, and actually seeing this girl, rather than hearing about her over the phone," Miles said quietly. "Otherwise, I'd be tempted to write you off as a certified nut case."

Ben smiled. "I don't blame you." He dropped onto the sofa and motioned Miles to join him.

"A sylph, huh?" Miles shook his head. "So all that stuff about a world of magic with dragons and fairy creatures was real after all. That right, Doc? Was it all real?"

Ben sighed. "Some of it, anyway."

"My God." Miles slowly sat down beside him, a stunned look on his face. "You aren't kidding me, are you? It really exists? Yeah, it does, doesn't it? I can see it in your face. And that girl . . . she's, well, she's beautiful, different, something like you'd imagine would live in a fairy world. Damn, Doc!"

Ben nodded. "We can talk about it some more later, Miles. But what about the information I asked you to get? Any luck?"

Miles was staring at Willow through the bedroom door as she undraped the bathrobe and stepped off into the shower. "Uh, yeah," he said finally. He unsnapped his briefcase and pulled out an orange-colored file. "Here's what the investigators got on this Michel Ard Rhi character. And, believe me, he's a character with a capital C."

Ben accepted the file, opened it, and quickly began to scan its contents. The first page offered general history. Michel Ard Rhi. Birthplace, parents, age, early history all unknown. A financier, mostly through private concerns. Net worth estimated at two hundred twenty-five million dollars. Lived outside Woodinville, Washington—Washington?—in a castle purchased and then shipped, block by block, from Great Britain. Unmarried. No hobbies, no clubs, no organizations.

"Not much here," he remarked.

"Keep reading," Miles said.

He did. On the second page, it began to get interesting. Michel Ard Rhi kept his own private army. He had helped finance several revolutions in foreign countries. He owned pieces of banking institutions, major arms corporations, even a few foreign government-subsidized industries. There was a suggestion that he might be involved in a good deal more, but there was no hard evidence. He had been charged with various criminal acts, mostly fraud related to SEC violations, although there was something about animal cruelty, but he had never been convicted. He traveled extensively, always with body-guards, always by private transport.

Ben closed the file. "Washington, huh? I don't get it. I was sure Las Vegas was where we would find . . ."

"Wait a minute, Doc," Miles interrupted quickly. "There's something more, something that just turned up yesterday. It's pretty farfetched, but it might tie in somehow with this guy being up there in Washington."

He dug through his briefcase and extracted a single sheet of typed paper. "Here we go. The investigators threw this in after I told them I wanted anything they could find on a talking dog. Seems one of them has some contacts in the scandal sheet business. Listen to this. Some fellow living in Woodinville, Washington—same place, right—tried to make a deal with *Hollywood Eye* for a hundred thousand dollars cash on delivery for an exclusive interview and photo session with a genuine talking dog!"

"Abernathy!" Ben exclaimed immediately.

Miles shrugged. "Could be."

"Did they give his name? The dog's?"

"Nope. Just the man's. Davis Whitsell. He's a dog trainer and showman. But he lives right there in Woodinville, same place this Ard Rhi keeps his walled tower. What do you think?"

Ben sat forward, his mind racing. "I think it's an awfully big coincidence, if that's all it is. But, if not, what's Abernathy doing with this Whitsell character instead of Ard Rhi? And what are Willow and I doing here? Could be Questor messed up with the magic and sent us to Nevada instead of to Washington. Damn! I suppose I should be grateful he didn't deposit us in the Pacific Ocean!" He was thinking out loud to himself now, and Miles was staring at him. He smiled. "Don't worry, I'm just trying to sort all this out. You did a heck of a job, Miles. Thanks.''

Miles shrugged. "You're welcome. Now are you going to tell me what's going on here?"

Ben studied his old friend a moment, then nodded. "I'm going to try. You deserve that much. You want a Glenlivet while we talk?"

Miles had his scotch, then another, then a third as Ben tried to explain the story behind Abernathy and the missing medallion. This, of course, necessarily involved some minimal description of Landover, and that, in turn, took them off on a variety of side trips. Ben didn't tell Miles everything, particularly where it involved anything dangerous, because he knew it would only worry Miles. Willow appeared from the shower, and Ben sent down for dinner. Miles seemed to grow more comfortable in the sylph's presence after a time, and she in his, and they began to talk with each other like real people. Much of what Miles had to say to Willow left her mystified, and much of what she had to say to him left him speechless—but they got along. The evening wore on, the questions mostly got answered, and the lights of the strip began to brighten the casinos and lounges against the night skies.

Finally, Willow drifted off to bed, and Miles and Ben were left alone. Ben poured them a brandy from the bar stock, and they sat together staring out the window.

"You have a place to stay?" Ben said after a time. "I never thought to check."

Miles nodded, his gaze distant. "Down a floor or two. Down with the commoners. I booked it with the plane tickets."

"That reminds me." Ben was on his feet. "I have to call the airport right now for a flight out tomorrow."

"Washington?"

Ben nodded. "Where the heck is Woodinville?" he called back as he crossed to the phone.

"North of Seattle." Miles stretched. "Make sure you make reservations for three."

Ben stopped. "Wait a minute, you're not going."

Miles sighed. "Sure, I'm going. What do you think, Doc? That I'm leaving just when this is getting interesting? Besides, you might need me. You don't have all the connections you used to. I do—not to mention credit cards and money."

Ben shook his head. "I don't know. This could be dangerous, Miles. Who knows what we're up against with Michel Ard Rhi. I don't like the idea—"

"Doc!" Miles cut him short. "I'm going. Make the call."

Ben gave up arguing, made the reservations on an early morning PSA flight, and returned to the sofa. Miles was staring out the window again.

"Remember when we were kids and we did all that pretending? Remember how we created all those make-believe worlds to play in? I was thinking about how lucky you were to find one for real, Doc. Everyone else has to live with the world they've got." He shook his head. "Not you. You get to live what others can only wish for."

Ben didn't say anything. He was thinking about how differently they looked at things. It was the difference in their realities. Landover was his reality; Miles had only this world. He remembered how desperately he had wished for exactly what he had now just two short years ago. He had forgotten about that. It was good to remember it again.

"I am pretty lucky," he said finally.

Miles did not reply.

They sat together in silence, sipping brandy and letting their private dreams take shape in the playground of their thoughts.

Their flight out of Las Vegas was at 7:58 A.M. on PSA flight 726, a smaller jet making a single stopover in Reno on its way north to Seattle. They arrived early at the airport, camped out in an empty terminal until boarding, and took seats at the rear of the airplane to avoid drawing any more attention than was necessary. Ben had bound up Willow's hair in a head scarf, covered her face with skin-toned foundation cream, and clothed her head to foot to hide her skin, but she looked like a walking sideshow nevertheless. Worse, she was more listless than ever. Her strength seemed to be simply draining away from her.

When they had taken off the second time out of Reno and Miles was dozing, she leaned over to Ben and whispered, "I know what troubles me, Ben. I need to nourish in the soil. I need to make the change. I think that is why I am so weak. I'm sorry."

He nodded and hugged her close. He had forgotten about her need to transform from human to tree every twenty days. Perhaps he had simply blocked it away when he had agreed to bring her on this journey in the misguided hope that it wouldn't prove to be a problem. But the twenty-day cycle had obviously come around again. She would have to be allowed to change.

But what would the elements in the soil of this world do to her body systems?

He didn't like to think about it. It made him feel helpless. They were trapped here now, trapped until he found Abernathy and retrieved his medallion.

He took a deep breath, gripped Willow's gloved hand tightly in his own, and leaned back in his seat. Just one more day, he promised silently. By tonight, he would be on Davis Whitsell's doorstep, and his search would be over.

The phone rang in the living room, and Davis Whitsell pushed back his bowl of Wheaties, got up from the breakfast table, and hurried to answer it. Abernathy watched him through a crack in the bedroom door. They were alone in the house. Alice Whitsell had gone to visit her mother three days ago. Show dogs were one thing, she had said on leaving—talking dogs were something else. She would be back when the dog—if that's what it really was in the first place—was gone.

Probably just as well, Davis had insisted afterward. It was easier to concentrate on things when Alice wasn't running the TV or her mouth.

Abernathy didn't know what he meant. What he did know was that as far as he could determine he was no closer to reaching Virginia than before. Despite his host's repeated assurances that everything would be fine, he was beginning to grow suspicious.

He listened as Davis picked up the receiver. "Davis Whitsell." There was a pause. "Yes, Mr. Stern, how are you? Uh, huh. Sure thing." He sounded very eager. "Don't worry, I'll be there!"

Davis placed the receiver back on its cradle, rubbed his hands together briskly, cast a quick look down the hall in the direction of Abernathy's bedroom, then picked up the phone again and dialed. Abernathy continued to stand at the door and listen.

"Blanche?" Whitsell said into the receiver. His voice was hushed. "Let me talk to Alice. Yeah." He waited. "Alice? Listen, I only got a moment. I just got a call from the *Hollywood Eye*! Yeah, how about that? The *Hollywood Eye*! You thought I was nuts, didn't you? One hundred thousand dollars for the interview, a few pictures, and out the door! When it's done, I put the dog on the plane, wish him luck, and we get on with our lives—a hell of a lot richer and a hell of a lot better known. The *Eye* will have the exclusive, but the other magazines will pick up the story afterward. I'll have more business than I know what to do with. We're gonna be in the big bucks, girl! No more scratching and scrimping for us!" There was a brief pause. "Sure, it's safe! Look, I gotta go. See you in a few days, okay?"

He hung up and went back into the kitchen. Abernathy watched him rinse the dishes and put them in the sink, then start down the hall toward the bedrooms. Abernathy hesitated, then moved back from the door to the bed and lay down, trying to look as if he were just waking.

Whitsell stuck his head through the door. "I'm going out for a bit," he advised. "That guy I told you about, the one who's going to provide the rest of the money we need to get you back to Virginia, is down at the motel waiting to talk to me. Then we'll be coming back here for the interview. If you check out, we're all set. So maybe you'd better get yourself ready."

Abernathy blinked and sat up. "Are you sure all this is necessary, Mr. Whitsell? I feel rather uncomfortable with the idea of talking about myself and having pictures taken. I doubt that the High Lord . . . uh, my friend, would approve."

"There you go with that 'High Lord' business again," Whitsell snapped. "Who is this guy, anyway?" He shook his head wearily when Abernathy just stared at him. "Look, if we don't talk to the man with the money and let him take your picture, we don't get the money. And if we don't get the money, we can't get you back to Virginia. As I told you before, the money Elizabeth gave you just isn't enough."

Abernathy nodded doubtfully. He wasn't sure he believed that anymore. "How much longer until I can go?"

Whitsell shrugged. "Day, maybe two. Just be patient."

Abernathy thought he had been patient long enough, but he decided not to say so. Instead, he stood up and started for the bathroom. "I will be ready when you return," he promised.

Whitsell left him there, passed back through the living room, pausing to scratch Sophie's ears affectionately, went out the side door into the carport, and got into his old pickup. Abernathy watched him go. He knew he was being used, but there was no help for it. He had no one else he could turn to and nowhere else he could go. The best he could do was hope that Whitsell would keep his word.

He walked into the living room and peered out the window

long enough to see the pickup back out the driveway and turn up the street.

He paid no attention at all to the black van parked across the way.

Somewhere down the hall, the old clock ticked methodically in the stillness. Abernathy stood in front of the bathroom mirror and looked at himself. Four days were gone since he had escaped Michel Ard Rhi and Graum Wythe, and Landover seemed as far away as ever. He sighed and licked his nose, rethinking his options. If this business of the interview and the pictures didn't produce results, he guessed he was simply going to have to bid Davis Whitsell good-bye and strike out on his own. What other choice did he have? Time was running out on him. He had to find a way to get the medallion safely back to the High Lord.

He cleaned his teeth, brushed his fur, and studied himself some more in the mirror. He was looking much better than he had on his arrival, he decided. Eating and sleeping like a regular person did wonders for one.

He toweled his paws absently. Too bad Mrs. Whitsell had felt it necessary to leave. He couldn't understand why she had been so upset . . .

He thought he heard something and started to turn.

That was when the immobilizing spray hit him in the face. He staggered back, choking. A cord wound about his muzzle and a sack came over his head. He was lifted off his feet and carried out. He struggled weakly, but the hands that held him were strong and practiced. He could hear voices, hushed and hurried, and through a small tear in the sack he caught a glimpse of a black van with its rear doors open. He was tossed inside and the doors slammed shut.

Then something sharp jabbed into his backside, and he was engulfed in blackness.

Love Song

Day slipped away into evening in the country of the River Master, and the fairy folk of Elderew put aside their work and began to light the lamps of the tree lanes and pathways in preparation for the coming of night. All through the massive old trees which cradled their city, they darted—along limbs and branches, up and down gnarled trunks, through steadily lengthening shadows and thickening mist. Sprites, nymphs, kelpies, naiads, pixies, elementals of all forms and shapes, they were the creatures of the fairy world that surrounded the valley of Landover, creatures who were exiled or had fled from lives in which they had found no pleasure, though such lives had lasted an eternity.

The River Master stood at the edge of a park fronting his hidden forest city and mused on dreams of paradise lost. He was a tall, lean man, dressed in robes of forest green, a sprite with grainy, silver skin, gills at the side of his neck that fluttered gently as he breathed, hair that grew thick and black on his head and forearms, and an odd, chiseled face with eyes that were flat and penetrating. He had come into Landover at the time of its inception, bringing his people with him, exiled forever by choice from the mists of fairy. Mortal now, in a sense he had never appreciated in his old life, he lived in the seclusion of the lake country and worked to keep its earth, water, air, and life forms clean and safe. He was a healer sprite, capable of giving back life where it had been stolen. But some wounds refused to heal, and the irretrievable loss of his birth home was a scar that would always be with him.

He walked a few steps closer to the city, conscious of the guards who trailed at a respectful distance to allow him his privacy. Five of eight moons glimmered full in the night sky, colors bright against the black—mauve, peach, jade, burnt rose, and white.

"Paradise lost," he whispered, thinking still of the haunting dreams of the fairy mists. He looked around. "But paradise gained, too."

He loved the lake country. It was the heart and soul of his people, the exiles and the wanderers who had banded with him to begin anew, to discover and build for themselves and their children a world of beginnings and ends, a world of no absolutes—a world they could not find within the mists. Elderew lay hidden within marshlands, deep within a sprawling maze of forests and lakes, so well concealed that no one could find a way in or out without the help of its denizens. Those who tried simply disappeared in the mire. Elderew was a haven from the madness of those in the valley that could not appreciate the value of life—the land barons of the Greensward, the trolls and gnomes of the mountains, the monsters driven from fairy who still survived after a millennium of war. Destruction and misuse of the land was the trademark of such beings. But here, in the sanctuary of the River Master, there was peace.

He watched a dance procession begin to form at the edge of the park before him, a line of children draped in flowers and bright cloth and bearing candles. They sang and wound their way along the paths, over the waterway bridges, and through the gardens and hedgerows. He smiled as he watched them, content.

It was better now in the lands beyond the lake country,

he reflected, than it had been before the coming of Ben Holiday. The High Lord of Landover had done much to heal the breach that existed between the disparate peoples of the valley; he had done much to encourage preservation and conservation of the land and its life. Holiday judged rightly—as the River Master did—that all life was inextricably bound together and that if one tie was cut, others were endangered as well.

Willow had gone with the High Lord, Willow his child— chosen, she claimed, in the manner of the sylphs of old, by fates that were woven in the grasses on which her parents lay at her conception. Willow believed in Ben Holiday. The River Master found her belief enviable.

He breathed deeply the night air. Not that his opinions mattered much these days with the High Lord. Holiday was still angry with him for attempting to trap the black unicorn and harness its powers some months back. Holiday had never been able to accept the fact that fairy power belonged only to fairy creatures because they, alone, understood its use.

He shook his head. Ben Holiday had been good for Land- over, but he still had much to learn.

There was a small disturbance off to his left, and it brought him about. Onlookers to the dancing of the children had moved rapidly aside as a pair of his marsh sentries stalked out of the gloom of the lowlands mist with a singularly frightening crea- ture between them. Hardened veterans, their grainy wood faces as fixed as stone, the wood nymphs nevertheless kept a fair amount of distance between themselves and their charge. The River Master's guards started to close about him instantly, but he quickly waved them back. It would serve no purpose to show fear. He stood his ground and let the creature approach.

The creature was called a shadow wight. It was a form of elemental whose physical self had been ravaged at some point in its existence for an unspeakable deed or misuse so that, while it did not die, all that remained of it was its spirit. That poor life was consigned to an eternity of nonbeing. It could sustain itself only within shadows and dark spots, never within light. It had been denied its body and so had no real presence. What presence it possessed it was forced to construct from the debris of its haunts and the remains of its victims. A succubus, it stole life from others so that it, in turn, could survive, thieving and robbing from the lost and dying as a scavenger would. There were few of these horrors left in the valley now, most having perished with the passing of the ages.

This one, the River Master thought darkly, was particularly loathsome.

The shadow wight came to him on spindly, warped legs that might have belonged to an aged troll. Its arms were the limbs of some animal; its body was human. It possessed gnome hands and feet, a human child's fingers, and a face that was a mix of ravaged parts.

It bore in one hand an old woven sack.

It smiled, and its mouth seemed to twist in a silent scream. "Lord River Master," it said, its voice an echo of empty caverns. It bowed crookedly.

"It came to us without being brought," one of the sentries informed the River Master pointedly.

The Lord of the lake country people nodded. "Why have you come?" he asked the wight.

The shadow wight straightened unsteadily. Light passed through its misshapen body at the ragged joining of its bones. "To offer a gift—and to ask one."

"You found your way in; find your way out again." The River Master's face was as hard as stone. "Life will be my gift to you; ridding yourself from my presence will be your gift to me."

"Death would be a better gift," the shadow wight whispered, and its empty eyes reflected the distant candlelight. It turned to where the children still danced, wetting its lips with its tongue. "Look at me, Lord River Master. What creature that lived in all the worlds of all the times that are or ever were is more pathetic than I?"

The River Master did not respond, waiting. The wight's empty gaze shifted again. "I will tell you a story and ask that you listen, nothing more. A few quick moments that might be of interest, Lord River Master. Will you hear me?"

The River Master almost said no. He was so repulsed by the creature that he had barely been able to tolerate its presence this long. Then something caused him to relent. "Speak," he commanded wearily.

"Two years now have I lived within the crawl spaces and dark spots of the castle of Rhyndweir," the shadow wight said, edging a step closer, its voice so low that only the River Master could hear. "I lived on the wretches the Lord of that castle cast into its keep and on those poor creatures who strayed too far from the light. I watched and learned much. Then, this past night gone, a ruined troll brought to Rhyndweir's Lord a treasure to sell, a treasure of such wondrous possibilities that it surpassed anything I had ever seen! The Lord of Rhyndweir took the treasure from the troll and had him killed. I, in turn, took it from the Lord of Rhyndweir."

"Kallendbor," said the River Master distastefully. He bore no great affection for any of the Lords of the Greensward, Kallendbor least of all.

"I stole it from his sanctuary while he slept, stole it from beneath the noses of his watch because, after all, Lord River Master, they are only men. I stole it, and I brought it to you— my gift for a gift in return!"

The River Master fought back the wave of revulsion that passed through him as the shadow wight laughed hollowly. "What is this gift?"

"This!" the wight said and pulled from the sack it carried in its withered pink hand a white bottle with red dancing clowns.

"Ah, no!" the River Master cried in recognition. "I know

this gift well, shadow wight—and it is no gift at all! It is a curse! It is the bottle of the Darkling!"

"It calls itself so," the other said, coming closer still, so close its breath was warm against the River Master's skin. "But it is indeed a gift! It can give the bearer of the bottle . . ."

"Anything!" finished the River Master, shying away despite his resolve. "But the magic it employs is evil beyond all words!"

"I care nothing for good or evil," the wight said. "I care only for one thing. Listen to me, Lord River Master. I stole the bottle and I brought it to you. What you do with it now is of no concern to me. Destroy it, if you wish. But first use it to help me!" Its voice was a hiss of despair. "I want myself back again!"

The River Master stared. "Back again? That which you once were?"

"That! Only that! Look at me! I cannot bear myself longer, Lord River Master! I have lived an eternity of nonbeing, of shadowlife, of scavenging and horror beyond all words because I have had no choice! I have stolen lives from every quarter, thieved them from every being that is or was! No more! I want myself back; I want my life again!"

The River Master frowned. "What is it that you expect me to do?"

"Use the bottle to help me!"

"Use the bottle? Why not use it yourself, shadow wight? Haven't you already said that the bottle can give the bearer anything?"

The wight was trying to cry, but there were no tears in its ruined body. "Lord River Master, I—can—give—myself—nothing! I cannot use the bottle! I have no being and cannot invoke the magic! I am . . . only barely here! I am only a shadow! All the magic in the world is useless to me! Look at me! I am helpless!"

The River Master stared at the shadow wight with new-found horror, seeing for the first time the truth of what its existence must be like.

"Please!" it begged, dropping to its knees. "Help me!"

The River Master hesitated, then took the sack from the creature's extended hand. "I will consider it," he said. He signaled back the watch. "Wait here for a time while I do so. And be careful you work no harm on any of my people, or the choice will be made for me."

He moved away a bit, holding the sack loosely, slowed, and looked back. The shadow wight was crouched upon the earth, huddled like a broken thing, watching him. He had not the power to heal such a being, he thought wearily. And if the bottle's magic should give him such power, had he even the right to try?

He turned sharply and walked away. He passed from the park into the city, passed by the dancers and the merrymakers, walked down pathways and along garden rows, lost in the barren landscape of his thoughts. He knew the power of the Darkling. He had known of its power for years, as he knew of the power of most magics. He remembered the uses to which it had been put by the old King's careless son and the dark wizard Meeks. He understood the way such magic wove bright-colored ribbons about its holder and then turned them suddenly to chains.

The greater the power, the greater the risk, he reminded himself.

And power such as this could do almost anything.

He reached the edge of the city before realizing where he was. He stopped, looked back momentarily for his guards, found them trailing at a respectful distance as always, and promptly dismissed them. He needed to be by himself. The guards hesitated, then were gone.

The River Master walked on alone. What should he do? The bottle was his if he chose to help the shadow wight. It never occurred to him simply to keep the bottle and send the wight packing; he was not that sort. Either he would keep the bottle and help the wight as it had asked, or he would give the bottle back and dismiss the unfortunate creature from his life. If he chose the latter, there was nothing more to consider. If he chose the former, he must decide whether he could use the magic to aid the wight—and perhaps even himself in some way—without falling victim to its power.

Could he do that, he wondered?

Could anyone?

He stopped within a clearing of Bonnie Blues that rose twenty feet above him and screened the night skies in a webbing of deep azure silk. The sounds of the city trailed after him, faint now and distant—laughter, singing, the music and dancing of the children. The old pines were close at hand, the grove in which the wood nymphs danced at midnight, the place where he had first met Willow's mother . . .

The thought trailed away in a wash of bitter memories. How long had it been? How long since he had seen her? He could still see her so clearly, even though he had been with her only that one night and lain with her only that once. She was the muse that tortured his soul still, a wondrous, nameless creature, a wood nymph so wild that he could never hope to possess her, not even for a single night more . . .

And then it came to him, a design so dark that it engulfed him as if he had been submerged in ice water.

"No!" he whispered in horror.

But why not? He stared down suddenly at the sack that contained the magic bottle—the bottle that could give him anything.

Why not?

The bottle needed testing. He must know if he could control it. He must know if he could help the shadow wight as it had asked him or if the magic was too strong to control. What harm, then, in indulging himself just this little bit, just this once.

Why not ask the Darkling to bring him Willow's mother?

He went hot and cold at the same time, warmed by the thought of her presence after so long an absence, chilled by the prospect of using the magic thus. Ah, but the heat was so much stronger! He longed for the nymph as he had longed for nothing in his life. It had been seemingly forever! Nothing was so missing from his life as what she could bring to him . . .

"I must try!" he whispered suddenly. "I must!"

He walked swiftly through the woodlands, through the great, silent trees where only the night sounds could reach him, until at last he stood within the grove of old pines. The stillness there was pervasive, and it was only in his mind that he could hear the children's laughter and see Willow's mother dance once more.

He would not ask much, he told himself suddenly. He would only ask to see her dance for him—just dance.

The need to have her there again burned through him like a fever. He set the sack upon the earth and lifted out the brightly colored bottle. Red harlequins gleamed like blood drawings in the moonlight.

Quickly, he pulled free the stopper.

The Darkling crawled into the light like some loathsome insect. "Oh, sweet are your dreams, master!" it hissed and began to writhe about the lip of the bottle as if possessed. "Sweet longings that need to be fulfilled!"

"You can read my thoughts?" the River Master asked, sudden apprehension flooding through him.

"I can read your very soul, master," the black thing whispered. "I can see the depth and height of your passion! Let me satisfy it, master! I can give you what you wish!"

The River Master hesitated. The gills at his neck fluttered almost uncontrollably, and his breathing was harsh in his ears. This was wrong, he thought suddenly. This was a mistake! The magic was too much . . .

Then the demon sprang upright on the bottle and wove its fingers through the air, conjuring from out of nowhere a vision of Willow's mother. She danced in miniature in a cloud of silver, her face as lovely as it had ever been in the River Master's memories, her dance a magic that transcended reason or restraint. She spun, whirled, and was gone.

The Darkling's laughter was low and anxious. "Would you have her whole?" it asked softly. "In flesh and blood form?"

The River Master stood transfixed. "Yes!" he whispered finally. "Bring her! Let me see her dance!"

The Darkling sped from sight as if one of night's shadows fleeing daylight. The River Master stood alone in the grove of old pines and stared after him, hearing again the music of the children, the bright, mesmerizing sounds of the dance. His silver skin glistened, and his hard, flat eyes were suddenly alive with expectation.

To see her dance again, to see her dance just once more . . .

Then, with the speed of thought, the Darkling was back again. It skittered through the ring of pines into the clearing, its laughter high and quick. It held in its hands lines of red fire that did not seem to burn, tugging on them in the manner of a handler.

The lines were secured at their other end to Willow's mother.

She came into the light as if a dog at its master's bidding, the lines of red fire fastened about her wrists and ankles, her slender form shaking as if from a chill. She was lovely, so small and airy, so much more alive than the pale vision the River Master still guarded deep within his memory. Silver hair fell waist-length and shimmered with every movement of her tiny limbs. Her skin was pale green like Willow's, her face childlike. A gown of white gauze clothed her body, and a silver ribbon cinched her waist. She stood there, staring at him, her eyes filled with fear.

The River Master saw nothing of the fear. He saw only

the beauty he had dreamed of all these many years, come finally to life. "Let her dance!" he whispered.

The Darkling hissed and jerked on the lines, but the frightened wood nymph simply crouched down against the earth, her face buried in her arms. She began to keen, a low, terrified cry that was almost birdlike.

"No!" the River Master shouted angrily. "I want her to dance, not cry as if stricken!"

"Yes, master!" the Darkling said. "She requires only a love song!"

The demon hissed once again, then began to sing—if singing it could be called. His voice was a harsh, rasping wail that caused the River Master to flinch from the sound and Willow's mother to jerk upright as if possessed. The lines of red fire fell away, and the wood nymph stood free once more. Yet she was not truly free, for the voice of the demon bound her as surely as iron chains. It picked her up and moved her about like a puppet, forcing her to dance, compelling her to move to the music. All about the clearing, she whirled and spun, a seemingly lifeless, if perfectly formed bit of workmanship. She danced, yet the dance was not a dance of beauty, but only of forced motion. She danced, and while she danced, tears ran in streams down her child's face.

The River Master was horrified. "Let her dance free!" he shouted in fury.

The Darkling glared at him with blood red eyes, hissed in loathing, and changed the shape and form of its song to something so unmentionable that the River Master dropped to his knees at the sound. Willow's mother danced faster, her speed of movement disguising now her lack of control. She was a blur of white gauze and silver hair as she spun recklessly, helplessly through the night.

She was destroying herself, the River Master realized suddenly! The dance was killing her!

Still she danced on, and the River Master watched, helpless

to act. It was as if the magic bound him, too. He was caught up in its feel, a peculiar satisfaction welling up within him at the power it released. He recognized the horror of what was happening, yet could not break free. He wanted the dance to continue. He wanted the vision stayed.

Then suddenly he was screaming without knowing how or why, "Enough! Enough!"

The Darkling abruptly ceased its song, and Willow's mother collapsed on the forest earth. The River Master dropped the bottle, rushed to where she lay, lifted her gently in his arms, and cringed as he saw the ravaged look on her face. She was no longer the vision he remembered; she was like some beaten thing.

He whirled on the Darkling. "You said a love song, demon!"

The Darkling skittered to the discarded bottle and perched there. "I sang the love song that was in your heart, master!" it whispered.

The River Master froze. He knew it was the truth. It *was* his song the Darkling had sung, a song born of selfishness and disregard, a song that lacked any semblance of real love. His impassive face tried to twist in on itself as he felt the pain well up from within. He turned to hide what he was feeling.

Willow's mother stirred in his arms, her eyes fluttered and opened, and the fear returned to them instantly. "Hush," he said quickly. "There will be no more harm done to you. You will be allowed to go."

He hesitated, then impulsively he hugged her close. "I'm sorry," he whispered.

His need for her in that moment was so great that he could barely bring himself to speak the words that would free her, but his horror at what he had done compelled him to. He saw the fear lessen perceptibly and the tears come again to her eyes. He stroked her gently, waited while her strength returned, then helped her to her feet. She stood there momentarily looking at him, glanced past him once in anguish at the creature who crouched upon the bottle's lip, then whirled and fled into the forest like a frightened deer.

The River Master stared after her, seeing only the trees and the shadows, feeling the emptiness of the night all about him. He had lost her forever this time, he sensed.

He turned. "Back into the bottle," he said softly to the demon.

The Darkling climbed obediently from view, and the River Master replaced the stopper. He stood there momentarily staring at the bottle and found that he was shaking. He jammed the bottle into the sack and stalked from the clearing back through the forest to the city. The sounds of the music and the dancing grew distinct again as he approached, but the feeling of joy they had given him earlier was completely gone.

He crossed torchlit bridges and wound down paths and garden walks, feeling the weight of the sack and its contents as if it were the burden of his guilt. Finally, he re-entered the park.

The shadow wight crouched where he had left it on the grass, dead eyes fixed on nothing. It rose at the approach of the River Master, impatience apparent in its movements. Poor soul, the River Master thought and suddenly wondered how much of his pity was meant for the wight.

He came up to the shadow wight and stood there for a moment, studying the creature. Then he handed back the sack with the bottle. "I cannot help you," he said softly. "I cannot use this magic."

"Cannot?"

"It is too dangerous—for me, for anyone."

"Lord River Master, please . . ." the wight wailed.

"Listen to me," the River Master interrupted gently. "Take this sack and drop it into the deepest pit of mire in the marshland you can find. Lose it where it can never be found. When you have done that, come back to me, and I will do what

I can for you, using the healing powers of the lake country people."

The shadow wight flinched. "But can you make me what I was?" it cried out sharply. "Can you do that with your powers?"

The River Master shook his head. "I think not. Not completely. I think no one can."

The shadow wight shrieked as if bitten, snatched the sack with the bottle from his hands, and fled wordlessly into the night.

The River Master thought momentarily to pursue it, then changed his mind. As much as he disliked risking the possibility that the bottle might fall into other, less wise hands, he hadn't the right to interfere. After all, the shadow wight had come to him freely; it must be let go the same way. There was nowhere for it to run in any case, if not to him. There was no one else who would wish to help it. Other creatures would be terrified of it. And it couldn't use the magic of the bottle itself, so the bottle was useless to it. It would probably think the matter through and do as he had suggested. It would drop the bottle and its demon into the mire.

Distracted by thoughts of what he had done that night, haunted by memories of Willow's mother in that clearing, he pushed the matter of the shadow wight from his mind.

He would regret later that he hadn't been thinking more clearly.

The shadow wight fled north all that night, escaping from the marshland forests of the lake country into the wooded hills surrounding Sterling Silver and continuing on toward the wall of the mountains. It ran first without purpose, fleeing the intangibles of disappointment and despair, then discovered quite unexpectedly the purpose it had lacked and ran toward its promise. It sped from one end of the valley to the other, south from the lake country, north to the Melchor. It was as quick as thought, the shadow wight, as quicksilver as a kobold like Bunion, and it could be anywhere in almost no time.

As dawn approached, it found itself at the rim of the Deep Fell. "Mistress Nightshade will help me," it whispered to the dark.

It started down the wall of the hollows, picking its way swiftly through undergrowth and over rock, the sack with the precious bottle held firmly in one hand. Light began to creep from behind the rim of the mountains, silver shards of brightness that lengthened and chased the shadows. The shadow wight pushed on.

When at last it reached the floor of the hollows, deep within the tangle of trees, scrub, marsh, and weeds, Nightshade was waiting. She materialized before him out of nothing, her tall, forbidding figure rising up from the shadows like a wraith's, black robes stark against her white skin, the streak of white that parted her raven hair almost silver.

Green eyes studied the shadow wight dispassionately. "What brings you to me, shadow wight?" the witch of the Deep Fell asked.

"Lady, I bring a gift in exchange for a gift," the wight whimpered, falling to its knees. "I bring a magic that . . ."

"Give it to me," she commanded softly.

It handed the sack over obediently, unable to question or resist her voice. She took it, opened it, and lifted out the bottle. "Yessss!" she breathed in recognition, her voice a serpent's hiss.

She cradled the bottle lovingly for a moment, then glanced back again at the shadow wight. "What gift would you have of me?" she asked it.

"Give me back my real self!" the wight exclaimed quickly. "Let me be as I was before!"

Nightshade smiled, her ageless face sharp and cunning. "Why, shadow wight, you ask so simple a gift. What you were before was what we all were once." She bent down and touched him softly on his face. "Nothing."

There was a flash of red light and the shadow wight disappeared. In its place was a huge dragonfly. The dragonfly buzzed and looped away as if maddened. It sped frantically across a bit of marshy swamp. Then something huge snapped at it from out of the mire, and it was gone.

Nightshade's smile broadened. "Such a foolish gift," she whispered.

Her gaze shifted. Sunlight streamed from out of the eastern skies overhead. The new day was beginning.

She turned with the bottle cradled in her arms and prepared to welcome it.

Lost and Found

*B*en Holiday turned the rental car into the drive of 2986 Forest Park, brought it to a stop, shut down the engine, and set the brake. He glanced briefly at Miles, who looked a little like what Bear Bryant used to on the sidelines, and then at Willow, who smiled at him through a mask of weariness and pain. Ben smiled back. It was becoming increasingly difficult to do so.

They left the car and walked to the front stoop of the small, well-kept ranch home and knocked on the door. Ben could hear the sound of his pulse in his ears and he shifted his feet anxiously.

The door opened, and a lanky, bearded man with hollow eyes and a guarded look stood facing them. He was holding a can of beer in one hand. "Yeah?" His eyes fastened on Willow.

"Davis Whitsell?" Ben asked.

"Yeah?" Whitsell's voice was a mix of fear and mistrust. He couldn't stop staring at the sylph.

"Are you the man who has the talking dog?"

Whitsell continued to stare.

"The one who called *Hollywood Eye*?" Ben persisted.

Willow smiled. Davis Whitsell forced his eyes away. "You from the *Eye*?" he asked cautiously.

Miles shook his head. "Hardly, Mr. Whitsell. We're
from . . ."

"We represent another concern," Ben interrupted quickly.
He glanced about the empty neighborhood momentarily. "Do
you suppose we could step inside and talk?"

Whitsell hesitated. "I don't think . . ."

"You could finish your beer that way," Ben interjected.
"You could let the lady rest a moment, too. She's not feeling
very well."

"I don't have the dog anymore," the other said suddenly.

Ben glanced at his companions. The uncertainty and concern mirrored in their faces was undisguised. "Could we come
inside anyway, Mr. Whitsell?" he asked quietly.

Ben thought he was going to say no. He seemed right on
the verge of saying it, closing the door, and putting them out
of his life. Then something changed his mind. He nodded wordlessly and stepped aside.

When they were inside, he closed the door behind them
and went over to sit in a well-worn easy chair. The house was
dark and still, the blinds drawn, and the ticking of the old clock
at the head of the hall the only sound. Ben and his companions
sat together on the sofa. Whitsell took a long pull at his beer
and looked at them. "I told you the dog was gone," he repeated.

Ben exchanged a quick glance with Miles. "Where did he
go?" he asked.

Whitsell shrugged, trying hard to be nonchalant. "I don't
know."

"You don't know? You mean he just left?"

"Sorta. What difference does it make?" Whitsell leaned
forward. "Who are you, anyway? Who do you represent? The
Inquirer or something?"

Ben took a deep breath. "Before I tell you that, Mr. Whitsell, I have to know something from you. I have to know if
we're both talking about the same dog. We happen to be looking

for a very particular dog—a dog that really does talk. Did this dog really talk, Mr Whitsell? I mean, *really* talk?"

Whitsell suddenly looked very frightened. "I don't think we should continue this," he said abruptly. "I think you should go."

None of them moved. Willow wasn't even paying attention to him. She was making a strange, birdlike sound—a sound Ben had never heard before. It brought a tiny black poodle out from under the couch with a whine and into her lap as if they had been friends all their lives. The dog nuzzled the girl and licked her hand, and the girl stroked the animal fondly.

"She's been badly frightened," Willow said softly, to no one in particular.

Whitsell started to get up, then sat back again. "Why should I tell you anything?" he muttered. "How do I know what you want?"

Miles was drumming his fingers on his knee impatiently. "What we want is a little cooperation, Mr. Whitsell."

They stared at each other for a moment. "You from the police?" Whitsell asked finally. "Some special branch, maybe? Is that what this is all about?" He seemed to think better of the question almost before he had finished asking it. "What am I thinking here? Police don't use girls with green hair, for Pete's sake!"

"No, we're not police." Ben stood up suddenly and walked about for a minute. How much should he tell this man? Whitsell had his eyes fixed on Willow again, watching the little dog nuzzle into the girl as she continued to pet it.

Ben made his decision. "Was the dog's name Abernathy?"

He stopped walking and looked directly at Whitsell. The other man blinked in surprise. "Yeah, it was," he said. "How did you know that?"

Ben came back and sat down again. "My name is Ben. This is Miles and Willow." He pointed to the other two. "Ab-

ernathy is our friend, Mr. Whitsell. That's how we know. He's
our friend, and we've come to take him home."

There was a long moment of silence as they studied each
other wordlessly, and then Davis Whitsell nodded. "I believe
you. Don't know why, exactly, but I do. I just wish I could
help you." He sighed. "But the dog's . . . but Abernathy's
gone."

"Did you sell him, Mr. Whitsell?" Miles asked.

"No, hell, no!" the other snapped angrily. "I never
planned anything like that! I was just gonna make a few bucks
off that interview with the *Eye*, then send him to Virginia, the
way he wanted. Wasn't no harm gonna come to him. But
it was the chance I'd waited for all my life, don't you see,
the chance to get a little recognition, get off the circuit, maybe,
and . . ."

He had leaned forward in the chair, but now he trailed off,
spent, and slumped back again. "It doesn't matter now, I guess.
The point is, he's gone. Someone took him."

He took another long pull on his beer and put it down
carefully on the table beside him, back into a glistening ring of
condensation that the bottom of the can had formed earlier.
"You're really who you say you are?" he asked. "You're really
friends of Abernathy?"

Ben nodded. "Are you?"

"Yeah, though maybe you wouldn't know it from all
that's happened."

"Why don't you tell us about it?"

Whitsell did. He started at the beginning, telling them
about how he had gone to Franklin Elementary to do his show,
how the little girl Elizabeth—hell, he didn't even know her last
name—had come up to him, asked his help. He told them about
the dog, about Abernathy, coming to his door that night, a
genuine talking dog walking upright like a man, saying the little
girl sent him, that he needed to get back to Virginia for some
reason or other, and that he couldn't use a phone because there

wasn't any. Whitsell hadn't believed a word of it. But he had agreed to help anyway, hiding Abernathy out in his home, packing Alice off to her mother's, then trying to line up that interview with the *Hollywood Eye* so he could raise enough money to pay the cost of sending the dog to Virginia and maybe make a few bucks for himself in the bargain.

"But I got fooled," he admitted sourly. "I was tricked out of the house. When I got back, Abernathy was gone, and poor old Sophie was stuffed in the freezer, half froze!" His gaze shifted momentarily to Willow. "That's why she's so skittish, Miss. She's a very sensitive animal." He looked back then at Ben. "I can't prove it, of course, but I know sure as I sit here that the same fellow that had your friend caged up in the first place found out about what I was doing and took him back again! Trouble is, I don't even know who he is. Not sure I want to, man like that."

Then he seemed to realize how that sounded and reddened. He shook his head. "Sorry. Fact is, I could find out about him from the school, find out the little girl's last name, where she lives. She'd know the man's name. Hell, I'll do it right now, mister, if you think it'll help that dog! I feel terrible about this whole business!"

"Thanks anyway, but I think we already know the name of the man," Ben said quietly. "I think we know where he is, too."

Whitsell hesitated, surprised.

"Is there anything else you can tell us?"

Whitsell frowned. "No, I guess not. You think you can do something to help the dog—uh, Abernathy?"

Ben stood up without answering, and the others followed suit. Sophie jumped down from Willow's lap and nuzzled her legs through her dress. The hem lifted slightly, and Whitsell caught a brief glimpse of silky emerald hair on the back of the sylph's slender ankle.

"Thanks for your help, Mr. Whitsell," Miles was saying.

"Look, you want me to go with you, maybe help out?" the other offered suddenly, surprising them. "This seems like pretty dangerous stuff, but I want to do my part . . ."

"No, I don't think so," Ben said. They moved toward the door.

Davis Whitsell followed. "I'd be worried about that little girl, too, if I were you," he added. Sophie had returned to his side now, and he picked her up. "She might have been found out."

"We'll look into it. She'll be all right." Ben was already thinking about what to do next.

Whitsell saw them to the door and outside. The late afternoon sun was sinking rapidly below the horizon, the dusk turning the light silver. Shadows from shade trees and utility poles dappled and ribbed the neighborhood houses. A man with an insurance sign pasted on the side of his car was just pulling into a driveway down the block, the crunch of his tires on the gravel sharp in the stillness.

"I'm sorry about all this," Davis Whitsell told them. He hesitated, then reached out to shake hands with the men, as if needing some small reassurance that they believed him. "Look, I don't know who you are or where you're from or what all this is about. But I do know this much. I never wanted anything bad to happen to Abernathy. Tell him that, will you? The little girl, too."

Ben nodded. "I'll tell them, Mr. Whitsell."

He was hoping as he said it that he would have the chance.

In the country of Landover, the wizard Questor Thews was hoping much the same thing. He was not, however, optimistic.

Following their escape from the castle fortress of Rhyndweir, Questor, the kobolds Bunion and Parsnip, and the G'home Gnomes Fillip and Sot had journeyed south and east once more to the sanctuary of Sterling Silver. Questor and the kobolds had gone home because there really didn't seem to be any alternative now that the trail of the missing bottle had come to an end. Questor still hadn't been able to fathom who might have stolen the bottle from Kallendbor; until he could figure that out, he really hadn't any idea where he ought to start looking again. Besides, affairs of state had been left alone for several days now and needed looking after in the High Lord's absence.

The G'home Gnomes tagged along because they were still too frightened after their ordeal with the band of trolls to do anything else.

A message from the Lord Kallendbor in the form of a threat of immediate reprisal for the imagined theft of the bottle almost beat Questor back to the castle, but the wizard was undaunted. Kallendbor was hardly likely to challenge the power of the High Lord—unless, of course, he was to discover that Holiday was missing, heaven forbid!—however irritated he was about losing the bottle. Questor penned off a strongly worded reply on realm stationery repeating once again that he was in no way responsible for the theft of the bottle, nor were any of those in his company, and that any hostile response would be dealt with severely. He stamped it with the High Lord's seal and dispatched it. Enough was enough.

During the next twenty-four hours, he met with a delegation of other Lords from the Greensward to address their grievances, including Strehan's concerning the destruction of his tower by Kallendbor, advised the newly formed judicial council on establishment of courts to enforce the King's Rule, studied irrigation charts that would enable farmers to cultivate portions of the arid eastern expanses of the valley, and heard ambassadors and others from all parts of the realm. He did this as representative of and advisor to the High Lord, assuring all that the King would give immediate attention to their concerns. No one questioned his word. Everyone still assumed that Holiday was somewhere in the valley, and Questor was not about to suggest otherwise. Everything went smoothly, and that first day expired without incident.

The first signs of trouble appeared with the next. Reports began to drift in of disturbances from all corners of the valley, a random scattering of raindrops that quickly grew into a downpour. Crag Trolls were suddenly, unexplainably skirmishing, not only with G'home Gnomes, but also with outlying residents of the Greensward, with kobolds and sprites, and even with each other. The lake country claimed it was being inundated with fouled water from the Greensward and infested by plant-eating rats. The Greensward complained that it was under siege from a flurry of small dragons that were burning crops and livestock alike. Fairy folk and humans were setting on one another as if fighting were a newly discovered form of recreation. As fast as Questor read one report, two more came in. He went to bed that night exhausted.

The third day was even worse. The reports had accumulated overnight, and on waking he was deluged. Everyone seemed to be at odds with everyone else. No one knew exactly why. There was hostility at every turn. No one knew what was causing it. Dissatisfaction quickly grew into a demand for action. Where was the High Lord? Why wasn't he dealing with this mess personally?

Questor Thews began to smell a rat. He had already begun to suspect that the Darkling was somehow behind all this sudden unrest, and now he was beginning to suspect that the demon was serving the interests of someone whose primary concern was getting back at Ben Holiday. It seemed obvious to the wizard that the one clear purpose of all these unrelated incidents was to focus everyone's anger on the High Lord. Excluding Kallendbor, who had already lost the bottle once and was unlikely to have gotten it back again so fast, the two who most wanted revenge on Holiday were the dragon Strabo and the witch Nightshade.

Questor considered the two.

Strabo was hardly likely to bother himself with magic where Holiday was concerned; he was more apt simply to try to flatten him.

Nightshade was another matter.

Questor left messengers and ambassadors alike to cool their heels in the reception rooms and ascended Sterling Silver's high tower to where the Landsview was kept. He stepped onto the platform, fastened his hands on the polished railing, and willed himself out into the valley. Castle walls and towers disappeared, and Questor Thews was flying through space, swept away by the magic. He took himself directly across the valley to the Deep Fell and down within. Safe, because he was only seeing what was there and was not himself present, the wizard began to search for the witch. He didn't find her. He took himself out of the hollows and crisscrossed the valley, end to end. He still didn't find her.

He returned to Sterling Silver, went back down to the various reception rooms, addressed another spate of grievances, went back up to the Landsview, and went out again. He repeated this procedure four additional times that day, growing increasingly frustrated and concerned as the valley's problems mounted, the outcry for an appearance by the High Lord grew, and his own efforts went unrewarded. He began to wonder if he was mistaken.

Finally, on his fifth trip out, he found the witch. He discovered her at the far north corner of the hollows, almost into the lower peaks of the Melchor, situated where her view of the valley was unobstructed.

She was holding the missing bottle, and the Darkling was rubbing its small, twisted, bristling dark form lovingly along one thin, white hand.

Questor returned to Sterling Silver, dismissed everyone for the day, and sat down to try to figure out what to do.

He couldn't escape the fact that this whole mess was his fault. He was the one who had insisted on trying the magic that

would have changed Abernathy back into a man. He was the
one who had persuaded the High Lord to give his precious
medallion to the dog so that it might act as a catalyst. He was
the one who had then permitted the magic to go awry. He
cringed at that admission. He was the one who had dispatched
the poor scribe into Holiday's old world and brought the bottle
and the Darkling into his. He was the one who had allowed the
bottle to sit unattended so that it might be stolen by the G'home
Gnomes, the troll thieves, Kallendbor, and in the end some final
unknown so that now it was in the hands of Nightshade.

He sat alone in the shadows and silence of his private cham-
bers and faced truths he would have preferred to leave alone.
He was a poor wizard at best; he might as well admit it. Sometimes he could control the magic—what little he had learned—
but, more often than not, it seemed to control him. He had
enjoyed a few successes, but suffered many failures. He was an
apprentice of an art that defied his staunchest efforts to master
it. Perhaps he was not meant to be a wizard. Perhaps he should
simply accept the fact of it.

He rubbed his chin and screwed up his owlish face in distaste. Never! He would sooner be a toad!

He stood up, paced about the darkened chamber for a time,
and sat down again. There was no point in bemoaning his life's
condition. True wizard or no, he was going to have to do something about Nightshade. The problem, of course, was that he
didn't know what. He could go down into the Deep Fell and
confront the witch, demand the bottle back, and threaten her
with his magic. Unfortunately, that would likely be the end of
him. He was no match for Nightshade in her own domain,
especially with the bottle and its demon in her service. She
would gobble him up like a sweetmeat.

He saw again in his mind the witch and the Darkling at
the hollows rim, a match if ever there was one, darkest evil and
her favorite child.

He clasped his hands before him, frowning so hard the

ends of his mouth almost disappeared below his chin. The Paladin was the only one who could master the witch—but the Paladin would only appear if the High Lord summoned him, and the High Lord was trapped in his old world until he could find the missing Abernathy, regain his medallion, and get back again.

Questor Thews gave a great sigh of disgust. It had all gotten so complicated!

"Well!" he snapped, coming abruptly to his feet. "We shall have to *uncomplicate* things!"

Brave words, he thought darkly. Uncomplicating things meant finding Holiday, Abernathy, and the medallion and getting all three safely back into Landover to deal with Nightshade and the Darkling. He hadn't the magic to do that. He'd told Holiday as much when he had sent him back.

There was another way, however.

A rather unlikely way.

He was chilled suddenly at the thought of what he had to do. He wrapped his gray robes with their bright-colored silk patches close about him for momentary warmth, then released them again to tug restlessly at his ear. Well, either he *was* Court Wizard or he *wasn't*! Better learn the truth of matters right here and now!

"No point in waiting, either," he whispered.

Determined, he went out the door and down the hall to find Bunion. He would leave tonight.

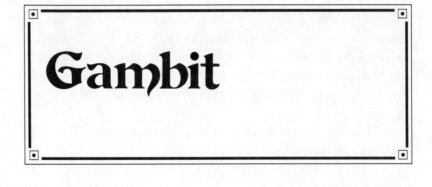

Gambit

"**I**'m telling you, it won't work," Miles Bennett insisted. "I don't know why I let you talk me into these things, Doc."

Ben Holiday leaned forward wearily. "You keep saying that. Why don't you try being more positive about things."

"I am being positive! I'm *positive* it won't work!"

Ben sighed, leaned back again, and stretched his legs out comfortably in front of him. "It'll work," he said.

They were speeding through the countryside north of Woodinville on 522 in a black stretch limousine, Miles driving, Ben sitting alone in the back seat. Miles wore a chauffeur's cap and coat at least one size too small, which was unfortunate because the whole scenario would have played better if the driver had been as immaculately dressed as his passenger. But there hadn't been time to shop for Miles—and even if there had, they probably wouldn't have been able to find a clothing store with chauffeur uniforms for rent or sale in any case—so they'd had to settle for what the original driver was wearing. Ben looked considerably better. There'd been time to shop for him. He wore a five hundred dollar three-piece dark blue suit with just a hint of pinstriping, a pale blue silk shirt, and a deep mauve silk tie with a scattering of blues and lavenders woven in. A matching scarf was tucked neatly into his breast pocket. He glanced surreptitiously at himself in the rearview mirror. Just your average millionaire businessman, he thought—with just a touch of the wheeler-dealer in evidence. Sitting in his stretch limo with his chauffeur and his fine clothes, he looked every bit the successful entrepreneur.

Which was the way he was supposed to look, of course.

"What if he's seen your picture somewhere?" Miles asked suddenly. "What if he recognizes who you really are?"

"Then I'm in big trouble," Ben admitted. "But he won't. He's had no reason to track down a picture of me. Meeks always handled the Landover sales by himself. Michel Ard Rhi was content to collect the money and let matters take care of themselves. He had his own interests to look after."

"Like running guns and overthrowing foreign governments." Miles shook his head. "This plan is too risky, Doc."

Ben stared out into the darkness. "True. But it's the only plan we've got."

He watched the dark shapes of the trees on either side of the highway rush past and disappear like frozen giants, the land sullen and empty, the night skies overcast and impenetrable. It was always smart to have a plan, he told himself. Too bad it couldn't always be a good one.

They had left Davis Whitsell knowing that Abernathy was again in the hands of Michel Ard Rhi. It didn't matter that Whitsell hadn't seen Abernathy's abductors. They were as certain as the trainer that it had been Michel Ard Rhi who had taken him. Abernathy was imprisoned somewhere in Ard Rhi's castle fortress, and it was up to them to rescue him—quickly. There was no telling what Ard Rhi would do to the dog now. There was no telling what he would do to that little girl either, once he found her out. He might even use the little girl as a weapon against the dog. Abernathy still had the medallion; Whitsell had mentioned seeing it. They had to assume that Ard Rhi knew about the medallion and was trying to get it back. If not, he would have done away with Abernathy long ago. He couldn't take the medallion by force, of course, but he could put an awful lot of pressure on the dog to persuade him to part with it willingly. The little girl would provide just the sort of pressure Ard Rhi would be apt to use.

That being the case, there simply wasn't any time to come up with the sort of elaborate, foolproof plan they might otherwise have envisioned. Abernathy and the little girl were in immediate danger. Willow was growing steadily sicker from the environment into which she had willingly placed herself in order not to be separated from Ben. God only knew what was happening back in Landover with the Darkling still on the loose and Questor Thews trying to govern. Ben seized hold of the first reasonable plan that came to mind.

It was going to take an awful lot of luck to make it work.

"Don't forget about Willow," he reminded Miles suddenly.

"I won't. But I don't see how she's going to have any better luck than you." He glanced quickly back over his shoulder. "There's bound to be lights all over the place, Doc."

Ben nodded. He was worried about that, too. How effective would Willow's magic be when she needed it? What if it failed her entirely? Under normal circumstances, he wouldn't have thought twice about it; he knew that, like all the fairy folk, the sylph could move about freely without being seen. But that was in Landover and that was when she was well. Willow was so weak, so drained by the attack on her system! She desperately needed the nurturing soil and air of her own world. She needed to make the transformation. But she couldn't do it here in this world. She had already told him so. Too many of the chemicals in the soil and air were toxins to her system. She was trapped in her present form until Ben could find a way to get her back to Landover again.

He tightened the muscles of his jaw. It was pointless to dwell on it. There would be no help for her until he regained the medallion—no help for any of them.

He turned his attention to the plan. It had been a fairly simple matter to have the rented limo and driver sent north out of Seattle to the little motel in Bothell that they had quickly made their base of operations. It had been equally simple to bribe the driver to part with the limo and his coat and cap for a few hours while he waited in the motel room and watched TV. After all, five hundred dollars was a lot of money. And it hadn't been too tough to track down the clothes Ben needed.

Finding Michel Ard Rhi had been easier yet. "Oh, sure, that nut that lives out in the castle!" the manager of the motel had eagerly volunteered when Ben asked. "Gramma White or some such, it's called. Looks like something out of King Arthur. Sits back in there behind the winery off 522. Can't even see it from the road. Guy runs it like a prison. Doesn't allow anyone close. As I said, a nut case! Who else would live in a castle in the middle of nowhere?" Then he had drawn Ben a map.

Finding the nut case was one thing; arranging to see him on short notice and at night was something else. Ben had made the call. He had spoken with a man whose sole position with Ard Rhi, it appeared, was to prevent people like Ben from disturbing his boss. Ben had explained that he was only in Seattle that one night. He had explained that the timing was quite important. He had even suggested that he was used to doing business at night. Nothing helped. Ben had talked money, opportunity, ambition, everything he could think of to persuade the man. The man was a stone. He had left the phone twice, presumably to confer with his boss, but each time he had returned as implacable as before. Perhaps tomorrow. Perhaps another day. Definitely not tonight. Mr. Ard Rhi never meets with anyone at night.

Finally, Ben had used Abernathy's name and alluded none too subtly to his own strong connection with certain government agencies. If he were not permitted to speak to Mr. Ard Rhi and speak with him now, personally, this night, he would have to consider turning the matter over to one of those agencies, and Mr. Ard Rhi might not find it so easy to refuse them.

That did the job. Grudgingly, the secretary had advised him that he would have his appointment. But must it be at night? It must, Ben insisted. There had been a pause, more background conversation, heated words. Very well, a few minutes only, nine o'clock sharp at Graum Wythe. The phone had gone dead. At the close of things, the secretary's voice had sounded very dangerous indeed. But that hadn't mattered to Ben. His meeting with Michel Ard Rhi had to take place at night, or the entire plan was out the window.

Miles slowed the limo abruptly, distracting Ben from his thoughts, wheeled left at a pair of stone block pillars with globe lights, and proceeded down a narrow, single-lane road that disappeared back into the trees. What little light there was from the headlamps of other cars, from the distant windows of solitary houses, and from the reflection of ground light off the clouded skies disappeared. The lights of the limo were lonely beacons in the gloom.

They drove on, a long, solitary journey through the night. The woods gave way to the vineyards, acres of small, gnarled vines planted in endless rows. The minutes slipped away.

Ben thought of Willow, hidden in the trunk of the car, carefully wrapped in blankets. He wished he could check on her, make certain she was all right. But they had agreed. No chances were to be taken. Once they had left Bothell, there was to be no stopping until . . .

Ben blinked.

Lights flared ahead from beyond the wooded hill they climbed—triggered, it seemed, by their approach. As they topped the rise, the spires of Graum Wythe lifted starkly before them. Though still far distant, they could see the castle clearly. Flags and pennants blew sharply in the night wind, their insignia unidentifiable in the shadows. A drawbridge had already begun to lower across a moat, and a portcullis was being raised. Breast-

works and spiked fences crisscrossed the open countryside surrounding the castle, dark scars on the grassland. The limo
crawled down the roadway toward a set of massive iron gates
that opened through a long, low stone wall that ran for miles
in either direction.

Ben took a deep breath and shivered in spite of himself.
How grotesque the castle seemed!

The iron gates swung open soundlessly to admit them,
and Miles eased the limo through. He had quit talking, rigid
in the driver's seat. Ben could imagine what he was thinking.

The roadway wound snakelike toward the castle, brightly
lit and flanked by deep culverts. That's probably so nobody
wanders off by mistake, Ben thought darkly. For the first time
since he had conceived this venture, he began to have doubts.
Graum Wythe hunkered down before him like some huge beast,
all alone in the empty countryside with its towers, parapets,
guards, spotlights, and sharp wire. It looked less like a castle
than a prison. He was going into that prison and he was going
in unprotected.

The full realization of where he was struck him suddenly,
a frightening and certain truth that left him shaken. He was
such a fool! He thought of himself as still being in a world of
glass high-rises and jetliners. But Graum Wythe wasn't part of
that world; it was part of another. It was part of a life he had
bought into when he had purchased his kingship nearly two
years ago. There wasn't anything from the modern world out
here. He could dress in suits and ride in limos and know that
cities and highways were all around him, and it wouldn't make
one bit of difference. This was Landover! But the Paladin was
not here to rescue him. Questor Thews was not here to advise
him. He had no magic to aid him. If anything went wrong, he
was probably finished.

The car reached the end of the winding roadway and pulled
onto the lowered drawbridge. They passed over the moat,
under the portcullis, and into a courtyard with a turn-around

drive that looped ahead to the main entry. Manicured lawns
and flower gardens failed to make up for the towering stone-
block walls and iron-grated windows.

"Charming," Miles whispered from the front.

Ben sat quietly. He was calm now, quite composed. It was
like old times, he told himself. It was like it had been when he
was a lawyer. He was simply going into trial court one more
time.

Miles pulled the limo to a stop at the top of the drive, got
out, and walked around to open the door for Ben. Ben stepped
out and glanced around. The walls and towers of Graum Wythe
loomed all about him, casting their shadows against the blaze
of lights that flooded the yard. Too many lights, Ben thought.
Guards patrolled the entries and the walls, faceless, black-garbed
figures in the night. Too many of them as well.

A doorman appeared through the heavy brass and oak
doors of the main entry and stood waiting. Miles closed the car
door firmly and leaned close.

"Good luck, Doc," he whispered.

Ben nodded. Then he went up the steps and disappeared
into the castle.

The minutes slipped past. Miles waited by the back door of the
limo for a time, then walked around to the driver's door,
stopped, and glanced casually about. The castle doors were
closed again and the doorman gone. The courtyard was de-
serted—discounting, of course, the spotlights that lit it up bright
as day and guards that patrolled the walls all around it. Miles
shook his head. He reached in the car under the dash and popped
the trunk, trying hard not to think about what he was doing,
trying to appear nonchalant. He walked back to the trunk, lifted
the lid, reached in, and took out a polishing cloth. He barely
glanced at the blanketed, huddled shape in one corner. Leaving
the trunk open, he moved to the front of the car and began
wiping down the windshield.

A pair of black-uniformed guards walked out of the shadows from one corner of the building and stopped, watching him. He kept polishing. The guards carried automatic weapons.

Willow will never make it, he thought dismally.

The guards strolled on. Miles was sweating. He released the hood latch, then moved to the front of the car and looked in, fiddling with nothing. He had never felt so entirely alone and at the same time so completely observed. He could feel eyes on him everywhere. He glanced surreptitiously from beneath the hood. Who knew how many of those eyes would catch Willow trying to sneak past?

He finished with the phony engine inspection and dropped the hood back in place. There hadn't been a sign of movement anywhere. What was she waiting for? His cherubic face grimaced. What did he *think* she was waiting for, for God's sake? She was waiting for a power outage!

That damn Doc and his hare-brained schemes!

He walked back around the car to the trunk, half-determined to find a way to call the whole thing off, certain the whole plan was already shot to hell. He was utterly astonished when he glanced in the trunk and found Willow gone.

Standing inside the front entry, the doorman patted Ben down for weapons and, presumably, wires. There weren't any to be found. Neither man said a word.

When the search was finished, Ben followed the doorman along a cavernous, vaulted corridor past suits of armor, tapestries, marble statues, and oil paintings in gilt-edged frames to a pair of dark oak doors that opened into a study. A genuine study, mind you, Ben thought—not a little room with a few shelves and bookcases and a reading chair, but a full-blown English-style study with dozens of huge, stuffed leather reading chairs and companion tables of the sort you saw in those old Sherlock Holmes movies in mansions where the characters retired to take brandy and cigars and talk murder. A fire blazed

in a floor-to-ceiling fireplace, the embers of charred logs smol-
dering redly beneath the iron grate. A pair of latticed windows
looked out into gardens that featured sculpted hedges and
wrought-iron benches and were disturbingly deep.

The doorman stepped aside to let Ben enter, pulled the
study doors closed behind him, and was gone.

Michel Ard Rhi was already on his feet, materializing from
out of one of the huge stuffed chairs as if he had miraculously
taken form from its leather. He was dressed entirely in the stuff,
a sort of charcoal jumpsuit complete with low boots, and he
looked as if he were trying to do Hamlet. But there was nothing
funny about the way he looked at Ben. He stood there, a tall,
rawboned figure, his shock of black hair and his dark eyes shad-
owing the whole of his face, his features pinched with displeasure. He did not come forward to offer his hand. He did not
invite Ben in. He simply viewed him.

"I do not appreciate being threatened, Mr. Squires," he
said softly. Squires was the phony name Ben had given over
the phone. "Not by anyone, but especially not by someone
looking to do business with me."

Ben kept his poise. "It was necessary that I see you, Mr.
Ard Rhi," he replied calmly. "Tonight. It was obvious that I
was not going to be able to do so unless I found a way to change
your mind."

Michel Ard Rhi studied him, apparently considering
whether to pursue the matter. Then he said, "You have your
meeting. What do you want?"

Ben moved forward until he was less than a dozen paces
from the other. There was anger in the sharp eyes, but no sign
of recognition. "I want Abernathy," he said.

Ard Rhi shrugged. "So you said, but I don't know what
you are talking about."

"Let me save both of us a little valuable time," Ben continued smoothly. "I know all about Abernathy. I know what
he is and what he can do. I know about Davis Whitsell. I know

about *Hollywood Eye.* I know most of what there is to know about this matter. I don't know what your interest is in this creature, but it doesn't matter as long as it doesn't conflict with mine. My interest is paramount, Mr. Ard Rhi, and immediate. I don't have time to wait for sideshows and the like."

The other man studied him, a hint of shrewdness displacing the anger. "And your interest is . . . ?"

"Scientific." Ben smiled conspiratorially. "I operate a specialized business, Mr. Ard Rhi—one that investigates the functioning of life forms and explores ways to make them better. My business operates somewhat covertly. You'll not have heard of either its name or mine. Uncle Sam aids in funding, and we exchange favors from time to time. Do you understand?"

A nod. "Experiments?"

"Among other things." Another smile. "Could we sit down now and talk like businessmen?"

Michel Ard Rhi did not smile back, but indicated a chair and sat down across from Ben. "This is all very interesting, Mr. Squires. But I can't help you. There isn't any Abernathy. The whole business is a lie."

Ben shrugged as if he expected as much. "Whatever you say." He leaned back comfortably. "But if there were an Abernathy, and if he became available, then he would be a most valuable commodity—to a number of interested parties. I would be prepared to make a substantial offer for him."

The other man's expression did not change. "Really."

"If he were undamaged."

"He doesn't exist."

"Supposing."

"Supposing doesn't make it so."

"He would be worth twenty-five million dollars."

Michal Ard Rhi stared. "Twenty-five million dollars?" he repeated.

Ben nodded. He didn't have twenty-five million dollars to spend on Abernathy, of course. He didn't have twenty-five million dollars, period. But then he didn't really expect that any amount of money could purchase his friend—not before Michel Ard Rhi had his hands on the medallion.

What he was doing was buying time.

So far, it hadn't cost him much.

Willow slipped noiselessly along the dimly lit passageways of Graum Wythe, little more than another of night's shadows. She was tired, the use of the magic that kept her concealed a drain on her already diminished strength. She felt sick inside, a pervasive queasiness that would not be banished. At times she was so stricken she was forced to stop, leaning back in dark corners and waiting for her strength to return. She knew what was wrong with her. She was dying. It was happening a little at a time, a little each day, but she recognized the signs. She could not survive outside of her own world for more than a short time—especially not here, not in an environment where the soil and the air were unclean and poisoned with waste.

She had not told Ben. She did not intend to. Ben had enough to concern him, and there was nothing he could do for her, in any case. Besides, she had known the risk when she had decided to come with him. Any fault was her own.

She breathed the close air of the castle, nauseated by its taste and smell. Her skin was pale and damp with perspiration. She forced herself from her hiding place and continued swiftly on. She was on the second floor and close to where she needed to go now. She could sense it. She must hurry, though. Ben could give her only a few minutes.

She reached a single door at the bend in the hall and pressed her ear against it, listening. There was breathing within.

It was the little girl, Elizabeth.

She placed her hand on the latch. It was for this reason that they had come to Graum Wythe at night—so that they could be certain the little girl would be there.

She pressed down on the latch until it gave, pushed the

door open, and slipped inside. Elizabeth was in her nightdress, propped up in her bed on one elbow, reading a book. She started when Willow appeared, her eyes going wide.

"Who are you?" she breathed. "Oh! You're all green!"

Willow smiled, closed the door behind her, and held a finger to her lips. "Shhh, Elizabeth. It is all right. My name is Willow. I am a friend of Abernathy."

Elizabeth sat bolt upright in the bed. "Abernathy? You are?" She pushed the covers back and scrambled out of the bed. "Are you a fairy? A fairy princess, maybe? You look like one, you're so beautiful! Can you do magic? Can you . . ."

Willow moved her finger to the little girl's lips. "Shhhhh," she repeated softly. "We do not have much time."

Elizabeth frowned. "I don't understand. What's wrong? Oh, I bet you don't know! Abernathy's gone! He's not here anymore! Michel had him locked in a cage in the cellars, but I sneaked him out and sent him . . ."

"Elizabeth," Willow interrupted gently. She knelt down next to the little girl and took her hands. "I have to tell you something. I am afraid Abernathy did not escape after all. Michel found him and brought him back."

"Oh, poor Abernathy!" Elizabeth's face tightened into a knot of anguish. "Michel will hurt him, I know he will! He was starving to death when I helped him escape! Now Michel will really hurt him. That's how he is! He'll really hurt him!"

Willow turned her toward the bed and sat with her on its edge. "We have to find another way to help him escape from here, Elizabeth," she said. "Is there anyone you can think of who could help us?"

Elizabeth looked doubtful. "My father, maybe. But he's gone."

"When does you father return?"

"Next week, Wednesday." Elizabeth's face knotted further. "It's not soon enough, is it, Willow? Michel was looking funny at me at dinner tonight—as if he knew something. He kept talking about dogs, and then he would smile, a mean smile. He knows I helped, I'll bet. He's just teasing me with it. He's going to hurt Abernathy, isn't he?"

Willow squeezed the small hands. "We will not let him. I have friends with me. We are going to take Abernathy away."

"You are?" Elizabeth was immediately excited. "Maybe I can help!"

Willow shook her head firmly. "Not this time."

"But I want to help!" Elizabeth said firmly. "Michel already knows I helped once, so I can't be in any worse trouble! Maybe you can take me, too! I don't want to stay here any more!"

Willow frowned slightly. "Elizabeth, I . . ."

"Michel's already said I can't leave my room! I have to stay up here all the time until he says different. He has to know! Tomorrow is Halloween, and I don't even get to go trick-or-treating! I practically had to beg to get permission to go to the school party tomorrow night. I even had to get Nita Coles to get her parents to call up and offer me a ride! With my dad gone, Michel wasn't going to let me go. But I told him everyone would wonder if I wasn't at the party because the whole school was going—so he gave in." She was crying. "I guess going to the party doesn't matter much now, not with Abernathy locked up again. Oh, I thought he was safe!"

Suddenly she stopped crying and her head jerked up sharply. "Willow, I know a way to get Abernathy out! If Michel's got him locked up again in the cellar, I know how to get him out!"

Willow touched the little girl's tear-streaked face. "How, Elizabeth?"

"The same way I got him out before—through the passageway in the wall! Michel doesn't know about that yet! I know because I was in it again after Abernathy got away, and it wasn't closed off or anything! And I could get a key to those cages again if I had to—I know I could!" She was excited now, her breathing rapid, her face flushed. "Willow, we could get him out tonight!"

For just an instant, Willow considered it. Then she shook her head. "No, Elizabeth, not tonight, Soon, though. And perhaps you can help. In fact, you already have. You have told me of a way to reach Abernathy. That was one reason I came to you—to see if there was a way. But we must be very careful, Elizabeth. We must not make any mistakes. Do you understand?"

Elizabeth was crestfallen, but managed a grudging nod.

Willow tried a wan smile. She had already stayed beyond her allotted time and she was growing dangerously weak from the effort. "You must not say anything about seeing me, Elizabeth. You must pretend I never came. You must act as if you know nothing about Abernathy. Can you do that?"

The little girl nodded. "I can pretend better than anyone."

"Good." Willow rose and started for the door, one of Elizabeth's hands still clinging to her. She turned. "Be patient, Elizabeth. We all want Abernathy safe again. Perhaps tomorrow . . ."

"I love Abernathy," Elizabeth said suddenly.

Willow turned, looked at the little girl's face, and then hugged her close. "I do, too, Elizabeth."

They held each other for a long time.

"Twenty-five million dollars is a lot of money, Mr. Squires," Michel Ard Rhi was saying.

Ben smiled. "We try not to put limits on the price of our research, Mr. Ard Rhi."

Still seated in the stuffed leather chairs, they studied each other in the silence and shadows of the study. No sound reached them from without.

"The subject of our discussion would have to be in good condition, of course," Ben repeated. "A damaged specimen would be useless."

The other said nothing.

"I would need to make an inspection."

Still nothing.

"I would need assurances that Abernathy . . ."

"There is no Abernathy, Mr. Squires—remember?" Michel Ard Rhi said suddenly. Ben waited. "Even if there were . . . I would have to think about your offer."

Ben nodded. He had expected that. It was too much to hope that he would have a chance to see Abernathy right away. "Perhaps if I were to arrange to stay a bit longer than planned, Mr. Ard Rhi, we might continue this discussion tomorrow?"

The other man shrugged. He touched something beneath the table beside him and rose. "I will decide the time and the place of any future meetings, Mr. Squires. Is that understood?"

Ben smiled companionably. "As long as it's soon, Mr. Ard Rhi."

Surprisingly, Michel Ard Rhi smiled back. "Let me give you some advice, Mr. Squires," he said, coming forward a few paces. "You should be more careful with your demands. This is a place of some danger, you know. That is its history. People have disappeared in these walls. They were never seen again. There is magic here—some of it very bad."

Ben was suddenly cold. *He knows*, he thought in horror.

"A life or two snuffed out, what does it matter? Even important lives—like your own—can be swallowed up and disappear. The magic does that, Mr. Squires. It simply swallows you up."

Ben heard the door behind him open.

"Be careful after this," the other warned softly, eyes hard with the promise that the threat was real. "I don't like you."

The doorman stepped into view and Michel Ard Rhi turned abruptly away. Ben walked quickly from the study, daring to breathe again, feeling the chill in his spine begin to fade. He passed back down the empty corridor to the front entry and went out, the doorman showing the way. As he stepped into the night, he thought he felt something brush against him. He looked but there was nothing there.

The door closed behind him. Miles was standing by the rear door, holding it open. Ben climbed into the car and sat back wordlessly. He watched Miles walk around the rear of the limo to the driver's door. The trunk was already closed. There was no sign of Willow.

"Willow?" he whispered urgently.

"I'm here, Ben," she replied, a disembodied voice from out of the pool of shadows at his feet, so close to him that he jumped.

Miles got in and started the car. Within minutes they were back through the portcullis, over the drawbridge, up the winding roadway, and out the iron gates. Willow sat up in the seat then next to Ben and related everything Elizabeth had told her. When she was finished, no one said anything for a time. The car's engine hummed in the silence as they passed back out onto 522 and turned south toward Woodinville.

When Miles turned up the heater, no one complained.

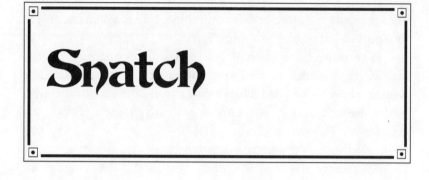

Snatch

October 31 was a gray, cloudy, drizzly day where the wind blew in sharp gusts, and the rain spit and chilled the air, as the whole western half of Washington State experienced a fore-warning of winter's coming. It was a gloomy day of shadows and strange sounds, the kind of day when people think about curling up next to a warm fire with a glass of something hot and a good book. It was a day when they found themselves listening to the sounds of the weather and to things that weren't even there. It was, in short, a perfect day for an Allhallows Eve.

Elizabeth was eating lunch in the school cafeteria when she got the message that a telephone call from home was waiting for her in the office. She hurried to get it, leaving Nita Coles to guard her double-chocolate-chip cookie; when she returned, she was so excited she didn't bother to eat it. Later, when they were at recess, she told Nita that she didn't need a ride to the Halloween party that night after all—although she might need one home. Nita said okay and told Elizabeth she thought she was acting weird.

Ben Holiday spent the better part of that blustery day south of Woodinville and Bothell in greater Seattle visiting costume shops. It took him a long time to find the costume he was looking for. Even then, he had to spend several hours afterward, back in the motel room, altering its appearance until it met with his approval.

Willow spent the day in bed, resting. She was growing steadily weaker and she was having trouble breathing. She tried to hide it from Ben, but it wasn't something she could hide. He was good about it, though, not saying anything, letting her sleep, forcing himself to concentrate on his preparations for that night. She saw that and loved him the more for it.

Miles Bennett visited several private airports until he found one with a suitable plane and pilot that could be chartered for a flight out that night. He told the pilot that there would be four of them and they would be flying to Virginia.

They all went about their business, right along with the rest of the world, but for them, it seemed, Friday was an endless wait . . .

Finally, dusk found Ben, Miles, and Willow back once more on 522 headed north out of Woodinville toward Graum Wythe. They were in the rental car this time, the limo long since dispatched back to Seattle. Ben was driving, Willow was beside him in the passenger seat, and Miles sat in back. The wind whistled and the weaving shadows of branches played along the car's dark shell like devil's fingers. The skies were slate gray, turning black as the final twinge of daylight slipped rapidly away.

"Doc, this isn't going to work," Miles said suddenly, breaking what had been a seemingly interminable stretch of silence.

It was like a replay of yesterday. Ben grinned, though Miles couldn't see it. "Why not, Miles?"

"Because there are too many things that can go wrong, that's why. I know I said the same thing about last night's plan and you still got away with it, but that was different. This plan is a hell of a lot more dangerous! You realize, of course, that we don't even know if Abernathy is down there in those dun-

geons or cages or whatever! What if he's not there? What if he's
there, but you can't get to him? What if they've changed the
locks or hidden the keys, for God's sake? What do we do then?"

"Come back tomorrow and try again."

"Oh, sure! Halloween will be over! What are we supposed
to do? Wait for Thanksgiving and go in as turkeys? Or maybe
Christmas and go down the chimney like Santa and his elves?"

Ben glanced around. Miles looked pretty funny sitting
there in that gorilla suit. But, then, he looked pretty funny
himself in the shaggy dog outfit that made him look somewhat
like Abernathy. "Relax, Miles," he said.

"Relax?" Ben could practically see him turning red inside
the heavy suit. "What if they count heads, Doc? If they count
heads, we're dead!"

"I told you how to handle that. It will work just the way
we want it to. By the time they figure out what's happened,
we'll be long gone."

They rode on in silence until they reached the stone pillars
with the lighted globes and Ben wheeled the car left down the
wooded, private road. Then Willow said, "I wish we didn't
have to take Elizabeth with us."

Ben nodded. "I know. But we can't leave her behind—
not after this. Michel Ard Rhi will know she was involved.
She's better off out of there. Her father will understand after
Miles has talked to him. They'll be well looked after."

"Humphhh!" Miles grunted. "You're crazy, Doc, you
know that? No wonder you like living in fairyland!"

Willow slumped back in the seat and closed her eyes again.
Her breathing was ragged. "Are you sure you can do this?"
Ben asked quietly. The sylph nodded without replying.

They drove through the vineyards and finally the electric
sensor that triggered the floodlights. When they reached the
low stone wall, the iron gates were open and Graum Wythe's
drawbridge and portcullis were already in operation. The castle
looked massive and forbidding against the mix of low-hanging

clouds and distant mountains, the outline of its towers and parapets hazy with the mist and rain. The wipers of the car clicked back and forth, blurring and clearing in brief intervals the sweep of the land ahead. Ben eased the rental car down the winding roadway, unable to escape the feeling that he had somehow managed to forget something.

They crossed the drawbridge, the tires thumping on the timbers, passed through the maw of the castle gates, and pulled around the drive. Lights blazed through the mist and gloom, but the guards they had seen the previous night were not in evidence. Doesn't mean that they're not out there, though, Ben thought and swung the car in close to the entry.

They stepped out quickly and hastened into the shelter of the front entryway, Ben holding Willow close to keep her from slipping. They knocked and waited. The door opened almost at once, and the doorman was there to greet them. He blinked in surprise.

What he saw was a gorilla, a shaggy dog, and a young woman dyed green from head to foot.

"Evening," Ben greeted through the dog suit. "We're here to pick up Elizabeth for her Halloween party at the grade school. I'm Mr. Barker, this is my wife Helen, and this is Mr. Campbell." He made the introductions quickly so the names wouldn't register, and they didn't.

"Oh." The doorman was not a conversationalist. He beckoned them inside, however, and they gladly went. They stood in the entryway, brushing off stray drops of rain and looking guardedly about. The doorman studied them momentarily, then went to a phone and called someone. Ben held his breath. The doorman put the phone down and returned.

"Miss Elizabeth asked if one of you could help her with her costume," he said.

"Yes, I can help," Willow offered, right on cue. "I know the way, thank you."

She disappeared up the winding stairway and was gone.

Ben and Miles sat down on a bench in the entryway, oversized bookends from a curio shop. The doorman studied them some more, probably trying to figure out how any sane adult could be talked into dressing up like that, then turned down the hall and disappeared from view.

Ben felt the heat of the two costumes he was wearing turn his back and underarms damp.

So far, so good, he thought.

Willow tapped lightly on Elizabeth's bedroom door and waited. Almost immediately, the door was opened by a small clown with frizzy orange hair, a white face, and an enormous red nose. "Oh, Willow!" Elizabeth whispered, grasping her hand and pulling her urgently inside. "It's all going wrong!"

Willow took her shoulders gently. "What's going wrong, Elizabeth?"

"Abernathy! He's all . . . strange! I went down to the cellars this afternoon after school to see if he was all right—you know, to make certain he was still there. I know I probably shouldn't have, but I was worried, Willow!" The words practically tumbled over one another. "I sneaked out of my room. I made sure no one saw me, then went down through the passage in the walls to the cellars. Abernathy was there, locked in one of those cages, all chained up! Oh, Willow, he looked so sad! He looked all ragged and dirty. I whispered to him, called to him, but he didn't seem to know who I was. He just . . . he sounded like he couldn't talk right! He said a bunch of stuff that didn't make any sense and he couldn't seem to sit up or move or anything!"

The blue eyes glistened with tears. "Willow, he's so sick! I don't know if he can even walk!"

Willow felt a mix of fear and uncertainty wash through her, but she forced it quickly away. "Do not be afraid, Elizabeth," she said firmly. "Show me where he is. It will be all right."

They slipped from the room into the empty hall, the tiny clown and the emerald fairy. An old clock ticked in the silence from one end, and the sound of very distant voices echoed faintly. Elizabeth took Willow to a cluttered broom closet. Closing the door behind them, she produced a flashlight, then spent a few seconds pushing at the back wall until a section of it swung open. Silently, they went down the stairs that lay beyond, navigating through several twists and turns, two landings, and one short tunnel, until at last they reached another section of wall, this one with a rusted iron handle fixed to it.

"He's right through here!" Elizabeth whispered.

She took hold of the handle and pulled. The wall eased back, and the rush of stale, fetid air caused Willow to gasp. Nausea washed through her, but she swallowed against it and waited for the feeling to pass.

"Willow, are you all right?" Elizabeth asked urgently, her brightly colored clown's face bent close.

"Yes, Elizabeth," Willow whispered. She couldn't give in now. Just a little longer, she promised herself. Just a little.

She peered through the opening in the wall. Cages lined a passageway, shadowed cells of rock and iron bars. There was movement in one. Something lay there twitching.

"That's Abernathy!" Elizabeth confirmed in a small, frightened voice.

Willow took a moment longer to check the corridor beyond for other signs of movement. There were none. "Are there guards?" she asked softly.

Elizabeth pointed. "Down there, beyond that door. Just one, usually."

Willow pushed her way out into the cellar passage, feeling the nausea and weakness surge through her once more. She went to the cage that held Abernathy and peered in. The dog lay on a pile of straw, his fur matted and soiled, his clothes torn. He had been sick, and the discharge clung to him. He smelled awful. There was a chain fastened about his neck.

The medallion hung there as well.

Abernathy was mumbling incoherently. He was talking about everything and nothing all at once, his speech slurred, his words fragments of witless chatter. He has been drugged, Willow thought.

Elizabeth was handing her something. "This is the key to the cage door, Willow," she whispered. She looked very frightened. "I don't know if it fits the chain on his neck!"

Her clown nose fell off, and she picked it up hurriedly and pushed it back into place. Willow took the key from her and started to insert it into the cage door lock.

It was at that same moment that they heard the latch on the door at the end of the corridor begin to turn.

Michel Ard Rhi came down the front hallway past the entry and paused momentarily as he saw the gorilla and the shaggy dog sitting there on the waiting bench. It was apparent that he wasn't sure what to make of them. He looked at them, and they looked back. No one said anything.

Ben held his breath and waited. He could feel Miles go rigid beside him. Suddenly, Michel seemed to realize what they were doing there. "Oh, yes," he said. "The Halloween party at the school. You must be here for Elizabeth."

A phone rang somewhere down the hall.

Michel hesitated, as if he might say something more, then turned and walked away quickly to answer it. The shaggy dog and the gorilla glanced at each other in silent relief.

The guard pushed his way wearily through the cellar door and came down the corridor of iron cages, boots clumping heavily on the stone block. He was dressed in black and wore an automatic weapon and a ring of keys at his belt. Elizabeth shrank further into the darkness behind the hidden section of wall where she was concealed, peering out through the tiny crack she had left open.

Willow was still out there in the corridor. But where? Why couldn't she see her?

She watched the guard pause at Abernathy's cage, check the door perfunctorily to make certain it was locked, then turn and walk back again the way he had come. As he passed her hiding place, the keys at his belt suddenly came free. Elizabeth blinked in disbelief. The snap that held them seemed to loosen of its own accord and all at once the keys were gone. The guard completed his walk down the corridor, pushed back through the metal door, and disappeared.

Elizabeth slipped quickly from her hiding place. "Willow!" she called in a muffled hiss.

The sylph appeared out of nowhere at her side, the ring of keys in one hand. "Hurry, now," she whispered. "We do not have much time."

They went back to Abernathy's cage, and Willow opened the door with the key Elizabeth had given her earlier. They hastened inside, moving to the incoherent dog and kneeling beside him. Willow bent close. The scribe's eyes were dilated and his breathing was rapid. When she tried to lift him, he sagged helplessly against her.

A moment of panic seized her. He was far too heavy for her to carry—far too heavy even if Elizabeth helped. She had to find a way to bring him out of his stupor.

"Try these until you find one that fits," she told Elizabeth, handing her the key ring.

Elizabeth went to work with the keys, trying one after another in the lock of the neck chain. Willow rubbed Abernathy's paws, then his head. Nothing seemed to help. Her panic deepened. She had to bring Ben down. But she knew, even as she considered the idea, that it wasn't possible. The plan wouldn't work with Ben down here. Besides, there simply wasn't time.

Finally, she did the only thing she could think to do to help the dog. She used her fairy magic. She was so weak that she had little to command, but she called up what she had. She placed her hands on Abernathy's head, closed her eyes in concentration, and drew the poison out of his system and into her own. It entered her in a rush, a vile fluid, and she worked desperately to negate its effects on her own body. She was not strong enough. It was too much for her. Some of it broke through her defenses and began to sicken further her already weakened system. Nausea mingled with pain. She shuddered and wrenched herself away, vomiting into the straw.

"Willow, Willow!" she heard Elizabeth cry out in fear. "Please, don't be sick!"

The little clown's face was pressed up against her own, whispering urgently, crying. Willow blinked. The red nose was gone again, she thought, distracted. She couldn't seem to organize her thoughts. Everything was drifting.

Then suddenly, miraculously, she heard Abernathy say, "Willow? What are you doing here?" And she knew it was going to be all right.

It was only after they were back in the passageway, safely clear of the cages, that Elizabeth rubbed her face where the clown's nose should have been and realized she had lost it. Panic gripped her. She must have dropped it while they were freeing Abernathy. It would certainly be found. She thought about stopping, then decided not to. It was too late to do anything now. Willow was too weak to go back and would never let Elizabeth return alone. She bit her tongue and concentrated on the task at hand, shining the flashlight's thin beam on the stairs ahead as they climbed toward the broom closet. Willow and Abernathy followed a few steps behind, hanging on to each other for support, both of them looking as if they would collapse with every step.

"Just a little farther," Elizabeth kept whispering to encourage them, but neither replied.

They reached the landing to the broom closet, worked the wall section open, and pushed inside. Willow's pale face was bright with perspiration, and she seemed to be having trouble focusing. "It is all right, Elizabeth," she assured the little girl, seeing the look of worry in her eyes, but Elizabeth was no fool and could clearly see that it was definitely not all right.

When they were finally back inside Elizabeth's room, the little girl and Willow worked hurriedly on Abernathy, combing his matted fur, cleaning him up as best they could. They tried to strip off his ruined clothes, but he protested so vehemently about being left naked that they finally agreed to let him keep the half pants and boots. It wasn't what Ben had wanted, but Willow was too tired to argue. She could feel herself withering a bit more with the passing of every second.

She surprised herself though. She wasn't as frightened of dying as she had imagined she would be.

The hall phone rang for what seemed to Ben and Miles an interminable length of time before the doorman appeared to answer it. There was a brief conversation, and then the doorman hung up and said to them, "Miss Elizabeth said to tell you that she would be right down."

"Finally!" Miles breathed in a hushed voice.

The doorman lingered a moment, then walked away again.

"I'm going out now," Ben whispered. "Remember what to do."

He rose and disappeared silently through the front door. He went down the front steps and got into the car. There, he stripped away the dog suit, straightened the costume beneath, and slipped a new mask into place. Then he got out again and went back inside.

The doorman was just returning. He frowned on seeing the gorilla now sitting in the company of a skeleton. "This is Mr. Andrews," Miles said quickly. "He was waiting in the car, but he got tired. Mr. Barker went upstairs to help his wife with Elizabeth."

The doorman nodded absently, still staring at Ben. He

appeared to be on the verge of saying something when Elizabeth, the green lady, and the shaggy dog came down the stairway. The green lady did not look well at all.

"All set, John," Elizabeth said brightly to the doorman. She was carrying a small overnight bag. "We have to hurry. By the way, I forgot. I'm spending the night with Nita Coles. Tell Michel, will you? 'Bye."

The doorman smiled faintly and said good-bye. The bunch of them, the gorilla, the skeleton, the green lady, the shaggy dog, and Elizabeth went out the door quickly and were gone.

The doorman stared after them thoughtfully. Had the shaggy dog been wearing pants when he came in?

By the time Ben Holiday pulled the rental car into the parking lot of Franklin Elementary, there were miniature witches, werewolves, ghosts, devils, punk rockers, and assorted other horrors arriving from everywhere, all dashing from their cars to the shelter of the lighted school as if truly possessed. The rain was still falling heavily. There were going to be more than a few disappointed trick-or-treaters this night.

Ben turned the wheel into the curb and put the gearshift into park. He looked over at Elizabeth seated next to him. "Time to go, kiddo."

Elizabeth nodded, somehow managing to look sad even with the painted happy face. "I wish I could go with you."

"Not this time, honey," Ben smiled. "You know what to do now, don't you—after the party?"

"Sure. I go home with Nita and her parents and stay there until my dad comes for me." She sounded sad, too.

"Right. Mr. Bennett will see to it that he finds out what has happened to you. Whatever happens, don't go back to the castle. Okay?"

"Okay. Good-bye, Ben. Good-bye, Willow." She turned to Willow, seated next to her, and gave the sylph a long hug and kiss on the cheek. Willow kissed her back and smiled, saying nothing. She was so sick it was hard for her to talk. "Will you be okay?" Elizabeth wanted to know, asking the question hesitantly.

"Yes, Elizabeth." Willow managed another quick kiss and opened the door. Ben had never seen her this bad, not even when she had been prevented from making the transformation into her namesake that first time she was taken into Abaddon. His patience slipped a notch.

" 'Bye, Abernathy," Elizabeth said to the dog, who was seated with Miles in the back. She started to say something, stopped, and then said, "I'll miss you."

Abernathy nodded. "I will miss you, too, Elizabeth."

Then she was out the door and dashing for the school. Ben waited until she was safely inside, then wheeled the car out of the parking lot and sped quickly back through Woodinville to 522 and turned west.

"High Lord, I cannot thank you enough for coming to rescue me," Abernathy was saying. "I had given myself up for lost."

Ben was thinking of Willow and trying hard to keep the car within the speed limit. "I'm sorry this had to happen, Abernathy. Questor is sorry, too. He really is."

"I find that hard to believe," the dog declared, sounding very much like his old self. The effect of the drugs had pretty much worn off, and the scribe was more tired than anything. It was Willow who was in trouble now.

Ben eased the speed of the rental car up a notch.

"He was trying to help you, don't forget," he said.

"He scarcely understands the meaning of the word!" Abernathy huffed. He was quiet a moment. "By the way—here." He took the chain with the medallion from his own neck, reached across the seatback, and placed it carefully about Ben's. "I feel much better knowing you have this safely back."

Ben didn't say so, but he felt much better, too.

He reached Interstate 5 twenty minutes later and turned

the car south. The rain diminished somewhat and it appeared to be clearing ahead. The airport was less than half an hour's drive.

Willow's hand stretched across the seat and found his. He squeezed it gently and tried to will some of the strength from his body into hers.

A car passed them in the left lane and a woman in the passenger seat stared over. What she saw was a skeleton driving a gorilla, a shaggy dog, and a lady dyed green. The woman said something to the driver and the car moved on.

Ben had forgotten about their costumes. He thought momentarily about removing them, then decided against it. There wasn't time. Besides, this was Halloween. Lots of people would be out in costumes tonight, going one place or another, trick-or-treating, attending parties, having fun. It was like that in Seattle; he'd read as much in this morning's newspaper. Halloween was a big deal.

He was feeling better about things by the time the lights of the city came into view. The rain had practically disappeared, and they were only moments from their destination. He watched the skyscrapers brighten the night skies and spread away before him in vertical lines. He took a deep breath and allowed himself the luxury of thinking they were almost safely home.

That was when he saw the lights of the state patrol car coming up behind him. "Oh, oh," he muttered.

The patrol car closed quickly, and he eased the rental car over onto the freeway shoulder by a bridge abutment. The patrol car pulled in behind.

"Doc, what's he stopping you for?" Miles demanded. "Were you speeding or something?"

Ben had a sick feeling in his stomach. "I don't think so," he said quietly.

He watched in the rearview mirror. The trooper was on the radio a moment, and another patrol car pulled up behind the first. The trooper in the first car got out then, walked up to Ben's window, and looked in. His face was inscrutable. "Can I see your license, sir?"

Ben reached for his billfold and belatedly remembered he didn't have it. Miles had signed for the car on his license. "Officer, I don't have it with me, but I can give you the number. It is a valid license. And the car is registered with Mr. Bennett."

He indicated the gorilla. Miles was trying to take off the head, but it was stuck. The trooper nodded. "Do you have some proof of identification?" he asked.

"Uh, Mr. Bennett has," Ben said.

"I do, officer," Miles hastily confirmed. "Here, right inside this damn suit if I can just . . ." He trailed off, struggling to get it free.

The trooper looked at Willow and Abernathy. Then he looked back at Ben. "I'm afraid I'll have to ask you to come with me, sir," he said. "Please pull your vehicle out behind mine and follow me downtown. The other patrol car will follow you."

Ben went cold. Something had gone terribly wrong. "I'm a lawyer," he said impulsively. "Are we being charged with something?"

The trooper shook his head. "Not by me, you aren't. Except maybe I'll issue you a warning ticket for driving a vehicle without carrying your license—assuming you have a license like you say. I'll want to check the registration on this vehicle as well."

"But . . . ?"

"There is apparently another matter that needs clearing up. Please follow me, sir." He turned away without further explanation and walked back to his car.

Ben slumped back and heard Miles say softly in his ear, "We've been made, Doc. What do we do now?"

He shook his head wearily. He didn't have the slightest idea.

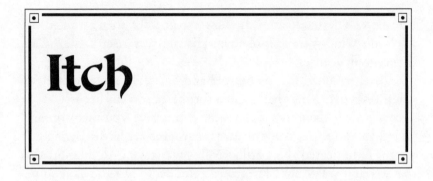

Itch

*I*t took Questor Thews the better part of three days to travel by horseback from Sterling Silver to the eastern edge of the Wastelands. He went alone, slipping from the castle before dawn of the first day, departing while the bothersome G'home Gnomes and all those annoyingly insistent ambassadors, couriers, and supplicants from one place or another still slept. Affairs of state would simply have to wait, he had decided, whether it was convenient or not. Bunion and Parsnip were there to see him off, anxious that they be allowed to accompany him, distressed at his insistence on going alone. Questor would not be swayed by the toothy grins and the furtive looks. This was something he must do by himself. Neither of them could help. It was best that they stay at the castle and look after things in his absence. He mounted his old gray and rode out, Don Quixote without his Sancho Panza, a scarecrow searching for his field of need. He went north through the wooded hill country of Sterling Silver, northeast across the fields and pastures of the Greensward, and finally east into the Wastelands.

It was nearing sunset on that third day when he finally sighted the distant glow of the Fire Springs.

"Come along, now," he urged his old gray, who had caught the scent of what lay ahead and was beginning to balk.

Questor Thews was a man who bore a very large burden of guilt. He knew that things would not be right again in the Kingdom of Landover until the High Lord was returned. Nightshade would continue her campaign of disruption and anarchy until someone found a way to deal with that bottle and its demon. Questor was not, unfortunately, the one who could do that. The High Lord was. But the High Lord was trapped in his old world and would not be able to come back again until he recovered his lost medallion—and even then would likely not come back if he could not bring Willow and the missing Abernathy with him. All of this was the fault of one Questor Thews, of course, and the wizard could not afford to stand by longer and allow matters to assume their own course when the course they assumed might well be the wrong one.

Therefore, he had come up with a plan to put things back the way they were. It was a very straightforward, if somewhat minimally developed plan—but a plan nevertheless. He would enlist the aid of the dragon Strabo to bring Holiday and the others back.

It was all quite simple, really, and he was surprised that he hadn't thought of it earlier. No one could journey in or out of the valley of Landover without passing through the mists of fairy, and no one could pass out of Landover and back in again through the mists of fairy without the magic of Holiday's missing medallion—no one, that is, except Strabo. Dragons could still go pretty much where they chose. Oh, they couldn't go deep into the fairy mists, of course, because dragons had been banished from there long ago. But they could go most places. The magic that allowed them passage through the mists was their own. That was why dragons were apt to pop up almost anywhere. Strabo was no exception. He had already taken Ben Holiday down into the netherworld of Abaddon for the purpose of rescuing Questor, Willow, Abernathy, and the kobolds from the demons. He could certainly make a second trip now to rescue Holiday.

Questor's face knotted. Strabo *could*, to be sure—but whether or not he *would* was another matter entirely. After all, the Abaddon trip had been made under extreme duress, and the dragon had made it quite clear on a number of occasions since that he would rather choke on his own smoke than lift a claw to help Ben Holiday again.

So while the plan's conception was indeed quite simple, its execution probably would not be.

"Ah, well," he sighed resignedly. "*Something* has to be tried."

He guided the gray to the edge of the hills that ringed the Fire Springs, dismounted, stripped saddle and bridle from the old horse, slapped him on the rump, and sent him home. No point in worrying about keeping the horse, he thought. If he couldn't persuade Strabo to help, he wouldn't be needing a horse.

He tugged at one long ear. How *was* he going to persuade Strabo to help anyway?

He thought about it a moment, then shrugged away his worry and began to make his way up the slope through the heavy scrub. Twilight descended gradually over the valley in darkening patches of blue and gray, and the sun diminished to a thin silver slash above the treeline along the western rim, then disappeared altogether. Questor glanced up. A bank of low-hanging clouds hung directly overhead, and its underside shimmered orange and red from the glow of the Springs. The wizard breathed in smoke and ash and sneezed. A sneeze, he thought irritably! That was how this whole mess had begun! He shoved ahead doggedly, heedless of the brambles and scrub that caught his robes and tore through fabric and skin. The explosions were audible now, short, booming coughs that lifted into the night like giant hiccups before subsiding into gurgles of discontent. The heat grew intense, and Questor began sweating freely.

At last he topped a rise and stopped, hands settling firmly

on his hips. The Fire Springs were spread out below him, a series of jagged craters in which a blue and yellow liquid bubbled and sizzled. Periodically, a crater would erupt in a geyser of flame, then settle back again discontentedly. The air was sulfurous and hot, its stench a mix of the burning liquid and the blackened bones of animals the resident dragon had devoured.

The dragon was eating now, it happened. He lay wrapped about one of the smaller craters at the north end of the Springs, busily gnawing on what appeared to Questor to be the remains of an unfortunate cow. Bones snapped and crackled loudly within the monstrous jaws, black teeth grinding contentedly. Questor wrinkled his nose in distaste. Strabo's eating habits had always annoyed him.

"Dragon, dragon," he murmured softly to himself.

Strabo seared a section of the cow with his fire, then tore it from the carcass and chewed loudly.

Questor Thews came forward to the very edge of the rise so that he was plainly visible. "Old dragon!" he called out. "I need a word with you!"

Strabo stopped chewing a moment and looked up. "Who's there?" he snapped irritably. He squinted. "Questor Thews, is that you?"

"It is."

"I thought so. How boring." The dragon's teeth snapped the air for emphasis. "And who are you calling 'old'? You're practically a fossil yourself!"

"I need a word with you."

"So you said. I heard you quite clearly. It comes as no surprise, Questor Thews. You always want a word with someone. You seem to delight in talking. I sometimes think that if you could manage to transform your unending conversation into magic, you would indeed be a formidable wizard."

Questor's brow furrowed. "This is quite important!"

"Not to me. I have a dinner to finish."

The dragon went back to work on the cow, gnawing a new portion free and chewing contentedly. He seemed oblivious of anything else.

"Reduced to stealing cows again, are you?" Questor asked suddenly, coming forward another few steps. "Tch, tch. How sad. Practically a charity case, aren't you?"

Strabo stopped eating in mid-bite and swung his crusted, scaled head slowly about to face the wizard. "This cow is a stray that wandered in and stayed for dinner," he said, grinning. "Rather like yourself."

"I would make a poor meal for you."

"Then perhaps you would make a decent dessert!" The dragon seemed to consider the idea. "No, I suppose not. There's not enough of you even for that."

"Not for a stomach the size of yours!"

"On the other hand, eating you would at least silence you."

Questor shook his head. "Why don't you just hear what I have to tell you?"

"I told you, wizard, I am eating!"

Questor hunkered down on his heels, smoothing his patched robes. "Very well. I shall wait until you are finished."

"Do anything you please, so long as you keep silent!"

Strabo returned to his meal, searing the flesh with quick bursts of fire, tearing off great chunks of meat and bone, and chewing ferociously. His long tail twisted and snapped as he ate, as if it were the impatient recipient of food that was too long in reaching it. Questor watched. Out of the corner of one eye, Strabo watched back.

Finally, the dragon discarded the carcass of the cow by spitting it into the mouth of the crater he was wrapped about and wheeled sharply once more toward the wizard. "Enough of this, Questor Thews! How can I eat with you sitting there and staring at me as if you were some harbinger of doom? You ruin my appetite! What is it that you want?"

Questor climbed gingerly to his feet, rubbing at his cramped legs. "I want your help."

The dragon snaked his way through the craters, his monstrous, cumbersome body impervious to the ash and fire, his tail and wings shaking off drops of liquid flame as he went. When he reached Questor's end of the Springs, he lifted himself up on his hind legs and licked his jaws hungrily with a long, split tongue.

"Questor Thews, I find it impossible to think of a single reason why I would want to help you! And do not, please, give me that tired old recitation about the close ties of dragons and wizards, how we have shared so much of history, and how we must do what we can for each other in times of need. You tried that last time, if you recall. It was nonsense then and it is nonsense now. Helping you in any way, frankly, is abhorrent!"

"Your help is not for me," Questor finally managed to get in. "Your help is for the High Lord."

The dragon stared at him as if he were mad. "Holiday? You want me to help Holiday? Why ever in the world would I agree to do that?"

"Because he is your High Lord as well as mine," Questor said. "It is time to acknowledge the fact, Strabo. Like it or not, Ben Holiday is High Lord of Landover, and so long as you live within the valley you are subject to his laws. That means that you are required to give aid to your King when he needs it!"

Strabo was in stitches. He was laughing so hard he could no longer hold himself upright; he collapsed in one of the craters, showering flames everywhere. Questor ducked a scattering and straightened. "There is nothing to laugh about here!"

"There is everything!" the dragon howled. He choked and gasped and belched smoke and fire. "Questor Thews, you are truly astounding. I think you even believe yourself sometimes. How droll!"

"Will you help or not?" Questor demanded indignantly.

"I should say not!" The dragon rose up once more. "I am

not a subject of this land or its High Lord! I live where I choose and obey my own laws! I am certainly not required to give aid to anyone—least of all Holiday! What utter nonsense!"

Questor was not surprised to hear Strabo speak like this, knowing perfectly well that the dragon had never willingly done anything to help anyone in his entire life. But it had been worth the try.

"What of the pretty sylph, Willow?" he asked. "She is in need of your help as well. You saved her life once before, re-member? She has sung to you and given you dreams to muse on. Surely, you would help Holiday if it meant helping her."

"Not a chance," the dragon sniffed.

Questor thought. "Very well," he said. "Then you must help Holiday for your own sake."

"My own sake?" Strabo licked his teeth. "What clever argument will you conjure up now, wizard?"

"An argument that even a dragon can understand," Ques-tor Thews replied. "Nightshade has gained control of a magic that threatens everyone in the valley. She has already begun to employ it, turning humans and the fairy folk against each other and causing disorder everywhere. If she is allowed to continue, she will destroy them all."

The dragon sneered. "What do I care?"

Questor shrugged. "Sooner or later she will get around to you, Strabo. Next to Holiday, you are her worst enemy. What do you imagine will happen to you then?"

"Bah! I am a match for any magic the witch might command!"

Questor rubbed his chin thoughtfully. "I wish I could say the same. This is a different magic, Strabo—a magic as old as your own. It comes in the form of a demon that lives in a bottle. The demon draws its strength from the holder of the bottle and can employ that strength in any way it chooses. You would agree, wouldn't you, that Nightshade's strength is formidable?"

"I agree to nothing!" The dragon was irritated. "Get out of here, Questor Thews! I tire of you!"

"As much as you hate Holiday, his is the only magic that can withstand the demon. Landover's High Lord commands the Paladin, and the Paladin can withstand anything."

"Begone, wizard!"

"If you do not agree to help Holiday, Strabo, there will be no Paladin to stand against Nightshade and the demon. If you do not agree to help, we are all doomed."

"Begone!"

The dragon breathed a stream of fire that seared the whole of the slope below where Questor Thews was standing and left the air smoking and filled with ash. Questor choked and gasped and retreated from the heat. When the air cleared, he saw the dragon turning sullenly away. "I care nothing for Nightshade, her demon, Holiday, you, or anyone else in this valley!" he muttered. "I barely care anything for myself! Now, go!"

Questor Thews frowned his deepest frown. Well, he had tried. No one could say that he hadn't. He had done his best to reason with the dragon and he had failed. The dragon was simply being his normal, intractable self. If he continued to press the matter now, it would mean a fight.

He sighed wearily. That was the way it was between dragons and wizards. That was the way it had always been.

He strode forward to the edge of the rise again and stopped. "Strabo!" The dragon's crusted head swung about. "Old dragon, it appears that we shall have to do this the hard way. I had hoped that common sense would prevail over innate stubbornness, but it now appears clear that will not be possible. It is necessary that you agree to help the High Lord, and if you will not do so willingly, then you shall do so nevertheless!"

Strabo stared at Questor in genuine amazement. "Good heavens, Questor Thews, are you threatening me?"

Questor drew himself up to his full height. "If threatening you is what it takes to gain your cooperation, then I will threaten you and worse."

"Really?" The dragon took a long moment to study the wizard, then slapped his tail in a crater of fire with a loud whack and sent the burning liquid flying everywhere. "Go on home, silly old wizard!" he snapped and started to turn away.

Questor brought his hands up in a broad sweep, fire gathering at his fingertips as he did so. With a lunge, he sent the fire hurtling at the dragon. It struck Strabo full along the length of his great body, lifted him from the earth, and sent him flying over several of the bubbling craters to land in a tangled heap. Rock and flames scattered everywhere, and the dragon gave an audible grunt.

"Dear me!" Questor whispered, surprised that he could muster such magic.

Strabo picked himself up slowly, shook himself head to tail, coughed, spit, and turned slowly back to the wizard. "Where did you learn to do *that*?" he asked, a hint of admiration in his voice.

"I have learned much you do not yet know about," Questor bluffed. "Best that you simply agree now to do as I have asked."

Strabo replied with a sheet of flame that lanced at Questor and sent him cartwheeling head over heels into a patch of brush. A second rush of fire followed, but Questor was tumbling back down the hillside by that time, out of sight, and the fire merely fried the landscape until it was black.

"Bah, come back here, Questor Thews!" the dragon called after him from the other side of the rise. "This fight hasn't even started yet and already you're running for home!"

Questor picked himself up gingerly and started back up the slope. This was going to require a considerable effort on his part, he decided grimly.

For the next twenty minutes, wizard and dragon attacked each other with a ferocity that was terrifying. They twisted and dodged and skipped about, hurdling craters that spit smoke and steam and flame, turning the whole of the Fire Springs into a blackened battleground. Blow for blow they traded, Questor employing every conceivable form of magic against the dragon, conjuring up spells he didn't even know he knew, Strabo answering back with bursts of flame. Back and forth they swung, pushing and shoving like fighters in a ring, and when the twenty minutes drew to a close, they were both gasping for breath and lurching like drunks.

"Wizard . . . you continually astonish me!" Strabo panted, slowly curling himself into a ball at the center of the Springs.

"Have you . . . given further consideration to . . . my request?" Questor demanded in reply.

"Most . . . certainly," Strabo said and sent a fireball hurtling at the wizard.

They resumed their struggle wordlessly, and only their grunts and cries and the occasional booming coughs of the craters broke the evening stillness. The clouds dispersed, and a scattering of stars and several of Landover's moons broke through the cover. The wind died, and the air warmed. Twilight passed away, and night descended.

Questor sent a swarm of gnats at the dragon, clogging his nose, eyes, and mouth. Strabo choked and gasped and breathed fire everywhere, thrashing as if chained. He began to swear, using words Questor had never heard before. Then he lifted free of the earth, launched himself at the wizard, and attempted to flatten him. Questor conjured a hole in the earth and dropped into it just before the dragon landed with a *whump* where previously he had been standing. Strabo sat there, looking about for him, not seeing him, so angry at his apparent miss he didn't realize what had happened. Then a six-foot bee stinger shoved at him from underneath and sent him lurching skyward again with a howl. Questor appeared from the hole, throwing fire; the dragon threw fire back; and both of them fell apart again, singed and smoking.

"Wizard, we are . . . too old for this!" Strabo gasped, licking away bits of ash that were crusted on his nose. "Give it up!"

"I will give it up . . . when you say 'yes'—not before!" Questor answered.

Strabo shook his blackened head. "Whatever . . . it is you wish, it cannot possibly . . . be worth all this!"

Questor wondered. He was black from head to foot with ash and burns, his robes were tattered and soiled beyond repair, his hair was standing straight out from his head, and the muscles and joints of his body felt as if they would never be right again. He had tried every magic he knew and then some, and nothing had fazed the dragon. He was alive, he thought, only by a series of flukes unparalleled in the history of wizardry. Much of the magic he had tried had misfired—as usual—and much of what he might like to do was beyond him. The only thing that was keeping him on his feet was the knowledge that if he failed now, he might as well forget about ever calling himself a wizard again. This was his last chance, his one opportunity to prove to himself—even if to no one else—that he really was the wizard he had always claimed to be.

He took a deep breath. "Are you . . . ready to listen?" he asked.

Strabo opened his maw as far as it would open and showed Questor all of his considerable teeth. "Step . . . inside, why don't you, Questor Thews . . . so you can better hear my answer!"

Questor sent a flurry of canker sores into the dragon's mouth, but the hide was so tough they couldn't even begin to settle before they were dispatched. Strabo responded with a blast that sent the wizard tumbling head over heels and burned off his boots. They traded fireballs for a moment, then Questor pinwheeled his arms until it seemed they might fly off and sent a ferocious ice storm at the dragon. Sleet and frigid wind beat against the dragon as he sought refuge in the fire of one of the larger craters. But the storm was so fierce it suffocated the flames and turned the liquid in the crater to ice. Strabo was trapped in the resulting block, the ice hammering off his head as he howled in rage.

Finally, the magic gave out and the storm subsided. A foot

of snow covered the dragon, but it was already melting from the heat of the other craters. Strabo poked his head out from beneath the covering and shook off the last of the flakes irritably. Then he heaved upward with a roar, and the ice shattered into cubes. The dragon was free once more, steam pouring from his nostrils as he swung about to face Questor Thews.

Questor stiffened. What would it take to overcome the beast, he wondered in frustration. What did he have to do?

He dodged another rush of flame, then another, and threw up a shield of magic against a third. Strabo was simply too strong. He wasn't going to win a test of strength against the dragon. He had to find another way.

He waited for Strabo to pause for breath, then sent an itch.

The itch started inside the dragon's left hind foot, but when he lifted the foot to scratch, the itch moved up to his thigh, then to his back, his neck, his ear, his nose, and back down to his right foot. Strabo twisted and grunted, flailing madly as the itch worked its way up one side and down the other, as elusive as buttered sausage, slipping and sliding away from him as he sought to relieve it. He howled and he roared, he writhed and he lurched, and nothing helped. He forgot about Questor Thews, working his serpentine body over the sharp edges of the craters, dousing himself in the liquid fire, trying desperately to scratch.

When at last Questor Thews made a quick motion with his hands and took back the itch, Strabo was a limp noodle. He lay gasping at the center of the Fire Springs, his strength momentarily spent, his tongue hanging out on the ground. His eyes rolled wearily until they settled at last on the wizard.

"All right, all right!" he said, panting like an old dog. "I have had enough! What is it that you want, Questor Thews? Just tell me and let's get it over!"

Questor Thews puffed up a bit and permitted himself a smile of satisfaction.

"Well, old dragon, it is really quite simple," he began.

Halloween Crazies

Chief Deputy Pick Wilson of the King County Sheriff's Department leaned forward cautiously across his paper-laden work desk and said to Ben Holiday, "So you and your friends were just on your way to a Halloween party at . . . What hotel was that again?"

Ben looked thoughtful. "I think it was the Sheraton. I'm not sure. The invitation should be in the car somewhere."

"Uh-huh. So you were on your way to this party, in a rental car, your suitcases packed in the trunk . . ."

"We were leaving right afterward for the airport," Ben interjected. The room smelled of new paint and disinfectant and was suffocatingly hot.

"With no identification, not even your driver's license?" Wilson paused, looking mildly baffled.

"I explained all that, Deputy." Ben was having trouble concealing his irritation. "Mr. Bennett has identification. Mine was left behind by accident."

"Along with that of Mr. Abernathy and the young lady," Wilson finished. "Yes, so you explained."

He eased himself back again in his chair, looking from the skeleton to the gorilla to the shaggy dog to the pale green lady and back again. None of them had taken off their costumes yet, although Ben had long ago removed his death's mask and Miles had finally gotten rid of the troublesome gorilla head. They sat there in that sterile, functional, bare-walled office somewhere in the bowels of the King County Courts Building, where the Washington State Police had deposited them nearly an hour ago, looking for all the world like candidates for "Let's Make A Deal." Wilson continued to look at them, and Ben could tell exactly what he was thinking.

The deputy cleared his throat, glancing down at some papers before him. "And the shaggy dog costume we found in the back seat . . . ?"

"Was an extra. It didn't fit right." Ben leaned forward. "We've been over this ground before. If you have a charge to make, please make it. You've seen our card, deputy. Mr. Bennett and I are both lawyers, and we are prepared to defend ourselves and our friends, if that should prove necessary. But we are growing very tired of just sitting here. Are there any more questions?"

Wilson smiled faintly. "Just a few. Uh, wouldn't Mr. Abernathy be more comfortable with his mask off?"

"No, he would not," Ben snapped irritably. He glanced sideways at Abernathy. "It took considerable effort to get it on him in the first place, believe me. And we still hope to make that party, deputy. So another five minutes and that's it. You'll *have* to charge us."

He was bluffing, but he had to do something to move matters along. He still didn't know exactly what Wilson knew or what sort of trouble they were in. Just a mix-up of some sort, the deputy had assured them. Just a matter of straightening it all out. But when it came right down to doing any straightening, they just seemed to continue running about in circles.

Willow sat next to him in something that resembled a trance. Her eyes were half-closed, and her breathing extremely shallow. Wilson had watched her with growing suspicion. Ben had explained to the deputy that she was just a little under the weather, but he knew Wilson didn't believe him. Wilson believed she was on drugs.

"Your lady friend doesn't appear to be doing so well, Mr. Holiday," the Chief Deputy said, as if reading Ben's mind. "Would she like to lie down?"

"I don't want to leave you, Ben," Willow said quietly, eyes flickering open briefly before closing again.

Wilson hesitated, then shrugged. Ben moved his chair closer to Willow and put his arm around her, trying to make it look as much as possible as if he were simply comforting her rather than holding her upright. She sagged against him weakly.

"I'm going to call local counsel, Deputy Wilson," announced Miles suddenly. He stood up. "Is there a phone I can use?"

Wilson nodded. "Next office. Dial 9 to get an outside line."

Miles glanced meaningfully at Ben, then exited the room. As he went out, one of several clerks working in the reception area outside stuck her head through the door and told Wilson he was wanted on the phone. Wilson got up and walked over. Ben could hear a couple of the deputies lounging outside talking about how the whole city was overrun like this every Halloween. Witches, goblins, ghosts, and God-knew-what, one said. Zoo animals everywhere, the other said. It was hard enough keeping the peace on normal nights, the first said. Impossible on Halloween, the other said. Bunch of nuts, the first said. Bunch of crazies, the other said.

Wilson finished his conversation with the clerk. "Excuse me a moment, Mr. Holiday," he said and went out. The door closed behind him.

Abernathy looked over worriedly. "What's going to happen to us, High Lord?" he asked in a whisper. He hadn't said a word since they got there because Ben had warned him not to. It was hard enough keeping up this charade about a Halloween party without trying to explain how the mouth in a dog mask could move so much like the real thing.

Ben smiled, trying to look reassuring. "Nothing's going to happen. We'll be out of here soon enough."

"I don't understand why they keep asking if I want to take off my mask, High Lord. Why don't I just tell them the truth?"

"Because they can't handle the truth, that's why!" Ben sighed, irritated with himself. There was no point in snapping at the faithful scribe. "I'm sorry, Abernathy. I wish we *could* just tell the truth. I wish it were that simple."

Abernathy nodded doubtfully, glanced at Willow, then leaned forward and whispered, "I know you came back for me and I am deeply grateful. But I think that, if we are not allowed to go soon, you must forget about me. You must cross back into Landover and help those whose needs are more pressing." His eyes flickered briefly to Willow and away again. Willow appeared to be asleep.

Ben shook his head wearily. "Too late for that, Abernathy. I'm as much a prisoner now as you. No, we'll all go back together. All of us."

Abernathy kept his brown eyes locked on Ben's. "I don't know if that's going to be possible, High Lord," he said quietly.

Ben didn't reply. He couldn't. He watched as Miles reappeared through the door and closed it again.

"Help's on the way," he said. "I reached Winston Sack, senior partner with the firm of Sack, Saul, and McQuinn. We did some business with them a few years back in that Seafirst case. He said he'd send someone right over."

Ben nodded. "I hope whoever it is hurries."

Wilson came back into the room, all business. "Mr. Holiday, do you know a man named Michel Ard Rhi?"

Ben had been ready for that question from the beginning. There couldn't be any other reason that they would be detained like this. He pretended to think a moment, then shook his head. "No, I don't think so."

"Well, it appears that Mr. Ard Rhi has accused you and your friends of stealing something from him. Some sort of medallion."

The room got very quiet. "That's ridiculous," Ben said.

"Mr. Ard Rhi has given a description of the medallion to us. The description is quite thorough. The medallion is silver and engraved with some sort of knight and a castle." He paused. "Do you have a medallion like that, Mr. Holiday?"

Ben felt his throat constrict. "Let's wait for the attorney that Mr. Bennett contacted to arrive before we answer any more questions. Okay?"

Wilson shrugged. "Up to you. Mr. Ard Rhi has contacted someone in the Attorney General's office. That's why you're here. Mr. Ard Rhi's coming down from up around Woodinville, I gather. Should be here in just a bit. The Attorney General's office already has a man in the building." He got up. "Maybe when everyone gets here, we can clear all this up."

He went out again, closing the door softly behind him. There was a moment of silence while he moved away, then Miles snapped, "Damn it, Doc, all he has to do is search you to find . . ."

"Miles!" Ben cut him short with a hiss. "What was I *supposed* to do? Tell him I had it? If he finds out I have it, we'll be charged for sure and the medallion confiscated in the bargain! I can't allow that to happen!"

"Well, I don't see how you can prevent it! They'll find it anyway the moment they search you!"

"Listen up, will you? He's not going to search me! He can't do that without probable cause, and he hasn't got any! Besides, it won't come to that!"

Miles' round face tightened. "With all due respect, Doc, you are not a criminal lawyer! You're a hell of trial lawyer, but your specialty is civil litigation! How do you know if he's got probable cause or not? Ard Rhi is going to say you took it, and that sounds like probable cause for a search to me!"

Ben felt trapped. He knew Miles was right. But if he admitted to having the medallion, they would be there in that Courts Building for the rest of their lives, or at least long enough to make it seem that way. He looked from Miles to Abernathy to Willow. Miles was beside himself with worry, Abernathy was within an inch of doing something that would blow his cover, and Willow was so sick she could no longer even sit upright without help. Landover was looking farther and farther away with the passing of every moment. His plan of escape was coming apart at the seams. He could not afford any further complications. He had to find a way to get them out of there right now.

He got up, walked to the door, and opened it. "Wilson," he called quietly, and the Chief Deputy left what he was doing to wander over. "I've been thinking," Ben said. "Why not put this whole matter over until tomorrow—or even until the first of the week. This isn't anything that won't keep. Willow seems to be getting worse. I want her to get some rest, maybe see a doctor. When that's done, I'll be happy to answer any questions you want. How about it?"

He meant it. He would come back, from Landover if necessary, and set things straight once and for all. He had already decided that he didn't care for the idea of Michel Ard Rhi running around loose in his old world after all.

But Wilson was already shaking his head. "Sorry, Mr. Holiday, but I can't do that. I might consider it if it were just me making the decision. But the order to hold you came right from the Attorney General's office. I can't release you until they say so. You're a lawyer; you understand."

Ben nodded wordlessly. He understood, all right. Somewhere along the line, Michel Ard Rhi had greased some political wheels. He should have expected as much. He thanked Wilson anyway and went back inside the office, closing the door once more. He sat down again beside Willow and cradled her against him.

"Well, you tried, Doc," Miles offered quietly.

Willow's head lifted momentarily from his shoulder. "It will be all right, Ben," she whispered. "Don't worry."

He did worry, though. He worried that time was slipping away. He worried that all the doors out of this mess were closing one after the other, and he wasn't going to be able to do a thing about it.

He was still worrying twenty minutes later when there was a brief knock, the door opened, and a young man in a neatly pressed, three-piece suit and carrying a briefcase appeared, spoke momentarily over his shoulder to Wilson, and stepped inside. This had better be the cavalry, Ben thought. The young man stopped. He was not prepared for what greeted him.

"Mr. Bennett?" he asked, looking doubtfully at the skeleton, gorilla, shaggy dog, and pale green lady facing him. Miles stuck out his hand and the young man shook it. "Lloyd Willoughby, Mr. Bennett, from Sack, Saul, and McQuinn. Mr. Sack called me and asked me to come over."

"We appreciate it, Mr. Willoughby," Miles said and proceeded to introduce the others. Ben shook his hand. Abernathy and Willow just looked at him, and he in turn looked back at them. Ben thought he looked awfully young—and that meant awfully green. You could tell from the way he was looking at them that he was thinking much the same thing Chief Deputy Wilson had been thinking a short time earlier.

Willoughby put his briefcase on Wilson's desk and rubbed his hands together nervously. "Now, then, what seems to be the problem?"

"The problem is simple," Ben offered, taking charge. "We are being held on a bogus theft charge—a charge made by a Mr. Ard Rhi. This man apparently has some clout in the Attorney General's office, because that's where the order to hold us originated. What we want—and right now—is to be allowed to go home and worry about this another time. Willow is quite ill and needs to be put to bed."

"Well, I understood that there was a possible theft charge pending," Willoughby said, looking increasingly nervous. "Some sort of medallion? What can you tell me about that?"

"I can tell you that I have it and that it is mine," Ben answered, seeing no purpose in pretending otherwise. "Mr. Ard Rhi has no basis for his charge that I stole it."

"Have you told this to the Chief Deputy?"

"No, Mr. Willoughby, because if I did, he would want to take the medallion, and I have no intention of giving it up."

Willoughby now looked as if he were waist deep in alligators. He managed a faint smile. "Certainly, Mr. Holiday, I understand. But, do you have the medallion on you? Because from what I understand, if they choose to charge you, they might search you, find the medallion, and take it from you anyway."

Ben fumed. "What about probable cause? Isn't it Ard Rhi's word against ours? That's not enough for probable cause, is it?"

Willoughby looked perplexed. "Actually, Mr. Holiday, I'm not sure. The truth is, criminal law is only a sideline in our firm's practice. I handle a small amount to satisfy those of our clients who want one of us to represent them, but I don't do much otherwise." He smiled weakly. "Mr. Sack always calls me to cover for him on these nighttime matters."

Green as new wood, Ben thought. We're doomed.

"You mean you're not even a criminal attorney?" Miles began, coming to his feet as if he might actually be the gorilla he was dressed as. Willoughby took a quick step back, and Ben restrained Miles with a hand on his shoulder, pushing him back down again into his seat with a quick warning glance in the general direction of the door that separated them from Wilson.

He turned back to Willoughby. "I don't want them to search me, Mr. Willoughby. It is as simple as that. Can you prevent it?" Willoughby looked doubtful. "Tell you what, then," Ben followed up quickly. "Let's play it by ear. You be local counsel, but I'll call the shots. Just follow my lead, okay?"

Willoughby looked as if he were considering whether or
not he was being asked to do anything unethical. His brows
were knit and his smooth, young face was deeply intense. Ben
knew he would be useless if push came to shove. But there was
no time to bring in anyone else.

The door opened to re-admit Wilson. "Mr. Martin of the
Attorney General's office has asked me to bring you up to Three
Court for a short meeting, Mr. Holiday. All of you, please.
Maybe now you can go home."

When cows fly, Ben thought dismally.

They took the elevator up several floors and got off in a
carpeted waiting area. The Chief Deputy led them down a short
hall to a pair of paneled doors and from there into an empty
courtroom. They stood at the head of an aisle that led down
through a dozen rows of a viewing gallery to a gate that opened
onto the trial floor and the judge's bench. The jury box and the
witness stand sat to the left, the reporters' stand to the right.
Further right, a bank of windows that ran the length of the wall
opened out onto the lights of the city. Shadows lay over the
room, broken only by a pair of recessed ceiling lamps that
spotlighted the counsel tables situated directly in front of the
gate.

A man with glasses and graying hair rose from one of the
tables and said, "Chief Deputy, would you bring Mr. Holiday
and his friends down here, please?"

Willoughby stepped to the forefront on their arrival, stick-
ing out his hand and announcing, "Lloyd Willoughby of Sack,
Saul, and McQuinn, Mr. Martin. I have been asked to represent
Mr. Holiday."

Martin shook his hand perfunctorily and promptly forgot
him. "It's late, Mr. Holiday, and I'm tired. I know who you
are. I've even followed a case or two you've tried. We've both
been around the block, so let me get right to the point. The
complainant, Mr. Ard Rhi, says you took a medallion from
him. He wants it returned. I don't know what the dispute is,

but I have Mr. Ard Rhi's word that if the medallion is returned, the whole matter will be forgotten. No charges will be filed. What do you say?"

Ben shrugged. "I say Mr. Ard Rhi is nuts. Is that why we're being detained—because someone says we stole a medallion? What kind of nonsense is this, anyway?"

Martin shook his head. "Frankly, I don't know. A lot of what happens anymore is beyond me. At any rate, you better think it over because if the medallion doesn't show up and Mr. Ard Rhi does—he's supposed to be on his way—you are likely to be charged, Mr. Holiday."

"On one man's word?"

"Afraid so."

Ben came right against him. "As you said, Mr. Martin, I'm a lawyer who's been around the block. So is Mr. Bennett. Our word ought to count for something. Who is this Ard Rhi? Why should you take his word? That's all you have, isn't it?"

Martin was unruffled. He stood his ground. "The only word I get, Mr. Holiday, is from my boss, who keeps me employed, and he says to charge you if Mr. Ard Rhi—whoever he is and whatever he does—signs a complaint. My guess is that if he doesn't get the medallion back, he'll sign. What do you think?"

Ben couldn't say what he was thinking without getting in worse trouble than he already was. "Okay, detain me, Mr. Martin. But how about letting the others go? Apparently I'm the one who's to be charged."

Martin shook his head. "No such luck. Your friends are to be charged as accomplices. Look, I've just finished a long, hard day in court. I lost the case I was trying, I missed my kid's Halloween party, and now I'm stuck down here with you people. I don't like this any better than you do, but that's the way life works sometimes. So let's just have a seat here while we wait for Mr. Ard Rhi. And maybe I can finish some of this paperwork I'm too damned tired to haul back to my office."

He motioned to the gallery. "Give me a break, huh? Talk it over. I don't want to mess with this thing."

He trouped wearily back to the counsel table and sat down, bending over a legal pad and notes. Willoughby motioned them all solicitously toward the gallery seats, where they sat in a row.

Martin looked up again. "Chief Deputy? Your people got orders to bring Mr. Ard Rhi up here when he arrives?" Martin waited for the affirming nod, then went back to his notes. Wilson drifted back up the aisle to the courtroom doors and stayed there.

Willoughby eased his way down the line to Ben and bent down. "Maybe you really should reconsider your decision not to give up the medallion, Mr. Holiday," he whispered, sounding as if perhaps Ben should realize that this would be best for all concerned.

Ben gave him a look that caused him to move quickly away. Willow's voice was a whisper in his ear. "Don't . . . give them the medallion, Ben." She sounded so weak it made his throat constrict. "If you must," she said, "leave me. Promise you will."

"Me as well, High Lord," Abernathy said, bending close. "Whatever happens to us, at least you must get back to Landover!"

Ben closed his eyes. There was that choice. He had the medallion back again. Alone, he could undoubtedly find a way to slip out. But it would mean abandoning his friends, and he wasn't about to do that, no matter what. Miles would probably be all right, but Willow wouldn't last the night. And what would become of Abernathy? He shook his head. There had to be another way out of this.

Miles leaned over. "Maybe you better think about hiding the medallion, Doc. Just for tonight. You can come back for it tomorrow. You can't let them find it on you!"

Ben didn't answer. He didn't have an answer. Hello, choice number two. He knew Miles was right, but he also knew that he didn't want to part with the medallion again for any reason. Twice now he had lost it, once before when Meeks had tricked him into thinking he had given it up when in fact he hadn't, and this time when he had given it to Abernathy in Questor's ill-fated effort to change the dog back into a man. Both times he had managed to retrieve it, but only after considerable difficulty. He was not anxious to risk a third mishap. The medallion had become an integral part of him since he had crossed into Landover, and while he didn't yet fully understand how it had happened, he knew that he could no longer function without it. It gave him the magic that made him King. It gave him power over the Paladin. And while he was reluctant to admit it, it gave him his identity.

He sat in the near-dark courtroom and thought about the medallion and all that he had become since it had been given to him. He looked at the trappings of the courtroom, symbols of his old life as a member of the bar, shards of the person he had been, and thought about how far he had gone away from them. Democracy to monarchy. Trial and error to trial by combat. A jury of his peers to a jury of one. No law but his. It had all been made possible by his acquisition of the medallion. His hand drifted to his tunic front. His smile was ironic. The trappings of his old life might be gone, but hadn't he simply exchanged them for new ones?

The doors pushed open and another deputy appeared. He spoke briefly with Wilson, and Wilson walked down to Martin. They in turn conversed, and then Martin got up and walked back up the aisle with the Chief Deputy. All three men pushed through the doors and disappeared.

Ben felt the hair on the back of his neck begin to prickle. Something was up.

A few moments later, they were back. Martin walked down the aisle to stand before Ben. "Mr. Ard Rhi is here, Mr. Holiday. He says you came to his house last night posing as a Mr. Squires in an attempt to buy the medallion. When he

wouldn't sell, you came back tonight with your friends and
stole it. Apparently, the daughter of his steward helped you.
He says she's admitted her part in the matter." He looked toward the courtroom doors. "Chief Deputy?"

Wilson and the other deputy pushed open the doors and
said something to someone outside. Michel Ard Rhi stepped
into view, his face impassive, but his eyes dark with anger.
Behind him appeared two members of Graum Wythe's watch.

Elizabeth stood disconsolately between them. Her eyes
were downcast and tears streaked her freckled face.

Ben felt sick. They had found Elizabeth. There was no
telling what they had threatened her with to force her to confess
to stealing the medallion. And there was no telling what they
would do to her if Ard Rhi didn't get it now.

"Do any of you know the little girl?" Martin asked quietly.

No one said anything. No one had to.

"How about it, Mr. Holiday?" Martin pressed. "If you
return the medallion, this whole matter can be dropped right
here and now. Otherwise, I have to charge you."

Ben didn't answer. He couldn't. There seemed no way out.

Martin sighed. "Mr. Holiday?"

Ben leaned forward, just to shift positions while he tried
to stall, but Abernathy misinterpreted the move, thinking he
had decided to give up the medallion, and hurriedly brought
up a paw to restrain him.

"No, High Lord, you cannot!" he exclaimed.

Martin stared at the dog. Ben could see in the man's eyes
what he was thinking. He was thinking, how can the mouth
on a dog costume move like that? How come he has teeth and
a tongue? How come he seems so real?

Then a ball of crimson fire exploded outside the bank of
courtroom windows, a black hole opened through the night,
and out of the hole flew Strabo the dragon and Questor Thews.

Dragon at the Bar

*I*t was one of those rare moments in life when everything seems to come to a halt, where movement is suspended, and everyone is trapped in a sort of three-dimensional still life. It was one of those moments that imprints itself in the memory, so that years later everyone still remembers exactly what it was like—what the feelings were, the smells, the tastes, the colors, and the lines and angles of everything around; and most of all, the way everything that happened just before and just after seemed focused on that moment like sunlight reflected off still water in colored threads.

It was like that for Ben Holiday. For that one moment, he saw everything as if it were captured in a photograph. He was half-turned in his seat in the front row of that courtroom gallery, Willow on one side, slumped down against his shoulder, Abernathy on the other, eyes shining, and Miles further left, still in his gorilla outfit, his cherubic face a mix of astonishment and dismay. Martin and Willoughby stood just in front of them on the other side of the gate, two generations of three-piece suits, their entire lives given over to a belief in the value of reason and common sense, the former looking as if he had just witnessed Armageddon, the latter looking as if he had caused it. Behind and to the rear, just visible in Ben's peripheral vision, were Chief Deputy Wilson and his brothers-at-arms, minions of the law, bent in half crouches that gave them the appearance of startled cats poised to run either way. Michel Ard Rhi had black hatred etched on his face, and his men were white with fear. Only Elizabeth radiated the pure wonder that was captured, too, somewhere in Ben.

Outside, pinned against the backdrop of the lights of the city of Seattle, was Strabo. His bulk seemed to hang in the air, wings outspread like a monstrous hang glider's, his black, crusted, serpentine form framed in the windows of the courtroom like an image projected on a screen. His yellow-lamp eyes blinked, and smoke trailed in streamers from his nostrils and mouth. Questor Thews sat astride him, patchwork gray robes so tattered they seemed to hang in strips, white hair and beard streaked with ash and flying in the wind. There was wonder mirrored in the wizard's face as well.

Ben wanted to howl with the exhilaration he was feeling.

Then Martin whispered, "Good God!" his voice like a small child's, and the moment was gone.

Everyone began moving and shouting at once. Wilson and the second deputy came down the aisle still crouched, slipping their guns from their holsters, yelling at everyone to get down. Ben yelled back, telling them not to shoot, glancing once over his shoulder to where Questor Thews was already making a quick circling motion with his fingers, then back again to see the astonished deputies staring at fistfuls of daisies where the guns had been. The hallway outside had become an impassable jungle, floor-to-ceiling deepest Africa, and Michel Ard Rhi and his men, trying desperately to flee, found their exit blocked. Elizabeth had broken free of them and was running down the aisle to greet Abernathy, crying and saying something about a clown nose and Michel and how sorry she was. Willoughby was pulling and tugging on Miles as if somehow Miles might get him out of this nightmare, and Miles was trying in vain to shove the other man away.

Then, suddenly, Strabo shifted positions outside the window, and his huge tail swung about like a wrecking ball and hammered into the bank of windows with an explosion that shattered glass, wooden frames, and half the wall. The city night rushed in, wind and cold, the sounds of cars from the streets and ships from the docks, and the lights of the adjacent high rises which now seemed magnified a hundredfold.

Ben went to the floor, Miles was thrown back into the gallery seats, and Abernathy and Elizabeth came together in a rush.

"Strabo!" Michel Ard Rhi screamed in recognition.

The dragon flew in through the opening like a dirigible and settled onto the courtroom floor, flattening counsel benches, the reporters' stand, and part of the gate.

"Holiday!" he hissed, and his tongue licked out from between the blackened spikes of his teeth. "What an ugly world you come from!"

Martin, Willoughby, Wilson, the second deputy, Michel Ard Rhi, and his men were climbing all over one another in an effort to get out of the way of the dragon, but they couldn't break through the wall of foliage that blocked the courtroom doors. Strabo glanced at them; his maw opened, and a jet of steam shot out at the five, who screamed in terror and dove for the cover of the gallery seats. The dragon laughed and clicked his jaws at them.

"Enough of that nonsense!" Questor Thews snapped. The wizard began climbing down from the dragon's back.

"You drag me here against my will, force me to rescue a man I despise, a man who is nothing less than what he deserves to be—the victim of his own foolhardiness—and now you would deprive me of the tiny bit of pleasure this pointless venture affords!" Strabo huffed and snapped his tail, taking out another row of gallery seats. "You are so tiresome, Questor Thews!"

Questor ignored him. "High Lord!" The wizard came forward and embraced Ben warmly. "Are you well?"

"Questor, I have never been better!" Ben exclaimed, pounding the other on the back so hard he almost knocked him over. "And I have never been happier to see anyone in all my life! Not ever!"

"I could not tolerate even the thought of you being here another moment, High Lord," Questor declared solemnly. He straightened. "Let me make my confession here and now. This entire mishap has been my fault. I am the one who made a mess out of things and I am the one who must put them right again."

He turned, his eyes settling on Abernathy. "Old friend!" he called over. "I have done you a grave disservice. I am sorry for what I did. I hope you will forgive me."

Abernathy wrinkled his nose with distaste. "Cat's whiskers, Questor Thews! There is no time for this nonsense!" Questor assumed a pained look. "Oh, for the . . . Very well! I forgive you! You knew I would! Now, get us out of here, confound it!"

But Questor had caught sight of Michel Ard Rhi. "Ah, hello, Michel!" he called up the aisle to where the other was crouched behind a line of benches. He smiled brightly, then whispered out of the corner of his mouth to Ben, "What is going on here, anyway?"

Quickly, Ben filled him in. He told him what Michel had done to Abernathy and tried to do to them.

Questor was understandably appalled. "Michel hasn't changed a bit, it seems. He remains the same detestable fellow he always was. Landover is well rid of him." He shrugged. "Well, this is all great fun, but I am afraid we must be going, High Lord. I suspect the magic I employed to close off this room won't last very long. Magic has never enjoyed much success in this world." He took a moment to survey his handiwork at the courtroom door, then sighed. "That's a much better than average forest wall I conjured, don't you think? I am quite proud of it. I have always been rather good at growing things, you know."

"A regular green thumb," Ben acknowledged. He had his eyes fixed on Michel Ard Rhi. "Listen, Questor, as far as I'm concerned, the quicker you get us out of here, the better. But we have to take Michel with us. I know," he added hastily, seeing the look of horror on the other's face, "you think I'm nuts. But what about Elizabeth if we leave him? What happens to her?"

Questor frowned. Clearly, he hadn't considered that. "Oh, dear," he said.

Elizabeth, a dozen feet up the aisle, was clearly thinking much the same thing. "Abernathy!" she begged, tugging on his sleeve. When he looked down, her eyes were huge. "Please don't leave me behind! I don't want to stay here anymore. I want to come with you."

Abernathy shook his head. "Elizabeth, no . . ."

"Yes, Abernathy, please! I want to! I want to learn magic, and fly dragons and play with you and Willow and see the castle where . . ."

"Elizabeth . . ."

". . . Ben is King and the fairy world and all the strange creatures, everything, but I don't want to stay here, not with Michel, not even if my father said it would be all right, because it wouldn't, not ever . . ."

"But I can't take you!"

They stared at each other in anguish. Then Abernathy bent down impulsively, hugged the little girl close, and felt her hug him back. "Oh, Elizabeth!" he whispered.

Outside the window, still in the distance, sirens sounded. Miles grabbed Ben. "You have to get out of here now, Doc— or you're liable not to get out at all." He shook his head. "I still think this whole thing is just a crazy dream. Green fairies and talking dogs and now dragons! I think I'm going to wake up tomorrow and wonder what I had to drink tonight!" Then he grinned. "Doesn't matter, though." He glanced at the dragon, who was chewing on a section of the judge's bench. "I wouldn't have missed a minute of it!"

Ben smiled. "Thanks, Miles. Thanks for sticking with me. I know it wasn't easy—especially with so many weird things happening all at once. But someday you'll understand. Someday I'll come back and tell you everything."

Miles put a big hand on his shoulder. "I'll hold you to that, Doc. Now get going. And don't worry about things here. I'll do what I can for the little girl. I'll find a way to straighten it all out, I promise."

Questor had been studying Elizabeth and Abernathy while Miles was speaking, but now suddenly he started. "Straighten things out!" he exclaimed. "That gives me an idea!" He wheeled and hurried up the aisle to where Michel Ard Rhi and the others still crouched behind the gallery seats. "Let me see," the wizard muttered to himself. "I think I still remember how this works. Ah!"

He muttered a few quick words, added a few curt gestures, and pointed, one after the other, to Chief Deputy Wilson, to the second deputy, to Michel's two henchmen, to Martin, and finally to Lloyd Willoughby of Sack, Saul, and McQuinn. All immediately assumed a rather blissful look and settled to the floor sound asleep.

"There!" Questor rubbed his hands together briskly. "When they wake up, they will have had a very pleasant rest and all this will seem a rather vague dream!" He beamed at Miles. "That should make your task somewhat easier!"

Ben glanced at Miles, who was studying the vacant look on Willoughby's face suspiciously. The sirens had settled underneath the Courts Building, and a spotlight was playing about the ragged opening in the wall.

"Questor, we have to get out of here!" Ben called sharply. He picked up Willow and cradled her in his arms. "Bring Michel and let's go!"

"Oh, no, High Lord!" Questor shook his head adamantly. "We can't have Michel Ard Rhi running about Landover again! He was much too much trouble the last time he was there. I believe he will do better here, in your world."

Ben started to object, but Questor was already approaching Michel, who was on his feet again and backed up against the courtroom wall. "Stay away from me, Questor Thews," he was snarling. "I'm not afraid of you!"

"Michel, Michel, Michel!" Questor sighed wearily. "You were always such a pathetic excuse for a Prince, and it seems you have not changed. You appear determined to bring unpleasantness into the lives of everyone around you. I simply don't understand it. In any case, you are going to have to change—even if I have to help you."

Michel crouched. "Don't come near me, you old fool. You play tricks with your magic that might fool others, but not me! You always were a charlatan, a pretend wizard who couldn't *begin* to do real magic, a ridiculous clown everyone . . ."

Questor made a short chopping motion, and the words ceased to come out of Michel Ard Rhi's mouth, even though he continued trying to speak. When he realized what had been done to him, he reeled back in horror.

"We can all improve ourselves in this life, Michel," Questor whispered. "You just never learned how."

He made a series of intricate motions and spoke softly. There was a wisp of golden dust that flew from his fingers and settled onto Michel Ard Rhi. The exiled Prince of Landover shrank back, then stiffened, and his eyes seemed to catch sight of something very far away, something that none of the others could see. He relaxed, and there was a strange mix of horror and understanding mirrored in his face.

Questor turned away and started back down the aisle. "Should have done that a long time ago," he muttered. "Simple sort of magic, best kind there is. Strong enough to last, too, even in this barbaric world of nonbelievers."

He stopped momentarily as he reached Abernathy and Elizabeth, and he put his gnarled hands on the little girl's shoulders. "I am sorry, Elizabeth, but Abernathy is right. You cannot come with us. You belong here, with your father and your friends. This is your home, not Landover. And there is a reason for that, just as there is a reason for most of what happens in life. I won't pretend that I understand all of what that reason is, but I understand a bit of it. You believe in the magic, don't you? Well, that is surely part of why you are here. Every world needs someone who believes in the magic—to make certain that it isn't forgotten by those who don't."

He bent to kiss her forehead. "See what you can do, will you?"

He continued down the aisle past Ben. "Do not worry, High Lord. She will have no further problem with Michel Ard Rhi, I assure you."

"How do you know that?" Ben asked. "What did you do to him?"

But the wizard was already through the gate and climbing back up on the dragon. "I'll explain later, High Lord. We really have to be going now. Right this instant, I think."

He motioned back up the aisle, and Ben could see that the wall of foliage blocking the courtroom entry was beginning to fade. In moments, the entry would be clear again.

"Get out of here, Doc!" Miles whispered roughly. "Good luck!"

Ben clutched the other's arm for a moment, then released him and carried Willow through the courtroom debris to where Strabo had swung about to face the opening in the wall. The dragon eyed Ben malevolently, hissed, and showed all of his teeth. "Ride me, Holiday," he invited menacingly. "It will be the last chance you will ever have to do so."

"Strabo. I would never have believed it," Ben marveled.

"I care nothing for what you believe," the dragon snarled. "Quit wasting my time!"

Ben cradled Willow tightly against him and started to mount. "It must have taken a small miracle for Questor to . . ." He stopped at the sudden sound of approaching helicopters, their rotors whipping through the night.

Strabo's lips curled back. "What is that I hear?" he hissed.

"Trouble," Ben answered, and hitched his way up quickly behind Questor. Willow opened her eyes briefly and closed them again. Ben squeezed her shoulders and pulled her close. "Hurry up, Abernathy!"

Elizabeth was hugging the dog once more. "I still want to go with you!" she whispered fiercely. "I still do!"

"I know," he whispered back, then broke free roughly. "I'm sorry, Elizabeth. Good-bye."

The others were calling out to him. He was halfway through the shattered gallery gate to join them when he heard Elizabeth call frantically, "Abernathy!" He turned at once. "Come back? Please? Someday?"

He paused, then nodded. "I promise, Elizabeth."

"Don't forget about me!"

"I won't. Not ever."

"I love you, Abernathy," she said.

He smiled, tried to respond, then simply licked at his nose and hurried away. He was crying when he pulled himself up behind Ben. "Sorry, High Lord," he said softly.

"Home, dragon!" Questor Thews cried.

Strabo hissed in response and lifted clear of the shattered courtroom. Wind blew and dust swirled with the beating of the great beast's wings; the lights that remained flickered and went out, and the dragon seemed to fill the whole of the night. A thing out of legend and bedtime tales, he was real for yet another instant to the man and the child who watched. Then he flew through the opening in the wall and was gone.

Miles walked back up the aisle to where Elizabeth was staring out into the dark. He stood there with her in silence, smiling as he felt her hand come up to take his own.

• •

Strabo burst through the opening in the wall of the Courts
Building five stories up and nearly collided with a helicopter.
Machine and beast veered away from each other, slicing
through the chill night air and the narrow beams of several
spotlights situated in the streets below. Neither was sure of what
the other had encountered, each a dark shape against the city,
and the confusion was evident. The helicopter disappeared skyward with a roar of its engine. Strabo dropped down between
the buildings, flattening out.

There were screams from the people in the streets.

"Climb, dragon!" Questor Thews cried frantically.

Strabo soared skyward once more, arcing between a pair
of tall buildings, steam rolling off his scaled hide. Ben and his
companions clung to him for dear life despite the fact that Questor's magic strapped them all securely in place. The helicopter
roared back around the corner of a building, lights searching. A
second ship followed. Strabo shrieked.

"Tell him not to use his fire on them!" Ben cried to Questor in warning, picturing flaming ships and buildings and Miles
and Elizabeth in jail.

"He can't!" Questor shouted back, head bent close. "His
magic is as limited in this world as my own! He has only a little
fire and he must save it if we are to make the crossover!"

Ben had forgotten. Strabo needed his fire to open a passage
back into Landover. That was how he had brought them out
of Abaddon when the demons had trapped them there.

They dodged and twisted, but the helicopters followed.
Strabo rounded the corner of a building and shot out toward
the bay. Wharfs, piers and jettys, shipyards with their dry docks
and containers of freight, giant cranes that looked like goose-
necked dinosaurs, and a kaleidoscope of vessels of all sizes and
shapes passed away underneath. Ahead, far beyond, loomed a
massive range of mountains. Below, the lights of the city
winked and flashed.

A ship whistle sounded with a shriek, frightening them all with its closeness. Strabo shuddered, twisted left, and began to climb. Ben squinted. Something huge loomed close behind, dropping rapidly, small red and green lights blinking.

"A jet!" he cried in frantic warning. "Look out, Questor!"

Questor screamed something to Strabo, and the dragon whipped aside, just as the huge airplane dropped past on its path of descent. Engines roared, the wind screamed, and every other sound disappeared into white silence.

Strabo came around again and started back for the city, blackened teeth showing.

"No!" Questor howled. "Climb, dragon—take us home!"

But Strabo was too infuriated. He wanted someone or something to fight. Steam blew in jets from his nostrils and there were strange, frightening sounds emanating from his throat.

He passed back over the harbor and spotted the helicopters. He roared in challenge, and now fire burned redly from his jaws.

Ben was wild. "Turn him, Questor! If he uses up all his fire, we'll be trapped here!"

Questor Thews shouted in warning at the dragon, but Strabo ignored him. He went straight for the helicopters, slashed between them so that they were forced to veer frantically aside to avoid a collision, then sped back into the midst of the city buildings. Spotlights whipped across the sky in search of them. Ben was certain he could hear people screaming. He was certain he could hear gunfire. Strabo, heaven help them, was flying blind.

Then, just when it appeared that matters were completely out of control, the dragon seemed to remember himself. With a shriek that froze the entire night into stillness, Strabo suddenly shot skyward. Ben, Questor, Abernathy, and Willow were thrust back viciously. Wind whipped and tore at them, threatening to unseat them, chilling them to the bone. Sound and sight disappeared in a vortex of motion. Ben held his breath and waited for them all to disintegrate. That was how this chase was going to end, he decided. They were simply going to come apart. There wasn't any doubt of it.

He was wrong. Strabo shrieked a second time and suddenly breathed out a rush of fire. The air seemed to melt and the sky to open. A jagged hole appeared, black and empty, and they flew into it.

The blackness swallowed them. There was a flare of light and a surge of heat. Ben closed his eyes, then slowly opened them again.

A scattering of colored moons and solemn, twinkling stars brightened the night like a child's picture book. Mountain walls rose all about and trailers of mist played hide-and-seek through craggy peaks and great, silent trees.

Ben Holiday let his breath escape in a slow hiss of relief.

They were home.

Stopper

*T*he little company spent the remainder of that night on the western slope of the valley just north of the Heart. They settled themselves in a grove of fruit trees mixed with a scattering of crimson-leaved maples, the smell of berries and apples mingling with hardwood bark and new sap in the cool night air. Cicadas hummed, crickets chirped, night birds called from near and far, and the whole of the valley whispered in the softest cadence that all was well. Sleep was an old and valued friend on such a night. For all but one of the worn and harried members of the little company, it came easily.

Ben Holiday alone remained awake. Even Strabo slept, curled up some distance off within the shelter of a low ravine, but Ben stayed awake. Sleep would not come for him. He leaned back against Willow and waited for the dawn, troubled and anxious. Willow was a tree now. She had made the transformation moments after they had eased her down off the back of the dragon, barely conscious. She had tried to reassure Ben with a quick squeeze of one hand and a momentary smile, and then she was changing. Ben remained unconvinced. He stayed awake next to her, wishing that it was not just in his imagination that he could seem to hear the sound of her breathing grow steadily stronger, smoother, deeper in tone. He knew she believed the transformation was necessary, that whatever the nature of the illness that had ravaged her in his world, whatever the form of the poison that attacked her, the soil of her own world would heal her. Maybe yes, maybe no, Ben thought. He had seen it work before, but that was before. He continued to keep an uneasy watch.

Even so, he tried several times to snatch a bit of sleep, tried to close his eyes and let it embrace him, but his thoughts were dark and filled with the promise of terrifying dreams. He could not shake the memory of how close they had all come to not making it back. He could not forget the sense of helplessness he had experienced there in that empty courtroom when all his options had been stripped from him, a trial lawyer whose arguments and appeals had finally been exhausted. He could not forgive himself for so completely losing control.

Questions whispered to him from the night. How far away from himself had he come in giving up his old life for his new? How much had he sacrificed to regenerate his sense of purpose? Too much, perhaps—so much, that he was in very real danger of losing his identity.

He drifted in and out of a sort of half sleep, through uneven bouts of self-recrimination and second-guessing, plagued by demons of his own making. He knew he should dismiss them, yet he could not find the means. He grappled with them helplessly, each encounter provoking new pain and doubt. He was too vulnerable, and he could not seem to protect himself. He simply drifted.

When dawn's light did begin at last to creep into the dark recesses of his consciousness, the eastern sky lightening and the night fading west, he found he had slept somehow, if only briefly. He jolted awake from a fitful doze, his eyes searching quickly for Willow, finding her asleep beside him, her color strong again, her life miraculously restored. There were tears in his eyes, and he brushed at them, smiling. Then, finally, the demons began to slip away, and he could feel again some small measure of hope that he might yet make sense out of who and what he was and take back into his own hands the lines that measured out his life.

He confronted then, for the first time, something he had carefully avoided that entire night—the prospect of dealing with Nightshade and the Darkling. The specter of such an encounter had been lurking at the edge of his subconscious ever since Questor had told him after landing what had become of the bottle, kept just back of where he would be forced to think about it. But now he must think of it, he knew. He could put it off no longer. Everything that had gone before in his long search for the medallion and Abernathy would be rendered pointless if he did not find a way, once and for all, to dispose of that damnable bottle. That meant he must face Nightshade. And that could easily cost him his life.

He sat in the gradually brightening clearing, feeling the pulse of the morning begin to quicken and the sluggishness of its night sleep begin to fade. He let his hand drift down to Willow's face and his fingers brush her skin softly. She stirred, but did not waken. How was he to do what must be done? he wondered. How was he to retrieve the bottle from Nightshade so that the demon could be put back inside? The doubts and fears had left him now, their needles withdrawn. He was able to think in clear, pragmatic terms. He must become the Paladin again, he realized, the knight-errant that was the alter ego of the Kings of Landover, that frightening iron juggernaut that seemed to claim a bit more of his soul each time he called upon its services. He shuddered involuntarily at the surge of ambivalent emotions that were stirred within him. He would need the Paladin's strength to withstand Nightshade's magic, not to mention the demon's. Questor Thews would help, of course. Questor would lend his own magic to the cause. The real question was, would the two of them be enough? Even forgetting Nightshade for the moment, how could they overcome the

Darkling? How could *anyone* overcome a creature whose power was apparently limitless?

Ben Holiday sat alone in the brightening dawn and pondered this puzzle. He was still pondering it when the others came awake, the solution he sought as elusive as summer frost.

He was pleasantly surprised, therefore, when halfway through a breakfast in which he was principally concerned with assuring himself that Willow was well again, the answer came to him.

He was surprised, too, when, following breakfast, Strabo offered to carry them all north to the Deep Fell. He needn't have been. The dragon didn't make the offer because he felt an obligation to do anything further to help, or because he felt Questor had any further hold over him either. He had no sense of responsibility or concern for the success of their endeavors. He made it because he was anxious to let Holiday and Nightshade have at each other and he wanted to be there to enjoy the show. Someone's spilled blood was necessary to satisfy his irritation at having been dragged into this conflict in the first place, and he could only hope that witch and King would both bleed freely in the battle that was to follow.

"You owe me, Holiday!" the dragon announced with a venomous hiss on making the offer to convey Ben to his own funeral. "This makes twice now that I have saved your worthless skin and twice now that you have given me nothing in return! If Nightshade dispatches you, I will consider the debt paid—but not otherwise! Think of what I have suffered for you! I was attacked, Holiday—chased and hounded by metal flying things, hunted with lights, screamed at and threatened by others like yourself, my system fouled by poisons I can only guess at, and my equanimity thoughtlessly disrupted!" He took a long, careful breath. "Let me put it another way. I find you the most annoying, bothersome creature I have ever had the misfortune of encountering and I *long* for the day you are finally no more!"

Having said that, he knelt down so that the object of his derision might mount him. Ben glanced at Questor, who shrugged and said, "What else can you expect from a dragon?"

Willow and Abernathy gave him fits as well by insisting that they should accompany him. When he had the temerity to suggest that he didn't think this was such a good idea, given the extent of the danger Questor and he would likely be facing from the witch and the bottle demon, both immediately suggested that perhaps he had better think again.

"I did not survive the acute discomforts of Graum Wythe's dungeons and the vicissitudes of Michel Ard Rhi's personality to be left behind now!" his scribe announced rather irritably. "I intend to see this matter through to its proper conclusion! Besides," he huffed, "you need someone to keep an eye on the wizard!"

"Nor do I intend to be left behind, either," Willow hastened to add. "I am well now, and you may have need of me. I have told you before, Ben Holiday—what happens to you happens to me."

Ben was hardly convinced by either argument; neither appeared to him to have fully recovered from the hardships of the journey over and back and neither would be of much help in dealing with Nightshade and the Darkling. But he knew there wasn't anything he could say that would change their minds and he decided it would be easier to take them than to try to force them to remain behind. He shook his head. Things never seemed to work out quite the way he wanted them to.

So they lifted skyward aboard the dragon, departing the grove of fruit and maple trees that had been their night's camp, leaving behind the Heart with its rows of flags, stanchions, and polished oak benches and the distant, tiny island where rested castle Sterling Silver, and passing finally out of the hill country of the south into the plains and grasslands of the north. They flew until the Greensward was behind them and the wall of the Melchor rose ahead. Then Strabo dipped earthward, sailing lazily across the dark, misted bowl of the Deep Fell, presumably so that Nightshade couldn't miss seeing them, settling at last on a small scrap of grassland a short distance from the hollows' edge.

Ben and his companions eased themselves down from the dragon's back, casting furtive glances toward the rim of the witch's home. Mist swirled sluggishly in the windless midday air as if stirred by some invisible hand, and silence masked all signs of whatever life waited below. The air was sultry and fetid, and the clouds were gathered thick across this stretch of the mountains. East, sunlight brightened the land; here, gray haze cloaked everything.

Signs of the wilt that had marked the land at the time of Ben's arrival in Landover were evident again. Leaves were withered and sick-looking; whole stands of trees and patches of scrub were black. The devastation spread outward from the Deep Fell for as far as the eye could see—almost as if some sickness had crawled out of the hollows and begun devouring what lay beyond in ever-widening circles.

"A fitting place for your demise, Holiday!" sneered the dragon, bending close. "Why don't you get on with it?"

He spread his wings and soared off into the mountains, settling comfortably upon an outcropping of rock that overlooked the hollows and gave him a clear view of everything below.

"I find him quite intolerable these days," Questor Thews said quietly.

"I find it hard to believe he was ever anything else," Ben said.

He positioned Willow and Abernathy in a broken stand of Bonnie Blues some distance back, pleading with them to stay out of sight until matters with the witch and the demon were resolved. He had no real expectation that his entreaties would be heeded, but he at least had to make the effort.

He returned to Questor and spoke quietly with him then,

explaining for the first time his plan for dealing with the Darkling. Questor was thoughtful for a moment, then announced, "High Lord, I think you may have found the answer."

Ben's smile was faint. "Finding the answer is one thing; applying it is another. You know what I mean, don't you? This will be tricky, Questor. It has to be done just so. Much depends on you."

Questor's owlish face was solemn. "I understand, High Lord. I won't let you down."

Ben nodded. "Just don't let yourself down. Are you ready?"

"Ready, High Lord."

Ben turned to face the Deep Fell and called out sharply, "Nightshade!" The name echoed and slowly died away. Ben waited, then called again. "Nightshade!" Again, the name echoed into silence. Nightshade did not appear. Beside him, Questor shifted his booted feet uneasily.

Then a swirl of black mist lifted out of the hollows, churning and seething as it settled on the parched grasses at its rim, and Nightshade appeared at last. She stood there against the mist, robes and hair black, face and hands white, a stark and forbidding vision. One hand clutched the familiar bottle, its painted surface luminescent in the gray air.

"Play-King!" she whispered with a hiss. With her free hand, she pulled the stopper on the bottle. The Darkling crept forth, wizened spider's body dark, sticklike, and covered with hair. Red eyes gleamed and fingers curled on the bottle's edge. "See, precious one?" the witch asked softly and pointed. "See what comes to amuse us?"

Neither Ben nor Questor moved. They became statues, waiting to see what would happen next. The Darkling crept about the lip of its bottle like an anxious cat, searching here and there, whispering and hissing words that no one but the witch could hear. "Yes, yes," she soothed, over and over, bent down now. "Yes, little demon, they are the ones!"

Finally, she looked up again. Her free hand slipped the stopper into her robes, and her fingers stroked the fawning demon. "Come play with us, High Lord and Court Wizard!" she called over. "Come play! We have games for you! Such games! Come closer!"

Ben and Questor held their ground. "Give us the bottle, Nightshade," ordered Ben quietly. "It doesn't belong to you."

"Anything I wish belongs to me!" Nightshade screeched.

"Not the bottle."

"Especially the bottle!"

"I will bring the Paladin, if I must," Ben threatened, his voice still quiet.

"Bring whomever you like." Nightshade's smile was slow and wicked. Then she whispered, "Play-King, you are such a fool!"

The Darkling shrieked suddenly, leaped upward, and thrust its tiny crooked fingers toward them. Fire and shards of iron flew at them with the blink of an eye, slicing through the hazy afternoon air. But Questor's magic was already in place, and the fire and shards of iron passed harmlessly by. Ben's hand was about the medallion, his fingers closed upon its metal surface, the heat beginning to surge through him. Light flared less than a dozen yards off, and the Paladin appeared, white knight on white charger, a ghost come out of time. Fire burned in the medallion, then surged outward through mist and gray to where the ghost took form. Ben felt himself ride the light, borne on its stinging brightness as if a mote of dust, carried from his body as if weightless. Then he was inside the iron shell, and the transformation had begun. A second more and it was completed. Iron plates closed about, clasps, straps, and buckles tightened, and the harness latched in place. Ben Holiday's memories faded and were replaced by those of the Paladin—memories of countless battles fought and won, of struggles unimaginable, of blood and iron, of screams and cries, and of the testing of courage and strength-of-arms on distant fields of

combat. There was that strange mix of exhilaration and horror—the Paladin's sharpened expectation of another fight, Ben
Holiday's repulsion at the thought of killing.

Then there was only the feel of iron and leather, muscle
and bone, the horse beneath, and the weapons strapped close—
the Paladin's body and soul.

The King's champion surged toward Nightshade and the
Darkling.

The lance of white oak dropped into place.

But the witch and the demon were already fusing hatred
and dark magic to produce something they believed not even
the Paladin could withstand. It climbed out of the hollows behind them, born of green fire and steam, clawing free of the
mists and the haze, a huge, lumbering thing as white as the
Paladin himself.

It was a second Paladin—of sorts.

From behind the shield of his magic, Questor Thews
blinked and stared. He had never seen anything quite like this
monster. It was a perversion—a joining of what appeared to
be a huge, squat, lizardlike creature and an armored rider twice
the size of the knight-errant, all twisted and sprouting weapons
of bone and iron. It was as if some impossibly warped mirror
had produced a distorted image of the Paladin, as if that image
had been reflected in the most loathsome way possible and given
life.

The monstrous creature—a single being—wheeled from
the hollows rim and lumbered to meet the charge of the Paladin.

They came together with a thunderclap of sound, white
oak and bone shattering, iron scraping and clanging, beasts
grunting and shrieking their pain and anger. They slid off each
other and passed by, dust and debris flying. Back around came
the Paladin, discarding the remains of his lance, reaching down
for the battle axe. The creature of the witch and demon slowed,
turned, and seemed to swell in size, growing as if fed by the
force of the conflict, lifting until it towered over everything.

All eyes were fixed at that moment on the creature.

Questor Thews made a slight motion with his hands. He seemed to shimmer, disappear, then reappear looking vaguely translucent. No one noticed.

The Paladin attacked, battle axe swinging. Nightshade and the Darkling fed their combined magics into their creation, shrieking with delight as it swelled even further, then lifted on its hindlegs and waited. It was as big as a house now, a mass of sluglike flesh. The Paladin rushed it, and the creature surged forward, trying to crush its attacker. The earth shook with the force of its weight as it struck. The Paladin just managed to slip past, the battle axe ripping along the beast's thick hide. But the wound closed over almost at once. Magic gave the creature life, and magic was not subject to the laws of man and nature.

Back came the Paladin, broadsword drawn now, the gleaming blade cutting and hacking with tremendous fury, carving lines of red along the length of the beast. But the wounds closed as quickly as they were made, and the creature kept lunging for the knight, waiting for its chance. Nightshade and the Darkling urged the monster on. The witch's face was rapt with pleasure. The demon's tiny body was stretched taut. Magic surged from both of them, feeding their creature, keeping it strong. They could see that the beast's lunges were getting closer now to the attacking knight. It would not be long now, they knew.

From within the cover of the decimated Bonnie Blues, Abernathy and Willow watched silently. They, too, could see how this fight was going and could tell how it was going to end.

Then something strange happened.

The creature suddenly lurched upward and began to shrink.

It shuddered as if stricken with a poison. The Darkling saw it first. The demon shrieked with anger and disbelief, raced down Nightshade's black robes, and thrust its spider arms out to feed its pet more magic. But the creature failed to respond. It continued to shrink, flinching back now from the blows of the broadsword struck by the Paladin, stumbling and tottering away as it felt its life drain from it.

Nightshade saw it now, too, screamed in fury, then made her own determination of the cause and wheeled suddenly on Questor Thews. Fire as dark as pitch flew from her outstretched hands and enveloped the wizard. Questor Thews erupted in a pillar of smoke and ash. Willow and Abernathy gasped in horror. The wizard had disappeared completely.

But the creature was still shrinking. And now something was happening to the Darkling as well. It was doubled over, writhing on the ground at Nightshade's feet, twisting as if the same poison that had infected its creature had infected it as well. It was shrieking something at Nightshade, who bent quickly to listen.

"The bottle, mistress!" it was saying. "The bottle has been sealed! I cannot find the magic! I cannot live!"

Nightshade still had the bottle in one hand. She stared at it uncomprehendingly, finding it unchanged, undamaged, the stopper pulled, the neck open. What was the demon screaming about? She was mystified.

A short distance away, the creature of the witch and demon's magic had breathed its last, crumbling completely into dust. The Paladin ground it beneath his charger's hooves and wheeled about once more. Nightshade looked up from the bottle in confusion. The Paladin was coming now at her.

Only then did she think to reach down to test the bottle's opening. Blue wizard fire sparked and bit at her, and she jerked her fingers back. *"Questor Thews!"* Willow heard her shriek in fury. The Darkling was barely moving, clinging to one sleeve. The witch snarled, clasped the bottle by its throat, and prepared to send her own magic surging into its blocked opening.

She was too late.

The Paladin was almost on top of her.

Then Questor Thews seemed to explode out of nowhere right in front of the witch, seizing the bottle before she could think to react, snatching it quickly away. Nightshade shrieked once and lunged for the wizard just as the Paladin reached her.

Fire seemed to erupt from everywhere at the point of impact.

No longer within the concealment of the Bonnie Blues, but running to reach Questor Thews and Ben, Willow and Abernathy drew up short, wincing from the sound and the heat. Fire flared, seemingly of all colors and shapes, exploding into the mist and gray like a geyser out of the earth.

Then the debris settled, and Nightshade and the Paladin were gone. Questor Thews was on his knees, both hands clutched tightly over the top of the bottle, watching stone-faced as the Darkling writhed on the scorched earth and turned to lifeless dust.

Ben Holiday returned to himself, lightheaded and dazed, with the medallion still warm against his chest. He started to sway and topple over, but then Willow was there, holding him upright, and Abernathy was beside her, and he managed to smile and say, "It's okay now. It's over."

The four friends sat quietly at the site of battle and talked about what had happened.

Nightshade was gone. Whether she had been destroyed by the Paladin or escaped to trouble them another day, none of them knew. They could recall the moment of impact—a flare of light and a glimpse of the witch's face. That was all. They were not willing to bet that they had seen the last of her.

Strabo was gone, too. He had lifted into the sky almost immediately at the battle's conclusion, winging his way east without a backward glance. They could only imagine his thoughts. They were certain they had not seen the last of the dragon.

The Darkling, they hoped, was gone for good.

So, with any immediate danger dispelled, Ben was able—
with occasional interjections from Questor—to explain to Willow and Abernathy how the puzzle of the Darkling had been
solved.

"The secret was the bottle," Ben said. "The Darkling lived
in the bottle and never left it completely for long, even when
freed from it, so there had to be some logical tie between them.
Otherwise, the demon, who was always so anxious to be let
out, would have simply abandoned its prison and gone its way.
I thought, what if it can't leave the bottle? What if that's where
it gets its power? What if the magic comes from the bottle, not
the demon, and the demon stays with the bottle because it has
to, if it wants to continue to use the magic? The more I thought
about it, the more sense it made."

"So the High Lord suggested to me," Questor broke in
eagerly, "that if the magic came from the bottle, then shutting
off the bottle would cut off the Darkling's power."

"The trick was in doing that without letting Nightshade
know what was happening—and then getting the bottle back
before she could do anything about it." Ben regained control
of his explanation. "So while the Paladin was engaged in battle
with the Darkling and Nightshade, Questor used the magic to
shrink himself down and slip over to hide in the bottle's neck.
He became its stopper. He left an image of himself so that
Nightshade wouldn't know what he was up to. What Nightshade ended up destroying, when she guessed that Questor was
behind the loss of magic, was just the image."

"You might have alerted us to that much, at least!" Abernathy interrupted heatedly. "You scared us to death with that
trick! We thought the old . . . Well, we thought he had been
fried!"

"Questor sealed off the bottle," Ben continued, ignoring
his scribe's outburst. "That shut off the source of the Darkling's
power and rendered Nightshade's own magic, which was focused on the bottle's, useless. It all worked exactly the way we

had thought. By the time Nightshade figured out what had happened, it was too late. The creature was done, the demon was too weak to help, and the Paladin was bearing down. Questor surprised Nightshade by jumping out at her the way he did, full-size again, and snatching back the bottle. She couldn't do anything."

"What we hadn't anticipated, of course, was the extent of the effect that sealing off the bottle would have on the Darkling," Questor cut in again. "The demon drew not only its magic from the bottle, but its life as well. Once it was shut outside, it could not survive."

The four glanced as one at the small pile of dust some dozen feet away. A fresh breeze had come up. Already, the flakes were beginning to scatter.

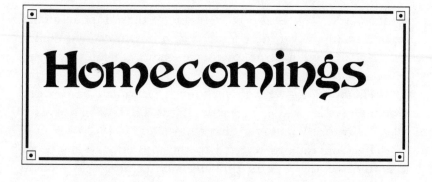

Homecomings

*I*t was Monday morning in Seattle, nearing noon. Miles Bennett sat in one of the waiting areas of the United Airlines Annex at SeaTac Airport waiting for the arrival of Flight 159 out of Chicago O'Hare. Elizabeth's father would be on that flight. It had taken Miles most of the weekend to track him down and arrange for his return. When he landed, they would drive out to Graum Wythe and begin making the necessary arrangements to dispose of Michel Ard Rhi's estate.

Miles stared out the Annex windows momentarily into the gray, overcast day. It was funny how things worked out.

Elizabeth was seated beside him, reading something called "Rabble Starkey." She was wearing a black and yellow knit skirt and blouse, and her jeans jacket was draped over the back of the seat next to her. She was immersed in the book and unaware that he was watching. He smiled.

Copies of the *Seattle Times* and the *Post Intelligencer* rested on his lap, and he began leafing through them idly. He had read the headlines and their various trailers a dozen times already, but each time it seemed he found something new. The events of Halloween night were far enough behind him already that he could hardly believe he had been a part of them. It was almost as if he were reading about something that had happened to

someone else. It was as if it were one of those foreign affairs
reports that he never quite felt had anything to do with him.

But that wasn't true, of course—not with foreign affairs
and certainly not with this.

The headlines were all very much the same. "Halloween
Goblins Invade Seattle." "Seattle Spirits Trick-Or-Treat City
Hall." "Spook Wars Over Elliott Bay."

The subheadings referred to the mysterious collapse of
a portion of the Courts Building, the sightings by police-
men, firemen, various city officials, and the ubiquitous man
on the street of some form of unexplained phenomenon, and
the strange state in which a number of lawyers and members
of the sheriff's department had been found in a courtroom that
looked as if World War III had been fought in it.

The stories beneath related the details, at least in so far as
anyone was able to relate them, given what little there was to
work with. The municipal police and fire departments had been
summoned on Friday night, Halloween, to the Courts Building
in downtown Seattle, following a report of an explosion. Upon
arrival, they found a hole apparently blown out of the side of
the building on the fifth floor. Attempts to reach that floor from
inside were unsuccessful. There were varying accounts as to why.
Several stories referred with tongue in cheek to the reports of
vast jungles of growth that later disappeared entirely. Helicopters were summoned. Firefighters eventually broke through and
found most of one courtroom in ruins, with an outside wall
gone entirely. A number of people working in the building were
found "in a dazed condition" but no one was seriously injured.

Farther down the page and often farther into the paper,
there were stories about the sightings. A dragon, some indicated
quite positively. A flying saucer, others said. A return of Satan's
hordes, some swore. Yes, there was something, agreed the helicopter pilots who had chased and been chased by whatever it
was. They didn't know what. Could have been some form of
sophisticated aircraft playing games, one city official theorized.

Sure, and maybe it was one of those close encounters that have their origins in Friday night taverns, another quipped. Come Christmas, we'll be getting sightings on Santa Claus.

Ho, ho, ho, Miles thought.

There were stories in which scientists, theologians, lay ministers, government officials, and one or two channelers were interviewed and asked for their opinions, which all were only too happy to give.

No one was even close, of course.

Miles finished with those stories and turned to the single column report on the front page of the *Northwest* section of Sunday's *Times*. There was a picture of Graum Wythe and a headline that read: "Millionaire Gives Castle To State."

Underneath, the accompanying story began:

Millionaire businessman Michel Ard Rhi announced at a news conference today that he was donating his castle home and surrounding lands to the state of Washington as a park and recreation area. A fund will be set aside to maintain and improve the facilities, and the balance of Ard Rhi's estate, conservatively estimated at three hundred million dollars, will be donated to various organizations throughout the world for humanitarian and charitable causes. Ard Rhi announced that the castle, Graum Wythe, will become a museum for pieces of art he has collected over the years and will be open to the public. Arrangements for readying the facilities will be handled by his private steward, whose name was not released.

Ard Rhi, a reclusive businessman who is thought to have made the bulk of his fortune in real estate and foreign trade, advised newsmen that he plans to retire to the Oregon coast to write or work on other projects. A small trust will be set aside for his support.

The story went on for several more paragraphs, relating Michel Ard Rhi's personal history and the reaction of a number of local and national notables. Miles read the story twice and shook his head. What *had* Questor Thews done to the man?

He put the papers aside, stretched, and sighed. Too bad Doc wasn't still around. There were just too many unanswered questions.

Beside him, Elizabeth looked up suddenly from her book, blue eyes intense. She seemed to read his mind. "Do you think they're all right?" she asked.

He looked down at her and nodded. "Yep, Elizabeth," he said. "Matter of fact, I'm sure of it."

She smiled. "Me, too, I guess."

"That doesn't mean we can't worry about them, though."

"Or miss them. I miss them a lot."

Miles looked out the windows again, across the broad expanse of the runways and taxi lanes, into the distant gray mix of clouds and mountains and sky. "Well, they'll be back," he said finally. "Someday."

Elizabeth nodded, but didn't reply.

A moment later, the arrival of Flight 159 was announced. Miles and Elizabeth got up from their seats and walked over to the windows to watch it come in.

Several weeks later, Ben Holiday and Willow were married. They would have been married sooner, but there was protocol to be observed in a wedding such as theirs, and it took awhile even to figure out what the protocol was, let alone to implement it. After all, hardly anyone alive could even remember a marriage of a High Lord of Landover. So Abernathy dug out his histories, and Questor Thews consulted a few of the valley's elders, and between them they finally figured out what had to be done.

Ben frankly wasn't interested in the formalities. All he knew was that it had taken him an impossibly long time to realize what Willow had known from the very first—that they should be together, joined as one, husband and wife, High Lord and Queen, and that whatever it took to get the job done, they should do it. Once, not so very long ago, he would never have allowed himself to feel that way; he would have considered such feelings a betrayal of his love for Annie. But Annie had been dead almost five years, and he had managed finally to lay her ghost to rest. Willow was his life now. He loved Willow, had known he loved her almost from the first, had heard her speak countless times of the foretelling of her destiny at the moment of her conception, and had learned from her the Earth Mother's prediction that one day she would bear him children.

Still he had hesitated to believe and to commit himself. He had been afraid, mostly. He had been afraid of a lot of things— that he still didn't belong, that he was somehow inadequate to be Landover's King, and that one day he would simply be gone, back again in the world he had wanted so badly to escape. The realization of the dream was greater than his expectations, and he had feared that he hadn't enough to give.

He was still afraid. Fears such as these lingered in the subconscious and would not be banished.

But it was another fear altogether that decided him on Willow. It was his fear that he was going to lose her.

He had almost lost her twice now.

It was not almost losing her the first time, when he had just come into Landover, that decided him. It was all too new then, and he had not yet put Annie behind him.

It was almost losing her this second time, when she had come back with him into his old world and he was forced to face the fact that she had come, not because she had to, but because she loved him enough to die for him. She had known that such a journey would endanger her and ignored the risk to herself because she knew that he might have need of her.

That was what decided him. She loved him that much. Didn't he love her just as much? Did he want to risk losing her before they had even tried to discover what sort of life they might have as husband and wife? At least he had shared that much with Annie. Didn't he want to share it with Willow as well?

Any fool could have given the right answers to those questions. And Ben Holiday was no fool.

So there was nothing more to say, nothing more to be decided. The marriage took place at the Heart. Everyone came: The River Master, uneasy as always in the presence of his child, still reminded too much of her mother by what he saw in her, and still searching for a way to reconcile the mix of feelings she generated within him; the fairy folk of the lake country, some almost human, some no more than faint shadows flitting through the trees; the Lords of the Greensward, Kallendbor, Strehan, and the rest, with their retainers and followers, an unsettled group that trusted no one, each other least of all, but who arrived and encamped together for the sake of appearances; the trolls and kobolds from the mountains far north and south; the G'home Gnomes, Fillip and Sot in the vanguard, proud of their part—the story varied as to what it was—in the making of this marriage; and common folk from cottages and farms, shops and villages—farmers, merchants, hunters, trappers, traders, peddlers, artisans, and workers of all sorts.

Even Strabo put in an appearance, flying overhead during the feast that followed the marriage ceremony, breathing fire across the sky and presumably taking some small satisfaction from the fact that women and children still ran shrieking at the sight of him.

The marriage was simple and direct. Ben and Willow stood at the center of the Heart on the dais of the Kings of Landover and told each other and those gathered that they loved each other, would be kind and good to each other, and would always be there for each other when needed. Questor Thews recited a few archaic vows of joining that High Lords and Queens might possibly have repeated years ago, and the ceremony was concluded.

The guests feasted and drank all that day and night and into the next, and all behaved themselves relatively well. Quarrels were kept to a minimum and quickly settled. Those from the Greensward and those from the lake country sat side by side and talked of renewed efforts at cooperation. The reclusive trolls and kobolds exchanged gifts. Even the G'home Gnomes took only a few dogs when they left.

Ben and Willow thought it all went pretty well.

It wasn't until several days later, when things had settled back down to normal, that Ben thought once again to ask Questor about what he had done to Michel Ard Rhi. They were seated in the chamber at Sterling Silver that housed the histories of Landover, a cavernous study that always smelled musty and close, trying to interpret some ancient rules on land ownership. Just the two of them were there, it was late at night, and the day's work was completed. Ben was sipping at a glass of wine and thinking about all that had happened the past few weeks; then his thoughts drifted to Michel, and he suddenly remembered that Questor had never finished his explanation.

"What *did* you do to him, Questor?" he pressed, after asking the question once and getting only a shrug for a response. "Come on, tell me. What did you do? I mean, how did you even know what kind of magic to use? I seem to remember you telling me that use of the magic was pretty uncertain over there."

"Well . . . most kinds of magic," Questor agreed.

"But not the kind you used on Michel?"

"Oh, well, that magic was mostly for effect. Not much real magic was necessary."

Ben was floored. "How can you say that? He was . . . he was . . ."

"Basically misguided, if you recall the story," Questor finished. "Remember, my half-brother was primarily responsible for making him into the disagreeable kind of person he was."

Ben frowned. "So what did you do?"

Questor shrugged once more. "He just needed his values rearranged, High Lord."

"Questor!"

"Very well." The wizard sighed. "I gave him back his conscience."

"You what?"

"I let the poor thing out from where Michel had locked it away. I used the magic to enlarge it and to give it a primary place of importance in Michel's thoughts." Questor smiled. "The guilt he felt must have been intolerable!" He smiled some more. "Oh. I did do one other little thing. I planted a small suggestion in his subconscious."

He arched an eyebrow, looking like the cat who had eaten the canary.

"I suggested that in order to atone for his guilt, he should give everything away immediately. That way, you see, if the magic gives out before his conscience has a chance to take hold permanently, it will be too late for him to do anything to reverse matters."

Ben grinned broadly. "Questor Thews. Sometimes you really amaze me."

The wizard's owlish face crinkled. They regarded each other with amusement for a moment, sharing the joke.

Then suddenly Questor jumped up. "Goodness! I almost forgot! I have some news that will amaze you indeed, High Lord." He forced himself to sit down again, clearly excited. "What if I were to tell you that I have found a way to change Abernathy back again? I mean, *really* change him back!"

He studied Ben eagerly, waiting. "Are you serious?" Ben asked finally.

"Certainly, High Lord."

"Change him back? Into a man?"

"Yes, High Lord."

"Like before?"

"Oh, no, not like before."

"But with magic?"

"Of course, with magic!"

"Have you tested it? This magic?"

"Well . . ."

"On anything?"

"Well . . ."

"So this is still just a theory?"

"A well-reasoned theory, High Lord. It should work."

Ben leaned forward until their heads were almost touching. "It should, should it? Have you told Abernathy about this?"

The wizard shook his head. "No, High Lord. I thought . . . uh, perhaps you might?"

There was a long silence. Then Ben whispered, "I don't think either of us should tell him just yet. Do you? Not until you've spent a little more time on it."

Questor frowned, then squinched up his owlish face thoughtfully. "Wellll . . . perhaps not."

Ben stood up and put a hand on his shoulder. "Goodnight, Questor," he said. Then he turned and walked from the room.

About the Author

Terry Brooks was born in Illinois in 1944. He received his undergraduate degree from Hamilton College, Clinton, New York, where he majored in English Literature, and his graduate degree from the School of Law at Washington & Lee University, Lexington, Virginia. He was a practicing attorney until recently; he has now retired to become a full-time author.

A writer since high school, he published his first novel, *The Sword of Shannara*, in 1977 and the sequels *The Elfstones of Shannara* in 1982 and *The Wishsong of Shannara* in 1985. *Magic Kingdom for Sale—Sold!* began a bestselling new series for him in 1986; Brooks presently lives in the Northwest.

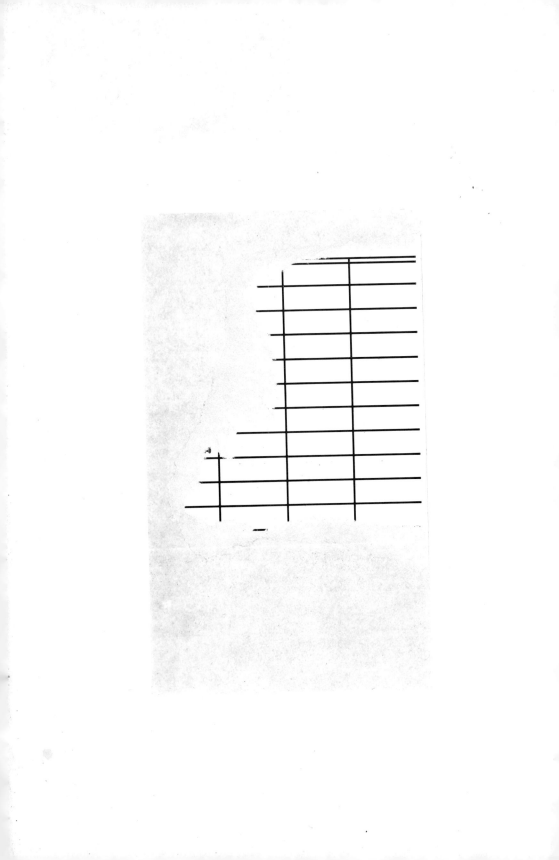